PULP CHAMPAGNE

Lorenz Heller sought to accomplish the same goal he sought in writing his novels, that is, create crime fiction that offered a more complex and nuanced story featuring richer characterizations than was normally regarded as "appropriate" to the audience or "typical" to the medium.

The thirteen stories included in this volume show Heller's work seeking a more mature expression of story, characterization and theme. These stories retain the pulp fiction characteristics of a simple story told using intriguing settings and engaging protagonists, but all the stories in this collection feature plots driven by character…

—Bill Kelly from his introduction

PULP CHAMPAGNE
•••••••••••••••••••
THE SHORT FICTION OF LORENZ HELLER

EDITED AND INTRODUCTION
BY BILL KELLY

Stark House Press • Eureka California

PULP CHAMPAGNE:
THE SHORT FICTION OF LORENZ HELLER

Published by Stark House Press
1315 H Street
Eureka, CA 95501, USA
griffinskye3@sbcglobal.net
www.starkhousepress.com

Copyright © 2023 Stark House Press. All rights reserved under
International and Pan-American Copyright Conventions.

"Pulp Champagne: The Short Crime Fiction of Lorenz Heller"
copyright © 2023 by Bill Kelly

ISBN: 979-8-88601-050-3

Book design by Mark Shepard, shepgraphics.com
Cover design by Jeff Vorzimmer, ¡caliente!design, Austin, Texas
Editing and Proofreading by Bill Kelly
Cover art by Walter Scott

PUBLISHER'S NOTE
This is a work of fiction. Names, characters, places and incidents
are either the products of the author's imagination or used
fictionally, and any resemblance to actual persons, living or dead,
events or locales, is entirely coincidental. Without limiting the
rights under copyright reserved above, no part of this publication
may be reproduced, stored, or introduced into a retrieval system
or transmitted in any form or by any means (electronic,
mechanical, photocopying, recording or otherwise) without the
prior written permission of both the copyright owner and the
above publisher of the book.

First Stark House Press Edition: November 2023

Contents

Introduction	7
I'll See You Dead!	23
Criminal at Large	29
Forger's Fate	35
Prelude to a Wake	47
If the Body Fits–	65
With Love and Bullets!	69
Death Brings Down the House	90
A Time for Dying	102
Living Bait	112
Don't Ever Forget	123
Bodyguard	133
Man With a Rep	164
Don't Wait Up for Me	176
Bibliography	242

ACKNOWLEDGMENTS

Bodyguard: *Thrilling Detective*, June, 1951
Criminal at Large: *Suspense Magazine*, Summer, 1951
Death Brings Down the House: *10-Story Detective*, April, 1948
Don't Ever Forget!: *Detective Story Magazine*, March, 1953
Don't Wait Up for Me: *Triple Detective*, Fall, 1955
Forger's Fate: *Dime Detective Magazine*, April, 1951
If the Body Fits–: *Dime Mystery Magazine*, December, 1947
I'll See You Dead!: *Detective Tales*, May, 1947
Living Bait: *Justice*, May, 1955
Man With a Rep: *Detective Tales*, December, 1949
Prelude To a Wake: *Dime Detective Magazine*, February, 1952
A Time for Dying: *Dime Detective Magazine*, August, 1951
With Love and Bullets!: *Detective Tales*, February, 1953

PULP CHAMPAGNE:
THE SHORT CRIME FICTION OF LORENZ HELLER

By Bill Kelly

Lorenz Heller (1910-1965) published novels and short fiction using the pseudonyms Dan Gregory, Laura Hale, Larry Heller, Larry Holden and Frederick Lorenz. Heller's first published work was the 1937 novel *Murder in Make-Up* for Julian Messner, written under the author's given name, Lorenz Heller. Heller would not appear in print again under any name for nine years until his short story, "Start With a Corpse" was published by *Mammoth Mystery* in their January, 1946 issue. He proceeded to make up for lost time by publishing over a dozen novels and fifty short stories through 1959. Stark House Press has published eleven of Heller's novels and this volume contains thirteen works representing the best of his short fiction. All but one of the stories in this collection was published under the pseudonym of Larry Holden, with only one, "Living Bait" as by Lorenz Heller. Heller, however used the Holden pseudonym for the overwhelming majority of his short fiction, with only four stories featuring other pseudonyms.

Lorenz Heller was of course one of hundreds of contributors required to fill the pages of the legion of magazines that would stock newsstands until the late 1950s, when pulp magazines were (for the most part) replaced by radio, television and paperback original novels. Critical studies of pulp fiction have become more numerous in recent years with a wide-ranging assessment regarding quality, as might be expected. As is true of all forms of expression, examples of the truly awful stand shoulder to shoulder with the great. American pulp fiction is no exception and the goal of this collection is to present some of pulp fiction's finest works by one of its finest practitioners. Literary criticism tends to be trendy and the lion's share of attention goes to the most notable, with "lesser lights" falling into undeserved obscurity. Heller is, I believe, one of these.

A typical "formula" for writing successful pulp fiction would include: simple stories (and sticking to them), engaging characters, fast pacing, stylized snappy dialog and the use of unusual or intriguing settings. Successful writers would often create or enhance existing publishing success by creating series characters that would appear in the pages of the same magazine over a period of years and thereby generate a niche market for both the author and the publisher. Heller (as Larry Holden) created one series character, Dinny Keogh, who appeared in seven early stories (six of his first ten published stories), but after a year and a half, Keogh disappeared and therein lies one premise of this essay: Lorenz Heller sought to accomplish the same goal he sought in writing his novels, that is, create crime fiction that offered a more complex and nuanced story featuring richer characterizations than was normally regarded as "appropriate" to the audience or "typical" to the medium. The Dinny Keogh stories (1946-1947) are often simplistic (a reader of pulp fiction crime stories would have seen these plots many times before) and the character himself is reminiscent of innumerable wise-cracking detectives in the Robert Leslie Bellem/Dan Turner vein. Although a popular character type, the wise-cracking detective's success depends, at least in part, on charm and (successful) humor and Dinny Keogh could be downright annoying at times and much of the humor seems forced and formulaic: almost imitative of 1930's B-movies, where one movie was often barely distinguishable from another. The most successful and polished of the Keogh stories is the last one Heller wrote, a long novella, "There's Death in the Heir" (1947), whose title illustrates the already outdated nature of the humor used in the Keogh stories. The thirteen stories included in this volume show Heller's work seeking a more mature expression of story, characterization and theme. These stories retain the pulp fiction characteristics of a simple story told using intriguing settings and engaging protagonists, but all the stories in this collection feature plots driven by character (vs. template plotting that drags the protagonist along with it) and the motivations of these characters are explored in a more complex fashion than in the Keogh stories.

An often controversial discussion topic of Pulp Fiction is the language chosen when writing dialog. To criticize the dialog found in many pulp stories as "unrealistic" is ignoring one of the intentions of those who wrote and published these stories: to entertain. The language chosen was complementary to another component of successful pulp fiction: pacing. Therefore wise-cracking characters in a Frederick Nebel Steve McBride story, for example, exchanging rapid fire, quip-filled dialog was never intended to mimic you or I in an argument or discussion with another citizen of this world. Pulp writers sought to entertain the reader and heighten the conflict of the situation simultaneously with larger than life and often humorous exchanges using typically short passages that also served to advance the story or aided in characterization development. As with any technique or style that gains the approval of the public, thereby gaining "must have" status for publishers, the application of this formula can be misused and abused with the resulting product producing unintended self-parody at best and silly buggers rubbish at the worst. Although clearly derivative in form, Heller's Dinny Keogh stories enabled him, after a long absence, to once again insert a foot in the publishing door and based on the post-Keogh stories he wrote afterwards, we can be grateful he did. Even while writing the Keogh stories, it is clear Heller made some effort to distinguish his creation from the hardboiled stereotype by making him physically roly-poly and reluctantly heroic and Keogh at his best does possess enough emotional depth and a uniquely individual style to make him memorable.

Heller abandoned Keogh (and the series character device) however, and began creating characters possessing personalities and psyches much richer than those of Keogh. Many of the characters seen in the stories featured in this collection face crises of conscience, moral dilemmas and experience personal awakenings that are generally atypical of pulp fiction where the protagonist and the story ride side-by-side, he/she doing what needs to be done and letting the chips fall where they may. In this collection, we find reluctant heroes and individuals obsessed with goals that are more critical to them as human beings than is the solving of a mystery or bringing justice to the bad guys. Some stories in this collection find Heller viewing the hardboiled milieu, a gold standard for much crime-based pulp fiction, somewhat askance—as illusion or a personality-crippling pose—and with "Forger's Fate", do as Raymond Chandler did with "Pearls are a Nuisance", and lampoon the hardboiled ethos into oblivion. In the story "With Love and Bullets", featured in this collection, Heller combines elements of the "comic mystery" with hardboiled action, as the story begins as a lark, but evolves into a portrait of ruthless greed and cold-blooded murder. As is typical with most of the other stories in this collection, we witness change and growth in the protagonists' self-development, as the events in the story shape and are shaped by their personalities and true natures. Heller's protagonists are not puppet masters of events, reacting to situations and shaping subsequent events through the application of will or sheer force of personality. Heller's characters are often more adaptive than controlling by nature, with aggressive attempts at resolution on their part often proving counter-productive.

As previously noted, pulp fiction readers were often offered stories that featured exotic/intriguing locations as an integral component of the escapist nature of the form. Only two of these collected stories feature "anonymous" locations, one for which location would add nothing to the story, and another, "If the Body Fits—" is obviously set in a rural area, but once again, added specifics would not enhance the story. Both stories are "shorts" that focus on the psyches of the principal characters. Five stories reside in the Newark/Hoboken area of New Jersey, a location Heller would have been familiar with in his younger days and six are set in Florida, where Heller spent much of his adult life. Elements indigenous to the New Jersey "big city" locations and the Florida coastal communities are more than window dressing however and play a meaningful role in the events unfolding in the story. In one story, "Death Brings Down the House", the decaying way-way-off Broadway Newark theatre is nearly as much of a character influencing events as any of the human characters.

In the hardboiled story "I'll See You Dead", Heller introduces us to a newly promoted and ambitious police detective who becomes more attuned to the human misery aspect of those whom he has previously regarded as mere players in the criminal tapestry he is daily exposed to:

> He slowly took his hands from his pockets and held them in front of me. I glanced down at them, then quickly away. It made me sick just looking at them. They were all twisted and curled and knotted like old dahlia bulbs forgotten in the cellar. He couldn't even have wiped his nose with those hands!

The detective intends to use this victim of a vicious gang punishment dispassionately as a stepping stone to bringing down one of the city's top criminals, heretofore immune from justice, but he begins to see that the victims of gang greed and ruthlessness are not only of today, but symptomatic of a more eternal ongoing pattern of life. He observes his young daughter asleep in her bed:

> I looked down at her blonde curls spread out on the pillow and for a minute I had the funniest feeling that she wasn't a baby anymore but was grown up and singing in a deadfall like the White Mule, then all of a sudden she was in the black water of the river, fighting the ropes that bound her hands and feet together.

Heller uses no abstract philosophy or hand-wringing sentiment as motivation to bolster the detective's determination to bring an end to those responsible for the murder under investigation. The detective is transitioning from a crime-busting machine to a human being that sees the pursuit of justice as more than adding numbers to his conviction rate. When the story ends he views the informant's role and his own experience in a different way than he had envisioned previously. Although the killer will be brought to justice, the end result is much more complicated (and less fulfilling) than he would have previously imagined:

> And that's the way it was. That's the picture. It bothers me.

With "Criminal at Large", Heller offers a Mark Twain/Bret Harte reminiscent tale of an escaped criminal who seeks vengeance on the man who fingered him to the police. Instead he finds the 12-year-old narrator and his Aunt at home on the proverbial dark and stormy night. This is a story where we know that the criminal will lose, but his undoing by the ingenuity of the Aunt and the teamwork between the two intended victims provides a "how it will be done" suspense and tension worthy of a Hitchcock tale. The relationship of respect and trust between the two family members enables their triumph and elevates this tale above an "ingenuity conquers brute force" story.

"Forger's Fate" stands the hardboiled macho hero concept on its ear and does it purely through characterization without relying on the hackneyed device of replacing one character stereotype with another. Every element in the story: plot, characterization, dialog, etc. contributes to a sendup of the type of story the reader may well have bought this particular issue of *Dime Detective Magazine* for in the first place. Wesley Smith is employed by Bankers Friend Automatic Check Writer Corporation to sell a machine designed to detect forgeries. He is an expert in "muscle forgery", demonstrating to potential clients how easy it is to forge their signatures. He is a man obsessed with his job, competing for a promotion to Regional Sales Manager and later in the story, when facing death from his heavily armed opponent:

> I was, at this point, actually hanging over the edge of the roof.
> Mr. Ganey had but to glance up and my career would have ended then and there.

Not his life ending, but his career! Smith is one of several reluctant heroes in this collection, but easily the most obtuse, which of course is where much of the humor lies. Heller uses language that matches the personality of his "hero": "In a trice, we were locked in a furious struggle." Possibly the first and last time the expression "in a trice" has appeared in US crime fiction. Other characters in the story, one of whom calls him "Reverend" view Smith as other-worldly:

> She looked at me as if there was something about me that was beyond understanding.

Smith himself narrates the story from a police station interview room. Smith's narration is juxtaposed with his increasingly violent outbursts aimed at a policeman who is heckling him and questioning the veracity of his story. Heller lampoons everything in sight, including Smith's employer who awards Smith the position he covets, declaring, "It's backbone, not wishbone that gets the soupbone." Cornball to the nth degree, but of course none of the corporate participants show any awareness of this.

In addition to all this there is murder, assorted acts of violence and romance, all of which Smith stumbles through with equal parts of naivete, Knight of the Roundtable save-the-lady-distress urgency and utter ineptitude, exhibiting, however, a resilient fortitude and courage that he himself seems totally unconscious of.

"Prelude to a Wake" is a down and dirty struggle between a soldier of fortune (Foyle) sitting on some loot gained from one of his adventures and a gambler (Routt) desperate to avoid retribution for an unpaid debt by extorting the money from the soldier-of-fortune in a seedy Hoboken, New Jersey bar. Added to the mix is the gambler's wife (Nora) who is looking to escape Routt and use Foyle as the means of doing so. The contest becomes a ballet of wits as Routt and his heavies try to pressure Foyle into handing over the loot, which is deposited in a bank. A fairly standard setup for the genre, but Heller, for the most part, eschews tough guy snarling and macho dialog and uses a series of ploys and counter-ploys enacted by the principals to effect an outcome. Additionally, there is a nice hook in the ending and two serio-comic characters who play significant supporting roles. Character change and development centering on the relationship between Foyle and Routt's wife adds some depth to the story.

"If the Body Fits—" is a macabre revenge tale about a father who hates his son for not dying at birth. The two live in mutual hatred for years, the son a virtual slave for the father:

> You don't have to be a psychiatrist to know that that's no life for a kid. Young Johnny was saving string and making one nail do the work of four when most kids are still playing with dolls, and at the age when he should have been teasing the young girls and offering them sodas in exchange for a furtive

kiss later, he was working sixteen and sometimes twenty hours a day, piling penny on top of penny, and nickel on top of nickel, watching them turn into precious dollars.

The revenge exacted on the father by the son is uniquely personal and appropriate to being his father's creation. When the father goes missing, others investigate and inquire after the old man's health. Johnny replies:

> "He drapped daid three-four days ago. Bury him t'morra—if I can spare time from the egg route."

The "like-father, like-son" adage gets a unique twist in this one.

Lorenz Heller was obviously heir to a long and rich pulp tradition by the time he started to produce his own stories. One of the stock characters encountered in pulp fiction is the Mean Old Rich Man, who also usually expands the range for any definition of eccentric. In "With Love and Bullets!" (one of three titles in this collection to bear an exclamation point—a treasured form of pulp punctuation) a PI is hired to transport a package for one such twisted millionaire:

> Trouble comes in all kinds of packages, but this particular package was in his sixties, had bristly gray hair like a Schnauzer, a pair of electric blue eyes that crackled like a short circuit, and a voice that should have been booked for assault and battery.

In his short stories, Heller could create the overripe metaphors and similes with the best of them, which add of course to the entertainment quotient when successful, but add to the annoyance factor when forced. Heller, of course, was aware of this and his later stories show less and less use of "snappy dialog", and rely more on dialog that reflected the inner conflicts of his characters. "With Love and Bullets!" is an unusual heist story with a ruthless femme fatale and a series of dupes, but Heller begins the story on a light note with a bizarre client and the client's even more bizarre set of instructions. The PI picks up his lothario brother for company during a long car journey and all seems for laughs until they arrive in Florida with the loot and are ambushed. The how of the femme fatale meeting her demise is unusual and well done, lending a nice twist to a story that could have been merely pulp template. A common crime fiction scene is that of the narrator describing what it is like to regain consciousness after being knocked out. In his rendition of this old chestnut, Heller displays his willingness to take a risk and try something different, using birth as an analog experience when describing recovery from a blow to the head:

> They say being born is a rough business—but coming back to consciousness after being slugged, really slugged, is worse because you can feel it with all your senses, which a baby can't. You can taste the salty blood on your tongue, all sounds tear at your eardrums, there is an acridness in your nostrils as if someone had shoved hot tar up them, and the light becomes splinters of glass in your eyeballs.

"Death Brings Down the House" is a tale of murder in a seedy Newark, New Jersey theatre, told somewhat tongue-in-cheek with the theatre folk, as usual, lending themselves to satire, although Heller doesn't push this aspect of the story very far. The principals involved are presented with some pathos and the motive for murder in this tale of thespian skullduggery is uniquely theatrical. The investigation of the murder of the show's star is police procedural light and the real suspense involves deciding whether one of the characters who seems harmless is the villain or if one of the obvious villains is indeed the culprit. A typical for the time short story twist ending well done here, though once again, with tongue-in-cheek.

"A Time for Dying" is a briskly paced noirish tale of a sailor (Woody) drunkenly celebrating the acquisition of his dream boat as a gift to his true love Gracie, but finds his joy short-lived as he is shanghaied into a murder frame. Woody struggles to escape the frame and do the only thing he can to clear himself—elicit a confession from the real murderer. Once again, a stock situation, but Heller uses a storm at sea and the incredibly hostile environment of a remote tiny island shared by the two adversaries to great advantage in playing out the resolution to the story. This story uses the "intriguing setting" component of Basic Pulp Fiction and non-stop action to great advantage. And as always in this collection of Heller stories, there are passages highlighting the human cost of it all as Woody ponders his fate:

> Stray thoughts scudded across his mind—thoughts of Gracie, incredulous, then delighted when she learned that he now owned the *Coquina*; thoughts of the *Coquina* riding calmly in a quiet bay on a sunlit afternoon, Gracie fishing off the bow, himself at the controls on the bridge; Gracie had never trolled for tarpon. In this crashing nightmare, it was sometimes hard to separate the visions from the reality.

Another Florida fishing boat tale is "Living Bait", the only story in this collection that bears the Lorenz Heller pseudonym. A charter boat captain (Roy) and his mate become involved with two wealthy competing business people, a man and a woman, the man coming into conflict with the mate over a lost fish. He is later arrested for throwing the mate overboard during a drunken brawl. The woman is the principal witness against the man, but Roy smells a rat and investigates. A "everything is not what it seems" type mystery with the mate emerging as the most interesting character. Heller frequently has his characters cast doubt on the advantage of wealth and here the mate eschews the "value of money" (as does a character in "Prelude To a Wake"):

> "Look at all the trouble Mr. Langler and Miss Starr got into on account of money. I don't want nothin' to do with that kind of trouble. There's only one thing to do with money, and I done it." He grinned happily and reminiscently. "And you know somethin', Roy? I met the nicest little old blonde gal down Miami. She had exactly the same idea about money as I did, and we did it together."

Just another corner of Pulp heaven.

At times, Heller would turn down the volume and produce a tale more brooding in nature than his more typical wall-to-wall action tales. "Don't Ever Forget!" (here the exclamation point runs counter to the basic tenor of the story) finds a retired sheriff dogged by a man posing as a newspaper reporter dogging him for an interview. The sheriff retired after being sickened by an arrest he had to make and believes himself totally unsuitable for police work and has instead become a charter boat captain. The "reporter" continues to dog the ex-sheriff, heaping praise on his abilities as a lawman, praise that is clearly mocking in nature. The sheriff is troubled by his inability to discover the real identity of the "reporter", a man whose face seems very familiar. This cat-and-mouse situation resolves itself in a totally unexpected finish, but the story is fairly clued nevertheless. "Don't Ever Forget!" is a low-key story of redemption and a solid mystery with good twists and spiced with some humor and an occasional pulpism:

> ... when the kingfish run started, and after that the tarpon, I'd be busier than a stripper's G-string in a four-a-day burlesque.

A tale that drips with pulp crime fiction characters, themes and language is "Bodyguard". A mostly inept PI (Chastain) is asked to gather new evidence to force an appeal of a child killer's conviction by plug-uglies working for the killer's brother, the city's crime kingpin. Allied to the crime boss are politicians and riding the fence between virtue and corruption is a judge whose daughter the PI wishes to marry, although the judge hates him because he is a PI, which the judge fears would tarnish his image.

> He [Chastain] knew damn well that all the love between the judge and me couldn't be fermented into a drink strong enough to intoxicate a fruit fly.

Approached by a corrupt lawyer (Moxie) with a bribe, Chastain, who at this point is only interested in marrying the judge's daughter, is astounded by Moxie's offer of so much "moolah":

> He [Moxie] folded back his jacket and showed a sheaf of brand-new bills in the inside pocket. He riffled them with his finger. They were all C-notes, and my eyes spread like a catfish's at the sight of the biggest worm in the world.

When bribery fails, the crime boss's goons try muscle. Chastain doubts his own courage after being threatened by the crime boss himself:

> I hung up fast before he could answer, and sat there breathing hard. Then the humor of it hit me. Brother, was I a hero! Iron-guts Chastain, that's me. Just show me a phone and I'll pick it up and get tough with anybody. I took out my gun and pointed it at the phone. "Bang," I said.
>
> That made me feel better. Not a lot, but some.

But as we of the pulp faithful expect, Chastain will get tired of being pushed around and rise to the occasion. He is another Heller reluctant hero, of modest intellect and abilities. This is easily the most complex of the stories in this collection with Chastain's reluctance, bumbling and faux bravado providing a lot of humor at each turn of events. Although containing real danger played out in a high stakes only-the-most-ruthless-survive milieu, this story is basically a romp: there is never any doubt that virtue will triumph, but Heller maintains suspense through a series of plot twists with several characters being not what they seem to be. Interlaced with all the peril and treachery are numerous pulp-flavored interjections:

> I wagged his hand enthusiastically. It felt like a shad fillet.
>
> Humor from him was like getting a hot foot from an undertaker.

We made the judge's house so fast that the clock owed us minutes when we slewed to the curb.

With the last two stories in this collection, "Man With a Rep" and "Don't Wait Up for Me", all frivolity comes to an end. To convince a man to talk in "Don't Wait Up for Me", a character is told:

> "Piet here knows some very useful tricks. Two minutes with Piet and a mother would eat her own baby, fried."

Both of these stories are hardboiled tales, but in each Heller explores the disillusionment felt by protagonists who, although successful, experience situations where the internal perils of self-doubt and self-recrimination pose as much threat to their continued existence as do the life-threatening situations they are confronted with. Typically, pulp heroes are not very introspective, but as any experienced reader of the genre knows, the tales that do contain a protagonist who sees more than a reflection when looking in the mirror can be a much more rewarding read than merely tagging along as a Race Williams guns down the bad guys.

The "Man With a Rep" is casino owner Dave Lait, who is faced with the consequences resulting from a loser not paying his debt. Lait must act quickly and decisively to keep the respect (and fear) of those always on the alert for any sign of weakness in order to maintain his position of power. By allowing losers not to pay up without retribution, he signals to those seeking to dethrone him as owner of the lucrative gambling den that he is weak. Lait has no stomach for murder, or, at this time in his life for the rackets. The quandary forced upon Lait is that the debtor must be killed, the maintenance of "respect" outweighing any financial loss. Lait's character cannot abide murder and he dreams, in a thirty second reverie, of escaping the life he is leading:

> In thirty seconds he had lived and loved. For a normal person, living and loving meant a whole lifetime. He had done it in thirty seconds.
>
> Tough Dave Lait—that was all finished. He could be a human being.

But the dream is not to be as his gal pal decides she does not want to give up the big money and engages a hit man to kill the debtor. Dave, is understanding, both of Tess's motivations and his own:

> He didn't blame Tess. She was protecting her capital. With the Club out of business, there wouldn't be any more mink, caviar

or filet mignon. She'd have to rough it on hamburger. She had acted according to her pattern. ... But he hated her, all the same. He hated the whole pattern, now that he'd had that brief insight into how it would be to be a human being again. Brief. Thirty seconds!

The man he is now cannot allow the murder to occur, so Lait frantically attempts to rescue the debtor and during his search for the intended victim he learns that he is also marked for death. In this story, Lorenz Heller presents the situational irony faced by a man who wishes to discard the prize he has worked so hard for and that others covet— and replace it with the dream of the man he wishes to become— a man who harms no one— but to do so, he may have to kill. This story features excellent chase suspense peppered with vivid confrontation scenes while presenting a theme unusual in a gangster melodrama: the rejection of material success for inner peace.

With "Don't Wait Up for Me" Lorenz Heller takes the risk of presenting the reader with an immediately unlikable "hero", the aptly named Clem Lasher. Unlikable protagonists à la Jim Thompson are calculated risks for the writer: the reader may ask, "Why should I care what happens to this creep? I certainly don't want to see him succeed." Heller is able to reward the patience of those willing to stick it out with the abrasive Clem as it soon becomes clear that he is headed for an attitude adjustment. Clem is a piano-playing gambler, a self-made man who has little patience for those he perceives as bumblers, their efforts on his behalf often meeting with abuse and he shows little remorse afterwards:

> I said I'm sorry, didn't I? I'll send you a singing telegram if you want, or would you rather sit in my lap?

Clem Lasher leads a full and rewarding life, but a seemingly trivial problem sends him into a spin: he has sponsored a singer by lending him $1000 on the condition that the singer appear at a club Lasher has made a commitment to, but the singer has disappeared. We gain some insight into Lasher's insecurity as he resolves to locate the singer to ensure he fulfills his commitment to the club owner:

> This was something he was going to have to do something about, personally—to keep his self-respect, to keep his nerve.

Clem's fear is sensed by his rejected lover and she responds to his snubs by doing her own lashing:

I know you now, Clem Lasher. You're tough only because you're afraid of losing your nerve. That's the one thing you're afraid of. You're not tough; you're just plain scared!

Clem sets out to find the wayward singer in a vividly portrayed 1950's Hoboken, New Jersey, but runs afoul of corrupt police and gangsters running a smuggling operation. Posing as a piano player of "gutbucket" music, Lasher sinks deeper and deeper into a situation that he has no control over, his self-doubt leading to some introspection, especially regarding how he treats others. He seems unable to resist wounding those who try to help him. A woman who cares about him tries to comfort him by explaining that he is too accustomed to being "self-sufficient":

> That's just a nice way of saying I've been an arrogant bastard. It's just come to me that ever since I've hit Hoboken, I've been helped by all kinds of people. I wouldn't have gotten to first base with my alleged self-sufficiency. The counterman at the lunchroom wanted to lend me money; that woman in the diner covered for me with the cops; McNulty gave me a job; you got me out of a bad spot. I've been kidding myself all my life. I can do all right, all by myself. The hell I can! The hell anybody can. Even poor Al Vance gave me a hand. Lasher the Great Lasher—the great jerk!

Undeterred by his protests, she continues to try and console him, but he has not yet emerged from the refuge of self-pity:

> "You're tired, darling," she touched his cheek. "You're just tired."
>
> "Tired? Yeah. Sick and tired. Sick and tired of me."

When he finally discovers a clue to the mystery, Lasher reasserts himself and resumes the pursuit. "Don't Wait Up for Me" is another Heller hardboiled tale where the lead character has a soft-boiled center (in Lasher, buried very deeply) and seeks to redeem himself by overcoming his doubts and fears in order to act effectively. In the end, Lasher falls back on one of his strengths, determination, to see him through. This is by far the longest story in the collection, but there are no dead spots and the narrative is enlivened by several well-drawn set pieces that advance both the story and Lasher's maturity. The mystery component is effectively preserved until the conclusion, with a surprising identity reveal of the puppet master behind all the mayhem. Throughout, the story is enlivened by fleshed-out "mean streets" characters and as usual, peppered with colorful slang and some purple prose.

The common thread linking these Lorenz Heller stories—beyond the pulpish style, colorful settings and quick pacing—is that the story and attendant plotting are less interesting than the people living the story. None of these stories are pure noir and are of a different age, where the good guy usually won, so we fully expect a positive outcome. But to be palatable to a "modern" audience however, a story written in the 1950s will have to strike other chords. For Heller, I suspect, achieving success was a two-fold challenge: write a story that was suitable for publication in a pulp magazine and get paid, but yet satisfy the artist within by writing a story superior to most—principally by creating complex characters easily distinguishable from those the reader was already familiar with. A story that leaves you thinking about (and remembering) the character(s) because of their complex internal struggles will appeal to any age. The story with the twist or surprise ending, the puzzle story, the shoot-em-up, etc. can be entertaining, but in the end, empty calories (if peopled with cardboard characters)—compared to a story with complex characters that forces you to care more (or at least as much as) about them as about the mystery component of the story. Lorenz Heller knew all the stories and recycled some of them in his pulp work, but his stories, at their best, exhibit more sensitivity and heart than many of those produced by his fellow pulp fictioneers.

—December, 2022
Mesa, AZ

···

Bill Kelly has proofread many Stark House releases since 2017 and recently has contributed introductions to several volumes, including the recently released *The Deadly Pay-Off* by William H. Duhart. Bill received a B.A. in English from Columbia University and was a technical writer and illustrator for several corporations. Bill's first exposure to crime fiction was the works of Raymond Chandler, Penguin UK editions, purchased in Singapore.

PULP CHAMPAGNE
THE SHORT FICTION OF LORENZ HELLER

I'LL SEE YOU DEAD!

I'm a mild guy. I have an even temper, a wife who never learned to spell n-a-g, a little girl about that big, and a dahlia garden I fuss over as if it grew beefsteak and butter. I'm a good steady plodder, and well thought of in the Department because I'm straight and keep my head. A little over a week ago they made me detective second grade, and me only thirty-seven. That's not bad.

But there always comes a time when you throw everything overboard and go completely haywire and ... I want to get it off my chest. I worry about it sometimes. It bothers me.

It was a month, two days and three hours ago. I remember the time to the minute. I have reason to. Five thirty-two in the afternoon. I was down in Charley's Bar and Grill on Market Street having my usual two beers before going home to dinner, after which I always read the funnies to the kid before shooing her off to bed. Charley and me were standing there exchanging the weather, when Charley leaned on the bar and said casually:

"That character down the end of the bar next to the phone booth, the tall, skinny crumb. Came in an hour ago, ordered a rye high and never touched it. He's been lampin' you steady since you came in. Know'm?"

I took a quick glance at him. He had a long gaunt face, all bone and angles like a piece of scaffolding, and he sat hunched over the bar, his big hands in his pockets, his hollow eyes fixed on us. He looked like something you'd find hanging next to the front door after a death in the family. There was something familiar about him, but maybe all skeletons look alike.

"Could be," I said to Charley. "But there's nothing like finding out for sure."

Charley strolled up the bar and I knew he'd throw out a front of conversation to hold the other customers while I did my chore. I picked up my beer, went down the bar and slid onto the stool beside the guy. Close to, he looked worse, sick—two coughs this side a lunger's grave.

"Something on your mind?" I suggested.

He didn't even stir to take his hands out of his pockets, and I had to look quick to see the movement of his lips.

"Al Crane?"

"That's me," I said.

His eyes folded for a minute, and he seemed to be praying over something, or maybe just making up his mind. Finally he said, "Let's go in the back."

"This is all the back there is, friend."

"The washroom, then. Let me go first."

He dismounted awkwardly from the stool and walked to the washroom with stiff, gangling strides, but that's about the only way you can walk if you keep your hands in your pockets. Maybe he was cold. I waited until I finished my beer, then followed him. He was leaning against the radiator under the window. I gave the empty stall a brief glance, closed the door and put my back to it. "Well?"

"I couldn't go down to headquarters or out to your house. I have to stay alive." He gave a brief shattering laugh, cut it off short and went on in his dead voice, "Then I found out you came here every day."

"Why me?"

"They say you're okay. Are you?"

"Sure. I've seen you around, haven't I?"

"Me? I guess so. I used to play piano over at the White Mule. Go there much?"

I shrugged. "Now and then." What the hell was he getting at?

"Remember a little blonde thrush called Mona Morgan?"

"Morgan? Yeah. Seems like. Deep voice, torchy. Pretty good."

"Well," a pain seemed to strike him and he squeezed his eyes until it passed. "Well," he said tightly, "she ain't no more. She's dead."

I looked at him sharply. It hadn't been physical pain. More as if Mona Morgan had been a voice and then some to him.

"That's too bad," I said carefully, watching him. "Flu or something?"

"She's in the river. No," he caught the tightening of my jaw, "you wouldn't know about it. She won't come up for a while yet. She was only put in last night." His mouth turned small and pinched the way it does when you're minding your own agony.

But I'll tell you right now, I thought he was unbuttoned someplace, and I wouldn't have given a nickel for his screwball story.

"You don't say," I said. "Who did it?"

"Brill."

My eyes must have stood out on stilts, for he looked into my face and laughed that short, shattering laugh again. "You'd like to tag that hood, wouldn't you?"

I still didn't believe him—not on the Brill angle. Not a slick operator like Brill, not that crook. "You actually saw him do it, no doubt?" I said.

"Not himself, no. A couple mugs named Moxie and Statts threw her in, all tied up like a birthday present. I saw it and couldn't do a thing about it. But Brill had it done."

I grabbed his lapels, jammed him hard against the wall and said harshly, "You saw this and didn't report it?"

He looked down at my hands as if I were pinning a flower on him, but even his amusement was sour. "Sure. I saw it," he said mockingly, "but how much you want to bet ten guys saw them not do it? How far did you get with Statts on that stickup last year?"

He was right about that. We hadn't got from here to there. He was Brill's man, and Brill could dream up alibis faster than a rabbit could get pups.

"And how long do you think I'd live after I ratted?" he asked fiercely. "Not that long!" he made an ugly noise with his mouth. "I want to stay alive long enough to hand you Brill, and that's what I'm going to do. Tonight! You'd like that, wouldn't you?"

I let him go. Now it was getting familiar. "You're going to give me Brill!" I jeered. "The hell you are! You only *want* to. He's slipperier than six feet up a greased pole. You ain't got a prayer."

"Listen. Wait. Listen a minute. He killed that girl. She was his woman till she got nosey, then he killed her."

"She was your girl first, wasn't she? And he beat your time. Is that the story?"

He stammered, "She wasn't my girl. I was just a beat in the piano while she sang. She had nothing to do with me. Nothing."

"Then why so generous? Or are you just stooling on general principles?"

He slowly took his hands from his pockets and held them in front of me. I glanced down at them, then quickly away. It made me sick just looking at them. They were all twisted and curled and knotted like old dahlia bulbs forgotten in the cellar. He couldn't even have wiped his nose with those hands!

"Six months ago I was nosey too," he said dully. "Moxie held one hand flat on the desk and Statts held the other, while a punk I'd never seen beat them with a gun butt. Brill was too smart to handle deals like that himself. I doubt if he ever knew just what did happen to me. But he knew I'd been taken care of—plenty!" He put them carefully back into his pockets, looked at me bitterly, then shuffled to the door. "They used to say," he mumbled, "They used to say I was a good as Tatum on boogie. That's what they used to say." The door opened, he shambled out, the door closed. I gave him ten minutes, and went home.

After dinner I read the funnies as usual to the kid, but my mind wasn't on it and she kept fighting and whining until the wife said reproachfully, "If you don't want to read to her, Al, why not say so, and I'll do it." But you know yourself you can't treat a kid like that, so I pulled myself together and finished off in style, then took her up to bed. I sang my usual four-five bars of "Rock-A-Bye-Baby" and turned off the light. But just before I did, I looked down at her blonde curls spread out on the pillow and for a minute I had the funniest feeling that she wasn't a baby anymore but was grown up and singing in a deadfall like the White Mule, then all of a sudden she was in the black water of the river, fighting the ropes that bound her hands and feet together. All this in a flash, all in the time it takes for a single, backward glance before reaching out for the light switch. It gave me the damnedest feeling. I've never been able to understand it.

Now it was over an hour and a half since I left Charley's, and I kept telling myself the guy was nutty as a peanut bar, and to forget it. Anyway, what could a guy like that turn up where the best cops in the whole city had fluffed?

But I couldn't get interested in my paper, and all I was doing was sitting behind it, waiting like a high school belle for the phone to ring. Then, when it did, I was out of my chair and on it before the wife could put down her sewing.

"Crane," I said. "This is Crane speaking."

"Al?"

"Yeah."

"Well say, listen. This is Ray Dorman, and I got four tickets for that Girlie Frolic over in Schuetzen Park. Sorry I didn't call you earlier but the guy just dropped them off. Couldn't go, or something. Suppose me'n Martha come right over to pick up you and the wife and …"

"Sorry, Ray. Another night."

"Hey, wait a minute. It's only one night, Al, and …"

"Sorry, Ray." I hung up as he was starting, "Now what the hell do you think of …"

I couldn't help it. I had to have the line clear for that one call no matter what—just on the outside chance that the guy did have something on the ball. Don't ask me why I didn't run him in when I had him pinned in the washroom. That's what I should have done. That's what any cop in his right mind would have done. But I had a pretty fair idea that if I put the arm on him then and there, he'd have clammed up so tight you'd have thought he was welded. And there was another angle, too. There was promotion in it. The guy who grabbed off Brill was up for more than a shiny red apple.

Sure. It's promotion. That's what I kept saying. It's promotion, Al. But deep inside, I knew it was something else, something personal between me and Brill.

The wife gave me a searching glance when I went back into the living room and sat on the edge of my chair again. She pursed her lips and didn't say anything, but when the phone rang for the second time, she was up before me. I heard her say, "Hello." Then, "Just a minute." She came to the door. "It's for you, Al," she said quietly.

I recognized that toneless flat voice the minute it hit my ear. "He just showed up. I been waiting. I'm down at the White Mule. How quick can you make it?"

"Half hour. Three quarters at the most."

"Okay. I'm down the end of the bar. I'll watch for you. Don't talk to me when you come in, but keep your eye on me. I'll go upstairs. Give me five minutes, then follow me. Got it?"

"Sure. But see here, fella, I want to know what I'm ..."

"See you then, Crane." He hung up.

Screwy. Screwy as they come. I swore as I checked my gun before slipping it in the underarm holster. That was the guy I was depending on to lead me to Brill—a consumptive hoople with a grudge. I was lucky if all they did was blow my head off.

I kissed the wife goodbye, and for a minute she held me tighter than usual. But all she said in her calm voice was, "I'll have a cup of coffee and a piece of pie for you when you get home, Al." She didn't say right out that she was going to wait up for me; she never wanted to let me know she worried. But she must have seen that business with the gun and the way I'd been acting. I felt like a heel walking out, leaving her there to eat her fingers till I got back. I walked out the door quickly.

The White Mule was one of those funny places. I mean, humorous. There were kicking mules and minstrel darkies all over the walls, and stuck here and there were fireproof plastic palms, and the orchestra, called Mickey Finn and his Eight Swallows, was beating the tar out of "Moanin' Low", and they had a dog that howled when you pulled its tail. The bar was called The Trough.

I mounted a stool, ordered a rickey and looked casually around. He was sitting down at the end where he said he'd be, curved hollow-chested over his glass, those useless hands hidden again in his clothes. His eyes looked closed, like he was praying again.

After a few minutes—when the barkeeps were busy down the other end—he got up and slouched over to the stairway that was partially hidden by one of those palms. At the top, he knocked at the first door. It opened slightly. I could see the crack of light. He put his shoulder to it and went in fast. The door closed.

My breath was coming faster. I put my left arm on the bar and kept my eyes tight on the minute hand of my wrist watch. I gave him five minutes to the second, then got up and followed him. I stopped outside the door, took the gun from the holster and put it in the side pocket of my coat. I leaned my ear to the door.

I heard him saying, "... time is now. That's all Brill. That's all I came to say. I wanted you to know why. She was a clean kid before ..."

Brill's harsh voice broke in, "And for the last time I'm telling you—get out! Get out while you're still together. Beat it!" But his voice didn't carry the usual authority. There was a tremble in it.

"Scared, Brill? I'm giving you better than an even chance. All you have to do is open that drawer in front of you. I don't care if you do or not. You only have until I count three, and then I'm letting go. One ... two ..."

I yelled, twisted the doorknob and lunged in as the gun roared. Brill sat white-faced behind the desk, and crouched in front of him was my guy, his hands sunk deep in his coat pockets. Then slowly he leaned to the left and slid toward the floor. He seemed to take forever. The gun in Brill's hand wove a small curl of smoke.

I snapped, "Drop it, Brill. You, too." The flat-nosed gorilla who stood behind the girl slowly drew his hand from under his coat and held it, empty away from him.

Brill said blandly, "Sure." And he laughed. He threw the gun on the rug in front of me with a derisive gesture. "Fingerprints and all. Go ahead and make something out of it, copper. It was self-defense. You can ask them." He waved his hand and grinned.

The girl said, "Self-defense. He's got a gun in his pocket."

I went down on my knees beside the body. I turned it gently on its back. I looked up at the girl.

"You'll swear to self-defense?" I asked.

"Why not?" she said lazily.

"This is why not!" I jerked the crippled, useless hand from his pocket and dangled it before their eyes. "What jury is going to believe he could hold a gun in *that*?"

And that's the way it was. That's the picture. It bothers me.

CRIMINAL AT LARGE

It was raining so hard that my Aunt Libby had to lean over the steering wheel so she could see the road ahead. Ordinarily, we would not have been out on a night like this. But my Uncle Steve was in a Paterson hospital with his appendix, and that's where we were coming from.

You've seen my Uncle Steve in the newspapers. Steve Moynihan. He's the one who showed the police where Howie Russ was hiding in the burned-out barge on the Passaic River, across from our house. Howie Russ is the man who killed his wife with a Stillson wrench. He was hiding in this old barge, and Uncle Steve noticed him two or three times coming on deck for air. Then my uncle got curious and looked at him with binoculars and recognized him.

A whole army of police came after Howie Russ, because he's a big man and dangerous. They were on the river in launches with Uncle Steve and a fleet of cars lined up on the Lyndhurst side. They captured him, all right, but he yelled at my Uncle Steve that he'd get him before he went to the chair.

My Uncle Steve laughed even before the police told him not to worry. People with freckles, like my Uncle Steve, never seem to worry about anything. Even in the hospital with his appendix he laughed and joked with us. My Aunt Libby was worried, though. I could tell by the way she was biting her lip as she drove through the rainstorm.

When we turned down our driveway toward the garage, the water spurted on either side of us, it was that deep. With newspapers held over our heads, we splashed into the house. My aunt was laughing when we burst into the kitchen with the newspapers plastered down on our heads and the rain running from our faces. Our feet made puddles on the blue linoleum. She winked at me as we shook out our coats and hung them on the porch to drip.

"Enough storm for you, boy?" she asked.

I grinned back at her. I was almost grown up. I was twelve. "Not enough thunder," I said.

I kept on grinning. But my aunt was standing with her curly wet head tilted to one side, listening.

"Aaaaah," she said with dreary patience, "It's pooped out again."

I knew what she meant. The sump pump in the cellar. We live so close to the river that whenever it rains hard, the water comes up in the cellar.

We have to keep a pump going.

She opened the cellar door and snapped the light switch. The pump was off, all right, and there was an easy ten inches of water down there. In the quiet, we could hear the stealthy whisper of it as it came through the stone foundation.

"Well," she said, "it's fix it or float, I guess."

And she could fix it, too. She could fix anything. Last Spring, when the level-wind on my reel jammed, she fixed it in nothing flat, and still got more trout than Uncle Steve and me.

I pulled on my high rubber boots. Aunt Libby hiked up her dress and pulled on hers, then put on a pair of heavy red rubber gloves, so she wouldn't get electrocuted fooling around the wires on the pump. We went down into the cellar. The water came up to my knees, and even the coal was floating.

The pump squatted in the center of the floor, and she bent over it, tucking her skirt into the tops of her waders. I stood next to her, holding Uncle Steve's tool box.

She reached for a screwdriver, then looked at me and said, "Almost put it over, didn't you, boy? It's time for bath and bed, and this doesn't count as a bath." She splashed water with her hand.

"But I have to hold the tools for you, Aunt Libby. You can't put them down in the water. Somebody's gotta hold them."

"'Got to,'" she corrected. She looked around, then pointed to a small keg beside Uncle Steve's work bench. "Bring that over here and set the tool box on top of it. It'll do pretty well, and I won't have to worry about it taking a bath and going to bed."

You can't win with my Aunt Libby. I set up the keg, kissed her good night and climbed up the cellar stairs as she bent over the pump again.

I closed the cellar door, then tiptoed over to the refrigerator. I opened it slowly so it wouldn't creak. We'd had baked beans for dinner, and there's nothing I like better than a baked bean sandwich. I was just taking the first bite when I heard the footsteps.

The rain was sweeping across the windows like a wire brush, and the wind roared in the trees outside, but the footsteps upstairs were just as plain as if they were inside my ear. I stood stiff with my mouth full of bread and beans. The footsteps came again—cautious, but with weight on them. They were in my room over the kitchen. I knew my room with my eyes closed. The footsteps went around my bed to the closet, to the window, back around the bed and out into the hall. Then they came down the stairs, slow and sneaky.

My heart seemed to swell up and, leaving the refrigerator door open, I dived for the cellar door and clattered down the stairs, breathing hard.

"Forget something?" asked Aunt Libby, raising her eyebrows.

My mouth opened and closed. I felt it open and close. I swallowed the beans. I pointed at the cellar door above us.

"There's a man," I finally managed. "There's a man up there. I heard him!"

She didn't make fun of me. She didn't laugh the way some grownups do. She stood and put her pliers back in the tool box.

"We'll take a look," she said calmly. "Give me your hand."

Together, we climbed the cellar stairs. She pushed open the door, and her hand suddenly tightened around mine. For just at that moment, coming through the doorway from the hall was Howie Russ.

Nobody could ever forget Howie Russ. Tall and heavy, with a thick mouth that ran right across his face and faded little blue eyes that kept blinking. He had no shave.

They faced one another, my Aunt Libby and he, both so surprised they didn't move. Then my Aunt Libby gasped, slammed the door and shot the bolt. There was a rush of heavy, clodding feet and the door creaked as he threw his weight against the other side of it and viciously rattled the knob.

"Okay, sister," he said, "stay down there. I'll wait right here for *Mister* Moynihan, and I can wait all the damn night."

Aunt Libby held me tight against her and watched the cellar door. It was only a little ten-cent bolt. We heard his footsteps cross the floor and stop.

Aunt Libby muttered, "Now what's he up to?"

"I think," I whispered, "he's up to the baked beans."

We heard him set something down on the porcelain-top kitchen table, then rattle the knife drawer. When he spoke again, his voice was thick, as if his mouth were full of food.

"In case you're thinking of yelling when he comes home, sister, you can't hear ten feet in this storm. And anyway, I'll be waiting at the door for him!"

He meant Uncle Steve. He was going to kill Uncle Steve, just as he had yelled he would when the police caught him on that barge.

I stammered, "He—he escaped from prison, Aunt Libby!"

She said, "I guess so."

"Does—does he have a gun?"

She squeezed my arm. "Probably. But he's not after us, Timothy. He's after your Uncle Steve, and we can't let him hurt Uncle Steve, can we? We can't let him find out Uncle Steve's in that Paterson hospital, can we? He might sneak in!"

Her hand was shaking, and her face was strained and white, but there was nothing scared about it. Then her hands tightened and she closed her eyes the way you do when you don't want to see something. Or think about something.

"Go down, boy," she said suddenly in a voice that sounded all flattened out, "and pull down the switch that turns off the electricity all over the house, the one on the right of the fuse box. Know which one I mean?"

"Yes. It curls over like the handle of a scissors."

"Go ahead, then."

I splashed over to the meter board and pulled down the switch. The lights went out, and the storm seemed to get louder. Upstairs, Howie Russ yelled something, then he understood. "Go ahead, sister," he jeered, "turn 'em off. It's all the better. I'll get him in the dark. He'll never know what hit him."

Aunt Libby didn't answer. I heard her pliers going click-click, and something made a ripping noise. She was working at something.

Maybe it was the dark that made me think of all the police it had taken to capture Howie Russ on that barge; and here we were alone with him. Uncle Steve wasn't coming home from the hospital for five days, and Howie Russ wouldn't wait that long. Sooner or later he was going to come down into the cellar, and that ten-cent bolt wasn't going to hold him back. I felt so scared I must have made a noise, trying to reach through the darkness to the safety of Aunt Libby.

She said soothingly, "Shhhhh ..."

But I was shaking and wishing Uncle Steve were there. Uncle Steve would know how to take care of Howie Russ.

Aunt Libby said softly, "Turn it on again, Timothy."

I pushed up the handle of the switch. Nothing happened. It stayed dark.

"Now," said Aunt Libby, "get up on the bench. Stand on it. Don't touch anything. This is important! Now do as I say."

I scrambled up on the bench and stood there. I don't know why she made me do this, but if Aunt Libby said it was important, it was important. My heart was going so fast that just breathing was like being sick.

I heard the stairs creak a little as she went up. She pushed back the bolt, and an oblong of yellow light from the kitchen, with her shadow in the middle of it, shot into the cellar as she threw open the door. I heard Howie Russ's chair scrape the floor as he jumped to his feet.

Aunt Libby said, "Stand where you are, Russ. I want to talk to you!"

"Talk to me?" he said heavily. "Talk me out of it? Don't make me laugh, sister!"

He sounded as if he had never laughed in his life.

"My husband won't be home tonight, nor tomorrow night, nor the night after. He's out of town."

"Sure."

"I want you to get out of my house. I'll give you five minutes' start before I call the police."

"*You'll* give *me!* Don't kid yourself, sister. You won't give me nothing. Waaaait a minute. You say the hero's out of town?"

"Yes. It's the truth."

"And you're all alone with the kid. Well, ain't that nice. I just thought of something that'll maybe hurt worse than plain killing. Suppose the hero comes home and finds the kid with his neck twisted? And his wife—" I heard him laugh, then. He could laugh, all right. He said, still laughing, "You're a cute little trick, at that!"

Cute? Why, my Aunt Libby is beautiful, anyone can see that.

"Really worth a man's time. And when your husband finds out— wouldn't that be too bad, now wouldn't that be a shame?"

What was he talking about, I wondered.

Aunt Libby said fiercely, "You'll get life for this—you wouldn't dare touch me—"

"Life! I'll get the chair, if I'm caught," he snarled, "Aaaaaa ..." and he must have lunged at her, because she jumped down a step, slammed the door, and ran down the rest of the way. I heard her splash in the water, just before the door opened again, shooting its oblong of light down into the cellar. He hesitated on the top step, probably looking, but he couldn't see Aunt Libby because she was standing beside the furnace to the left of the stairs.

I saw his foot take the first step. The cuff of his pants was frayed. Why do you remember a thing like that? I remember his frayed cuff and how thick his bare ankle looked. He took another step, then a third and fourth, and stopped ... waiting, poised to leap back or forward. He still wasn't sure that Aunt Libby might not have a gun or something, I guess. He came down another step, his foot reaching slowly for the tread.

I made out the gun in his hand as he stepped off the stairs into the water. It was a short gun, hardly any barrel at all. He couldn't see me standing stiff on the bench; I was in the dark corner. He splashed another two steps, and my Aunt Libby cried out desperately.

"That's far enough. Come another step and I'll kill you!"

In the oblong of yellow light, I saw him swing around toward the sound of her voice. He still hadn't found her.

"Come on, come on!" He sounded mad because she was making him look for us. "You're just making it tougher on yourself, sister. Where are you?"

Aunt Libby said shakily, "Put down your gun, Russ. I'm giving you a chance."

She seemed to be pleading with him, begging him almost!

He turned toward the furnace. He had her spotted now. He stood up straight and I could see his teeth when he grinned and threw up his head.

To my horror, Aunt Libby stepped out from behind the furnace with nothing in her hands to defend herself but a thin three-foot brass curtain rod. Her face looked awful.

She cried hysterically, "I'm warning you, Russ. I'm warning you …"

But the rest was lost in the splashing surge he made toward her.

My Aunt Libby screamed, and there was a cracking blue flash from the curtain rod.

She hadn't pushed it at him. She'd just held it in front of herself, and he'd grabbed it. And electrocuted himself. When she moaned and dropped the rod, I saw the wire from the cellar light attached to the other end of it, and when he'd grabbed it with his bare hands, the juice went right into him. And, standing in ten inches of water, it killed him.

Aunt Libby was all right because she had been wearing rubber gloves and waders. And I was all right because Aunt Libby had made me stand on the bench, and I was wearing waders, too. But Howie Russ had been standing in ten inches of water.

The next day, the newspapers all said she was a hero, but I remember how she sat in the kitchen, shaking so hard she couldn't stand, with the tears running down her face, even after the police came.

FORGER'S FATE

Verbatim statement of Wesley Smith; taken by stenographer in the office of the District Attorney, Saturday, June 16:

My name is Wesley Smith. I am twenty-seven years of age, six feet in height, weight one hundred and seventy-five pounds, and was educated in the public schools of lower Jersey City, augmented by night courses in the YMCA. I now live in Nokomis, Florida, which is on Dona Bay and not on the banks of Gitcheegoomee, as Sergeant O'Shea has implied.

Until this morning I was a salesman in the employ of the Bankers Friend Automatic Check Writer Corporation. Circumstances, which I shall explain, have altered this association. I swear that the facts contained herein are the truth, the whole truth, and nothing but the truth.

On the afternoon of Thursday, June 14, at approximately 6:00 P.M., I entered the premises of the Gulfshore Club for the sole purpose of selling the management a check writing machine. The Gulfshore Club is the lone structure, excepting a boathouse, on Bonito Key, which can be reached only by the causeway.

As I entered the Tap Room, I saw several persons imbibing, and at the far end of the bar, a dark heavy-set man was talking in angry undertones with a very pretty girl, who was drinking milk.

"What'll it be, Reverend," the bartender greeted me, possibly because of the conservative cut of my clothes.

"I am not a Reverend," I assured him. "I represent the Bankers Friend Automatic Check Writer Corporation. Is the manager in?"

He said, "Let us pray," and walked up the bar to the dark heavy-set man. He was brusquely dismissed and returned. "Mr. Ganey's busy, Reverend," he asserted. "But he says to give me the pitch. I'm his assistant."

I have always found it good policy to impress a subordinate, so I looked him straight in the eye and said significantly, "Do you realize that within one week, with less than fifteen minutes practice per day, the average man can learn to forge your name to a check so perfectly that your own bank would cash it without hesitation?"

I have found that this declaration usually arouses interest.

"Think of that," said the bartender, astounded.

"A sobering thought," I said placing a pad and pencil on the bar before him. "Just write your name and I'll prove how easily it can be duplicated by the simple exercise of muscle forgery."

He put his tongue into his cheek and quickly wrote, "Poor Lew, the barkeep," on the pad. His handwriting was florid. I turned the pad so that the words were upside down as I faced them, and immediately beneath them and also upside down, I rapidly made a perfect replica. The reason for doing it thusly, I must explain, is that the principle of muscle forgery, aside from the fact that the action is solely from the forearm muscle, lies in its total disassociation from personal foibles in the formation of the letters of the alphabet.

Yes, Sergeant O'Shea, I am speaking English! I have taken courses in Business English and spend thirty minutes a day at Vocabulary Building. I shall enunciate more clearly if you wish.

To continue, I tore the sheet of paper in half, shuffled the pieces and, smiling, defied the bartender to tell them apart.

He could not and said suspiciously, "You do this for a living?"

I laughed heartily and assured him that I used muscle forgery only as a sales argument. "However," I said gravely, "forgery is exactly what our machine will protect you against."

"Sure, sure. But where're you staying, Reverend?"

"At the De Soto Hotel in Sarasota," I gave him one of my cards, which he put in his pocket. "Mr. Ganey can reach me …"

"He'll reach you all right if you pass around any samples of his signature. Have one on the house before you go, Reverend?"

Again protesting that I was not a Reverend, I selected a dry aperitif sherry, then continued to my hotel in Sarasota.

After dinner, I consulted my appointment book for Friday, and found that I had fifteen callbacks to make. I desperately needed ten orders. The Company was conducting a competition for the post of district sales manager for the south Florida area, and Mr. Zimmer, a go-getter himself, had hinted that no one but a go-getter would be considered. Ten orders would, as they say, put me over the top.

I had not abandoned hope of selling the Gulfshore Club, but I did not expect Mr. Ganey to send for me at 3:00 A.M. A heavy knock on my door was followed by the voice of Lew, the bartender.

"The boss wants to see one of them gadgets you're peddling, Rev."

"At this advanced hour?" I said suspiciously. "Why can't I contact him in the morning?"

"Because he'll be in bed. You gotta get Ganey when he's hot; Reverend. That's the gin mill business for you."

Had I not needed every order I could muster at this critical moment, I would have demurred. As it was, I went.

We drove in his car, and when we arrived, the building was entirely dark. I had found his manner increasingly nervous and furtive, and I admit to a certain uneasiness as I followed him through the hushed and gloomy Tap Room.

He opened a door at the rear of the Club, and the sudden brilliance of light dazzled me.

Mr. Ganey's voice roared, "Get him out of here, dammit!" and this was followed immediately by a feminine scream.

Lew muttered, "Hold it, Rev," and attempted to close the door in my face.

I thrust him aside and strode into the room, and as I did so, a girl hurtled toward me, crying, "Get me out of here. He killed Whitney!"

It was the girl who had been drinking at the bar. Distorted by fear though her face was, she was still lovely.

Mr. Ganey took a long step and slapped her sharply across the cheek, his own face congested with rage. I have never been able to stand by and permit a woman to be maltreated, and I started toward Mr. Ganey with the intention of giving him some of his own medicine. My arms were grasped from behind and Lew whispered:

"Relax, Reverend. She's a little hysterical."

I felt that this explanation was inadequate, for at this moment I caught sight of an overturned game table at the far end of the room and among the scattered cards and chips I saw a pair of legs lying in such a way that their owner could only be recumbent on his face.

"Is that," I asked, "Mr. Whitney?"

There was a moment of silence, and then Mr. Ganey said, "That's right, Reverend. He had a heart attack."

"Don't believe him," the girl cried, again appealing to me. "They were playing poker. Whitney caught him stacking the deck, and Ganey hit him."

I heard Lew draw in his breath, but Mr. Ganey, though his eyes were furious, was smiling.

"That little tap I gave him wouldn't kill anybody," he said. "He was a heart case. He even carried nitro pills with him. Everybody can tell you that. That little tap didn't mean a thing."

"The police," I said coldly, "may differ." Wrenching myself free of Lew's grasp, I sprang for the door. Something struck me violently from behind, and I fell unconscious.

Sergeant O'Shea, I resent your remark! That was the first and only time I was unconscious. All right, Mr. District Attorney, I'll continue, but this guy's ... Sergeant O'Shea is trying my temper.

How long I was unconscious, I do not know, but when I opened my eyes, I was lying on the chartreuse leather sofa at the window, and Lew, the young lady and Mr. Whitney were no longer in the room.

Mr. Ganey sat facing me in a chair, idly holding a gun by the trigger guard. My senses were confused, and a little incoherently I stammered, "Where—where's Mr. Whitney?"

"In the refrigerator," answered Mr. Ganey coolly. "I want him to keep for a while."

This callous statement sent a shiver through me.

"And now, Reverend," Mr. Ganey continued, "you and me, we're going to make a deal. You know what an I.O.U. is?"

I faltered that I did.

"Good. Whitney left me with a mittful of them when he kicked off. He had a million and I thought he was good, but now it looks like I'm stuck for something like twenty grand. I don't like it. That's too much sugar to be stuck for. So I'm cutting you in, Reverend."

Startled, I cried, "I?"

"Yeah, you. Lew tells me you're quite a genius with the pen. Muscle forgery, you call it? It must be quite a knack."

Aghast at what he was suggesting, I could only stare.

"I got Whitney's signature all over the place," Mr. Ganey said. "All you gotta do is put it on a check, and we're set."

I sat up. "No!" I said indignantly.

"Did I mention," Mr. Ganey murmured, "that we're making this check out for twenty-five grand? That extra five is your cut. Look, Reverend, if I keep Whitney in the deep freeze until say Tuesday or Wednesday, there isn't a doc in the world who'd be able to say he was dead before the check was made out.

"On Tuesday or Wednesday I'll drop Whitney on the beach somewhere, but in the mean time we'll cash the check and everything'll be copacetic."

It was an ingenious scheme, and had I assented, the bank would have undoubtedly cashed such a check without question, for I am exceptionally proficient in the science of muscle forgery. I had no intention, however, of lending myself to his plot.

On the other hand, I faced the prospect of being held prisoner, which meant that I would miss my last selling day before the close of the contest, lose those vital orders, and with them every chance of being named district sales manager for the south Florida area.

Had not the flutter of the drapes that masked the window to my right caught my eye, my dilemma would have been insoluble. I would not forge that check, and Mr. Ganey would not release me until I did. I turned and dived for the division between the drapes, hoping that the window behind them was open widely.

Fortunately, it was. I scrambled to my feet in the soft sand and ran precipitately through the palm trees and shrubbery toward the causeway.

I confess that my sensation at the sound of the first shot was that of profound shock. I could not believe that Mr. Ganey was actually shooting at me, but when his second bullet struck the tree immediately beside me, I realized with horror that he would actually kill me if he could.

In fact, I realized that he would have to kill me, anyway. He could not permit me to go to the police with the facts about the death of Mr. Whitney, and there was only one way that he could be certain that I would not.

This realization gave rise to another, equally as dismaying. I was not the only one who had to be silenced. There was the young lady who had appealed to me for assistance.

All right, Sergeant O'Shea, perhaps she did not know to whom she was appealing, and look, I'm getting tired of the way ... I'm sorry, Mr. District Attorney. I did not realize I was shouting. I'll go on as soon as you tell Sergeant O'Shea to keep his big mouth ... Thank you.

As I was saying, I could not run away knowing that I was leaving another in danger. I stopped and turned back toward the Club. As I did, the car roared by and thundered over the causeway, and I glimpsed Mr. Ganey's dark face bent grimly over the wheel.

Seeking me.

I made my way cautiously toward the building, taking advantage of all possible cover. Unfortunately, I was not wary enough, and in the darkness, I collided with the burly figure of Lew. In a trice, we were locked in a furious struggle. I struck him several times before he closed with me, swearing. I hooked my heel behind his and when we fell to the ground, I was astride him. It was not until then that I realized he was making pacific gestures.

"Hold it, Reverend," he pleaded. "For the love of Mike, hold it. I'm with you. If I wanted to, I could of plugged you a dozen times."

To my consternation, I saw that he was grasping a gun in his right hand. l rose stiffly. He did likewise, brushing the sand from him and grumbling:

"Why don't you listen to a guy before you try to tear his head off?"

"I thought you were swearing," I stammered.

"I was. You pack a stiff right, Rev. But listen. I don't want any part of this. I'm levelling with you. I didn't know Ganey had knocked Whitney off, and that's the honest truth, Reverend."

"What do you propose to do?" I asked, not entirely convinced.

"We gotta get the car away from Ganey. He took the keys away from me. He don't trust nobody. Peggy twisted her ankle when he smacked her down, so we need the car to get out of here. I got her stashed in the boathouse for the time being."

He pointed and I could see the small, flat-roofed building at the edge of the Bay about a hundred yards distant.

The sky was becoming lighter in the east. Lew's face was clearly visible to me. It was haggard and there was fear in it. He clutched my arm and cocked his head at a listening angle. The car was slowly returning over the causeway. We exchanged an apprehensive glance.

"You stay here, Rev," Lew whispered. "I'll go to meet him. He don't know I've dealt myself out. He won't have an eye out for trouble if I go alone."

I wanted to protest, but his logic was unassailable. Cautioning me to silence, he stood and walked boldly through the trees toward the Club. I was wretched because I wanted to help, yet I knew that any overt act on my part would endanger his life. I lay concealed behind the hibiscus bush, my heart pumping violently.

I heard him hail the car and there was a grinding slide as Mr. Ganey applied the brakes. I could not distinguish their words, but I could hear that they were talking together. The car door slammed and their footsteps crunched in the shell driveway. Suddenly there was a cry, a scuffle and then the abrupt sound of a shot. The world seemed to stand still in the thick silence that followed.

Then Lew came walking slowly through the gray light; and I surged to my feet in a wave of relief. He raised his arm—but a moment later I saw that it was not in greeting, for he bent slowly forward, toppled to the ground and lay motionless. Before I could stir, Mr. Ganey burst through the bushes and, making an ugly sound in his throat, stood over Lew and fired two more shots into his defenseless body.

He had not seen me, and I dropped hastily behind the hibiscus bush again, sick with the impotent rage that rose within me at the sight of that savage act. It was only by clenching my teeth that I restrained myself from rushing out and attacking Mr. Ganey with my bare hands. Trembling, I circled away. When I thought I was clear, I sprinted for the boathouse.

Mr. Ganey opened fire almost immediately, and the bullets were spurting sand at my feet when I flung myself at the door of the boathouse and tumbled inside. I slammed the door and bolted it.

Turning, I saw Peggy crouched against the wall, her face pale behind an upraised oar. In the meager light that filtered through the only window, I saw another oar at my feet. Giving her a pallid smile of reassurance, I picked up the second oar and broke off the blade, leaving me a sizeable and dangerous club.

I scarcely dared breathe as Mr. Ganey's running footsteps approached the boathouse. The doorknob turned and the dry wood creaked a little as he leaned against it. Then I heard him creep along the wall, and I went toward the window. The moment his head showed through the glass, I swung at it with my club. In my haste and over-anxiety, I misjudged my swing and achieved nothing but a broken window.

He swore savagely and disappeared from sight. I heard him walk around the boathouse, and he returned within a few minutes apparently satisfied that we had no way of escape except the small door and the window. The huge double doors, that opened to admit the passage of a boat to the Bay, had a metal grill that extended down into the water, effectively blocking it as a means of egress. There was no boat.

"Come on, Reverend," called Mr. Ganey, "use your head. This isn't doing either of us any good. What's so tough about signing that check? There isn't a chance you'd get caught. Be smart."

"I am smart," I said. "Smart enough not to sign any name to a check but my own."

"There's five grand in it for you, Reverend."

"No."

"Ten grand."

"No!"

"Okay. Think it over. I got all the time in the world."

He did not have, I felt, all the time in the world. Sooner or later, someone would come looking for Mr. Whitney. All we had to do was wait.

"What are you feeling so good about, Reverend?" asked Peggy, giving me a curious glance.

"I am not a Reverend," I protested, for, somehow I did not want her to call me that. "My name is Wesley Smith."

"Right, Wes. But what's the secret?"

I told her my thought about Mr. Whitney. She slowly shook her head. Dejectedly, she told me that there was little chance of anyone coming to look for Mr. Whitney.

Though he was wealthy and had all a man could wish, at periodic intervals he disappeared for as long as a week at a time to drink and gamble, despite his heart condition, and even Mrs. Whitney had long since resigned herself to her husband's profligacy.

"Ganey wanted me to keep Whitney interested while he trimmed him," she said, "but I didn't want any part of that."

"Naturally not!" I said.

She gave me an odd glance, then unexpectedly she said, "You're sweet."

I did not understand that at all. There was no sound from outside, and apparently Mr. Ganey was content just to wait. Very well. We could wait, too.

But as the sun climbed higher and higher, the flat-roofed, uninsulated boathouse became hotter and hotter, and I would have given much for a plain glass of cold water. I glanced sidelong at Peggy and saw her run her tongue over her dry lips. She, too, was feeling the first pangs of thirst. It was obvious that this discomfort would increase, so I looked about for a means of escape.

The large double doors opened to the Bay, so I knew there had to be a channel. If I could open those doors just wide enough to permit the passage of my body, I knew that I could swim underwater for a considerable distance, having won several prizes at the YMCA for my aquatic ability.

There was a bar across the doors. It could easily be reached from a boat, but standing at the edge of the enclosed dock I could just barely touch it with my splintered oar. Peggy watched me.

"And what's that going to get you?" she asked despondently.

I told her my plan of swimming underwater, and added, "But even if I am apprehended, I hope to draw off Mr. Ganey sufficiently to permit your escape. You could telephone from the Club and summon assistance."

"If he catches you in the water, Wes, he'll shoot you like a fish in a barrel!"

"I don't think so," I said with an assurance I was far from feeling. "He needs me to forge that check."

"And he'd cut you down," she retorted emphatically, "before he'd let you get away."

I shook my head stubbornly. It was, I felt, a necessary risk.

I gave the bar a preliminary prod. It was firmly wedged, but by squatting and prodding beneath it, I could feel it give just a little. Before very long, my muscles were aching from holding the heavy, broken oar at arm's length. I could work no more than ten minutes at a stretch, and each time I thrust, I lifted the bar no more than a fraction of an inch. The perspiration was pouring from me, and the intervals between thrusts grew longer. What made it more difficult was that I could not make a sound to arouse Mr. Ganey's suspicion.

It took fully two and a half hours of the most arduous labor to raise that bar the necessary four inches. Breathing heavily, I stripped off my shoes, socks, trousers, jacket and shirt. It was no time for false modesty. I let myself down into the water. It was about five feet deep. I waded silently to the door and inched it open.

I swear that the small squeak it made would not have aroused a bird, but almost instantly Mr. Ganey's feet thudded outside and a bullet through the door sent splinters flying into my face. I hastily splashed away from it as he laughed.

"Try again, pal," he called. "I was getting bored out here."

Discouraged, I climbed out of the water. His vigilance, it seemed, was greater than my ingenuity. Peggy patted my cheek.

"Don't take it so hard," she said with forced cheeriness. "At least you've had a refreshing dip."

I smiled weakly and started to dress again. As I picked up my wristwatch, I saw the time and uttered a small cry of consternation. It was 1:30 P.M.

"What's the matter?" Peggy asked anxiously.

"The time," I said dully. "I had to get ten orders today."

I told her about the contest and the post of district sales manager that I had hoped to win. "If I can get out of here," I said, "there's still a chance!"

She gave me another odd look, then said, "You're all business, aren't you?"

"The chance of becoming district sales manager does not occur every day."

"Yeah, and the chance of getting your head blown off doesn't occur every day, either."

She limped away from me and sat down on the floor with her back against the wall. I wanted to tell her that I was far from being "all business", but at that moment, Mr. Ganey called out again.

"I'm pushing a check under the door, pal. Take a look at it. Think it over. All you have to do is sign it. How else can you get five grand?"

I saw the yellow oblong of paper slide under the door, and I snatched it up. I tore it angrily into several pieces and flung them through the open window. He gave a cry of rage as he saw them flutter to the ground.

"Okay, pal," he said harshly, "I'm giving you till three o'clock and that's all. Three o'clock."

Peggy sat up tensely. "He's thought of something!" she said. "He's figured a way to get in."

I picked up the splintered oar. It seemed pitifully inadequate against a gun. However, there was nothing else.

"I don't see how he could get in." I tried to sound confident.

"You don't know Ganey. He's shrewder and tougher than anyone you've ever met before. Say ... how did you manage to get away from him in the first place, Wes?"

"I—I jumped out the window."

"Just like that?"

"I ran and he shot at me."

She looked at me as if there was something about me that was beyond understanding. "You got away from him," she said slowly, "and ... you came back. Why?"

I said hurriedly, "We've got to keep our eyes open now. We cannot afford to permit Mr. Ganey to surprise us."

I shouldered my club and began a slow patrol of the walls, listening for any untoward activity outside.

All right Sergeant O'Shea, so I didn't actually shoulder the club! What difference does it make, anyway? Now listen, I've taken just about as much from you as I ... All right, Mr. District Attorney, I'll sit down, and I'll finish my statement, but under protest, understand? Under protest!

The walls of the boathouse were very flimsy, nothing more than boards nailed to uprights, and in some cases the cracks between were more than an inch wide in width.

I felt increasingly apprehensive. If Mr. Ganey could manage to insert his gun between the boards of the wall, shooting us would be merely a matter of pulling the trigger. I posted myself in a corner and tried to watch all the walls at once. I couldn't think of any other way.

It was Peggy who first heard him. "Wes," she beckoned urgently. "He's up to something at the door."

I listened. Something scratched against the wood. There was a brief silence, and something scratched down the side of the door again. I looked at Peggy, and she shook her head. I couldn't understand it, either.

Mr. Ganey called heavily, "Last chance, pal. What's the word?"

I licked my lips. "No," I managed to sputter out.

This time he did not answer. I watched tensely. Nothing happened—then suddenly there was a crackling and a roar and a puff of smoke came under the door. He had piled dry palm fronds against the door and set fire to them. All he had to do was sit outside and shoot us as we ran out, through the water door or the window. Or—

My eyes lighted. He would be exceptionally vigilant, I knew, and we could use that as a weapon against him. I rapidly outlined a plan to Peggy, anxious, I admit, for her approval. To my astonishment, she stood on tiptoe, kissed me and whispered, "That's for luck, Wes."

Taking the second oar, she limped to the wall opposite the window and inserted the blade between the boards. She did it with caution, but nevertheless, the pried nails screeched, as I knew they would. I heard Mr. Ganey move rapidly outside as he went to investigate. I knew that I would have to act quickly.

Grasping my club, I scrambled through the window, grasped the edge of the flat roof and, panting, swung myself up. I tiptoed across. I peered over the opposite edge. There at the corner, a gloating smile on his lips, Mr. Ganey was watching, his gun ready in his hand to shoot us down as we came through the aperture Peggy was ostensibly making in the wall.

I was, at this point, actually hanging over the edge of the roof. Mr. Ganey had but to glance up and my career would have ended then and there. My heart hammering wildly, I raised my club and brought it down squarely on top of his head....

I'm afraid Peggy exaggerated my part in the incident when she gave her version at Police Headquarters, for I admit now that no one could have been as badly frightened as I. I slipped out of Headquarters in the confusion. It was 5:30. I went through the motions of calling on two prospects, two I had considered sure sales, but somehow, my heart was not in it, and I sold neither of them.

I felt very badly at having deserted Peggy at Headquarters. She alone would know why. "All business," she would say. I wanted desperately for her to know that I wasn't "all business," but now it seemed that there was no longer anything I could do about it.

The next morning, I slunk into the sales meeting, glancing glumly at the chart on the wall that showed the progress of each salesman. I was third on the list, though only four sales behind the leader. I sat down in the back row of chairs as Mr. Zimmer mounted the platform and rapped for order with a rolled-up newspaper firmly held in his hand.

"Well, fellas," he said in that inspirational voice of his, "today, as you know, is the big day. Yessir. Today one of you goes up another rung on the ladder of success, proving what I've always said— It's backbone, not wishbone, that gets the soupbone!"

Kelly, the high-ranking salesman, was already being congratulated by his neighbors.

"But first," said Mr. Zimmer, unrolling the newspaper, "I want to read you a little something ..."

I felt myself blushing as he read the news account of my belated capture of Mr. Ganey. Mr. Zimmer slapped the newspaper down against the table when he finished, and I jumped because it sounded uncomfortably like a pistol shot. He raised himself on tiptoe as he always does when he is putting across a message. It was his method of calling for attention.

"Wesley Smith," he said in a voice that grew in volume as he continued, "was offered a bitter choice—his life in exchange for his integrity—yet he steadfastly refused to forge that check. And what did he prove? I'll tell you what he proved. He proved that the integrity of a company can be as great and no greater than the integrity of the men who represent it to the public.

"I want each and every one of you to go out and buy this newspaper. I want you to read the story of Wesley Smith on the front page. There's a message in it for each and every one of you. Two columns long, and the name of the Bankers Friend Automatic Check Writer Corporation mentioned four times, telling the world that there must be something great about a company for which a man will risk his life to safeguard its name.

"Stand up, Wesley. Get up on your hind legs and give the boys a good look at the new district sales manager of the Bankers Friend Automatic Check Writer Corporation."

Well, that's all, Mr. District Attorney. I just wanted you to know why I left Police Headquarters instead of staying to make my statement at that time. If you're finished with me, I'd like to go, because Peggy's waiting for me outside.

That's the end! That's the last wisecrack I'm taking from you! Come on, O'Shea, put up your hands. You've been dishing it out, now let's see if you can take it …

PRELUDE TO A WAKE

Foyle stared at the spread of IOU's that lay on the table soaking up the spilled drinks—twenty-two thousand dollars' worth of them, all signed by George Bascule. He hadn't seen George in years, not since that South American business, but he knew George's signature. A careless slash of ink, typical of George. Foyle raised his eyes to the man sitting opposite him, reflecting that they were all alike, these men, from Hongkong to Hoboken, the big and the little. In the little ones, the panhandlers on the street, the predatory gleam was pretty dim, but in the big ones, like this fellow, it burned hot and fierce with the refusal to be denied.

This one's name was Routt, a round-headed blond with popping blue eyes and a thin, sucked-in mouth. He had brought a girl with him, and now she sat in the corner of the booth, smoking a cigarette and sullenly indifferent to both of them.

She was a brunette and worth every dollar, Foyle thought, that Routt had spent on her. But she was another predatory character. They seemed to run in pairs, on this level—men like Routt and their women.

Foyle reached out and picked up his glass of lime and rum, taking a sip before answering the question that had been put to him.

"What makes you think," he asked indifferently, "that I'm responsible for George Bascule's gambling debts?"

Routt shrugged and reached into a pocket, as if he had been expecting this question, and slid a newspaper clipping across the table. Foyle picked it up between his second and third fingers. His bony face was wooden as he read it.

It was datelined Tampa, Florida, and it said that the bullet-riddled body of a man, identified as Matthew Lund, had been found floating in Old Tampa Bay at the eastern foot of Gandy Bridge. There was a brief description of Lund, and according to a Sheriff Sublette, the old man had been the victim of a gang killing and was suspected of smuggling aliens from Cuba into Tampa, posing them as seamen from the shipping lines. That part of it sounded like the old man. He had been a former resident of Newark, New Jersey, and the clipping was from the *Newark Evening News*.

A muscle bulged in Foyle's jaw, but otherwise his face was unchanged as he dropped the clipping in the middle of the table between them.

"What about it?" he asked.

"You've got twenty thousand dollars belonging to Lund."

"I have?"

"There were five of you," said Routt, writing the figure 5 on the wet top of the table with his forefinger. "Soldiers of fortune, you called yourselves ..."

"What gave you that damn fool notion?" interrupted Foyle drily. "We didn't call ourselves anything." Then he laughed. "Oh, Bascule. Yes, George might have said a thing like that."

"May I continue?" asked Routt coldly.

Now that Foyle had laughed, it stayed close to the surface of his gray-green eyes. "You haven't finished?" he grinned.

"No."

"Then," he made a lordly, derisive gesture with his hand, "you may continue."

"This isn't a joke, Foyle."

"Oh, I don't know. I thought you wanted to continue."

The girl laughed suddenly and sharply, and her eyes gleamed sidewise at Routt, enjoying the pinch of anger that showed white at the flange of his nostrils. She leaned toward Foyle.

"Watch yourself," she said. "Routt doesn't have a sense of humor."

Routt looked at her. "That's your last crack," he said.

He turned back to Foyle. "There were five of you," he said, as if nothing had happened since the first time he made that statement. "You hired out to the government of Palmagua, in South America, to fight the guerillas under Montoya. There were ten of you, actually, who went out on reconnaissance patrol in the hills where the guerillas hid, but only five of you lived after your attack on the paymaster's mule train. You got a hundred thousand dollars out of that raid, and you were the one who carried it in the retreat. Matthew Lund was wounded, and he made you leave him behind, or all five of you would have been captured. Your retreat," Routt's voice became momentarily ironical and he traced two x's on the wet wood of the table with his finger, "carried you all the way to the seaport of Jurua, where you took the first banana boat to New York. Not forgetting the hundred thousand dollars, of course."

Foyle forked his fingers through his harsh red hair and laughed. "It was a tough trip," he confided. "We had the guerillas *and* the federal troops after us every jump of the way. But go on. I got a feeling you're just coming to the interesting part of the story."

The girl laughed softly, but this time Routt ignored her.

"Yes," he said. "The interesting part was your division of the money. You held out a full share for Lund, saying it was his by rights, if he came out alive, but that it would be divided if he didn't."

Foyle murmured, "You can't help liking George Bascule, even if he does talk his head off. But you must have gotten him drunk, or was he already drunk and babbling when you picked him up? I think that must have been it." Foyle nodded and flicked the IOU's with his finger. "Otherwise you wouldn't have let him get this deep into you. Did he also tell you that the money is banked in the Newark and Essex Trust? He must have. George always told everything when he was drunk. But go ahead and finish, now that you've come to the really interesting part."

"Lund is dead," said Routt flatly. "Two others of the five are dead, too. You and Bascule are the only ones still alive, so you've got ten thousand dollars belonging to Bascule. I want it. He owes it to me, and I want it."

"Naturally. If a man owed me money, I'd want it, too." Foyle drained his glass. He set it down very carefully in the same wet ring from which he had lifted it. "You want it pretty badly, I suppose?"

"You have it. I want it."

"Suppose I said the hell with you?"

"You won't. If you were honest enough to hold Lund's share all this time—three years, isn't it?" Routt's first smile was a mocking pursing of his lips. "You'll be honest enough to give Bascule what's coming to him."

"If I gave George what's coming to him," said Foyle with sudden violence, "he'd be in the hospital for a month. For blabbing to you. What kind of a damn fool do you take me for, anyway? You show me a scrap of paper torn out of a newspaper, and expect me to hand you ten thousand dollars. Well, I'm not going to, bucko!"

"Lund is dead."

"Is he? Did you have him embalmed and bring him along with you? I don't *know* that Lund is dead, and until I do, neither you nor George Bascule, nor anybody else, is going to get a smell of that money."

The girl had stopped smoking and was leaning forward, watching Foyle with interest.

"Would you take the word of the Tampa police?" asked Routt.

"Maybe."

Routt's temper cracked again. "Believe me, Foyle," he snapped, "the Tampa police are not in my employ. Are you willing to take *anybody's* word for his death?"

Foyle flushed. "I'll confirm it my own way," he said.

"And in your own time, Foyle? The way you've waited three years to give Lund his share of the money?"

"I didn't *wait* three years. I was offered a job in India and I took it."

"You could have banked the money in Lund's name so he could draw on it. But you didn't, did you? You banked it in your own name. You didn't touch it, I know. But no one else could, either. Are you going to wait another three years, Foyle?"

Foyle half rose from his chair, his face clotting. Routt's right hand darted under his left lapel and he leaned back.

Foyle said harshly, "Pull that gun, Routt, and I'll slap you silly with it!"

Routt's hand came slowly out from under his coat.

"Well?" he said challengingly.

Foyle dropped back in his seat and put both fists on the edge of the table before him. They were big, bony fists, white across the knuckles.

"We'll settle it tonight," he said heavily "My way. Give me a piece of paper. I'll send a telegram to a friend of mine in Tampa."

"Why not call him on the phone?"

"He's in the Tampa Hospital for Paraplegics," said Foyle shortly. "But he has contacts. Do you have a piece of paper or don't you?"

Silently, Routt handed him a small leatherbound notebook and a pen. Foyle scribbled out the telegram, hesitating at the end.

"What's the address of this gin mill?" he asked.

"Seven-six-three River Street, Hoboken. It's called Ed and Shorty's."

"I know what it's called. Here, you send it." Contemptuously, he tossed the notebook across the table at Routt. It struck the man's chest and slid into his lap.

Routt's nostrils whitened, but he took the notebook and slid out of the booth. As he stood, Foyle looked up at him and asked softly:

"Tell me, Routt, was it you who had Lund killed?"

"Talk sense," said Routt and started toward the phone booth. He stopped and looked back over his shoulder. He tapped the notebook. "And this had better be answered tonight before closing."

"If you're worried," drawled Foyle, "add 'urgent' to it."

Routt walked away without another word.

The girl started, "If you want me to leave …"

Foyle held up his hand, stopping her. "Just a minute," he murmured.

He stood and leaned over the partition between his booth and the booth behind him. Two men were sitting there—one bald and squat, very broad across the shoulders; the other young, with wavy black hair, a self-satisfied expression and an obviously expensive chalk-striped blue suit.

Foyle looked down at them and said, "Beat it."

They sat stock still for a moment, surprised, and then the young one began angrily, "Who the hell do you—"

The squat man backhanded him casually across the mouth and said, "Shut up, punk." He looked up at Foyle with eyes as brown as melted chocolate. "Beat it why?" he asked mildly.

Foyle grinned at him with appreciation. He knew this kind of man. In a sense, Foyle was the same kind.

"Because," he said, "all we do now for a while is wait. Your boss is phoning a telegram. He won't be coming back here. He won't like my company. You two better join him at the bar. I want some privacy."

The squat man considered this thoughtfully. "Or else?" he asked.

"Or else," Foyle agreed cheerfully.

The man sighed, "Oh hell," and slid out of the booth. "Come on, punk."

The boy said hotly, not taking his eyes from Foyle, "You can go if you want to, but me. I'm staying."

"Suit yourself, but if he takes that gun away from you, the boss'll crucify you."

Chuckling, the squat man walked toward the bar. The boy sat undecided for a moment, then scrambled angrily out of the booth. He faced Foyle and for a minute it looked as if he might spit straight at him, but his eyes wavered and he spat on the floor in front of Foyle's booth instead.

"Tough boy," he jeered. "Real tough."

Having vindicated himself, he swaggered across the room to the bar. The two regulars, who had been drinking beer at the far end of the bar, quietly put down their glasses and just as quietly turned and walked out. The bartender hurriedly walked down, took their glasses, mopped the bar and looked anxiously out into the darkness of River Street. There was nothing across the street but the high fence that surrounded the docks and warehouses of the steamship lines. Routt's two henchmen were now the only ones at the bar.

Foyle turned and slipped back into his seat, grinning at the girl. "Hell, no," he said, as if just answering her question, "I don't want you to leave. It's not very often that I get the chance of buying cheap drinks for something as expensive as you. What's your name?"

Her chin lifted. "I'm not Routt's woman and never was," she said defiantly.

"And never will be, I guess. He just gave you the kiss-off, and with a guy like him I'd say it's permanent. Why'd you feel you had to needle him all the time?"

"I wasn't his woman. You don't believe me, but I wasn't. I just went around with him. Things happen where he goes. I thought I'd like that."

Foyle rubbed his chin and gave her a searching glance. Apparently satisfied, he nodded. "Yes," he said, "I've done some things I wasn't proud of, too, just because I wanted to be where something was happening. Is that why you needled him—because you'd gotten in, couldn't see a way out, and weren't very proud of yourself? Is that it?"

"There's more to it than that," she said wearily. "It's not that simple. All right, I was his woman, but I didn't have the guts to walk out on him. I needled him so he'd kick me out. Does that satisfy you?"

"Satisfy me?" Foyle looked surprised. "What have I got to do with it? The point is, does it satisfy you?" Then he laughed. "There's an old song," he said, "about a bear. It went over the mountain, but there was always another mountain, and the bear always kept going over the next one, just to see the other side. It sounds pretty pointless, until you consider that he must have seen a helluva lot of mountains and become a pretty well-traveled bear after a while.... Now, can I buy you a drink?"

"But you don't understand," she said with a bleak kind of earnestness. "Everybody knew I was Routt's woman. Nora Logan, Routt's girl, me. And yes, I can use a drink."

Foyle called the bartender with a careless wave of his arm and said, "There's something you can tell me. I got back in New York a week ago from India, where I spent some of the best years of my life teaching Mr. Nehru's soldier boys to shoulder arms. I got a room up in Myer's Hotel here in Hoboken, but I don't like the bar there because it's always full of tourists from East Orange. I like this gin mill. Until their ship sailed, it was full of Dutch sailors who like to sing Dutch songs. So. Tonight you and Routt walked in on me, and this is what I want to know—who the hell is this Routt?"

Her mouth fell open at the unexpectedness of the question, and when she realized the implication, she said wryly, "Nice try, Foyle. Very nice try but you can ask about Routt, and they'll tell you, in Miami and in San Francisco and in Chicago and in New York ..."

"Yeah, but I'm asking in Hoboken. Who *is* he?"

"He's a gambler."

"That much I guessed. A big shot?"

"A *very* big shot."

"But right now he's broke, eh?"

Nora Logan's eyes sprang wide, then narrowed suspiciously. "I thought you didn't know him."

"I don't, but a big shot wouldn't be making such a college try for ten thousand bucks if he weren't broke. He'd send somebody to collect it. And he wouldn't have fooled around with somebody like George Bascule, in the first place. So he's broke."

"He won't be for long," said Nora bitterly. "He never is. He just needs a stake."

The bartender came to the table and nervously asked what it would be. Foyle told him to bring a bottle of Royal George scotch. Tonelessly, the bartender said the best they had was Vat 69 and it was eight bucks, would that do or wouldn't it? Foyle cocked an eyebrow at him.

"Why not make it ten bucks while you're at it?" he asked.

"Okay. Ten bucks." His eyes were passively hostile.

"Bring it. And for the same ten bucks you can bring us a bucket of ice and two or three bottles of plain soda. Roger?"

"Roger," said the barkeep with disgust. He walked away.

"He doesn't like us," whispered Nora.

"Can you blame him? We cleaned out his bar for him. And Routt'll keep it clean 'til this is settled. He doesn't like a mess any more than—" Foyle grinned wryly "—most people."

Nora looked at him and her young face was suddenly tired. "You can include me," she said. "I'm tired of messes, too."

"Too?"

"How old are you, Foyle?"

Foyle winced and unconsciously his fingers touched his temple where the gray had begun to seep into the angry red of his hair.

"Maybe you're right," he said. "Maybe you're right."

"If I'm not, then all the happy tourists from East Orange all over the country are wrong."

Foyle, suddenly harsh, said, "Hold your hats, kids, here we go again."

Routt had come out of the phone booth and was standing at the bar beside the squat man, and the two of them were looking expressionlessly toward the booth while the boy in the two-hundred-dollar chalk-stripe suit slowly crossed the intervening space with reluctant feet. His cockiness was gone. The squat man had obviously and sadistically told him a few things about Foyle.

Foyle felt the impulse to slide out of the booth just to see the boy jump, but he grimly checked it. He waited until the boy came up to the table and said to Nora, with a jerk of his head toward the bar:

"He wants to see you."

Before Nora could answer, Foyle grabbed the front of the boy's double-breasted jacket, jerked him against the table, fanning him quickly for a gun. There wasn't any gun. The squat man at the bar laughed, but it was a laugh of respect and satisfaction, as if he had learned something he had wanted to find out and now had things well in hand.

Foyle shoved the boy back roughly, swearing to himself. They had wanted to find out if he was carrying a gun, and now they knew he wasn't, or else he wouldn't have fanned the boy.

But he was totally unprepared for what happened next.

The boy staggered back three hard-heeled paces, his face veal white, gave his right arm the peculiar straight-arm jerk of a knife fighter with a knife up his sleeve, and lunged at Foyle with the knife blade gleaming between his thumb and forefinger.

Foyle swore and kicked up the table with his knees, deflecting the boy's arm, and he saw the wickedly gleaming blade go past his eyes and heard the thunk as the point stabbed into the high wooden back of the booth. He grabbed the boy's wrist, and if Nora had not been sitting there, her mouth rounded in horror, he would have wrenched down, breaking the boy's arm across the edge of the table. Instead, he bounced the boy's elbow twice against the table edge, then released his grip and pulled the knife out of the wood over his left shoulder. It was a beautiful, balanced knife with an ivory handle—the kind you either make for yourself or have made to order for fifty dollars.

Foyle hefted it familiarly and said, "Tell *Mr.* Routt that *Mrs.* Routt does not care to join him at the moment." He said it gravely, without any hint of a smile.

The boy stood white-faced, holding his elbow, then turned and walked back to the bar. The squat man patted him patronizingly on the shoulder, and Routt said something to him. With a look of hatred toward Foyle, the boy walked out of the bar, not holding his elbow but squeezing his arm against his side so he wouldn't have to swing it as he walked.

Foyle muttered, "I'm getting old. I should have known you can't play around with a young buck. I shouldn't have fanned him. I should have smacked him. If you hadn't been here, it would have been different. You can't shame that kind in front of a woman. I thought I'd have to kill him at the end."

A little hysterically, Nora cried, "Getting old!" Then, "How did you know Routt and I were married?"

"How did Mr. Bessemer know what made steel?" Foyle asked sourly. His hand flicked and the knife flew across the table, pinning the collar of Nora's sport coat to the wood of the high seat behind her. "Good knife." Before she could even gasp, he reached out, wrenched the knife loose and bounced it appreciatively in his hand. "Good knife."

The bartender came to their table with the scotch, ice and soda. He was not hostile any longer. He was scared and there was no room for anything else. He knew now that the bar was divided into two camps, and that he was the innocent bystander who always got it in the neck, and that there was no hope for him unless a policeman dropped in, which was unlikely. The police went down River Street in prowl cars.

Foyle took the scotch bottle and under the cover of opening it, he said, "Can you get me a gun?"

The bartender had already made up his mind against Routt. He nodded. "In the till," he whispered back.

"Can you get it to me in a tray of sandwiches?"

"I can try, buddy. Any particular kind of sandwiches?"

Nora laughed hysterically. "Ham," she cried. "Ham and Swiss on rye with mustard!"

"With mustard," muttered the barkeep. "And, brother, I hope you know what you're doing!"

He walked quickly away, twitching his towel against his leg. He did not have to go into a back room to make the sandwiches. All the makings were at the end of the bar next the hamburger grill and coffee urn.

Nora grasped the edge of the table, leaned over it and said a little wildly, "You're not going to do it, are you? You're not going to do it."

"Do what?"

"Give Routt that ten thousand dollars. You're not going to do it no matter what happens. Isn't that right?"

"That depends."

"Depends on what? The answering telegram from Tampa? I don't believe that."

Foyle' drew his mouth together and glanced sideways at Routt's back. The man was leaning over the bar, talking to his henchman.

"There won't be any answering telegram from Tampa," he said. He grinned a reckless, lilting grin. "I don't know if Tampa has a hospital for paraplegics, but if it does, I don't have any friends in it."

Aghast, Nora said, "*What!*" Her fingers clawed on the tabletop, and she stared at him incredulously.

He shoveled ice into the two clean glasses the bartender had brought, measured the pour of scotch with his eye, then added soda for a strong drink. He handed her one of the glasses.

"Well," he said, "let's try the dive from the twenty-foot board. I think your husband killed the wrong man, Mrs. Routt."

"Don't call me that!"

"All right. I apologize."

"I mean it," she said fiercely. "He may kill me before this is over tonight, but you've got to know how I feel!"

Impulsively, he took her outstretched hand, looked down at it, then, with a rueful grin, kissed the palm of it.

"Yes, Nora," he said gently.

She jerked her hand away from him. "Don't pity me!" she cried tearfully. "I don't want pity. I wasn't the underprivileged child, I wasn't a slum kid. I went in with my eyes wide open. My father was a school teacher in White Plains, New York. I was wild, you understand. I was just plain no good …"

"Maybe that makes two of us. My old man was a mechanical engineer. Worked in a furnace factory. The only thing I can say for myself is that I've never fought against my country, though I've fought under every flag except my own. Call us two of a kind."

Nora's hands, both of them, now closed convulsively around his. "I want to know something," she asked feverishly. "I want to ask you something. About that twenty thousand dollars. I know you've never touched it—but did you ever intend to give it to Matthew Lund?"

He said very carefully, "That's a funny question."

"Three years you waited. Three years! You could have found him before. You knew he escaped. You must have known, but you waited three years. Why? Why did you wait? You didn't want to turn it over to him, did you? You wanted to keep it!"

"I was in India. If Lund is dead. I *will* divide it with George Bascule."

"You will divide with Bascule?"

"If Lund is dead. I don't think he's dead."

She said, "Oh," and her shoulders seemed to slump a little. "You don't think Lund is dead, but instead of trying to verify the report of his death, you sent a telegram to a fictitious man in a fictitious hospital. You're never going to give that money up, are you, Foyle? To Bascule, Routt, or anybody. Why did you send that telegram?"

His gray-green eyes snapped and he said angrily, "What is all this anyway? Why all the questions? Have I applied for a job, or something?"

"I just thought you were somebody, that's all," she said dully. "I just thought I had finally met somebody who wasn't like Routt and the rest of them."

He stared at her and slowly a lopsided grin dug into his right cheek. "Think of that," he murmured. "After all this, you still think there's an honest man."

She picked up her bag from the table and started to slide out of the booth. "Oh, let me out of here," she said. "At least Routt never pretended."

Foyle put out his long arm and stopped her. "Stick around," he said. "Maybe you were right the first time. That wasn't Matty Lund they found in Tampa Bay. Matty Lund had only one arm, and when they described that guy in the newspaper story, they didn't say anything about only one arm. They wouldn't have missed that in a description, would they?"

"Then who—who did they find?"

"Ask Routt. He had it done so he could show me proof that Matty Lund was dead. I sent that phony telegram because I need time. I sent Matty a telegram five days ago, telling him to meet me here tonight. I'm waiting for him."

Her face showed only horror. "You fool!" she said. "You fool! Do you think that's going to stop Routt now? Do you think he's going to let you get away with that money? He needs more than a stake. He's in the hole, and if he doesn't pay up, he knows what they'll do to him. He won't be the first gambler they took for a ride because he didn't pay up. Foyle. Listen to me, Foyle."

She clutched his hand in both of hers. "Give him the ten thousand dollars. This is his last chance to get the money, and he's desperate. You haven't looked outside since we came in, have you? Well, I'll tell you what's out there for Routt. There's death out there unless he gets the money, or the definite assurance of it—*tonight!* Maxon and Tony aren't his men. They're here to see that he gets the money or—the other thing."

"Maxon and Tony?"

"Maxon's the one standing at the bar with Routt. Tony's the young one who went out. Their car is waiting outside, and there's another man in it. They'll help Routt get the money from you, if they have to. They'll hurt you, Foyle. They'll hurt you dreadfully, and in the end you'll give them the money, anyway. Give it to them now, before anything happens. Give it to them now!"

She saw Foyle's head jerk around and his eyes become very intent. She turned and saw that a uniformed policeman had just walked in, thrusting back his cap and wiping his forehead with a handkerchief. Routt and the squat man, Maxon, stood frozen as the bartender walked quickly down the bar toward the cop. Foyle grasped Nora's arm and whispered harshly:

"You keep your mouth shut, understand?"

She tried to free her arm. "You're hurting me."

"You keep out of this. Let me handle it."

"All right, but let me go, please. You're hurting me."

He muttered, "Sorry," and released her arm, watching the policeman stroll toward their booth.

The policeman stopped at the table and looked down at Foyle. He was a big man, middle-aged and gone to fat. His blue coat strained at the buttons across his middle.

"What's the trouble, buddy?" he said to Foyle. "The barkeep says those two guys at the bar have you behind the eight ball."

Foyle looked surprised. "Trouble? There's no trouble now. I had a little trouble a while ago with a wise kid, but he's gone."

"Now wait a minute, buddy. The barkeep said you wanted a gun."

"A gun!" Foyle blinked, then roared with laughter. "What would I do with a gun? I'd probably shoot myself in the foot, or something. If you ask me, the barkeep's been sampling his inventory."

The policeman's face turned fiery red. "And it wouldn't be the first time," he said angrily. "Sorry to have bothered you, buddy."

He turned, and glowering at the barkeep, walked out of the bar. The barkeep stared at Foyle, then walked back to the sandwich counter and deliberately threw the two ham and Swiss sandwiches into the waste can.

Nora breathed, "And you could have walked out of here ..."

Foyle shook his head. "How far do you think they'd have let me go? And how much good do you think that fat cop would have done? His badge wouldn't save him from a clout over the head, and we'd be out of here and in that car you told me was waiting outside."

"But you can't just sit here!"

Foyle glanced toward the door. "It's beginning to rain," he murmured.

As if to verify his observation, a peal of thunder reverberated across the night, and out on the river, a wallowing tugboat hooted twice. Foyle gently patted the girl's hand.

"Will they let you walk out of here?" he asked.

She shook her head. "Not now. Not anymore."

"Try going to the john. There may be a window or a door back there. The going may get rough, and I don't want you to get hurt."

"They won't let me, Foyle."

"Try it."

Obediently, she slid out of the booth and walked steadily across the floor toward the door marked *Ladies*. Under the sign, some prankster had penciled, *Ha-Ha*. Routt did not stop her. He followed her and when she went into the room, he quickly stopped the door with his foot before she could close and lock it. She jerked it open, her face red.

His lips puckered in his pursy smile and he said, "Don't mind me, darling. After all ..."

She slapped him furiously, thrust past him and strode back to the booth. Maxon followed the movement of her hips with his chocolatey eyes and put his tongue in his cheek.

Foyle stood as Nora came back to the booth; then he sat and tipped the scotch bottle over her glass. He smiled at her.

"I'll bet that did you good," he said, "that slap."

"I wish I'd had a club!" Her hands were shaking.

He glanced up at the wall, at the clock that advertised Four Roses. It was ten-thirty.

"Three and a half hours till closing," he murmured. "Am I going to see you again, after this is all over?"

She raised her eyes to his face and silently began to cry. Foyle patted her hand, then looked up quickly as the street door opened again. There were three men, obviously members of the engine-room crew of a docked freighter. All three wore black caps and grease-stained dungarees and skivvies. They rapped noisily on the bar and called for beer.

Maxon stopped the bartender and spoke a few words to him. The bartender wet his lips and rolled his eyes toward the three men clamoring for beer, and when he walked toward them, he looked scared.

"Sorry, fellas," he said, "no tap beer. The keg run out."

"Okay, give us some bottles."

"All I got's the imported. That's seventy-five cents a bottle."

They swore at him, telling him what to do with his bottles of imported Holland beer at seventy-five cents a bottle, and stamped out, slamming the door. The bartender just stood there, staring after them, not looking back at Maxon, who was watching him with a small smile on his round face.

Maxon's the man to watch, thought Foyle, Maxon's the tough one. Routt's desperate, but Maxon'll be the one to swing the ax.

But aside from keeping the bar clear of transient customers, Maxon seemed to be keeping himself aloof, his attitude saying very plainly that, until the deadline, it was Routt's party. Once or twice he glanced curiously at Foyle, as if the big red-headed man had him puzzled. He had been like that since Foyle had gotten rid of the policeman. Maxon and Routt hardly spoke, and when they did, it was always Routt who initiated the conversation, and Maxon answered him only in monosyllables. At twelve-thirty he was yawning and seemed to be getting drowsy, but Foyle knew better. Maxon was just coasting, taking it easy, waiting.

Nora had not said anything for an hour. She sat hunched in the back corner of the booth, watching Foyle with tragic eyes. Foyle was watching the door. His eyes sharpened when the door opened at one o'clock and a gray-haired Salvation Army man walked in with a black, shiny raincoat thrown over his shoulders like a cape. The man took off his red-banded cap, set it down on the bar and wiped the rain from his face, his glance wandering from Foyle to Routt and Maxon and then to the bartender. Foyle sighed and sat back in his chair.

The Salvation Army man tried to order a cup of coffee, but the bartender, with a sidelong glance at Maxon, shook his head.

"Sorry," he said gruffly, "all outta coffee."

"Then give me a cup of that brown stuff that's bubbling away in there." The Salvation Army man pointed at the coffee urn. A finger of steam was coming from the top of it, and the coffee could plainly be seen on the tubular glass gauge at the side.

Maxon growled, "Give him a cup of coffee and shut up. Here, pal, put this in your hat." He spun a half dollar down the bar.

The Salvation Army man picked it up and put it in his pocket. "Thank you and God bless you," he said gravely.

Maxon said sure, and laughed, as if he found it very funny.

The phone rang and Routt jumped for it. He came out of the booth and crooked his finger at Foyle.

"For you," he said. "Western Union."

Foyle muttered to Nora, "Here we go. Stay here."

Nora's eyes became enormous as she watched him cross the room to the phone booth. Routt stepped in front of him. His face was shiny with perspiration.

"I want to hear this, too," he said tightly. "Have them repeat it to me."

Foyle shrugged and picked up the receiver. He felt his stomach tighten just a little, the way it always did before an action. He knew what Western Union was going to say to him—*sorry, but we could not deliver your telegram. There is no Tampa Hospital for Paraplegics.*

"Yes?" he said into the mouthpiece.

The voice began to talk and his harsh, red eyebrows lifted. Then he grinned. Western Union was giving him an "answer" to his telegram. "Body positively identified as Matthew Lund. Anything else you want to know, pal? Why don't you drop in and see a guy once in a while?" It was signed with the fictitious name to which Foyle had sent the original telegram, and it had come from Tampa.

Foyle said solemnly, "Would you mind repeating that, please?" and handed the receiver to Routt.

Routt, the man who thought of everything, the man who had acquaintances all over the country, including Tampa, would have an acquaintance who would, as a favor, answer one fictitious telegram with another.

Routt hung up and faced Foyle. "Well," he said with satisfaction, "are you convinced now?"

Foyle felt a tingling in his legs. Maxon was standing away from the bar now, watching them. Foyle gave his head a short nod.

"If I can't trust that guy," he said, tilting his chin at the phone, "I can't trust anybody. But you're still not getting the money, Routt. It goes to Bascule and nobody else."

Routt's mouth pursed and he walked to the front door. He opened it and waved his arm. He stood there until the young hoodlum, Tony, walked in, pushing a staggering, unshaven man before him.

Foyle's heart turned over at the sight of this drunken derelict. It was three years since he had seen George Bascule, and at that time George had been a laughing, good-natured braggart. Whatever had happened in those three years, it had left Bascule a bleary-eyed wreck.

Foyle cried poignantly, "George!"

Bascule raised his head and looked dimly around. Spying Foyle, he rubbed the back of his hand across his mouth and grinned loosely.

"Hiya, Foyle," he said thickly. "Heard you was back. How's about buying a drink for an ol' friend?" He lurched to the bar and stood there blinking and grinning foolishly at Foyle.

Routt said sharply, "Here's a check, Foyle. Give him his money."

Foyle looked down at the check Routt was offering. It was a Newark and Essex Trust counter check. Foyle raised his eyebrows and took it. Routt did think of everything. He laid it on the bar and bent over it with the pen Routt had thrust at him. He looked up at Bascule.

"Do you want me to make this out to you, George?" he asked softly. "Or shall I make it out directly to Routt, here?"

Bascule clung to the bar with both hands and his mouth fell open.

"Ten thousand dollars, George," said Foyle. "Half of old man Lund's share."

Bascule swallowed. He stammered, "Foyle, I swear I didn't mean to get you mixed up in this, but I'm always a damn fool when it comes to likker. I ..." His hands clawed on the edge of the bar and he cried, "Don't give it to him, Foyle. He gypped me. He got me soused, and when I woke up he said I owed him. I don't even remember playing poker with him. Don't give it to him!"

He shoved himself away from the bar and fled clumsily toward the door.

Tony took two lithe strides and chopped him savagely across the back of the neck with his clubbed fist. Bascule went down on his face, twitching. Tony raised his foot to kick him in the side and, with a roar, Foyle flung Maxon out of his way and lunged. He caught Tony by the arm, twisted him around and hit him in the stomach as hard as he could. Gagging, Tony doubled up, and Foyle hit him in the face, driving him back against the bar, chopping again and again at the gagging face, refusing to let Tony fall.

The bartender cried, "Oh, God," and Maxon flung himself at Foyle, locking his arms behind him at the elbows. Tony slid to the floor and lay still.

Maxon grunted, "Take it easy, pal, or I'll let you have it, so help me."

Foyle took a breath. "You can let me go."

Maxon released him and stepped back warily. Routt had not moved from his place at the bar.

"Are you going to finish making out the check or not?" he asked sharply.

Foyle balanced on the balls of his feet. He looked over his shoulder. Maxon was behind him, his head cocked to one side as if he were still very, very curious about Foyle.

Foyle laughed and thrust out his finger at Routt.

"I'll make you a deal," he cried liltingly. "If Lund is dead, there's twenty thousand dollars floating around loose. I'll cut cards with you. Twenty thousand or nothing. What do you say, Routt?"

Routt's eyes seemed to bulge and his glance flickered at Maxon. His pale tongue darted out across his lips. He showed his teeth.

"That's a deal," he said hoarsely. "But we'll use his cards." He jerked his head toward the barkeep.

The bartender said shakily, "All I got's a pair of dice." He reached under the bar and put a leather dice cup on the bar. "Here you are."

Foyle shook it out and picked up one of the dice, grinning into Routt's sweating face.

"One roll," he said. "Want me to go first?"

Routt swallowed. "Yes."

Foyle flipped his dice. It bounced down the bar, caromed off Routt's glass, spun for a moment and turned up a six.

Routt cried, "No dice! It wasn't a free roll. It hit the glass."

"I never heard that rule before. Just make it up? I suppose if I had turned up a six without hitting the glass, you'd have accused me of using educated dice. I think George was right. I think you did clip him."

Routt swung his arm, sweeping the dice and glass from the top of the bar. "The hell with this!" he said hoarsely. "Give me my ten thousand."

Foyle smiled into Routt's convulsed face, then turned his head just a little and said over his shoulder, "Tell them who you are, bucko!"

"Why," said the Salvation Army man, "the name's Lund. Matty Lund, old man Lund himself, in person." He whirled and dived straight at Maxon, and his raincoat falling off showed his left sleeve pinned emptily to his shoulder.

Routt cried out and scrambled back, his hand darting under his coat for his gun. Foyle's open-handed swing caught him across the face and sent him staggering and flailing across the floor. Foyle bounded after him and slapped again, then again and again, driving Routt across the room. Routt crushed against the wall and Foyle finished him off with a short, hard hook to the jaw.

Foyle bent over him and swiftly flipped out the gun from under his left arm. He whirled. Maxon was sitting on the floor, dizzily shaking his head, and old man Lund was standing over him.

"Butted him right in the kisser," the old man cried gleefully. "I always did have the hardest damn head. Here's his cannon, you crazy mick." He swept Maxon's gun down the room to Foyle with a flip of his foot. Foyle picked it up, grinning.

"Old man," he said, "I've just had a sweet time saving your twenty thousand dollars for you."

The old man walked over to the bar, picking up his raincoat on the way. He put on the red-banded cap of the Salvation Army. He gave the visor a little tug, setting it jauntily on his head. He looked at himself in the mirror.

"Now I got the strength to tell you what I came all the way up from Tampa for," he said. "I don't want the money, Irish. I'm a reformed character, but if I got my hands on that much money, I'd go right back to being unreformed. I think I like it better being reformed. I could say give it to the Salvation Army, but I ain't gonna, because it'd always be an awful temptation for me to tell somebody the money came from me, and I'd start getting a big head, and there's nothing like a big head to start you on the way to getting unreformed again. Now I want to get out of here. You're a bad influence, Irish. For two years I've been decent and God-fearing and now, after only a half hour around you, I've been fighting and rolling around on barroom floors and swearing."

"You're kidding!" gasped Foyle.

"No sir, I'm not kidding. All I want is to go back to Tampa and get back to doing good, and I hope the good Lord will forgive me for lifting my hand against a fellow man even if that fellow man was as sinful and ugly as a moth-eaten gorilla. My advice to you is to keep that money. You always were unreformed and you always will be unreformed, so it can't do you any harm. And in case you do decide to get reformed, maybe the money'll help you stay that way, because you ain't like me, content just to do good. As I remember, you've never been content unless you had that big hairy fist of yours in somebody's kisser. So long, Irish. And so long, ma'am," he said to Nora. "I seen you looking at him like he was something, special. Well, he is."

He turned and walked quickly out of the bar, his raincoat flapping behind him.

The bartender had been standing, gaping, behind the bar. Now he vaulted over it and ran for the phone booth, muttering, "This time I'm calling the cops." He stopped at the booth and glowered back at Foyle. "Don't you understand, stupid?" he shouted angrily. "I'm calling the cops. Get that dame outta here before she gets mixed up in this, too."

Nora came running from the booth. Foyle put his arm around her and hurried her out of the bar. As they stepped out on the sidewalk and started up the street, they heard a car door slam and saw a man come sprinting from it toward them. Foyle waved the gun he had taken from Routt and the man sheered off sharply, darting now for the door of the bar.

Foyle lengthened his stride and carried Nora along with him. They turned the corner and started up toward Hudson Street, hearing the sound of the police siren. Foyle looked back, and as he did, a car roared north on River Street and he caught a glimpse of Routt's white face in the rear window as the car flashed under the street light. There was a flat crack, like the bark of a gun; the door of the car opened and something tumbled out, flapping limply like a scarecrow. Nora gave a cry, but Foyle tightened his arm around her and hurried her forward.

"No, honey," he said, "don't go back." Then, "Don't ever go back."

IF THE BODY FITS—

"For three days now …" Joe was saying thoughtfully. "He ain't showed for three days on that old wagon of his, and it got me to thinking. He's dead."

"And it hasn't been reported?" I asked. Joe was chief of police, and he'd know.

He shook his head. "No. That's what got me to thinking. Between you and me, there's more funny business going on out at that farm than we know about, them two hating one another's gizzards the way they do. Let's get Doc and take a run out."

I stammered, "You—you think he was murdered, Joe? Is that what you think?"

He shrugged. "What's *your* guess?"

Old Jake Stence was a miser.

He wasn't merely economical, thrifty, parsimonious or even just stingy. He was a fanatical, money-crazed miser.

Let me give you an example of the kind of thing he did. Eighteen years ago, just after young Johnny was born, his wife dropped dead with the baby in her arms. She rolled down the stairs from the second floor, and the baby wasn't expected to live. Jake hitched the horse to his wagon and disappeared for twelve hours. When he came back, he had two battered, paintless coffins in the back of the wagon—a large one for his wife and a little, four-foot one for the baby. How or where he had gotten them was anybody's guess, but from the looks of those old relics, you knew darned well he had gotten them for a song.

But there was a joke in it—if you can imagine a joke in a pair of coffins. The baby didn't die, and Jake was stuck with that second four-foot coffin on his hands. He went out one morning with it in the back of the wagon again, but when he returned that evening his face was as dark as midnight in a wolf's throat—and the coffin was still in the wagon.

From that day on he hated young Johnny. There are charitable folks around who said he hated the baby because he blamed his wife's death on it. Me, I know better. He hated the baby because it didn't die and use that coffin. Jake never forgot a wasted penny, and he never forgave it, either.

The kid got through as much school as he had to, and every extra minute he spent working on old Jake's poultry farm. And not learning the poultry business, as you might think. No. Learning the business of being a miser. Jake drilled it into him from morning till night, sixteen hours a day, until in the end Johnny was just as miserly as old Jake himself.

And don't think for a minute that Jake ever let the kid forget that useless little four-foot coffin. He kept it in the parlor so he could brood over it, so he could beat his breast every time he looked at it—so it would be a continual reproach to the kid for being alive.

You don't have to be a psychiatrist to know that that's no life for a kid. Young Johnny was saving string and making one nail do the work of four when most kids are still playing with dolls, and at the age when he should have been teasing the young girls and offering them sodas in exchange for a furtive kiss later, he was working sixteen and sometimes twenty hours a day, piling penny on top of penny, and nickel on top of nickel, watching them turn into precious dollars. As I said, it was no life for a kid. It was no life for anybody.

They were a familiar sight around town, young Johnny and old Jake, perched side by side on the hard seat of that old wagon. Every day they came through to sell their eggs from door to door because they could squeeze out a few extra pennies that way. And they were as alike as brothers, both six feet tall, as skinny and bony as a piece of scaffolding, dressed in rag-ends and tatters, their hair home-cropped to the skull to save barber bills. The horse was spraddle-legged and tottering, and the wagon moaned as if haunted by all the weary years it had spent past its prime.

In the evening they returned, sagging with fatigue, the wagon empty, old Jake driving and young Johnny sitting beside him, carefully counting a handful of loose change and dropping it piece by piece into a small leather sack under the old man's steely eye.

They lived on the refuse of the garden they kept, eating the chickens that died of old age, or any other way except chopping their heads off. I sometimes wondered if Jake made the kid eat dinner on the lid of the coffin just to remind him what a dirty trick he had played by insisting on staying alive; and sometimes I was darned near to being convinced that if the kid had had his choice, that little four-foot coffin would have been under the turf of the cemetery these eighteen years.

Those were idle thoughts, though, and I had no proof. So I kept my mouth shut.

But Joe had a fact that day when he came through my front gate, fanning himself with his hat. Joe was chief of police. He and I hunted duck and deer in season, and whenever he had a job in which he had to depend on a steady hand with a gun, he usually called on me to go along.

"Harry," he said, "have you noticed anything funny about old Stence's wagon these past few days?"

I laughed. "Don't tell me he's gone and got a new one."

"Not much chance of that. But I been watching it for three-four days and he ain't been on it."

"Maybe he's sick."

"Jake's never too sick to ride that wagon, never too sick to let young Johnny make the collections without his being there to keep one eye on the accounting."

We looked at each other.

"For three days now ..." he said thoughtfully. "He ain't showed for three days on that old wagon of his, and it got me to thinking. He's dead."

A half-hour later the three of us—Joe, the Doc and I—were riding in silence out toward the Stence farm on the Pike. We stopped at the rickety fence, and Joe got out of the car soft and easy, went up the path, not making a sound. There was a feeble, flickering light in the kitchen, and when we peered through the window we saw young Johnny sitting there, listlessly turning over the pages of an old magazine someone had given him. On the table, stuck in its own grease, stood about an inch of candle. It threw an eerie light, fitful and shallow, and it filled young Johnny's gaunt face with darkness. He looked as if the bones of his skull were impatiently thrusting against his skin.

But there was no sign of old Jake. It was too early for bed and old Jake would certainly not have been in another part of the house when one candle would have done for two.

Joe opened the door without knocking and walked in.

He said casually, "Hello. Johnny."

Johnny looked up. "Hello. Joe." His voice was creaky and rusty, as if he were just as miserly about using it as he was about everything else.

Joe went on, "I notice Jake ain't been to town these past few days, and I dropped in to see if anything was the matter."

Keeping his finger in the magazine to mark his place, young Johnny said emotionlessly. "He drapped daid three-four days ago. Bury him t'morra—if I can spare time from the egg route."

Six feet tall, harsh-boned and scrawny, the image of the old man, you'd never have taken him for eighteen. He looked a hard-used forty. And his words, as calmly as they were spoken, were callous enough to have curdled lead. But what else could you expect, when everything had been squeezed out of him except the bleak desire for money?

"Mind if I take a look at him?" Joe's voice hardened.

Johnny shrugged. "Go right ahead," he said disinterestedly. "He's in there." He tossed his thumb limply toward the parlor.

Joe gave him a sharp glance and he and Doc went into the other room, while I stayed in the kitchen to keep an eye on young Johnny. I had a gun stuck in my waistband, under my coat.

From the tail of my eye, I saw the beam of Joe's flashlight flick around the parlor; then I heard both of them gasp. I sharpened my ears. Johnny hunched over his magazine.

Having difficulty with his tongue. Doc mumbled something about a stroke. Joe stumbled through the doorway with a small hatchet in his hand, his face the color of spoiled veal.

He said hoarsely, "You chopped him off at the knees!"

Johnny didn't even look up from his magazine. "What of it? He was dead, wasn't he?" Then, with sudden, blazing hatred. "That was the only way I could get him in that little coffin. Now he should feel better, damn him! Now that he knows that little coffin didn't go to waste after all!"

WITH LOVE AND BULLETS!

Trouble comes in all kinds of packages, but this particular package was in his sixties, had bristly gray hair like a Schnauzer, a pair of electric blue eyes that crackled like a short circuit, and a voice that should have been booked for assault and battery. His name was Jesse C. Kuykendall, and he was as crazy as they came—uncommitted.

We were sitting in the law office of Bert Campbell. That is, Bert and I were sitting. This other character kept jumping up and down as if he had a hot foot in the seat of his pants.

"Mr. Kuykendall has a little job for you, Lew," said Bert, trying to keep from laughing.

"That's right, a job," yelled Kuykendall, leaping to his feet and glowering at me. "Are you honest?"

"Reasonably," I said.

"That's a lie! Nobody's honest. You only think you're honest because nobody's offered you your price yet. I'm not honest. I'm a dirty crook. Always was. And Campbell here, he's a shyster that uses the law to keep his crookedness legal. But I don't care if you're honest or not. You'll be bonded."

He plumped back in his chair and leered at me, as if he'd put over a fast one and was proud of it.

"Mr. Kuykendall," said Bert, "has a certain package that you are to deliver to his ex-wife, who is now living on Manana Key in Florida—"

Kuykendall sprang from his chair as if he were coming out of his corner to try for a first-round knockout. "What are we beating around the bush for?" he snarled. "All this about certain packages and this, that, and the other thing. Tell him what's in the package. Scare the pants off him. That's the way to keep 'em honest! Scare them!"

"In the package, Lew," sighed Bert, "there will be fifty thousand dollars in negotiable Power and Light bonds. They will be insured for full value."

Kuykendall said, "Ha!" and grinned triumphantly at me. He had put over another fast one.

"Mr. Kuykendall," I said to Bert, "could save himself a lot of trouble, expense and worry if he simply sent the bonds by registered mail, insured."

I thought Kuykendall would have apoplexy. His arms exploded in all directions, his eyes bugged out and he began to beat on the desk with both fists.

"I wouldn't spend one penny," he howled, "to enrich those bloodsucking crooks down in Washington. I wouldn't spend one penny on a stamp even to send them a time bomb to blow them to Kingdom Come. I wouldn't spend one penny on a match to set them afire. Let them stew in their own juice. Let them be hoist on their own petard!"

"Mr. Kuykendall," said Bert, sneaking in a wink, "has just written a pamphlet proving that the U. S. Mail is a sink of iniquity."

"A disgrace!" growled Kuykendall. "I wouldn't sully my conscience by using it. I've been using special messengers for years."

"Furthermore," said Bert, "you are not to deliver the bonds to the ex-Mrs. Kuykendall until she hands over to you the patent rights on a dual carburetor that Mr. Kuykendall invented. Mr. Kuykendall will pay you thirty-five dollars a day and expenses. You will drive down, leaving for Florida at exactly six o'clock tomorrow morning. You have, on Mr. Kuykendall's instructions, already been bonded without your knowledge so that you would have no opportunity whatever of tampering with the bond."

I said, "Drive down! Why can't I take a plane?"

"Nobody in my employ," said Kuykendall ominously, "ever sets foot in a plane."

"Mr. Kuykendall," Bert explained, "is suing several of the airways for infringement of patent and he refuses to enrich them further until the suit is settled. In his favor, of course. Anyway, Lew, it will be a pleasant drive, three days down, three days back, with one day allowed for a swim in the Gulf of Mexico. Altogether, seven days at thirty-five dollars a day and expenses. Lord love me, Lew, I'd jump at a chance of a free, Florida vacation like that, myself."

"I wouldn't trust you twelve hundred miles with fifty thousand dollars worth of negotiable bonds," sneered Kuykendall.

I hate long drives. Some people get a kick out of them, but to me they're nothing but a dreary grind. I made up my mind to take Jerry, my kid brother, who was just back from Korea. I didn't say anything about this to Kuykendall or Bert. Kuykendall would probably have hit the ceiling. Once I had made up my mind to that, I didn't mind the idea of the drive. The kid would enjoy it.

Kuykendall had it all figured out for me. I would drive exactly four hundred miles each day; I would stop for the night at the motor courts he designated; I would drive at a fixed rate of speed; and I would arrive on Manana Key at 10:10 p.m. on Friday, the twenty-third. His ex-wife would be waiting, at that time, with the patent rights, all ready to exchange them for the Power and Light bonds.

"But Friday's the twenty-second, not the twenty-third," I said.

"I said she'll be waiting for you!" he said belligerently. "I sent her a letter. Don't argue with me. I never argue. Anybody gives me an argument, I fire him! She'll be waiting for you. You will deliver the bonds in a steel mesh bag chained to your wrist by a handcuffs. I have sent the keys to the bag and the handcuffs to the local chief of police. He will be a witness when the bag is opened. I have also sent him a fifty-dollar gratuity, so possibly he might be able to tear himself away from swilling liquor in his favorite gin mill for an hour or two. Do you have a gun, Sonny?"

Bert was making pacifying gestures at me, so I said yes, I had a gun.

"Then take it with you," said Kuykendall grimly. "That ex-wife of mine is a cold-blooded female tigress! Keep your gun in your hand every minute you're talking to her, and don't turn your back on her. She'll tear your throat out and laugh in your face while you're dying. She's a succubus. She doesn't have a drop of blood in her veins. It's all rattlesnake venom. Now goodbye to both of you."

He tramped to the door, turned and showed us his teeth. "But don't start cashing in those bonds until you've stolen them, and always remember, it's not me you'll be diddling; it'll be the insurance company, and they'll see you in hell before they'll let you get away with it!" He gave us a mean, superior laugh and strutted out.

I looked at Bert.

"Where do you get them from?" I asked.

He shook his head gloomily. "I don't know," he said. "But that old goat isn't as crazy as he sounds. He's made more than a few millions, so he must have more in his head than butterflies. That ex-wife of his must really have him over the hip. He'd rather part with an arm and a leg than those Power and Light bonds. They're his pets. I know, because I've been handling his investments. He's turned down some offers for them that made my fingers itch, but he won't sell. He gets spells like that. Of course, he does need those patents. He turned them over to her some years ago when he was being sued. To protect them. He needs them for this suit against the Airways."

"He wasn't serious about that gun business, was he?"

"Well," Bert grinned at me, "his ex-wife did shoot her first husband. Claimed he tried to clamp a bear trap around her neck. The bear trap was right there on her bed, and his fingerprints were all over it, so the jury acquitted her. She made a cool quarter of a million on that deal—which she ran through in no time at all, and then married Jesse C. Kuykendall. They stayed married three years, then she divorced him and got a whopping settlement. It seems she ran through that, too. She's expensive. Beautiful woman, absolutely the most beautiful woman I've ever seen, but if you stuck a thermometer in her mouth, I'd give a hundred to one she'd register somewhere around sixty below zero on the Fourth of July. She's as cold, my friend, as the Arctic ice cap, and twice as hard. So watch yourself. She'll diddle you if she can."

"Charming," I said drily. "And I'm the private eye who won't take divorce cases because they're too dirty."

"Dirty!" Bert laughed. "You should have seen the receipt Kuykendall wanted me to draw up for her to sign on delivery of the bonds. It was six pages long and all in fine print. He wanted me to stick in so many jokers that she'd not only have to return the bonds to him, but she'd have to spend the rest of her life in court fighting to keep herself out of the pokey for ninety-nine years. He's a vindictive little skunk, and he loves litigation.

"Nothing would make him happier than doing her out of the bonds and hauling her into court for extortion on top of it. However, I wouldn't draw it up for him. He practically climbed the walls and tore out the ceiling with his teeth, but I finally convinced him that she'd have a shyster of her own, and we wouldn't be able to put anything like that over on her. So I drew up a simple transfer that she'll sign and give to you with the patent papers. No jokers in it. Her own lawyer will undoubtedly be there, and he'll advise her to sign, so you'll have no trouble."

"And do you really think he sent those keys to the handcuffs and the bag to the local chief of police?" I asked incredulously.

Bert smiled wearily. "That's the kind of thing he does all the time. Will we see you at six in the morning? I'm actually ashamed to ask you to do a thing like this—a stooge job—but it's good pay, and nothing to worry about. After all, Lew, think what I have to go through with this comedian. I have to deal with him all the time!"

"Why can't I fly down and not say anything about it?" I asked.

"Uh-huh. Those motor courts, where you're supposed to stop, will send him a telegram when you arrive. He's got that all arranged. You can't fool him. Be a good guy and drive down and arrive there on schedule at ten p.m. on Friday. Take my word for it, he'll know if you arrive even five minutes early. I'm not supposed to tell you this, but I've got a thousand dollar check here for you—he's generous when it suits him. Do it the way he says, and the thousand is yours. Do it any other way and you'll spend the rest of your life in court trying to collect even a penny. That's the way he is. Okay?"

"What the hell," I said, thinking of Jerry, the kid brother, "it'll be a nice vacation."

Six o'clock the next morning, in Bert's office, was quite a circus. Kuykendall was there with about fourteen witnesses while Bert brought out the steel mesh bag from his safe, unlocked it, and in the presence of everybody, put in the bonds one by one, and clamped it around my wrist. I felt as if I were about to carry the word to Garcia. But Kuykendall was not quite satisfied.

"Let me see your gun," he barked at me, holding out a stubby hand that looked as if it would rather take me around the neck.

By this time, he merely amused me, so I dropped my .38 Bankers Special into his palm. It was a neat and wicked little piece of hardware, a real pal at close range.

He wrinkled his nose and turned the gun in his hands as if it were made of bubble gum. He tossed it into Bert's waste basket and said contemptuously, "No stopping power, no shock—a target pistol." Then he handed me an Army .45 automatic that you almost required an engineer's degree to operate.

"Where am I supposed to be going?" I asked him with lost irony. "On a moose hunt? Wouldn't it be better if I mounted a machine gun on the hood of the car, or dragged a caisson with a hunk of field artillery? I've got to protect myself, you know."

"A smart aleck, eh?" he jeered. "Wait till you have to use it, then you'll thank me. Give him the license, Campbell."

With a perfectly straight face, Bert handed me the license, plus another piece of paper that made me a U.S. Marshal, entitled to carry a gun anywhere in the U.S. and possessions, including the Virgin Islands. I laughed.

"Now I'm a G-man," I said.

Kuykendall nodded smugly. "That's right," he said. "And it's twenty years to life in Leavenworth if there's any funny business, Sonny."

It gave me a very chilling feeling down the humps of my backbone, the way he said it. He meant it, and any guy who could get me appointed, even temporarily, a U.S. Marshal just to run a simple errand for him, would have the necessaries to make a federal rap stick.

Jesse Kuykendall wasn't a comedian. He was a dangerous lunatic. I began to wish I had taken an easier way to earn my biscuits.

They all saw me down to the car. Bert handed me a package and said gravely: "A little going-away gift, Lew. A bottle of after-shave lotion." It turned out to be a pint of dear old Grandad's best bourbon, for which I was duly grateful that night when we stopped in Virginia.

Kuykendall leaned in the window and insisted on shaking hands with me. He squeezed once as if he wanted to make sure I hadn't palmed any of his hundred-dollar bills, and said sourly, "I'd go myself, but I wouldn't be found dead in the same state with my ex-wife. In fact, that's what I'm afraid of. Good luck, sonny, and if you find her especially cordial, reach for your gun. If she smiles at you—run!"

I stepped on the starter, put the car in gear and eased up on the clutch. Kuykendall kept his hand on the window edge and trotted half way down the street beside the car, barking advice at me, most of which had to do with shooting first and asking questions afterward.

I picked up the kid brother, Jerry, on Broad Street in Newark. I'm big, but he's bigger. Six-foot-two, blond, built like a fullback, and with a grin that would melt the scruples of angels.

"Move over, Junior," he said. "Driving's a man's job."

He loved to drive, and I had no objection. I showed him the Army .45 automatic that Kuykendall had given me.

"What do you think of this?"

"Put it away. You're only bragging. That's a man's gun, Junior. The first time you pull the trigger, you'll wish you had your water pistol back."

He laughed, a big hearty laugh that made my own laugh sound like a school girl's.

We had lunch in Baltimore and camped for the night in the Virginia motor court Kuykendall had designated. I was not surprised to find that Kuykendall had already paid our bill for the night. Bert had warned me that he was thorough. Within fifteen minutes after hitting the town, Jerry had a lovely young blonde giggling on his arm, looking up into his face as if he were a young maharajah. I don't know how he does it, or where he gets the energy. Me, I was so ready for the sack, it seemed to leap up to meet me as I approached it. He introduced her as Margot and insinuated that she had a friend.

I said, "I don't believe it, because a real friend would never have let you pick her up. Good night, girlie. I'm going to hit the sack, and if you're smart, you'll stay on your toes."

The next night we were in Georgia, where we had Southern fried chicken and hush puppies for dinner. It was Southern fried chicken that would make the Great Stone Face drool.

But when I patted my belly and mentioned it to Jerry, he grinned and tilted his chin at the cashier of the restaurant.

"Now there, Junior," he said, "is what I call real Southern chicken. You're getting old."

Ten minutes later he was hanging over her counter with a toothpick in his mouth, and her black eyes were full of happy laughter. He didn't hit the sack that morning until four a.m. But he was fresh as a daisy during the drive the next day, laughing and singing, and advising me to buy a new rocking chair.

CHAPTER II

We were right on Kuykendall's schedule all the way through. I was very careful about that. We had stopped in both the motor courts he had demanded, and we hit Manana Key at 9:30 that night. We stalled around for fifteen minutes, watching the fishermen on the bridge—down in Florida they call them causeways—hauling up those big black-and-silver striped fish they call sheephead, but which really look like a heavyweight angel fish, and a villainous-looking thing, with barracuda jaws, called a snook.

We had strolled up on the bridge—or causeway—just to kill time so I could keep to the timetable, and Jerry nudged me with his elbow.

"Look at that moon," he said.

I looked. It was fabulous, as big and yellow as a fried egg.

"What a moon!" I said. Then suddenly suspicious, "Wait a minute, since when ..."

But he was already grinning and waggling his thumb at a custom-made redhead, who was hanging over the rail with a baitcasting rod in her hand. Two minutes later, Jerry had the rod in one hand and the redhead in the other arm, showing her how to cast, but nobody can tell me that a redhead would laugh that way just at the idea of catching a fish.

When my wristwatch told me that it was time to be pushing on to be on schedule, I went over to them and growled, "Okay, All-American Boy, let's shove off. You can earn your merit badge tomorrow."

Jerry waggled the redhead's cute little nose between his thumb and forefinger, grinned, "See you, honey," and ambled peaceably back to the car with me.

"Dames," he said. "I love them. Why don't you latch onto a dame once in a while yourself, Junior? You might like it. You never can tell. What's the matter, did you promise Mother never to look at one, or something?"

"Drop dead!" I snarled.

He grinned.

Kuykendall had given me a map to his ex-wife's place at the end of Manana Key. There was a private road that branched from the main road, and her place was at the extreme southern tip of the island. The private road was a daisy, composed chiefly of sand dunes, and surrounded by mangrove, sea grape, and cabbage palms. I should have brought a jeep.

We came finally to rest, with the front wheels squarely against a palm log placed across the road. Over the palm log was a chain stretched between two trees and a little sign hung from the middle of it saying Private. This was the beginning of Kuykendall's ex-wife's property. He had marked it on the map, including even the palm log.

Jerry and I got out of the car to remove it and lift the chain so that we could drive through. We were bending over to lift it by either end, when two floodlights sprang on, illuminating us like the first-act chorus of *The Desert Song*, and a voice roared out of the trees overhead:

"Just straighten up, boys, and stand still. Be good and nothing will happen to you."

It wasn't a human voice. It was a roaring, distorted voice coming from an amplifier concealed in the palm fronds above us. I ground my teeth. That Army .45 that Kuykendall had given me was back in the glove compartment of the car because it was too bulky to wear.

I saw Jerry slide me a sidelong glance and I quickly shook my head at him.

The amplifier roared, "Here's a key." It spattered into the sand in front of me, tied to a four-inch length of one-by-two so that I could not miss it. "Unlock that bag from your wrist, then get back in your car and drive over to the beach. Stay there a half hour—"

Jerry whirled and dived for the car. I cried, "No, kid, no!" but I was too late. A shot rang out and I saw him throw up his hands, stagger in the heavy sand and go down with a shawl of blood spilling over his face.

"Hold it!" the amplifier roared sharply as I stiffened in a surge of insane fury. "Hold it or you'll get the same. Pick up that key and unlock the bag and be quick about it. I'll count to three. One ... two ..."

I picked up the key and unlocked the bag. I couldn't do anything else. He, she, or it, whatever it was, could just as easily have shot me down and unlocked the bag anyway. I dropped the bag into the sand, but slipped the key into the palm of my hand.

"Now walk backward to the rear of your car!" I was ordered.

I slid an agonized glance toward Jerry's body lying face downward in the sand, but obeyed slowly.

I heard a dry rattle as someone slipped through the palmetto at the side of the road and I tried to turn and meet the charge, but he, she or it must have had a sap three feet long, because it came down on the side of my head before I could see anything but the empty waste of palmetto, mangrove, and sea grape that lined the road.

I plunged down into the roaring vortex of a whirlpool of darkness, crying out from the despair within me: "Jerry, Jerry, kid ..."

They say being born is a rough business—but coming back to consciousness after being slugged, really slugged, is worse because you can feel it with all your senses, which a baby can't. You can taste the salty blood on your tongue, all sounds tear at your eardrums, there is an acridness in your nostrils as if someone had shoved hot tar up them, and the light becomes splinters of glass in your eyeballs.

I tried to groan as I was coming out of it, because I felt that if I could only groan, it would ease the pain and clear the nasal passages so that I could breathe again, but it was like trying to breathe after being hit hard in the solar plexus. I could not, no matter how hard I tried, emit a sound. I was lying on something. I could feel it under my fingers—short, harsh, yet resilient, a rug. A rug with cut loops. Not an uncut-loop rug, like a pebble-twist, but a cut-loop like an Oriental. I felt like a blind ant crawling voiceless and hurt.

I heard a feminine voice, beautiful and crystal-clear saying, "But for heaven's sake, Harry, what are we going to do with them?"

The masculine voice rumbled uneasily in return, "Nina, please, control yourself."

"I won't control myself. There's a dead man out in the roadway, and there's this other one over here. I'm sure they're the messengers from Jesse. But where are the bonds? He said he would send me the bonds. What happened?"

"Nina, please! Stop acting. I can always tell when you're acting, and you're acting. Stop it! I've got to think. And you've got to tell me the truth. Did you have anything to do with that dead man out in the roadway?"

"Don't be a fool! I'm not acting. There's a dead man out there in the roadway. Is that something I'd be likely to act about? I didn't call you up to bleat at me like a sheep. I want some advice—fast!"

I could open my eyes and I could see painfully. I was lying on a rug in front of a sofa. My hands were tied, and so were my feet. The two who were talking were standing tensely in front of a large fireplace, a fireplace with an opening big enough to roast a pig. She was dressed in white. She was dark. Her hair was black and her skin was sun-toasted to a deep coffee. Bert Campbell had said she was beautiful, but my idea of beauty stopped at the pony line of the Frou-Frou Club in Newark. She made every woman I have ever seen look like an insipid, washed-out frump.

Kuykendall had called her a tigress, but she wasn't. She was a panther of a woman, as vital as a sinuous, tawny, animal. Her head was small, beautifully shaped, but her mouth was wide, and thin-lipped, promising passion. Her eyes, even at that distance, flashed green in the lamplight. She was standing with her legs apart and I could see the thrust of her full thighs against the white nylon of her skirt.

She was breathing heavily and her high, proud breasts were trembling. Her head was thrown back, her expression angry and contemptuous. She had a glass clasped in her hand, and I expected any moment to see it exploded from the pressure of her fingers. That was the effect she had. She was beautiful. But supercharged and dangerous.

In comparison to her, the man facing her, with his hands sunk in his pants pocket, was an unhappy—as she called him—sheep. He was good-looking in a fleshy, easy-going way, double-chinned, brown-eyed, and the beginning of a pot under the bulge of his vest. The collar and leash were not apparent, but they were there all the same.

"Now, Nina," he groaned. "The thing for us to do is call the police. There's a dead man out there in the—"

"Oh, use your head, you idiot! Suppose we called the police, and then they decided that Jesse killed that man out there. He's fully capable of it! Where would I be? The bonds are gone, and he'd be in jail. I wouldn't have that much chance of collecting. These papers I hold, these patents, aren't worth a nickel to me. They're only worth something to him in his lawsuit against the Airways. I want my money, Harry. If Jesse killed that man out there, I want to be sure, so I'll have something to hold over his head for the rest of his life, and he'll pay and pay and pay. I want evidence against him! You're a lawyer. I'm paying you. Get me that evidence!"

"But Nina, if your ex-husband killed that man—"

She threw up her arms to whatever God she had, to bear witness to what she had to suffer from this fool. "Listen to me! Please, if you have any intelligence, which I doubt, use it now! Jesse sent me fifty thousand dollars worth of Power and Light bonds. They're gone. I want those bonds. I can resell them for a hundred and fifty thousand dollars. I know that Jesse had this man killed out there in the roadway and had the bonds stolen. Are you listening, Harry?"

I moved. Not much. Just a hand. But she saw it instantly. I don't think she ever missed a thing with those green cat's eyes of hers. She put her hand on Harry's arm and smiled at him.

"Forgive me, Harry. I'm upset. Do something for me, will you? That dead boy out there. Cover him with something. Put some palmetto branches over him. We'll inform the police when the time comes, but not right now. I have to think."

She was cold-blooded enough to make you shiver, but she had Harry right where she wanted him. He protested feebly, but he went.

She came directly down the room to me. She pulled over a chair and sat regarding me. She lit a cigarette, leaned over and touched the glowing end of it to my ear. I tried to move away from it, but I couldn't.

"Sorry," she said pleasantly. "I thought you were shamming."

She went to the server and came back with a bottle of Scotch and a glass. She held my head as she poured the liquor drop by drop between my lips. She was so gentle you might almost have mistaken her for Florence Nightingale.

"Thanks," I said hoarsely. Strength was coming back.

"Better?"

Yes, better—except for a splitting head and an icy rage. I wanted to cry thinking of Jerry out there with a bullet through his head. I was going to get somebody for that.

"Now," she said, "what do you know about this? You did bring the bonds down from my ex-husband, didn't you?"

For the first time I saw the empty steel mesh bag lying on the floor by her chair, and she stirred it with her foot.

"What happened?" she demanded. "You were supposed to come tomorrow. Jesse sent me a telegram saying that you'd be here at ten p.m. on the twenty-third...."

"Didn't he say Friday, the twenty-third?" I interrupted, remembering how Kuykendall had shut me up when I pointed out his mistake in the date. Friday was still the twenty-second.

She shook her head. "He merely said the twenty-third at ten o'clock."

I laughed harshly. "He meant the twenty-second."

"You're lying. He never makes a mistake like that. Unless," her eyes turned thoughtful, "he did it on purpose. He sent the police chief a telegram saying the same thing. I'll bet he had something up his ... exactly what happened out there on the road?"

"You wouldn't know, I suppose."

"I wouldn't ask if I knew, so please don't annoy me. I dislike flip men. The next time," she held up her cigarette, "I might push this into your ear." She laughed. "And you'd just love to get your fingers around my neck, wouldn't you? Don't worry, my friend, I'm not going to give you the opportunity. Now tell me how you could possibly have managed to lose the bonds."

I wasn't going to let her have a field day pushing cigarettes into my ear, so I told her, briefly, what had happened, including the amplifier up in the trees.

"That's nothing, that amplifier," she said. "Jesse had it installed when he lived here. It's an intercom between the house and the entrance to the estate. There's a mike on the tree. He could have put in a telephone just as easily, but that was too prosaic for him. But your holdup man—

if there was one—must have been in front of you then. You must have seen him."

"He was behind us."

She nodded. "Of course. Jesse is clever. He would have used an extension on the mike. I actually believe you're telling the truth...."

An outer door slammed, and a second later Harry ran into the room, panting.

"He's gone!" he cried. He looked as if he were about to faint.

She grimaced and said, "Oh, stop shouting, will you. Who's gone? The dead man?"

"Yes. Somebody dragged him to the car, and the car's gone, too."

She smiled. She actually smiled. "Well," she said, quite cheerfully, "that simplifies things."

He pointed a trembling finger at her.

"I'm not going any further with this, Nina. I am going to inform the police—right now."

"Suit yourself, my dear Harry. However, I shall deny it. I shall tell the police you were drunk, as usual, and were seeing things. And they'll believe me, too. The police chief, as you know, is a very good friend."

"This man here will confirm my story!"

"What man, Harry?" pretending not to see me lying there on the floor. "There's no man. You're upset. Go home. Lie down. Take a sleeping powder. You'll feel much better in the morning."

"We'll see about that!" He turned and rushed hysterically from the room.

Nina Kuykendall sat perfectly still, her face cold and furious. She leaped up and ran to the fireplace, over which hung a rack of hunting rifles and seized one. She threw up the window at the far end of the room, carefully rested the rifle on the sill, and fired.

Harry screamed shrilly. She fired again. She ran out of the room.

I tried to break or loosen the rope that bound my wrists, but it bit into me like wire, though it wasn't wire. It was probably fishing line. I lay there sweating, waiting my turn.

She came back in about ten minutes without the rifle. She was not even breathing hard, and her beautiful cold face was composed. After staring at me for a moment, she went out of the room again. When she came back, she was carrying some cloths and a table knife. The sweat poured from me, but she had no intention of having two corpses on her hands. She slipped the knife blade between my teeth.

"Open up," she ordered, "or I'll break your teeth."

I opened up and she thrust a ball of cloth into my mouth, tying it in with another cloth. She noticed the way my eyes were blazing at her.

"Don't worry," she told me contemptuously, "you're not going to live long enough to do anything about it. I'll take care of you later."

She tried to drag me, but that was something else again. She didn't have the muscle for it. She straightened up and bit her lip, glancing around the room. I was lying in front of a sofa, so she dragged me around the end of it and dumped me behind. Without wasting another glance on me, she walked briskly down the room.

A dial phone whirred as she dialed a number.

"Police headquarters? Give me the Chief, please ... Charlie? Thank heaven you were in. Something awful has just happened out here, something entirely unforeseen. Come out right away. Alone, please! No, no. I'll tell you when you get here ..."

She hung up. Then I heard the clink of a bottle against a glass. Even her icy nerves needed a little reinforcement.

I lifted my tied legs and brought them down gently on the floor. The Police Chief was obviously a pal of hers—but not so much of a pal that she wanted him to find me. Good. When he walked in, I'd hammer on that floor with my heels till it boomed like a bass drum.

That brilliant idea lasted exactly two seconds. Like many of those Spanish-type houses down in Florida, the floor was made of unglazed red tile and my rubber heels bouncing against it made no more noise than if I'd snapped my fingernail against a tombstone. Less. I tried to break my wrists loose again, but the cut of that tough thin line brought the sweat out on my forehead. It would cut down to the bone before it would break. I could see it now around my ankles—white nylon fishing line, almost as tough as steel wire.

I stiffened as four shots exploded in the silence after her drink. They came from outside the house. I waited, scarcely breathing, but nothing happened. There was no other sound, no voices, nothing, and within a few minutes I heard her walk back into the room. She poured herself another drink.

Had she gone outside and put four more shots into Harry? Even nightmares weren't as horrible and crazy as this! I raged against the line around my wrists. I knew I was tearing the flesh. I could feel the greasy flow of blood, but I didn't care. Slowly the momentary insanity passed and I lay back, breathing heavily. I would have to figure out another way....

CHAPTER III

It seemed endless hours before Charlie came. He was young. His voice sounded young and worried.

He cried, "Nina ..."

"Oh, Charlie! No, no, please don't kiss me now. Something ... awful has happened. Sit down. I want to tell you about it. I feel as if I'm going crazy. You know that messenger with the bonds from my ex-husband was supposed to arrive tomorrow? We both got telegrams saying the twenty-third. He arrived tonight while I was in town. He was here when Harry and I drove in. Look, here's the steel mesh bag Jesse sent the bonds in.

"Well, as Harry and I drove up, this man ran out of the house. Harry yelled at him and the man turned and fired twice at Harry with a rifle. I don't know how he ever did it with two bullets in him, but Harry fired four times at the man. He must have hit him, because I saw him stumble just before he disappeared into the palmetto. I was terrified. I rushed in and locked the door and called you right away...."

Now I understood the meaning of those four unexplained shots. Later, she meant to put four shots into me, and I would be found dead somewhere in the palmetto. Shot by Harry!

Charlie's young voice rumbled, "Did you see this other man, darling?"

"Very clearly. He was about six feet tall, had curly black hair, he was wearing a gray suit...."

She went on describing me exactly and in detail. No Arctic blast could have been as cold as the wind that seemed to rake me. I was the next corpse, all right. She had everything planned.

Charlie's voice came slowly and heavily, "Nina ... are you sure you didn't have anything to do with this? Remember, I know what you had in mind for this messenger when he came."

"Oh Charlie! That was something entirely different. Jesse Kuykendall has cheated me of thousands and thousands of dollars. I was simply going to get back a little of what was rightfully mine. I'd never kill anybody, Charlie! I was just going to put him to sleep and take the bonds that were rightfully mine in the first place. But this ... this ..."

She began to sob. I heard him murmuring comfortingly, and she said brokenly, "Please don't kiss me now, Charlie. Please ... oh, Charlie, Charlie ..."

I knew, just as surely as if I had been able to see them, that she had led him into kissing her and taking her into his arms. And this hardly an hour after she had finished putting two bullets into poor old Harry! Then l heard her saying firmly, "No, Charlie. That's enough. I blame all this on myself, darling. I wish I had never made you give me that key to Jesse's steel bag, and I should never have left it lying around so carelessly. See, it's still up there on the mantel over the fireplace. That awful man must have found it and opened the bag. Fifty thousand in negotiable bonds. No wonder he was tempted...."

Oh, she wove a web around him all right, and he didn't even struggle. He was a gone goose as far as she was concerned. I felt sorry for him. Harry had been useful to her too, I suppose, and now look at Harry— She never let anybody who could talk back hang around for long. Look at what she had planned for me!

After she had that young police chief all wrapped up and wanting to take her in his arms again, she maneuvered him outside to look at the remains. I had not the slightest doubt that within thirty minutes my description would go out on the teletype to every police headquarters in the state. She was that good.

They weren't out of the house two minutes, when I heard these slithering sounds, as if someone were creeping across the floor on his hands and knees toward me, and I turned my head.

I could have broken right out into tears. In fact, I did. Happy, grateful, thanksgiving tears—for there was Jerry, grin and all, creeping across the floor toward me from the doorway, that big fat Army .45 in his right hand. There was a shallow gutter of dried blood across his forehead, and it must have hurt, for his grin had a little trouble staying put.

I actually started to blubber, "Oh, kid—"

He put his finger to his lips. He cut me loose, and for about five minutes I could have danced with the pain as the circulation of blood needled back into my hands and feet, but by this time he had helped me stagger out into the big kitchen at the rear of the house. He gave me a bottle of brandy he had found in one of the closets and I took a deep pull from it. Jerry clucked around me like a worried hen.

"Gosh, Lew, you ought to see your wrists, cut to ribbons!"

I punched him affectionately on the chest. "And you should see your noggin'. But what I'm really sorry for is the bullet that bounced off you. It must have screamed in agony when it smacked that solid concrete."

"Aaaah, you can't kill us Riordans, Lew. But what do we do now? I got the car hid down the other side of the bridge. What's going on here, anyway? And who's the beautiful Borgia? My God, did you see her put two slugs through her boyfriend?"

"You're young yet, kid. You don't understand these things. Those were only love shots. She was crazy about him. And you've got it all wrong.

She didn't shoot him at all. I did. In thirty minutes you can ask any cop in Florida and they'll tell you the same thing."

"Let's get out of here, Lew!"

"Nix, kid, nix. If I start running now, I'll be running till the end of my life. She's got me sewed up. What we've got to figure is a way to cut the stitches."

"She the one that held us up down there at the beginning of the road, Lew?"

I shook my head. "Uh-uh. She says she was in town with that poor old Harry character, and you can depend on it that she really was. Somebody else pulled that one. But she knew all about it. Don't ask me how I know, but I know. She was in on it. The police chief and Harry are, or were, just a pair of stooges. Dammit to all hell!" I gritted my teeth in a surge of impotent anger. "I've been set up for a sucker, and I can't see any way around!"

Jerry was standing at the window when we heard the sound of the car. He peered out into the bright moonlit night.

"There goes the police chief," he said. "She's coming back to the house by herself. Say," he pushed out his jaw, "let's you and me work on her. We've got her here alone. Lew. We'll scare the nylons off her!"

"Scare her!" I laughed bitterly. "Kid, she's tougher than you, me and anybody else you can name all rolled together. We wouldn't get a thing out of her, and on top of that I have a pretty fair idea that when it's all over the pair of us would be lying at the bottom of a six-foot hole staring straight up while they shoveled us over. Only we wouldn't know anything about it. We'd be a pair of very dead Riordans. You couldn't scare her unless you'd be willing to go all the way, and we're not tough enough for that. Could you, for instance, shove a lighted cigarette into her ear?"

He muttered, "God!"

"Yeah, and she's as tough as that," I told him. "I'm on the hook. I've got a story to tell, but nobody'll believe me. Unless I can lay those bonds on the line, together with the guy who hijacked them, even if it's Kuykendall himself."

"But Lew, I can tell them you didn't shoot that Harry character and—"

"Sure you can, and when you get all finished, if they wanted to be nice, they'd let you have the cell next to mine. Since when is one brother's word enough of an alibi for another brother? They wouldn't even bother laughing at you. They'd throw the book at you and you'd just about start recovering consciousness when they were strapping you in the electric chair on my lap. Wait a minute." I looked at him. "I seem to remember a rumor that you're a great hand with the ladies. True or false?"

"Aw, Lew ..."

"No. I'm serious. They say that all you have to do is show that All-American snoot of yours and strong women faint and weak ones succumb without a struggle. Right?"

"It's just a line I give them," he mumbled.

"But it works, doesn't it? How would you like to try that line out on some real competition, kid? And I'm talking about Dracula's little sister in there. Do you think you could work it? It's a chance, kid, and you'd have to watch yourself every second. What do you think? I'll be covering you."

His grin grew slowly. "It sounds like an idea, Lew."

"Okay. Now here's the idea. You walk in on her. I'll cover you from the other end of the living room. You tell her you saw her knock off that Harry character, and tell her that you know the bonds were hijacked down at the entrance of her private road. She gave the police chief a different story. At first, all you want are the bonds, then gradually work up to the point where you have her thinking that you want her and the bonds. Kid, if you've got that old black magic, now's the time to work it. But look, any time you feel you're not making your points, drop out. Pull out, or you'll have a knife in your back. Let me have that hunk of artillery so I can cover you. I'll have my eyes on her every minute, and I won't have any gentlemanly feeling against letting her have a slug if she asks for it."

He grinned and slipped the heavy butt of the Army .45 into my hand. He hitched up his belt.

"Duck, dames," he said, "here comes Riordan."

He slipped out the kitchen door.

I ran lightly across the kitchen and out into the small butler's pantry that separated it from the living room. I held the door open a fraction and peered into the living room. Nina Kuykendall had stopped for a drink. As I watched, she put the glass down on the cocktail table. She looked back over her shoulder and walked swiftly down the room, knelt on the sofa and peered over the back of it. It must have been a terrific shock not to find me there, but her expression did not change by as much as the twitch of a muscle.

She crouched frozen, and then carefully pushed herself to her feet. She glanced toward the fireplace where three more rifles hung in the rack over the mantel. She walked quickly toward them. I had the door open about six inches and the sights of the .45 squarely on her right shoulder when Jerry walked into the living room through the doorway at the opposite end. He had the rifle with which she had shot Harry cradled over the crook of his left elbow. His finger was on the trigger and the muzzle was pointed directly at her. He gave her his big All-American grin.

"Hiya, sweetheart," he said. "Look what I found buried out in the sand. Uh-uh. Look but don't touch. Those nasty old guns up there might be loaded."

God! She must have had nerves like reinforced concrete! She did not even start. Turning slowly toward him, she dropped her arms from the rifles, smiling.

"Well," she murmured, "the dead man!"

"You can't kill a Riordan," he grinned. "Sit down, honeybun. I've got a little chore to do."

She sank down into the wing chair beside the fireplace. Jerry walked over and took the rifles down from the rack. He lifted each one by the barrel and with a full-arm swing smashed each one hard against the floor.

"I hate to do this to valuable merchandise," he said, "but I've been shot at enough for one night."

"You're big," she said. "You're the biggest man I've seen in a long while."

"That's right, honeybun. Big and generous."

"Generous?"

"That's right. There are some bonds. You see, I happened to be riding along with the guy who was delivering them, so I know all about them. I'll settle for those bonds. How's about it, honeybun?"

"I don't know anything about them," she answered calmly. "They were stolen by the man who was supposed to deliver them—"

"Intercepted pass, honeybun. You'll have to try again. I found that guy tied up behind your sofa down there at the other end of the room. He didn't have anything to do with it. I've got him stashed away outside. And he didn't have anything to do with knocking off that Harry character, like you told the chief of police. So what's a few bonds between friends? You'll live a lot longer, honeybun, if you pass them over to me."

"You're mad. You're absolutely, thoroughly mad."

"That's right, honeybun," he grinned at her. "And not only that, I can get downright sore if I don't get my own way. I'm a spoiled brat."

"Do you realize that the police will be back at any moment? After all, there is a dead body out there."

"Another intercepted pass. You're just not in form tonight, are you? The cops won't be back till tomorrow. You sold that yokel chief a bill of goods, and he's going to let you discover that body all over again tomorrow. No more cops tonight. Like to try again, honeybun?"

I was filled with admiration for the kid. That was fast thinking, and he had hit it right on the nose. That police chief would never have left the scene if she hadn't sold him a bill of goods, and it was a good guess that he was going to let her discover the body tomorrow.

I was so wound up that I had twisted the doorknob in my hand and in my relief at the kid's answer, I let it go. It made a slight snick that no ordinary person would have heard three feet away—but she whirled and cried: "What was that!"

He turned. She made a grab for the barrel of his gun. She was out of that chair so fast, that she was hardly a blur, and there wasn't a thing I could do, because Jerry was between us, as big as a barn door with those shoulders of his. But there was nothing wrong with the kid's reflexes. The moment her hand touched the gun, he reversed it and butted her under the chin with the walnut stock.

It looked like a casual, almost lazy gesture, but there must have been some muscle in it, for her head jerked back, her feet flew up and she crashed against the wing chair, collapsing on the floor, with a flash of ivory thighs above her stocking tops, her eyes glazed. But even sprawled like that, she was lovely.

The kid looked aghast at what he had done. He had reacted automatically. He bent over her. I wanted to yell out for him to watch himself, but he was okay. He saw immediately that he had not really hurt her.

He stood his rifle against the fireplace and lifted her in his arms. He looked around unhappily, not knowing where to put her, and then he came down the room toward me and laid her on the sofa—behind which so recently I had been gagged and bound. I opened the door a little wider and gave him a warning flash, but he just winked and trotted to the server and came back with the scotch bottle and a glass. He sat on the edge of the sofa and bent over her. He was sweating.

I heard her whimper, "You hurt me ..."

"You're just lucky," he told her toughly, "that I didn't crack your jaw. Grab for a man's gun, and things happen to you."

I saw her slim arms come up and encircle his neck. "Kiss me!" she whispered. "Kiss me. Quickly! Kiss me!"

He bent deeper and all I could see was the hunch of his heavy shoulders. It was quite a kiss. I saw her fingers writhe, convulse and dig into the thick muscles of his neck. The kid had more than just a line. When she spoke again, she was all his.

"God!" she said huskily.

His voice wasn't quite steady either. "You're a lot of woman, honeybun."

"Kiss me again! Kiss me hard!"

Her fingers were talons, pulling him deeper and deeper into the kiss. They murmured things to each other, and if I hadn't known the kid was faking, I'd have exploded from behind that door with the gun in my fist. But even at that, I was perspiring. She was dynamite.

A long about four in the morning, she whispered, "I'll have to make a phone call, darling. We'll get the bonds. We'll go to South America. You will go with me, won't you?"

"I'll go with you!"

But all the same, he followed her up the room and stood between her and the rifle that he had leaned against the fireplace while she phoned, sitting in the wing chair, taking the phone from the commode beside the chair.

I could not hear a word she said, but the kid looked startled. He did not dare try to signal me at this point. They came back to the sofa, their arms around each other's waists.

"Only five hours more, darling," I heard her murmur to him as she pulled him down into the sofa as she sank into the cushions. "Kiss me again, darling. Oh, darling!"

I swear, never did I spend such a five hours in all my life, nor do I ever want to spend such a five hours again. I felt like a cross between a Peeping Tom and a condemned killer waiting for zero hour. Five hours! And I was so ashamed for having pushed the kid into this that I wanted to go away some place by myself and be sick.

In the gray and morning light, when he sat up on the sofa, he looked exhausted and bitter. He did not even glance toward the door behind which I had crouched all night. He simply let his head lay back against the back of the sofa and closed his eyes. For just about a second. He would, I am sure, have fallen asleep had she not shaken him awake, saying urgently, "Darling, darling! Don't fall asleep now. He'll be here any moment. Get the rifle and hide behind the sofa. Don't miss. Get him on the first shot!"

"Right, right," he mumbled.

She actually ran up to the fireplace and brought the rifle back to him. My kid brother!

It was quarter to six when the doorbell rang. Jerry shambled around the sofa and knelt behind it with the barrel of the rifle resting on the back of it. She bent, kissed him swiftly, smiled and walked quickly up the room.

I opened my door and whispered, "Okay, kid?" By this time, from all that had gone on during the night, you can't blame me for not being sure.

He nodded, gave me a wan grin and tightened as she came back into the room—with Bert Campbell, Kuykendall's own attorney.

Bert was saying worriedly, "But what happened, Nina, darling?" She evaded his arms. "Everything happened. Do you have the bonds?" "Of course." He patted his brief case. "You told me to bring them...." And then I remembered. Back in Newark, *he* was the one who had brought the steel mesh bag out of *his* safe, and *he* was the one who had unlocked it before the bonds were put in, and *he* had known all about that silly timetable Kuykendall had given me. Three days it had taken me to drive down by car. He had flown down by plane. He had the key to the bag, and he had held me up at the entrance to Nina's private road. He was just another of Nina's suckers ...

"Thank heaven you brought them," she said. "Kiss me, darling...."

He moved toward her like a starving man toward a full course dinner. She struck him on the chest with her out-thrust hands, sending him staggering backward, as she cried out to Jerry:

"Shoot! Shoot! Shoot! Kill him!"

I walked through the doorway with the gun in my hand at the same time Jerry rose from behind the sofa, covering both of them with his rifle.

From there on in it was something I would just as soon forget. They accused each other, they screamed; they would even have fought to lay the blame on the other—but they had been in it together and there was no doubt of it. And in the middle of it all, the chief of police walked in on them, a very disillusioned yokel. The most horrible part of it was when she turned to him and he slapped her with a vicious backhand swing. She was done....

It was a week later before Jerry and I got finished signing things in triplicate, and repeating our stories over and over again to the same hard, official faces. They were both, Nina and Bert Campbell, indicted for the murder of Harry.

It was a day after that when the kid and I stopped for a hamburger in Georgia. The cashier of the lunchroom was a very luscious blonde.

I nudged Jerry.

"She's trying to give you the eye, kid," I said.

He bit grimly into his hamburger. "Let her keep it," he said stonily. "It's probably glass."

DEATH BRINGS DOWN THE HOUSE

She had never been beautiful, and now what was left of her flamboyant charm lay huddled and smashed on the sidewalk. The hotel roof was a long way up, and she had come all the way down, her shriek streaming behind her like the tail of a comet. The crowd bubbled around her. Binnie Bailey had made a dramatic exit—but there was no applause, no whistling, no stamping of feet, no cheering.

And there were no encores.

The detective from headquarters slapped his hand with the folded theater program and scowled down at it. His name was O'Grady and he looked it—red hair, freckles and a bulldog jaw, a tough cop. Only this time he didn't look so tough; he just looked unhappy.

The program said:

BINNIE BAILEY
in
"EARLY TO RISE"
With Joey Coy
Produced by
Sam Bennett

Sam Bennett sat hunched on the edge of the bed in his hotel room, his hands dangling between his plump thighs. He had a round face, plump cheeks and blue eyes, a face made for jollity. He, too, looked unhappy. As did the miniature, cigar-smoking comedian, Joey Coy, who restlessly prowled the room, touching everything in it, lifting lamps, moving chairs, looking behind the very pictures on the walls. Even on the stage, Joey Coy was never still for a minute.

Sam made a weary gesture with his hands and looked up at O'Grady. "It's a serious thing, calling it suicide, lieutenant," he said reproachfully. "How can you tell it was suicide? Did she have a sign around her neck? There are things to consider."

Joey Coy poised for a moment, waved his heavy cane and squeaked, "The insurance!" He glowered at O'Grady, then trotted across the room and peered into the wastebasket.

"Comes suicide," said Sam, "comes no insurance."

O'Grady raised his head and said sharply, "You two seem to have got yourselves in an uproar over the insurance. How come?"

Sam protested, "Not for us, lieutenant. It's for Binnie's little girl. She's with the show too. Ten thousand is a lot of money."

With gloomy amazement, O'Grady watched Joey Coy empty the wastebasket on the rug and poke through it with his cane. He shook himself and looked back at Sam Bennett.

"I'll look at it your way for a minute," he said. "If it wasn't suicide, what was she doing up on the roof at this time of night?"

Joey Coy screamed, "She *liked* roofs!"

Sam was again the interpreter. "Always after opening night Binnie goes up on the roof, sits on the edge and swings her legs. It quiets her down, she says. She feels like she was flying right up into the sky, and the sky, she says, is the most peaceful thing there is. Anyway," he pointed out, "why should she do the dutch? She comes out of retirement and everybody says, don't do it, Binnie, you're too old.

"So what happens? She's a hit. On top of that, she owns twenty-five percent of the show, and the show's a hit, too. Ten weeks already we're sold out in New York, and we just opened in Newark. We killed them in Newark opening night. We killed them in Buffalo, and we killed them in Albany. We'll kill them in New York." His face twitched. "Would have," he amended.

Joey Coy interrupted savagely, "We'll kill them in New York. Look, Sam, I got it all figured out. I take over most of Binnie's business in all three acts. I dress up like a dame and come out and do her songs. I'll be sensational!"

Sam looked resigned, hopeless. He moved his hands about a quarter of an inch. "We hope," he muttered.

"I'll kill them," Joey told O'Grady. "Ask Sam. He knows. I've been in his last fifteen turkeys."

"Now, Joey, be serious. Please."

Joey was serious. "Ten turkeys," he said. He picked a scrap of cloth from the wastebasket, admired it and thrust it into his pocket. He turned around and looked at Sam. "I'll tell you what," he said. "I'm going to bed." He trotted out of the room.

Sam caught O'Grady's puzzled glance. "You don't want to mind Joey," he said. "All he ever thinks of is the show, and he's always picking up props, like that wastebasket business. He finds the damnedest things and makes them look funny. To me. On the stage his stuff's getting a little familiar. He can't carry the show in New York.

"I'll have to get a new lead," he went on despondently. "Someone like Merman. Someone you can hang a show on and she carries it. Did you see Binnie? Terrific! She carried the show. Without her it's just another turkey. Ten weeks in New York and we fold. She was as good as

Merman. I thought I had a winner this time. Haven't had one in years. And I'm tired of turkeys." Sam had aged.

O'Grady had the program all smoothed out in the palm of his hand and he was staring at it thoughtfully. "Maybe it wasn't suicide," he conceded. "How many people knew she went up on the roof all the time?"

"Comparatively speaking, nobody. There are over a hundred million people in the country, and only a hundred of us knew about it." His eyes suddenly flew wide with thought. "What's that again? You mean, she was pushed?" he said incredulously.

"You've eliminated all the reasons for suicide, haven't you?"

"Yes, but I didn't say—"

"I'm saying it. I'm saying it's a possibility that has to be looked into. This daughter of Binnie Bailey's, for instance. She gets that quarter interest in the show now, doesn't she?"

"And what's it worth? Strictly the neck of the turkey."

"Is she a talented kid?"

"Talented? How should I know? Maybe she could cook."

"In other words, she couldn't carry the show in Binnie Bailey's place. Is that the idea?"

"She couldn't carry programs for the show. For ten weeks maybe people come because she's Nora Bailey, Binnie's kid. She sings and she understudied. Binnie wanted it that way. Between you and me, lieutenant, that little girl didn't want any part of the show. Of any show. She's strictly from mustard. Talent? No talent. But Binnie snapped the whip and the kid's on the stage, hating it. Only because she loves her mother."

O'Grady accepted the last statement as propaganda. "I think I'll have a little talk with her," he said. He folded the program and put it in his pocket.

Sam went to the door with him, his shoulders sagging, his eyes mournful. "I should talk to you some more," he said. "Binnie didn't jump, and she wasn't pushed. She fell. You'll see." He shook hands solemnly with O'Grady before closing the door.

And the moment it closed, the door of the room beside it opened and Joey Coy skipped out, looking like a musical comedy conspirator. He put his finger to his lips, rolled his eyes and beckoned O'Grady into his room.

Inside, he stood close to the detective and whispered, "The old man." He prodded O'Grady's stomach with his forefinger, winked significantly.

O'Grady said, "What old man?"

"What old man!" Joey Coy looked surprised, "Nora's old man, the guy Binnie was hitched with. Stuck with. A souse. He follows the show around like a bad debt."

He stepped back and interestedly riffled through a wallet he held in his hand. Startled, O'Grady recognized the badge pinned to it and snatched it from the comedian's hand.

"Another stunt like that," he said grimly, "and you'll be wearing your ears in your pocket. Now cut the comedy and stop hinting around. What about this old man?"

Joey Coy grinned impishly. "A souse, see? A barfly." He staggered in a circle around O'Grady, illustrating a drunk. Any other time it might have been funny. "What happens is this." He poked at O'Grady's stomach again and the detective stepped back. "What happens is this, whenever he thinks Binnie is looking the other way, he comes to the stage door and mooches a sawbuck from Nora.

"Last night Binnie catches him promoting his buck, she bats him down to an inch and a half and they square off. 'You're ruining my daughter,' he weeps. Tears run down his face." Joey Coy shed a tear. "'You're ruining her reputation, you souse. Begone!' Binnie says." Joey struck a pose and pointed a stern arm "'Begone!' The old man pleads, holds out his arms. 'Give me back my daughter,' he sobs. 'I'll reform. I'll show her how to lead a normal life. She will be happy and married with kids.' Binnie curls a scornful lip and turns her back. 'You'll be sorry,' he shrieks—"

O'Grady interrupted impatiently, "Never mind the act. Where can I find this guy?"

Joey Coy stopped grinning and suddenly, despite his funny cigar and out-sized cane, he looked normal. "I'm not as screwy as I seem, lieutenant," he said in a natural voice. "It's a habit I get into. I think it would be a good idea if you looked up Nora's father. Right now I think you'll find him in the Star Hotel over on Mulberry Street, a flophouse. He'll be soused, but there are ways around that."

Then, as if regretting his temporary sanity, he reached into his pocket and put on a pair of enormous black-rimmed glasses. "I'll have other ideas from time to time," he announced importantly. "Make me an offer."

O'Grady left.

Nora Bailey, Binnie's daughter, was in Room 304, and O'Grady found her in exactly the condition he had expected, for she had seen the body. She was lying stiffly in bed, as mute as a tombstone and just as colorless. Her eyes were dark, wide and fixed, and the tears welled up in them, rolled down her cheeks and fell unchecked to the pillow as steadily as the ticking of the clock on the night table.

A motherly looking woman bustled indignantly across the room as

O'Grady entered, but before she could loose the tirade that was bursting at her lips, he showed his badge.

"You couldn't wait," she said bitterly. "Look at her. She's in no condition." O'Grady could see the girl was in no condition. But that was all the better from his angle, if there was something to be dug for.

The bathroom door opened and out stepped one of the handsomest men O'Grady had ever laid eyes on.

He was six feet tall, had a lean, tanned face, wide shoulders and slim hips. But on second glance he fell to pieces. His eyes were too close, his mouth too small and his nose too long and predatory. His smile didn't reach his eyes by inches.

He looked arrogantly at O'Grady and said, "Yes?"

"Mr. Tony Reagan," the motherly woman said drily to O'Grady. "The juvenile lead in the show. For fifteen years now he's a juvenile. In the show I'm his mother. I should be found dead. He's got the girl mesmerized, the Svengali." Then sweetly, "This is a policeman, Mr. Reagan, not a reporter. You can go back into the bathroom and uncomb your hair."

Reagan smiled thinly at O'Grady. "Quaint old guernsey, isn't she?" he drawled. "I'm Miss Bailey's fiancé."

The woman said darkly, "See?"

O'Grady's eyes flickered from the silent, sorrowing girl to Reagan's shallow face. Reagan ran his hand over his hair and straightened his tie, and he was very fond of his fingernails.

"I protest," he said unconvincingly. "I protest against your disturbing Miss Bailey at a time like this."

O'Grady murmured, "You don't say."

The woman muttered, "The hell he doesn't. He says all the time. Binnie had a word for him. Phonograph needle. If you don't mind, I think I'll go back to my room and get sick." She gave Reagan a venomous glance and marched out of the room.

O'Grady lifted a cigarette to his lips. "On second thought," he said, "maybe I won't disturb Miss Bailey. I just wanted a little information, that's all. Perhaps you'd help me, Mr. Reagan?"

Reagan was flattered. His vanity was colossal. He accepted this as a tribute to his intelligence. "Gladly," he said graciously.

"Suppose we hash it up over a cup of coffee?"

"Delighted, Mr.—ah—?"

"Just call me Chief."

Reagan had been in Newark exactly twenty-four hours, O'Grady for twenty-four years, but it was Reagan who showed O'Grady where to get the best coffee in town. *He* said. It was good coffee, almost half as good as the coffee O'Grady was accustomed to drinking at Mike's Lunch, across the street from headquarters. He wagged his spoon in his cup as if to stir some life into it.

"I suppose," he said thoughtfully, "you'll be marrying Miss Bailey now."

"Oh, not immediately, Chief—ah—?"

"O'Grady."

"Not immediately, Chief O'Grady. One has to observe a decent period of mourning, doesn't one?"

"Naturally, naturally. You know, a handsome guy like you, Reagan— how come you and the little lady didn't tie it up before this?"

Reagan's small mouth thinned. "If it had been up to me, Chief O'Grady—"

O'Grady nodded sympathetically. "The mother, eh?"

"A termagant, a virago, a fishwife. Meaning, of course," Reagan added on hurriedly, "no disrespect to the dead."

"Of course not," O'Grady agreed. "Opposed to the match, eh?"

"Opposed to everything. The merest suggestion she opposed. For instance, she made the show the rowdy free-for-all it is. How often I said to Mr. Bennett. 'Mr. Bennett,' I pleaded with him, 'the public is tired of these musical fistfights. They want something romantic and nostalgic.'"

O'Grady's spoon kept stirring and stirring, but he hadn't touched the coffee. Reagan's story seemed to fascinate him. "That romantic angle," he observed, "I'll bet you could handle that in a breeze."

"Naturally." It was a statement of fact embroidered with no false modesty. "And I'm pretty sure you'll see some changes in the show before we reach New York. Miss Bailey owns twenty-five percent interest, and she'll have something to say about it. We'll throw out all the slapstick, including that gruesome little comedian, Joey Coy. I can't look at him without reaching for the Lysol."

"You and Miss Bailey will play the romantic leads?"

"Naturally."

"Talented little girl, I hear."

"Beautiful talent, Chief O'Grady. Beautiful. Fragile, dainty ..."

"Nostalgic? Romantic?"

"More sentimental than romantic. I've been coaching her. When her mother wasn't around, of course. That was another thing she opposed. She was ruining the girl. Binnie," he added maliciously, "belonged strictly to the semaphore school of acting."

O'Grady pushed back his untasted cup of coffee and stood. "I won't keep you any longer, Mr. Reagan. As a representative of the police department, I'd like to offer my profound gratitude for your assistance."

Reagan beamed.

O'Grady stopped in the corner cigar store and called headquarters. "I'm going over to the Star Hotel on Mulberry Street. Have the boys get there before me and cover all exits. You know how it is when a cop walks into that flea bag."

The clerk at the desk turned pale when O'Grady plodded across the murky lobby. They were old acquaintances.

"A guy named Bailey," O'Grady said without preliminaries.

The clerk fumbled with the register. O'Grady cocked his ear and delightedly listened for the familiar sounds. They came—a scamper of furtive feet down the back hallways, a scuffling of feet, curses at the doors. The boys had the exits covered. The clerk also heard it.

He wet his lips and said, "Room 211," and seemed ready to duck.

O'Grady moved, unhurried, toward the stairs. If Bailey had run, it might mean something. But Bailey hadn't run.

He lay open-eyed on his crummy bed, his hands clasped behind his head. He jumped up when O'Grady walked through the doorway.

O'Grady said, "Sit down," and showed his badge again. He leaned against the door as Bailey slowly sank back.

Bailey's mouth twisted. "She really meant it," he said bitterly. "She really did sic the cops on me. She said she would."

"Your wife—Binnie Bailey?"

"She said she would, but she's ruining my kid. I couldn't stay away. I know I'm not much good, but tonight I made up my mind to lay off the bottle. See, I'm sober. I'm going to get a job. Publicity. I used to be one of the best. I can do it again. Maybe if I show her I can take care of Nora."

O'Grady said abruptly, "Your wife's dead, Bailey."

Bailey's hands and shoulders jerked. He said, "Good!" then mumbled, "God forgive me."

"She was pushed off the hotel roof. How long have you been in your room?"

Bailey's hands shivered. "A half hour," he said in a muffled voice. He blurted desperately, "I was walking down by the river, taking a good look at myself, making up my mind to pull myself out of it. I'm not something to be proud of. I panhandle my own kid for liquor money. I want to help Nora ..."

"How are you going to help Nora?"

"She doesn't belong on the stage. She never belonged on the stage, but Binnie trained her for it since the cradle. It—I guess it would have broken Binnie to bits if the kid ever quit. She couldn't face it that Nora was no good and was just eating her heart out. She wants to live like other girls—if she's still able."

O'Grady said, "Hmmmmm," and polished his nails on his lapel. "I hear you had quite a scrap with your wife tonight."

"We always scrapped when we saw each other. Always. Not just tonight."

"But tonight was kind of special, wasn't it?"

Bailey sat up and looked steadily at O'Grady. "Am I under arrest?" he asked. "You can take me in. It doesn't make any difference to me. I don't give a damn. I didn't kill her. She's dead and the kid's free to go as she pleases. That's all that counts." He swung his legs over the side of the bed. "I'll be dressed in a minute."

O'Grady watched him cynically as he fumbled with his shoes.

"You know," he observed, "I never saw a guy so anxious as you to get himself pinched. Most guys'd be jumping out the window to get away from it. Maybe you're just queer. Or, on the other hand, maybe you know something I don't know. Could that be it, Bailey?"

Bailey looked up with a shoe in his hand. He said stupidly, "What was that?" as if he hadn't heard all of it.

"I said, you're in a hell of a rush to get yourself tossed in the clink."

"I'm not in a rush. You said you were arresting me."

"*You* said that," O'Grady pointed out. "You told me I was arresting you, and the next thing I knew you were jumping into your clothes like an overslept fireman. I just wanted to know, how come? It didn't seem natural. I'm not used to it. You'd do anything for your daughter, wouldn't you, Bailey?"

"Except stay sober."

"That was then. I mean now. Suppose you got the screwy idea she was mixed up in the murder somewhere. You'd break a leg to crucify yourself for her. See what I mean?"

Bailey dropped the shoe. "No," he whispered, horror-stricken. "You don't think that! You don't think Nora—"

O'Grady said mildly, "I said it was a screwy idea, didn't I?" He opened the door. "Hang around awhile. I may drop in tomorrow."

Bailey darted from the bed and grasped O'Grady's arm. "Wait a minute," he pleaded. "You've got Nora all wrong. She didn't have anything to do with it. She couldn't. She loved Binnie. That's the reason she stayed on the stage all these years. She'd do anything for Binnie. Honestly, she'd—"

O'Grady pushed him gently back into the room. "Go to bed," he said. "And if I find you drunk in the morning, I *will* throw you in the can."

He closed the door. He looked thoughtfully at it, rubbed his chin, then turned toward the stairs, shaking his head.

O'Grady was at the morning rehearsal of the *Early To Rise* cast the next day. The cast moved listlessly, conscious that the ax had fallen. Nora Bailey was pale but composed. Tony Reagan was at her side constantly, talking, arguing, impatiently tossing his dark curls—and getting nowhere. The pianist poked woodenly at the keyboard. It sounded like a dirge. At last Sam Bennett climbed to the stage and made a sad little speech. He looked like a pink baby, ruthlessly deprived of his bottle.

"I know it's going to be tough without Binnie in there, kids," he said, "but we got a great little comedian in Joey Coy, and Joey's going to be giving all he's got, and you know that's plenty. I want you to back him to the hilt. Do that and we'll have the sparklingest little musical that ever hit Broadway." He waved his hand and climbed down to the auditorium and sat beside O'Grady in the fifth row.

The stage cleared, the piano tinkled out the cue, and Joey Coy, cigar and all, dashed out, crouching low, dragging a dressmaker's dummy at the end of a rope. He turned, looked surprised, then leaped on the dummy, winding his arms around it.

"At last, Hortense!" he screamed. "At last we are alone. Tell me that you will never leave me. Say that you'll be mine forever. I missed the last payment on you, and the finance company's at my throat."

The rehearsal was on.

O'Grady whispered, "Where'd he get that thing from? It looks like my grandmother, bustle and all."

"From an ash can, maybe. From the gutter, from the city dumps. Heaven knows where he gets his props from. He never stops looking. Great little comedian. Look at that. Nobody but Joey Coy would think of a thing like that and make it funny."

Joey had pulled a phony pig's head from a burlap sack and had spiked it atop the dummy. He gave it a horrified glance and shrieked.

"You don't love me! Don't speak. I can see it in your face."

O'Grady didn't think it very funny.

As a matter of fact, he couldn't make head or tail of the whole rehearsal. It looked like hash to him. The director never let a song be sung through to its end, the dancers pattered on for a few steps, stopped and started all over again. Tony Reagan didn't have a good voice, but it was certainly one of the loudest O'Grady had ever heard. The whole thing looked and sounded like rush hour in the subway.

And Nora Bailey. The kindest thing that could be said of her was that she was miscast, but no matter what part she took, it would have been a miss. She moved like a well-trained terrier, and the job she turned in was just as human.

But Sam Bennett seemed more and more pleased as the rehearsal clattered on. "It's got a chance," he whispered to O'Grady. "It's got better than a chance."

O'Grady said frankly, "It looks lousy to me."

Sam was hurt. "But all rehearsals look lousy. Come and see it tonight."

"Thanks."

As Sam had promised, the finished show did look different. It was smooth and polished, but it lacked sparkle. The songs were ordinary and the dancing usual. O'Grady watched from the wings, and by the end of the second act he could tell it was headed for the warehouse. The applause was as thin as Sahara rain.

Joey Coy was working like a beaver. He clambered over furniture, ran up the scenery and produced an endless amount of garbage from his pockets.

He got one laugh when he ran into Tony Reagan and they both fell over the sofa and disappeared. It was a laugh of sheer gratitude.

As the second curtain came down, Joey Coy ran into the wings, sweating. He panted to O'Grady, "It can't live without Binnie. Right now it's strictly from cheese."

"Sam Bennett doesn't seem to think so."

Joey turned to look at Sam, who was noisily congratulating everyone as they came from the stage. "He knows," Joey said. "He's been in the business long enough to know what a turkey smells like." He hesitated, then said in a low voice, "I got something for you."

He dug under his costume and brought out a small handkerchief, smeared with orange lipstick. "Orange," he pointed out. "Binnie had orange hair and had all her lipstick made special to match."

O'Grady said drily, "You had your back turned to Sam at the time, but I saw you pick it up. What were you saving it for?"

Joey shrugged. "Self-protection, Jack. I had a chance to put the show on its feet, and I wasn't going to throw any monkeys. I've been slipping for too long, and this was a chance to show stuff, but I guess there ain't none left no more."

"Would you have turned this over to me if the show had gone over?"

"Don't ask me, Jack. If you saw me pick it up, you know what that nose rag means."

"Yep, but I don't see how it helps. I've known who the killer is for quite a while, but pinning it on him is a different thing. She must have been in his room last night when she dropped this handkerchief. What were they doing—scrapping?"

"Like they was married. The walls are thin in that hotel, Jack. I could hear."

O'Grady said, "You're going to do something for me, Joey, and if it turns out, I'll forget you suppressed evidence. Now listen ..."
Joey listened.

The roof was dark, illuminated only by the reflection from the harsh neon lights from the street far below. From where he stood at the chimney, O'Grady saw Joey Coy only as a hunched silhouette on the parapet, and beside him a heavy, round-shouldered figure. Their voices were low, but distinct.
"Another turkey," Joey was saying.
Sam Bennett's voice protested, "You can't tell yet, Joey."
"I can, and you can. We gotta make changes, Sam."
"No changes. It goes as it stands."
"You sound as if you want it to flop, Sam."
"Don't talk like a screwball."
"In fact, Sam, I'll put it this way. I know you want it to flop, for the same reason all your other turkeys flopped. I know how you financed the show, Sam. It came to me tonight when I saw how you had deliberately ruined this one. It came to me that all your shows were alike. You sold about five hundred percent of this one, Sam. You're a slick talker, you make a lot of contacts, and years ago you had a hit or two. You sold big chunks of it to about twenty-five guys, subtracted the cost of production and pocketed the difference. Then you set out to make sure it flopped. You're a crook, Sam."
O'Grady saw Bennett step back from the parapet and heard him say dangerously, "You're a screwball. You always were a screwball."
"Was Binnie Bailey a screwball, too? She knew you were needling the show. She had dough sunk in it and she got sore. That's why she scrapped with you last night."
"What's on your mind, Joey?" Bennett purred.
"You killed Binnie, Sam. Not because she scrapped with you, but because she was making a success of the show. You didn't expect that when you put her in the lead—an old has-been like Binnie. And if she put the show in the big-money brackets, you were going to have one sweet time when all those guys came around for their twenty-five percents of the profits. You know what I'm going to do to show you up, Sam? I'm going to put an ad in *Variety*. I'm going to say, 'Special meeting of the backers of *Early To Rise* will be held in—'"
Bennett lunged with his arms thrust before him. Joey Coy's legs flew up and he disappeared over the edge of the roof. Sam turned and stumbled toward the stairway. O'Grady stepped from beside the chimney and turned on his flash.

He snapped, "Hold it, Bennett!"

Sam gave him a glance of pure terror and threw up his hands as if to ward off the searching, accusing finger of light. Then, with a shriek, he turned and sprang headfirst over the parapet. O'Grady jogged across the roof and peered over the ledge, grinning.

One story down, Joey Coy and Bennett were floundering in the safety net O'Grady had the fire department string up for him. Sam clawed toward the edge of the net and, as O'Grady yelled, Joey raised his heavy cane and brought it down heavily on that shining, bald head. Then, reverting, he reached over and flicked an invisible speck of dust from it.

A TIME FOR DYING

The murderer, Marmot, picked Woody up in a gin mill at one A.M., and after that he stayed with him, watching, calculating, waiting for the exact moment of drunkenness at which Woody would be manageable without being unconscious.

Woody realized none of this. The night was full of faces, floating happily by, like jellyfish on a summer sea. Woody was celebrating; he was on a vast, joyous toot of triumph, for that very afternoon old man Haskins had signed over the charter boat, *Coquina*, to him, and had formally and finally retired. The terms were so unbelievably generous that every time Woody lifted his glass he grinned a toast. The world was such a delightful place that there were many toasts, and by one A.M. he was really looping.

Marmot found him in the gin mill sitting privately at a side table beaming at the empty chair opposite. Marmot had come in as if walking hand in hand with fear, and terror only a step behind. He had been drinking steadily and desperately, but it needed more than liquor to change the fact that his wife lay dead in the stateroom of their cruiser, anchored at the Yacht Basin dock, more than liquor to change the fact that he had swung the fire extinguisher that had bloodily crushed her skull. But the sight of Woody, happily toasting the empty chair, brought Marmot's aimless flight to a sharp and sudden focus.

A face swam into the line of Woody's vision and hovered there. He knew it was a face because there was a hole in it that opened and closed and voice sounds came forth. He could not distinguish Marmot's weak, fleshy chin, or his petulant mouth, but it did not matter. Everything was so wonderful.

"Gonna get married now," he announced happily. "Wonderful girl. Big s'prise."

Fresh drinks appeared on the table. The mouth opened and closed. The voice said, "Can you swim?"

Swim? Go swimming? He could swim like a trout, but he didn't want to go swimming. He wanted to drink another toast to old man Haskins. And one to Gracie. But swim? He laughed and said, "No."

"Can you run a boat, a cruiser?"

Woody gave the face a chiding glance. The *Coquina*, his very own now, was a cruiser. What did this face want, anyway? To go out in the *Coquina* at this hour of night?

He shook his head and said, "No." Then mysteriously, "Gracie," meaning that Gracie was to be the first to go out in the *Coquina* under his skippership.

To Marmot, all this meant something entirely different. It meant that Woody could neither swim nor run a boat. That Woody was, in fact, made to order. Marmot had the bottle brought to the table.

The gin mill closed at three. Woody lurched from his chair and looked hazily around the emptying room.

"Gonna get married," he said solemnly. "Big s'prise."

He did not seem a whit drunker than he had at one. Marmot's face was whiter and his hands trembled as he slipped the waiter a ten-dollar bill in exchange for two flat pints. Dawn was a bony finger of gray in the eastern sky when Woody reeled all but helplessly out on the Yacht Basin dock, clutching an envelope Marmot had thrust into his hand.

The watchman yelled, "Hey, you! Where you think you're going?" and plodded up the dock in the thinning darkness. He recognized Woody at six paces and growled, "What's got into you?"

Woody beamed foolishly on him and swayed. "Ferg'son," he said with an air of triumph. Ferguson was the watchman's name.

"What's this?"

The watchman took the envelope Woody was carrying and read the note inside.

> Mr. Ferguson: This is Johnny Woods, who is going to repair my boat. Please pass him. Orin Marmot.

Marmot let out a harsh breath as the watchman took Woody's arm and led him up the dock, talking sternly to him.

"Oughta be ashamed getting soused like this. Woody. You never got soused before. What's got into you …?"

He watched until he saw the watchman help Woody into the cockpit of the cruiser. That was as far as they'd get. The salon, with its grisly occupant, was securely locked.

Marmot slipped into the warm water and silently swam under the dock. Overhead, he heard Ferguson's plodding footsteps returning. He waited until they stopped, as Ferguson went back into his shack, then swam over to the side of the cruiser. He climbed the swimming ladder and slipped over the side. There was no apparent reason for it, but the moment he touched Woody, he began to tremble violently again, as if he had touched a corpse.

As swiftly as he could, he pulled off Woody's striped Basque shirt and drew it on himself. He dragged Woody into the salon, then came out and securely locked the door again, rattling the knob several times as if to reassure himself that it was really locked. He stepped to the controls of the cruiser and took a deep breath. He almost fainted when he remembered that the boat was still moored with both bow and stern lines. If he had started the engines then, Ferguson would have come running and it would have been all over.

Stealthily he cast off the lines and staggered back to the controls. He ransacked his mind. Was there anything else he had overlooked? He couldn't think. The words, *anything else, anything else, anything else*, spun senselessly until his head reeled. He stretched out a faltering forefinger and pressed the starter button. The motors roared thunderously. Without giving them time to warm up, Marmot headed out into the bow at the pass between Dinghy Key and Treasure Island, purposely steering such a crazy course that it would be obvious to anyone watching that there was a drunken man at the wheel.

The watchman came pounding up the dock, shouting angrily, "You damn fool, come back here! Damn it, Woody ..."

Marmot licked tremulously at the sweat that pebbled his upper lip. He glanced back over his shoulder and saw Ferguson standing at the end of the dock, futilely brandishing his arms. He turned back to his course and gave the engines full throttle. He leaned precariously over the side and peered through the window into the salon. His heart lurched as he saw Woody roll over on his side, then heavily push himself to a sitting position. Marmot pulled himself hurriedly back to the bridge and felt for the .45 automatic that hung beside the controls in a leather holster. Then, to relieve the terrible tension, he threw back his head and screamed at the top of his lungs.

The scream came to Woody as the cry of a hungry gull. He was sitting up, leaning now in the angle of the lounge seat and the side wall. He felt the throb of the engines, and he was trying to puzzle it out.

Out of his alcoholic haze came the awful thought that the *Coquina* was running wild, helmless, while he lay down here in the cabin. He lunged to his feet with a cry, already half sobered. The pitch of the cruiser sent him staggering across the salon and he crashed into the dropleaf table. He clutched the table and stared at it. A table? There wasn't any table in the cabin of the *Coquina*. This wasn't the *Coquina*. This was too big, too luxurious. But how ...

He rubbed his chin, half grinned and said, "Whew!" The things that happened when you were on a toot!

In little snatches, he began to remember. Ferguson. He remembered Ferguson. Ferguson had put him aboard. But why? Ferguson knew he belonged to the *Coquina*. A note, a note in an envelope. Somebody had given him a note in an envelope, something to do with the cruiser he was on, but he couldn't figure that one out. He was still too fuzzy for such close reasoning.

The cruiser was pitching quite heavily. He glanced through the window. They were going through the pass out into the Gulf, Treasure Island to starboard, Dinghy Key to port. A half mile beyond was Pelican Key, a God-forsaken strip of mangrove, Spanish dagger, scrub pine, horseshoe crabs and water moccasin. What were they doing out here—going fishing? He didn't want to go fishing. He wanted to get back to the *Coquina*. He grinned again, remembering that he was now master of the *Coquina*. He wanted to go back to the dock and admire it. He wanted to stand on the tiny flying bridge and be monarch of all he surveyed, or something. He wanted to call Gracie up, as soon as she returned from Miami, and casually—oh, so casually!—invite her out for a cruise among the Keys, and watch her face when she learned the stupendous news.

He didn't know whose boat he was on, and he didn't care. He wanted to get back to the *Coquina*. He bent over the basin in the galley and splashed his face with water to wash the cobwebs out of the uneasy corners of his mind.

The cruiser was in the Gulf now, and she was rolling badly and pitching. She was taking the seas heavily on her slim, aristocratic nose, and standing there in the salon was like standing inside a well-beaten bass drum. Something in the forward stateroom rumbled and thudded against the door. A good sailor, Woody knew the damage it could cause, and he opened the door ...

Two paralyzed minutes later he closed it again and unconsciously wiped his right palm down his thigh, feeling slightly sick at what he had seen in there on the floor. It was the heavy fire extinguisher that had been banging against the door, but at that moment he would not have touched that ugly encrusted thing if it had been battering holes in the hull.

He turned and sprang for the door that opened to the cockpit. It was locked and he rattled the knob savagely. A face appeared in the port to his right, twitching. A hand appeared with a gun and violently ordered him back from the door.

Wholly sober, Woody stepped back from the door. He glanced at the windows. They could be slid open, but open or closed, they were too small for anything larger than a trout to wriggle through. There was no way out to the forward cockpit—and, anyway, that maniac out there at the controls had looked as if he meant everything the gun had implied.

He clenched his fists and looked around the salon for something he could use as a weapon. There were pots and pans in the galley, an electric iron; in the salon there was the dropleaf table, a bronze ashtray, a pair of copper lamps. He lifted the hatch cover in the middle of the floor and found a collapsible rubber boat and a pair of aluminum oars. But there was nothing that was proof against bullets.

With the suddenness of murder itself, the engines stopped. Woody leaped to the window. Aft, Pelican Key was a thin line of white and green and the sea between was serried with whitecaps, like rows of teeth. The sky was a smoldering gray, and the wind was coming up strong. A series of rending crashes came from the outside, as if someone were hacking the cruiser to bits. Woody lunged to the porthole and flattened his right cheek against it.

Panting, Marmot gave the controls a final, smashing blow, then tossed the fire axe over the side. Ignoring Woody at the port, he stripped down to a pair of swimming trunks and lashed a cushion-type life preserver around his waist. His face was contorted, and he kept throwing anxious glances at the sky, at the tossing sea. Tripping and staggering in his haste, he gathered up an armful of life preservers he had piled in the cockpit and threw them over the side. He hesitated over the .45, then it, too, followed the life preservers. He threw one last glance at the locked salon, and Woody saw in full the drained, fleshy face, the weak, tremulous mouth, the muscle jerking in the sagging cheek. Then Marmot turned and, in a stumbling run, dived over the bow and struck out for shore with a clean, powerful stroke.

Woody stared, unbelieving. First, that the man thought he could live in that mounting sea. The gale was coming up fast, and already Marmot's bobbing head was lost in the fierce chop. No one could outswim what was coming.

Then the full significance of his own position burst upon Woody. The helpless cruiser was wallowing drunkenly, and it would soon be obviously in distress, a signal for the Coast Guard to pull up alongside— and find him aboard with the murdered woman!

That was it, that was the whole strategy. Grimly, Woody glanced toward the window and wondered if the murderer were enjoying his triumph, as stroke by stroke he began to realize the hopelessness of his struggle to reach the shore.

Not once did it occur to Woody to throw the body overboard, and he would not have done it if it had occurred to him. He had seen the condition of bodies washed ashore and, though she was dead and past caring, he would not have thrust her into that final degradation.

But he had to get out of the salon, off the boat. Big as the cruiser was, she was disabled and the coming storm would play cat and mouse with her. The dropleaf table was of heavy birdseye maple. It went through the locked door as if the door were made of glass. Woody squeezed through, scratching himself on the splinters. One glance at the wrecked controls told him there was nothing to hope for there. And there wasn't a life preserver aboard. Woody felt a rising tide of helplessness as he stared at the sea. It would have been suicide to attempt to swim for it, as Marmot had done, especially without a life preserver.

Marmot had had the cunning of desperation. Woody was imprisoned with the corpse, and all he could do was wait for the Coast Guard. How fantastic would his statement of facts sound to the cold-eyed officer who would find the body? To the police? To the jury? Even to Gracie?

But Woody's anxiety was not mixed with the gibbering fear that had scourged Marmot. He could still think with a semblance of calm, he could still spot the one thing that Marmot, in his haste to spring his trap, had overlooked—the inflatable rubber boat in the hatch under the salon floor.

Woody's last act, before he launched the little boat, was to cast off the bow anchor. The cruiser was a beautiful craft, and it would have been sacrilege to let the coming storm wreck her. There was no bottom here for the anchor, but as the cruiser was driven toward the shore, there were coral ledges on which it could catch and hold.

He lashed himself to the built-in rubber oarlock, then shoved off. His hands tightened on the shore oars. It was going to be a muscle-cracking job.

He wasn't twenty lengths from the cruiser when he remembered Ferguson. Ferguson had put him aboard the cruiser, and when the police asked their questions, Ferguson would remember. Dismay seemed to drain him of strength. He was actually worse off now than if he had stayed aboard, for now he had to fight the angry sea as well, to remain alive.

He looked over his shoulder, straining for a glimpse of Marmot amid the waves. His only hope lay with Marmot, the real murderer. Alive, Marmot was his alibi. Dead, the police could say Woody had killed him as well.

He rowed. At times the height of the sea hid the cruiser from him entirely, and then, finally it was gone. The little rubber boat was so light and bobbed so crazily that half the time Woody was thrashing the air emptily with his oars and he seemed to be getting nowhere in a nightmare of water and wind. The rain came, slanting stingingly into his face, and that alone told him that he was still heading for shore. He had no other way of knowing, for he had no horizon but the jagged peaks of the surrounding waves. The wind came driving hard. Finding Marmot in that maelstrom would have been nothing but crazy, fantastic luck. He rowed. Fatigue was just another thing that came out of the rising storm, like the tear of the wind, like the fist of the waves, another thing he had to battle. Stray thoughts scudded across his mind—thoughts of Gracie, incredulous, then delighted when she learned that he now owned the *Coquina*; thoughts of the *Coquina* riding calmly in a quiet bay on a sunlit afternoon, Gracie fishing off the bow, himself at the controls on the bridge; Gracie had never trolled for tarpon. In this crashing nightmare, it was sometimes hard to separate the visions from the reality. He had been out in a storm before, but never in a ten-foot rubber boat. His mind reeled with the immensity of it.

He did not recognize the final wave that seized the little boat in its teeth, but suddenly he was amid the roar and violence of the surf. Somehow, the boat had struck something and capsized, leaving him choking and flailing in the green water. Frantically he tried to pull himself free of the line that tied him to the boat, for it was dragging him out to sea again. He was tumbled into the branches of one of the dead, fallen trees that spiked the tiny beach of Pelican Key, and he clung to it, holding his face barely above water, sobbing for breath and strength.

The boat was still a powerful drag on the line, and, catching sight of it as it streamed seaward, he could see why. The wave had flung it into the tree and it had been ripped open from bow to stern. It lay flat on the water like the carcass of a manta ray. Clinging to the branches with one arm, he worked his knife out of his pocket and cut himself free. It immediately disappeared into the sea. He waited until he saw the rhythm of the waves, waited until the big one thundered by, then scrambled for the shore as the smaller one raged after him like a terrier. He staggered into the soft sand and fell full length.

The sounds of the storm receded from him. He lay with his head cradled in the bend of his arm. It was sheer luxury, not having to move. Then, slowly, that passed and he could no longer lie still. He sat up. A few feet away from him, one of the hollow aluminum oars had been tossed ashore, but of the boat there was no sign. The breakers snarled along the shore, but it was a changed world, looking at it from the land.

He was astounded. It was a storm, all right, but nothing even approaching the hurricane intensity he had thought it. The waves were not mountains, and the wind did not have a maniacal shriek, though it was strong enough to chill him to the bone.

He thrust himself to his feet and winced as his right ankle buckled under him. He had gotten that when he was flung into the tree. He hopped over to the oar and picked it up. In this soft sand it was a bad crutch, but it was better than nothing. And, anyway, he did not want to go exploring; all he wanted was shelter from the wind.

He was on the southernmost tip of Pelican Key, a scrap of beach hardly as large as half a city block.

Wryly, he muttered, "Thank God for small mercies." But it was more than a small mercy, for the rest of the Key was nothing more than a water moccasin-infested mangrove swamp. Even without the snakes, to have been flung into the tough tangle of mangrove roots would have gotten him worse than a twisted ankle. The mangrove was a tree that grew on a multitude of stilts.

Woody laboriously hobbled toward the dunes, skirting the murderously pointed clusters of Spanish dagger plants. Panting, he hoisted himself up on the shelf of sand the sea had made. He rounded the dune and stopped dead, his jaw dropping.

There, in the lee of the dune, sat Marmot, huddled miserably over his knees. At the sight of Woody, Marmot's face turned gray. With a hoarse cry he scrambled to his feet and pelted up the beach, throwing terrified glances over his shoulder, as if Woody were not real, but a monster.

Woody yelled and flung the oar end over end. It caught Marmot across the knees and brought him down, but before Woody could close the gap between them, Marmot lurched to his feet and, limping, pounded across the sand toward the mangrove. Woody retrieved his oar and grimly swung himself after the fleeing man. Marmot stopped at the grove and looked back. He ran up and down before the mangrove, as if seeking another avenue of escape, but the grove covered the Key solidly from side to side. In a frenzy, he ran to the raging edge of the water, then back along the mangrove. Finally, whimpering, grasping the trunks of the trees, he fearfully edged into the grove. He was ten feet in and clinging desperately with both arms when Woody hobbled up. Woody stared at him. With his twisted ankle, it was impossible for him to follow. He planted the oar before him and leaned on it.

"That's just where you're going to stay, fella," he said heavily. "You come out here and I'll brain you. But maybe you'll think it's worth it when the water moccasins come swimming around. They're very nosy, and you'll interest them, but if you stand perfectly still, you'll be all right. They won't strike unless you move."

Marmot's terror was so obvious that it was a weapon to be used against him. He threw a horrified glance at the black water below his feet. The tangle of mangrove root seemed to writhe, and each root became a snake.

Woody sat down stolidly in the sand with the oar across his knees. He wanted to keep Marmot in there. After finding the abandoned cruiser and its bloody cargo, the Coast Guard would make a search of every Key, and Woody did not want Marmot to see them land.

Marmot shifted on his perch to get a better view of the water below.

"That's right," Woody called, "commit suicide. There are probably ten or twenty moccasins swimming around you right now."

Marmot moaned and looked up at the slender trunk of the tree. He could climb up a little way, but beyond that the branches were too frail to support him. He would have nothing but the trunk to cling to, nothing to stand on, and it would not be very long before he would drop off.

"Help me out of here, Woods," he begged. "I'll clear you. I'll tell them I framed you. I'll tell them I killed my wife. Help me out of here!"

"I'll help you out—with the butt end of the oar."

Marmot, he felt, would promise anything. If there were pen and paper, he would write anything, confess anything Woody demanded. But he wasn't to be trusted. He had to be kept in a state of constant terror until there were witnesses to his confession.

Marmot, still pleading, took a tentative step toward the edge of the grove, lifting his legs very high. Woody rose and ominously hefted the oar. It was so light that if Marmot forced the decision it probably would not even stun him.

But there was no force in Marmot. He stopped and hugged the tree, openly weeping. His pleas became so abject, so groveling that Woody turned sick just listening.

Marmot tried twice again to come out of the grove, but each time Woody drove him back with the oar. Marmot cowered there and shrieked. He shrieked until Woody, unable to bear it any longer, leaped to his feet and cried,

"Damn it, come on out. Come out, but for the love of God, stop yelling!"

Marmot either did not hear or he did not understand. He started to laugh.

"Ah, you had me fooled, Mona," he giggled. "You really had me fooled. You were punishing me, weren't you? You were angry with me. I'm sorry, Mona. I didn't mean it. I lost my temper. You know what a bad temper I have. You should have given me the money when I asked you. You'd never have missed it. I know you said I shouldn't gamble, but just this last time you should have given it to me."

Woody felt his heart contract as the chill closed around it. He had pushed Marmot too far. He had gone crazy....

The storm traveled slowly north and by the midafternoon a long pennant of clear blue floated over the southern horizon. The Coast

Guard came ashore an hour later, four men and a lieutenant, all wearing sidearms. Woody stood and waved his oar. Marmot was lying on the sand beside him, sleeping. Woody knew the lieutenant. His name was Thompson.

He called, "Hiya, Tommy."

Thompson barely nodded. "We found the cruiser," he said shortly. "The police want you, Woods. Ferguson told them you took her out this morning. Let's go."

Woody said, "Wait ..." and bent over to shake Marmot. There was a tension in him that hummed shrilly. Marmot had been sleeping, and he might wake up sane.

"Wake up, Orey," he whispered—he had learned that Marmot's wife always called him Orey. "Wake up."

Marmot stirred and sat up, sleepily digging his knuckles into his eyes. He looked at Woody and broke into a big, foolish smile.

"You're not mad at me?" he wheedled. "Say you're not mad at me."

"No. I'm not mad at you, Orey."

"I didn't mean to hit you, you know. But all of a sudden the fire extinguisher was in my hand and you were on the floor. Anyway, you shouldn't be mad at me. You punished me enough, pretending to be dead. I almost went out of my mind." He waggled a horribly playful finger.

Woody shuddered. The Coast Guard lieutenant stared.

"He thinks," said Woody dully, "that I'm his wife, that he didn't kill her after all. I can get him to tell more, if you want."

The lieutenant just looked at him. Words were not necessary.

LIVING BAIT

I could see that Mr. Langler was boiling. He had no reason to be mad. He'd brought two tarpon to gaff. Miss Starr had only caught one, but Miss Starr's had been a good thirty pounds heavier. All three tarpon were too light for the tournament, and we turned them loose.

There's lots of guys like Mr. Langler. No matter what they do, they got to win every time or they don't like it. He was big and red-faced and built like a fullback, and you could see that he was a real tough man about everything. He seemed to have the idea that when he'd hired my boat he'd hired the tarpon, too, and he was mad because they wouldn't do exactly what he wanted them to do, like everybody else who worked for him. He was some kind of big executive. Big executives, for some reason or other, always seem to think they're bigger than life size.

Miss Starr was a big executive, too—she owned some kind of cosmetics company—but you wouldn't think it to look at her. She was the most beautiful woman I have ever seen. Wearing those shorts and halter, there was an awful lot of Miss Starr visible to the naked eye. She had the kind of legs a man had an awful time keeping his mind on what he was doing, and the shape of her halter only made it worse. But it was Mr. Langler she was after, not me. Mr. Langler was mad at the tarpon, so nobody was getting nowheres. It was a kind of a mess.

And Wiley wasn't helping things out any either, kidding around the way he was. He didn't have much sense. I should never have brought Wiley along, I thought. He didn't mean any harm. He thought he was making Mr. Langler feel better about not catching the biggest tarpon. Still, Wiley could bait-up faster than any mate I'd ever had, even if he didn't have but only one arm. He could gaff a tarpon without ripping it to pieces, the way some of them do.

I was just about to call him up to the flying bridge to keep him out of trouble, when Mr. Langler hooked into another tarpon. He grunted and the tip of the rod dipped down over the transom. A few minutes later the tarpon came up out of the water with such a surge it looked like a fountain glittering in the sun. He was big and silver, and he shook himself like a bulldog to throw the hook. His heavy underslung jaw was wide open and his mouth looked like you could put your head in it. He was a big tarpon, a hundred and fifty pounds easy, big enough to win a tournament and then some. He was really a tarpon to make you catch your breath.

Mr. Langler fought him like it was life and death and the most important thing in the world. His mouth was fixed in a kind of snarl. He cursed and ground his teeth and jerked on the rod. The way he carried on, you'd of thought that tarpon was his worst enemy.

That tarpon was really something, though. I never seen a tarpon jump the way that one did. He was up, and, no sooner he came down, he was up again with that wrenching shake that almost pulled Mr. Langler's arms out of their sockets.

For the next two hours, that tarpon was in the air more than it was in the water. The sweat poured off Mr. Langler like rain off a tin roof. His arms were beginning to quiver from the strain, and if it kept up I knew the tarpon was going to pull that two-hundred-dollar rod and reel right out of his hands. I helped him all I could with the boat, but fighting a tarpon that big is mostly up to the fisherman.

Miss Starr stood at the side of the cockpit out of Mr. Langler's way. If it'd been me, I'd of lost that tarpon a dozen times, the way she stood there her legs all round and rich in the sun, and her chest so deep and curved.

"Oh, you're doing splendidly!" she cried. "You've almost got him. He's tiring. You fought him beautifully!"

Mr. Langler snarled, "Keep out of my way, dammit!" though she wasn't within three feet of him.

She was right. The tarpon was tiring. I came down from the bridge, pulling on a pair of gloves to grip the leader when Mr. Langler got the tarpon to the boat. Wiley leaned over the transom with the gaff.

Then it happened. Mr. Langler was just plain bushed. The tarpon had one hard jump left—and when he got to six feet of the boat, he made it. He gave his big, bulldoggy head a snap, and the hook whizzed right into the cockpit. He splashed back. I leaned over the transom and watched him swim down and down in the water till he wasn't even a shadow anymore. He was one tired fish.

Mr. Langler's eyes bulged at his slack line. He turned on Wiley and began to call him everything he could lay tongue to. He called him a one-armed clown.

"Really it wasn't the man's fault," Miss Starr tried to soothe Mr. Langler. "And it wasn't your fault, either. The tarpon threw the hook."

Mr. Langler threw down the rod and stamped into the cabin, grinding his teeth some more.

Wiley picked up the rod and looked at the reel. "He might of bent it," he said in a disapproving voice.

A few minutes later, Mr. Langler came out of the cabin with a bottle of scotch. "Tomorrow's another day," he said, and poured us all a drink.

That was as close as he could get to an apology, I guess.

I took the boat through Novidades Pass and anchored in the bay. The tide was beginning to run out and it was moving along at about fifteen miles an hour. There was a dock at the fishing village, but they soaked the hell out of you during the tarpon season. Anyways, it was too buggy with mosquitoes and things.

Wiley came down to the cabin to help me with dinner. We could hear Mr. Langler and Miss Starr arguing in the cockpit. They were always arguing, it seemed.

"What were they squabbling about all day?" I asked Wiley.

"Big business deal." He grinned. "Miss Starr, she's got a company that makes lipstick and stuff, and she wants to sell it to Mr. Langler. Mr. Langler says he's got a company that makes lipstick and stuff and he don't need another one. Can you imagine that Mr. Langler having a company that makes lipsticks?" He laughed.

"Is everything a joke to you, Wiley?"

"You got a boat to worry about, Roy. Mr. Langler and Miss Starr, they got a big business deal to worry about. Me, I ain't got nothin'. So I don't worry. It's more fun just kidding around."

"Well stop kidding around Mr. Langler. He gets sore."

"That's a fact, Roy. You hit the nail right on the head. He's a mean man. And that Miss Starr, she's a mean woman."

"You're crazy!" I said. "You must be getting old or something. That Miss Starr is just about the most gorgeous piece of female I ever seen."

He looked at me and laughed. "Man," he said, "you get mixed up with that female and you'll have first-, second-, and third-degree burns before you can even put on your fire hat. Maybe she don't mean no harm, but when she tells you to do something, like bait-up for instance, she looks about three feet over your head like it hurts her eyes to look at us common people. Is that the way when you're a big executive, Roy?"

"That's the way when you kid around too much, like you do. Big executives don't like to kid around with nobody but other big executives."

"Well now, that changes everything, Roy. I thought they didn't like me personal. It's just because they don't know I'm a big executive, too. A big executive is a feller that's got a monopoly on something, ain't he? Well, I got a monopoly on all the nothing on the west coast of Florida. I got more nothing than anybody. I better go right out and tell them, and get things straight."

I couldn't help laughing at him. "You know, Wiley," I said, "when you lost that one arm, I think you lost half your brains with it."

"That's a fact, Roy. I did. The worst half. When I had all my brains, I used to worry about big business deals like Miss Starr and Mr. Langler.

You'd of thought I had a million dollars, the way I used to worry. Then I lost my left wing and half my brains, and now I ain't got a worry in the world. But all the same," he looked sore for a minute, "he don't have no call saying I'm a one-armed clown."

I patted his shoulder. "Take it easy."

We had grouper steaks, home fries, and canned string beans for dinner. Afterwards, Mr. Langler brought out the scotch bottle again, but I excused myself. I went to my berth in the forepeak, leaving Wiley telling them how he was a big executive because he had a monopoly on all the nothing in West Florida.

Maybe I slept and maybe I just dozed, but all of a sudden I was wide awake. There was cursing and fighting in the cockpit. I jumped out of my berth and ran through the cabin. Wiley and Mr. Langler were swinging away at each other right at the transom.

I yelled, "Cut that out—" and tripped over something. I came down hard with my chin on the arm of the bed lounge, and passed out cold.

When I came to, I heard Mr. Langler swearing and Miss Starr saying sharply, "Let me do it, please!" Mr. Langler swore again. I sat up, only half there.

"Whass the matter?" I mumbled.

Miss Starr said worriedly, "Wiley's overboard. Where's the searchlight switch?"

That brought me around. I jumped up and pushed them away from the controls. The switch was way underneath. I reached in and snapped it on. We were facing into the out-going tide. The light was on the bow, so it didn't do much good. If Wiley went overboard, he would've been swept out Novidades Pass, not up into the bay, and we couldn't turn the light astern. We had to pull up the anchor, start the engine and run it in reverse to hold our position as we pointed toward the pass. I played the beam over the dark water but I didn't see a thing that looked like Wiley's head.

I shoved the controls into forward and ran toward the Pass, working the beam all the way. I took her out into the Gulf and cruised up and down, listening and looking, but there wasn't any sign of Wiley.

"Perhaps he swam to the fishing village, Captain," Miss Starr said later.

"Could be," I said, not believing it. "We'll go see." There wasn't much point looking for Wiley in the Gulf anymore. We'd been looking for an hour now, and the water was choppy. We could of missed him a dozen times.

Mr. Langler didn't say anything. He looked pretty sick. We chugged in to the fish-house dock. There was a gang of commercial fishermen sitting there drinking bottle beer. None of them had seen hair nor hide of Wiley. In ten minutes, there were twenty boats all over the bay looking for him. By this time we all knew there wasn't much chance of finding Wiley alive anymore, but we kept at it till two in the morning. Miss Starr and a couple of the fishermen scoured the shore for a mile in both directions.

When we got back to the fish-house dock, I was surprised to see the sheriff there with a deputy. We hadn't told the fishermen about Mr. Langler having the fight with Wiley in the cockpit, so there was no reason for them to have called him in. As far as they were concerned, Wiley had just fallen overboard. These fishermen weren't the kind who went running to the sheriff for every little thing. I had an idea right then and there that it was Miss Starr that'd done the calling. She was standing there on the dock talking to the sheriff and looking very upset.

"That poor man," I heard her say to the sheriff. "That poor, poor man!"

Mr. Langler stood with them, looking numb.

The sheriff took the three of us inside the fish-house and told the fishermen to stay out. "Now let's get to the bottom of this," he said, looking straight at Mr. Langler. "What happened out there?"

Mr. Langler didn't say anything. He was slumped against the wall and his eyes looked like they were kind of rotting away. You could see he couldn't feel worse.

"Come on, what's the story?" the sheriff demanded, looking at Miss Starr this time.

Miss Starr shook her head. "Well," she said in a small, unwilling-sounding voice, "Wiley and Mr. Langler were drinking in the cockpit when I went to bed. They were rather drunk and were bickering about a large tarpon that Mr. Langler had lost that afternoon. I called to them to lower their voices. Mr. Langler just swore louder and called Wiley a one-armed moron who had no right on a boat. They started fighting. Just as I was getting out of bed to stop them, the Captain came running from his berth. He ran into me and fell down and knocked me back. Then Mr. Langler cried out that Wiley had fallen overboard. We made every effort to find him. But I'm certain, Sheriff," she gave him the big-eyes, "that Mr. Langler didn't do it on purpose."

Mr. Langler raised his head and stared at Miss Starr, and she smiled back at him sadly.

"Is that the way it went?" the sheriff asked Mr. Langler.

Mr. Langler made a limp little movement with his hands. "Yes," he said. "That's the way it went."

"You called him some names and you hit him because you were sore about losing that tarpon. Is that right?"

"I was angry at having lost the tarpon and I called him names, but I didn't hit him until he swung the gaff at me."

For the first time I saw that there was blood on his shirt under his left arm.

The sheriff saw it, too. "Is that where he got you?"

Mr. Langler pulled up his shirt and there was a narrow gash across his ribs like a gaff would make. The sheriff's face changed. Things were a little different, now. Before, it was just Mr. Langler knocking Wiley overboard because he was sore, and that would have made it tough for Mr. Langler. But now with that gash on him, it was self-defense, more or less.

"Do you know anything about that part of it?" the sheriff asked Miss Starr.

Miss Starr still gave him the big-eyes. "I was in bed. I didn't see any of it. Wiley said something after Mr. Langler called him a one-armed moron, and Mr. Langler said, 'Shut your stupid mouth or I'll shut it for you.' Then there was the sound of a slap. I don't know which of them struck the other." Her voice was low and had a throb in it and you could tell she was all broken up inside because of this.

The sheriff gave Mr. Langler a very hard glance. That piece about the slap had sure put a hole in the gaff story. Wiley wasn't the kind that went around slapping people. He might make a pass with the gaff if he was drunk enough and sore enough, but he sure wouldn't slap anybody. It just wasn't his way of doing things, and the sheriff knew that as well as I did. When Wiley got sore, he didn't fool around with fluff-stuff like slaps. He let you have it, and he had a lot of strength in that one arm. It was Mr. Langler that slapped Wiley first, and that was just too bad for Mr. Langler.

You could see by the sheriff's face that he didn't like Mr. Langler for nothing. "I'm going to take you in," he said flatly to Mr. Langler, "and if you want my advice, you'd better get yourself a damn good lawyer."

Miss Starr cried, "Oh, please don't take my word for any of this, Sheriff! I didn't actually see anything, you know."

The sheriff patted her hand and told her not to worry about a thing. I stood there trying to think of something so I could pat her other hand.

Before they took him away, Mr. Langler asked to have a private word with me. He looked shamed at what he'd done and hopeless because he knew he didn't have a leg to stand on. He told me to look after Wiley's family and draw on him for any amount of money. He gave me the name of his lawyer in Tallahassee and said he'd tell the lawyer to give me whatever Wiley's family needed in the way of money. I didn't tell him Wiley didn't have any family that I knew of because he might of had somebody someplace.

Then Mr. Langler said dully, "I want you to know, Captain, that I'd give a fortune if this hadn't happened. I must have been out of my head to have struck a one-armed man."

He embarrassed me because he was really all broken up about it and I couldn't feel any sympathy for him.

"Well," I said lamely, "maybe Miss Starr had it mixed up a little. Maybe it didn't happen quite that way."

He gave me a funny look and said, "That's very possible."

"Well—I'll see if there's anything I can do."

"Thanks, Captain."

After the sheriff took Mr. Langler away, Miss Starr said regretfully that she thought it would be better if she spent the night at the Inn instead of on the boat alone with me. The way she put it made me sort of tingle all over, like she really *wanted* to stay on the boat but that if she did and I tried to kiss her or something there wouldn't be anything she could do about it except give in because she couldn't resist me and it wouldn't be fair to either of us until she knew me better. She didn't say any of that, you understand, but that was the feeling I got when she looked at me. She was the most beautiful woman in the world.

I went out early the next morning in the boat. I didn't have much hope, but I hated to think of Wiley's body floating around in the Gulf. He was probably miles down the coast by this time, if the sharks hadn't got to him first. There's always a mess of shark around during tarpon season. Sometimes I think they come from all over the United States just for the season from May to August because the rest of the year you hardly see them at all.

There was one especially big shark, a twenty-footer we called Whitey on account of he's a light gray. He's turned up regularly every year for five years. I've taken dozens of shots at him with the .30-.30 but nobody can seem to knock him off. He's got a mouth like a manhole, and I've seen him take three quarters of a record tarpon in one bite. We all hated him. All Whitey's got to do is sniff blood and he's there.

If Wiley was bleeding, he wouldn't of had much of a chance with Whitey around.

The whole commercial fishing fleet hunted with me for a couple hours. Then they went off with their nets after mullet. They had a living to make. The Coast Guard had been notified, and they'd be on the lookout for a body. In the end, I had to quit too. I put down the hook just about where we'd anchored the night before.

I never felt lower in my whole life. Aside from being the best mate I'd ever had, I really liked poor old Wiley, his happy-go-lucky ways and funny sayings. I really hated Mr. Langler right then. I went down into the cabin and had a drink from one of the other bottles of scotch Mr. Langler had left, a thing I never do out on the boat.

After the second drink, I put the bottle away because I was too much in the mood to get drunk. I didn't hate Mr. Langler so much anymore. I had the feeling that maybe he was all right underneath when he wasn't excited. The way he said to take care of Wiley's family, for instance. He could of made a big thing out of it in front of everybody to get sympathy for himself, but he had told me privately and had really seemed all broken up.

I went up on deck and looked out over the water. The tide was coming in strong, making a ripple over the bar from the end of Jarrett Key to the south. Every year that bar got longer and longer and the channel from the Gulf to the bay through Novidades Pass got more crooked. I looked at the bar a long time. I began to think, and get a little excited. The more I looked at it with the tide rippling over it, the more excited I got.

If the out-going tide got a man, it *could* of swept him right up on that little old bar out there—and he could walk ashore to Jarrett Key. But it didn't seem hardly likely because Wiley would of seen us looking all over the bay for him and he would of yelled. Yet, I couldn't get it out of my mind. Finally, I hauled up anchor and chugged over to Jarrett Key. I dropped the hook in the shallows.

I waded in and climbed over the spider-leg roots of the mangrove. It was pretty much of a wilderness in there—mangrove, sea grape, cabbage palm and palmetto. A pair of raccoons scurried into the underbrush, waddling like little fat men. A blue heron flew up with heavy flaps, his long legs trailing. I went along slowly, watching the sand in the open spaces. I came to where the bar joined the Key. My heart flopped right over—because there were the marks of Wiley's sneakers in the sand. I knew they were Wiley's because of the crisscross pattern on the soles. I followed them down the beach, and saw where they turned into a big clump of sea grape.

"Wiley!" I called. It came out like a squeak. I called again, "Wiley!" I waited and listened.

Then I heard him say cautiously out of the sea grape, "You alone, Roy?"

"What're you hiding in there for, you dumb clunk?" I asked.

"Are they still looking for me, Roy?"

I went around the bush. He was standing by a cabbage palm with a driftwood club in his hand.

"What's the matter with you anyways?" I asked. "We looked for you all night."

"I know. I seen you. Is it all right now?"

"Is what all right?"

"They gonna stick me in the jail?"

"In the jail! If they stick you anywheres, it'll be in the looney bin. Why should they stick you in the jail?"

"On account of I hit Mr. Langler with the gaff." Then incredulously, "He didn't say nothin' about it?"

"Mr. Langler's in jail for drowning *you*, you dumb ox. Now come on, let's get him out of there." I started to go but he didn't move. "Come on," I said.

He pressed his mouth together and looked stubborn. "I ain't going. Let him stay in jail."

"Are you crazy? You don't do things like that. Now come on before I get sore, Wiley."

"I ain't going."

"Okay," I said. "I'll go back and tell them you're here."

"I won't be here when you get back. There won't be no sign of me. He can stay in jail. He called me things I don't take from nobody, and he knocked me overboard. The hell with him. He can stay in the jail for the rest of his life."

"And are you going to stay here for the rest of your life?" I asked him.

"I'll go down Key West or someplace. I got nothin' to keep me around here. I ain't getting Mr. Langler out of no jail just to do him the favor. He's got it coming."

He meant it. His face was set and stubborn. I knew there was nothing I could say to change him. He didn't care about right or wrong. He meant just what he said. He'd let Mr. Langler rot in jail.

He must of guessed what was in my mind because he tightened his hand around his driftwood club and said, "Now don't make me hit you, Roy. I ain't going back there with you."

I said, "Yes you are, Wiley," and measured him to see how I could get in under that club.

He lifted it and stood clear of the cabbage palm so he could get a good swing. "Don't make me do it, Roy," he pleaded. "If Mr. Langler's in jail, he's getting what's coming to him. I can't help it if I only got one arm, and a man that throws a thing like that in your face twice ain't no kind of man. I ain't going back to do him no favors. That's final, Roy."

I could see I didn't have a chance of getting at him. He was fast on his feet and he had a lot of strength in that one arm. I looked around for a club of my own, because I was going to take him in, no matter what.

When I turned, there was Miss Starr. She was holding the .30-.30

taken from my boat.

"Neither of you is going back," she said. "Get over there by that tree with Wiley, Captain."

I thought she was making a joke or something. I mean, she looked so beautiful in her shorts and halter, you couldn't take that gun serious. Then her voice cracked, "Get *over* there, Captain!" and it wasn't no joke. I got over there.

Wiley's jaw sagged. "What's she mean, Roy? What's she mean?"

It came to me in a flash. "She wants Mr. Langler in jail, too," I said, "on account of that business deal they were squabbling about all yesterday."

"She came with you?" Wiley asked, dumbfounded.

Miss Starr said crisply, "No, the Captain didn't bring me. The Captain just led me here. I hired a boat and followed him. I had the same idea he had, that you were still alive."

"Well," I said, "what're we going to do, just stand here?"

"I don't know," Miss Starr said, frowning. "This situation just came up. It requires thought."

"You can't hold us here forever."

"That's very true. But on the other hand, I can't let you go back either. It's purely business. Langler owns a company that is in direct competition with mine. He's driving me out of business, and he won't buy my company. I'll be bankrupt in another six months. However, with Langler in jail, I have nothing to be afraid of. His company will break up without him. I have a lot of money at stake, Captain. A *lot* of money!"

"Is she going to shoot us, Roy?" asked Wiley, wide-eyed. "Is that what she's going to do?"

Just as he spoke, Miss Starr lifted the gun and fired. I jumped at her with Wiley's yell ringing in my ears. She tried to bring the gun around, but I knocked it up. The barrel caught her across the nose and the blood poured. I tried to grab her, but she gave me the butt of the gun on the jaw. I went down.

By the time I got up groggily, she was a hundred yards down the beach, her beautiful long legs flashing in the sun. I got to the shore of the bay as she was roaring away in her hired speedboat. Wiley was in my boat, getting it started. We went after her.

She looked back over her shoulders and there was blood all over her face. Her nose must of been broken. She turned the speedboat and headed for the open Gulf where we'd never catch her.

Wiley gasped, "She's crazy!"

I knew what he meant. It's really rough going through the Pass to the

Gulf on an incoming tide, and even the big boats had to watch themselves. Miss Starr hit the Pass wide open, doing around thirty-five knots. The little speedboat leaped in the air like a struck tarpon and flipped over. I saw her go sailing out, spread-eagled. I eased into the rip, the boat rolling and pitching so hard we had to hang on with both hands.

All of a sudden, Miss Starr half rose out of the water with a terrible scream. We saw the flash of a long white shark belly as she was dragged under. She never came up again. She didn't have a chance with a twenty-foot shark like Whitey and that blood all over her face.

A half hour later we tied up at the fish-house dock. I went to the telephone booth and called the sheriff.

Mr. Langler gave Wiley a thousand-dollar check to make up for how mean and nasty he'd been.

Wiley disappeared twenty minutes later.

It was two weeks before he turned up on my boat, flat broke and wanting his job back.

"You mean you spent all that money?" I demanded incredulously.

"Now don't be like that, Roy," he said contentedly. "Look at all the trouble Mr. Langler and Miss Starr got into on account of money. I don't want nothin' to do with that kind of trouble. There's only one thing to do with money, and I done it." He grinned happily and reminiscently. "And you know somethin', Roy? I met the nicest little old blonde gal down Miami. She had exactly the same idea about money as I did, and we did it together."

DON'T EVER FORGET!

I was having a cup of coffee and a sandwich in the lunch wagon with Vance Chandler, our new police chief, when this fellow got up from the end of the counter and came down to us. He was a big, tough-looking man with black eyebrows that ran straight across his eyes and gave him always the effect of scowling.

"Chief McMahon?" he said to me; his voice was deep in his chest and kind of rumbling.

"Ex-chief," I told him. "This is the man you want—Chief Chandler. He took over last month."

The fellow gave Vance a disinterested glance and held out his hand to me.

"My name's Brown," he said. "George Brown. Chief Eccles from Tallahassee told me to look you up if ever I got down this way."

That made me feel pretty good. Chief Eccles is a big wheel, not only in Tallahassee and the state, but in the National Police Chiefs Association as well. I never thought he'd remember me, ex-chief of a blowhole like Sarabay. As a town, the best thing you can say of Sarabay is that it has one of the few fifty authentic and genuine fountains of youth in Florida.

I was a little embarrassed, too, and as I shook Brown's granite hand, I said lamely, "And how is Chief Eccles these days? Fat as ever?"

"Fatter. I'll tell you what's on my mind, Chief ..."

"Ex-chief," I corrected him again, seeing Vance's face begin to curdle; Vance is a very touchy man.

Brown said, "Sure. It's like this, Mr. McMahon. I'm doing a feature on the typical police chief for the *Tallahassee News*, and if you don't mind giving me a little of your time, I'd like to use you as the example. On Chief Eccles' recommendation."

I shot a side glance at Vance. I was starting to feel very uneasy. "You don't want to talk to me, son. You want to talk to Vance, here. As a typical police chief, I was strictly subhuman. That's the reason I resigned."

When you came right down to it, that was the reason I had resigned. It was the last job I had worked on that showed me that, inside of me, I was anything but a cop. There was this kid. Mickey Tate. He was wild and mean, and he'd been in several minor scrapes around town before he hit the jackpot. He got likkered up one night and killed a hitchhiker with his car on the Tamiami Trail. I'll never forget the scared, sick look on his face when I took him in. It haunted me day and night. I couldn't get it out of my mind. I knew he had to be taken in, but I didn't want to be the one to do it to anybody. And I never wanted to see that awful look on a human's face again. Tate got twenty years, and when he was sentenced, he screamed right out in court:

"I'll get you for this, McMahon! Don't ever forget it! I'll get you!"

I didn't pay any attention to the threat, but there were things about being a cop that I didn't like anymore, so I resigned.

Before Brown could open his mouth, Vance got up, leaving his unfinished coffee. "See you around, Tod," he said shortly, and walked out.

"You shouldn't have slighted Vance like that, Brown," I said. "He's a good chief, but he's touchy."

Brown shrugged his big shoulders. He had the unsmilingest face I'd ever seen. "I'm not interested in Chandler," he said. "I'm interested in you."

There was something strange in that tough voice of his, and I gave him a sharp look. His face was impassive.

"Why me?" I asked. "Why me in particular?"

"Any objection? I'm offering you free publicity. Maybe you'll even get your picture in the paper."

"Not interested. Talk to Chief Chandler." I was beginning not to like Brown. "I'm not a cop anymore, and I don't want to talk about it."

"Come on, Mac. Think it over. Everybody likes to see his name in the newspaper. All I want to do is talk over a couple of your old cases with you. You'll be a hero all over again."

I said angrily, "Beat it. I'm not talking to you now or any other time."

He gave me a long look, the kind that turns your ears red. "You're just kidding yourself, Mac," he said. He turned his back and walked away. Even his back looked tough.

I had the funny feeling for the rest of the day that he was following me around, but it was just a feeling. I looked once or twice, but he wasn't there.

I went down to the Sarabay public dock in the afternoon and fixed up a couple rods and reels for grouper and snapper fishing. I've got a little 27-foot half cabin cruiser and I take charters out into the Gulf of Mexico. Right then things were a little dull, but when the kingfish run started, and after that the tarpon, I'd be busier than a stripper's G-string in a four-a-day burlesque.

That night, I ran into Vance Chandler again. Or rather, he ran into me. I was having the seafood platter in Mooney's Grill, and he came over and sat down at my table.

"Talk much to that guy Brown, Tod?" he asked.

"Didn't talk to him at all. He rubbed me the wrong way."

Vance gave a thin laugh. "Listen to this. I called the *Tallahassee News*. Spoke to the managing editor, and he said there wasn't any George Brown working for them. What do you think of that? He's a phony?"

That gave me a very funny feeling. "What do you suppose he's up to, Vance?"

"I wouldn't know, but I'm keeping my eye on him. Know what he did all day? Went around town asking questions about you."

There's a mean streak in Vance, and he was getting a bang out of telling me this. Maybe not mean, exactly, but jealous because I still had a kind of reputation around town for cleaning up a case without having to call in the county police.

"What kind of questions, Vance?" I asked mildly.

"Well, for instance, he asked Frank, the barkeep down at the Gulf Breeze, where you got the boat, how much you paid, what kind of political connections you had, and things like that." He didn't take his eyes off my face. "Maybe he's an income tax man."

"I won the boat in a box of cornflakes; and as for political connections, last election, I voted for Francis X. Bushman."

It wasn't anybody's business but the bank's that the boat was mortgaged to the gunwales, nor anybody's affair what way I voted.

Vance pressed his thin lips together.

"There's something I think you ought to know, Tod. There's been a lot of talk going on around town about you resigning as chief so suddenly, then turning up with a fifteen-thousand-dollar boat. They think there's something funny. I just telling you this—as a friend."

"I didn't mean to be funny," I said. "I was just kidding about winning the boat in a box of cornflakes. It was a box of crackerjack."

"Have it your own way, but there's talk."

Sure, I thought, looking at his pale, malicious eyes, and if there's talk I have a pretty fair idea where it started. He was telling me all this as a friend—just to see me squirm.

"Thanks a lot, Vance," I said earnestly. "I sure appreciate you coming to me instead of talking behind my back. But that's what friends are for."

He sat there with his thin face all pinched together with the spiteful things he wanted to say. "Well," he said finally, "I hope you don't have to watch your step. If Brown's an income tax man ..."

He let it dangle, watching me for a reaction, but I just grinned.

I watched him walk outside and climb into the familiar black-and-yellow police car. He walked with quite a swagger. I felt a little gloomy, because I knew that nothing would make Vance happier than being able to run me in for something—and that he was going to make the chance if he could.

That kind of thinking led me right back to this George Brown, and all of a sudden I realized what a fake-sounding name that was. Like John Smith. And I realized, too, that if Vance really believed Brown to be an income tax man, I'd have been the last one he'd have told it to.

I sat there thinking about George Brown and how he had recognized me in the lunch wagon. With the kind of mind Vance has, he must have thought there was something funny about that, too. Hell, I'd never seen Brown before in my life and ... then it struck me. I had seen Brown somewhere. There was something damned familiar about that tough face. I chased it around and around in my mind, but I couldn't pin it down.

I got up without waiting for my coffee and dessert, and went down to headquarters. Sarabay is a small town, and "headquarters" is nothing but a small room in the firehouse—a room with a desk, a chair, and a small iron safe that would open by itself in a light breeze. I used to keep cigars in it because it was at least bugproof.

I didn't expect Vance to be there, and he wasn't. I resisted the impulse to see what he kept in the safe, and instead took the stack of Wanted readers from the top of the safe and started going through them.

I went through the whole stack, and some of them were from '47 and '48, which was silly. I never had that memory for faces that has to be standard equipment for a good cop. I had a feeling that Brown's picture should have been among them, but it wasn't. Unless Vance had removed it for some reason of his own.

I looked at his desk and had taken one step toward it, when I heard him say nastily, "What the hell are you doing in my office, McMahon?"

I must have started guiltily, but I covered by waving a stack of readers I still held in my hand.

"Just going through these, Vance. I had half an idea I might find Brown among them."

"You'll find Brown down at the Gulf Breeze Bar, flashing a roll that would choke a porpoise. And from now on I'd be obliged if you'd keep your nose the hell out of here. If you wanted to be chief, you shouldn't have resigned."

I looked at him. "But Vance," I said, "don't you want to know why I thought Brown might be among these readers?"

"That's your business," he said shortly. "And hereafter I don't want you in this office unless I'm here, too."

I was incredulous. This character was supposed to be the police chief. I know that Sarabay's not much to be chief of, but as a cop he should have been at least curious!

And this is the citizen I resigned in favor of! I thought.

I said, "Okay, Vance," and put the readers back on top of the safe. But as I did, I gave the door a nudge near the hinge with my knee and it swung open, as I knew it would. As I reached down to close it, I saw a whiskey bottle standing up in there like a sentry waiting to be relieved. In fact, it looked like a sentry who'd been relieved many times. I grinned into Vance's pinched, angry face and walked out.

I went down to the Gulf Breeze Bar, but George Brown had gone. I ordered a beer, and after a while Frank, the barkeep, came back and said casually:

"Are you looking for another job or something, Tod?"

"Not that I know of. Why?"

"Well, there was a fella in here asking a lot of questions, like what kind of cop you were—when you were a cop—and like that. Sounded as if he was looking for a character reference or something. I told him as far as I was concerned you were a helluva nice guy. You're not looking for a job?"

"Not me. Maybe they're putting me in *Who's Who*."

Frank scratched his ear. "I didn't like to say too much, Tod. After all, I didn't know the fella, and he was pretty toughlooking. Know what I mean?"

"I know just what you mean."

I tried a few other bars, but wherever George Brown was, he wasn't where I was. I tossed and turned so much in bed that night that you could have called me Revolving McMahon. It wasn't Brown himself that bothered me; it was just that I couldn't figure out where I had seen that face before.

I was down on my boat the next morning about eight, just kind of fooling around and hoping for a charter, when I saw Brown come walking down the dock carrying a rod and a tackle box. He was dressed in a T-shirt and shorts. His legs were heavy, but not fat-heavy, and the muscles on his thick arms looked like the kind of stuff they plate battleships with. He was scowling, as usual—or maybe it was that black bar of eyebrows over his eyes that made him look that way.

"I want to hire your tub for the day, Mac," he said.

"That's what it's here for," I said. "It'll be forty bucks in advance. But I might as well tell you right now that there's nothing out there but grouper. The kingfish run won't start for another week or two."

"I like grouper, whatever they are," he said.

He jumped down into the cockpit and, for all his solid bulk, landed as light as a feather. He handed me a fifty and told me to lay in some ice and a case of beer.

When I got back with it, he had the engine hatch open and was looking down at my power plant.

"Twenty-four jewel movement," I said. "At great expense, I had the bearings replaced with blue sapphires."

He gave me a look that could have been quarried in Vermont. "What the hell are you talking about?" he demanded. "Let's get out of here."

No sense of humor. But neither had the Barkers, Dillinger, or Mad-Dog Coll.

I went in to the controls and loosened the .30-30 in its scabbard. I carried it to scare off sharks during the tarpon season.

He stood outside in the cockpit, watching the shore, until we were across the bay and through the pass into the Gulf. Then he came inside and sprawled on the bunk, smoking a cigarette.

"Change your mind, Mac?" he asked indifferently.

"About what?"

"About giving me a story for the papers."

"Yeah," I said slowly, "I changed my mind. What do you want to know?"

"I thought you would. Nothing like publicity, eh, Mac?"

"That's a fact. What paper you say you were from?"

"The *Tallahassee Trib*."

"I thought it was the *Tallahassee News*."

"Same difference. It's all publicity and it's free. Everybody likes publicity, even your pal, Chief Eccles."

"That's a fact. Is the chief as skinny as ever?"

"Skinnier. Let's hear about a few of your hot cases, Mac. I'll write them up big."

So he didn't know Chief Eccles, either. Yesterday he had said Eccles was fatter than ever, and today he said he was skinnier than ever. It did not surprise me—but I felt a tightening all over, as if every muscle were readying itself.

"I never had any hot cases," l said evenly. "Sarabay's a pretty small place."

"Come on, Mac. You must have solved something in your life. All cops solve something. You can read it every day in the magazines. What'd you solve?"

He said, "cops," just about the way I expected him to say it—flat, hard, without inflection.

"I never solved a thing," I said.

"You don't have to be modest with me, Mac. I don't believe in it. Like Santa Claus. A lot of guys around town seem to think you're a better solver than Bogart. Tell me about it."

"Nothing to tell. A kid named Mickey Tate got plastered one night and killed a hitchhiker on the trail with his car. I took him in the next morning. That's all there was to it."

"That must have taken some solving, Mac. A guy gets knocked off on the highway, and the next morning you turn up with the killer. How'd you do it, with bloodhounds?"

I went along with him to see what he was really leading up to; this business of interviewing me was just the camouflage.

"No bloodhounds," I said. "Not even police methods. Just common sense."

"You got a senser too, Mac? A solver and a senser, that's quite a combination. No crystal balls?"

"Call it luck. This hitchhiker was killed at the intersection of the trail and the Sarabay main street. The body was thrown west on the main street, showing that the car that hit him must have been coming into town across the trail. The boy—he was only fifteen—was wearing a green and white sport shirt with a palm tree pattern, and half of it had been torn away. I had an idea it was a drunken driver, and that he lived in town. It's a small town, and I know most of the people. I spent all night calling on the phone, asking them to report any car with a piece of green-and-white cloth hanging from the front of it.

"The next morning, at nine-fifteen, Reverend Brinkerhoff of the First Methodist Episcopal Church called in and said there was such a car parked in the kids' playground behind his church, and that there was somebody asleep in it. I went over. There was part of the shirt, all right, and the right front fender was smeared with dried blood. We had the blood typed.

"Tate was still a little drunk when we took him in. If anybody solved that one, it was the Reverend Brinkerhoff, because Tate had driven through a sapling hedge of Australian pine which had sprung back when the car passed over, and nobody but the reverend would have spotted it in the playground because it was completely hidden from all sides."

The sick, scared face of Mickey Tate rose in my mind again.

"That was the case that soured me on police work," I said. "I had to take Tate in, and it was like taking in my own kid brother. I didn't sleep for weeks ..."

In the remembrance of it, I forgot about Brown until his heavy, tough voice broke my reverie.

"Tell me about some of your other arrests, Mac. Tell me ..."

"The hell with this! You're not a newspaperman, and you don't know

Chief Eccles. What's on your mind?"

"Now you're beginning to sound like a cop, Mac. Tough."

"You've been asking a lot of questions about me around town, and I want to know why."

"I guess I'm just nosy. And I take that back. You're not tough."

"I'm tough enough …"

"Mac, you don't even know how to spell it. Me, I'm tough and I know it. Some guys think they're tough, and they ain't. You don't even think it. Let's go fishing."

He walked out into the stern cockpit and stood with his back to me. I took him out to the twelve grouper banks and dropped the hook. We didn't say a word to each other. I had some mullet, and I cut it up for bait. He stood there watching me impassively.

"You can use one of my rigs if you want," I said.

"I'll use my own. I want to get my thirty-five bucks' worth out of it. I got some hooks, too,"

As he opened his tackle box, I saw the snub-nosed gun lying in the bottom, the kind they call a belly gun, a .38 with a two-inch barrel.

"You got a permit for that thing?" I asked toughly.

"This thing?" He hefted the gun in his hand—and after the longest moment I have ever spent, dropped it back into the box. "Sure. I'm not that dumb. What kind of hook you want? I bought a buck's worth, all kinds."

He fished for about two hours and brought up twelve grouper—reds and blacks—the biggest about ten pounds, which was quite a grouper this close in.

Finally he said, "Hell, they come up like old boots. Let's go home."

All the way back to the dock, I felt his flinty gray eyes boring a hole between my shoulder blades. He stayed out in the cockpit, and he didn't say a word, but I felt him there every minute of the way. Still, if he'd had anything in mind, he could have let me have it that time out in the Gulf when he held that belly gun in his hand and I had nothing but my fists.

I felt all wrung out. I went back to my place, had a hot shower, built a drink.

I stopped trying to figure it. I went to my dresser drawer and got my old Police Positive. I checked the loads and stuck it into my waistband.

I whipped up some bacon and eggs for dinner. Then I got an idea and called Harry Jamieson at the *Sarabay Herald*, our weekly newspaper, and asked him if he could tell me where a guy named George Brown was staying. The *Herald* always prints the names of visitors, which it gets from the hotels, motels, and so forth. He told me that Brown had taken the cottage at Point Of Rocks on the Gulf.

Along about ten, I was on my third scotch and soda when the radio said something that jerked my head around.

"... since noon today. Georgia police have been alerted, since Mickey Tate was last seen heading north. Tate is a killer. I repeat, Tate is a killer. Take no chances. If you think you have seen him, inform your nearest police station at once. Do not attempt to stop him unaided. He is armed and desperate. He has killed two guards in escaping from ..."

It was as if something had exploded in my mind and—just like that!—I knew where I had seen George Brown before.

I had never seen him.

But I had seen his kid brother, Mickey Tate. Now that I had tied it up, the family resemblance was unmistakable. If I'd had a memory for faces, the way, say, Vance Chandler has, I'd have known right away.

And suddenly, too, I knew that Mickey Tate wasn't heading for the Georgia border.

I went down the stairs to the street, the gun in my waistband digging into my belly at every step. I climbed into my jalopy and drove out to Point Of Rocks. There was only one cottage there. It was a narrow tongue of land, jutting out into the Gulf. It was a very famous place because there wasn't a better spot for snook or sheepshead fishing on that whole coast.

I left my car up the road and walked over the noiseless sand with my gun in my band. There was a light in the cottage, and I saw Brown's heavy silhouette go from the living room into the kitchen. I took off my shoes and leaped up on the porch. I opened the front door and walked in. I was standing there with my gun pointed when he came from the kitchen with a glass of milk and a sandwich in his hands. I couldn't have caught him flatter-footed.

"Relax, Brown or Tate or whatever your name is," I said grimly. "We're going to stay right here and wait for your kid brother. I've been ..."

I never got to telling him what I'd been because right that second a voice told me exactly what I was—a fish in a barrel.

It was Mickey Tate's voice, and it was right beside me, gloating. "Drop your heater, McMahon. Tha-a-at's right. Now turn around, chum. I told you I'd get you, didn't I? I told you not to ever forget, and here I am. Turn around, chum. I'm gonna give you one in the belly for every month you made me spend in that dirty lousy hole of a jail. Turn around, McMahon!"

I didn't turn, but I instinctively sucked in my stomach as if to protect it from the slugs. Then—incredulously—I saw Brown move, and I had never seen anyone move faster. One moment he was standing at the kitchen door under the muzzle of my gun, and the next moment he was at the sofa, his arm slinging and a sofa pillow flying across the room. He was moving again before the pillow had caught Mickey full in the face.

Mickey's gun went off, but I had moved by that time, straight down. From the floor, I saw Brown crash into Mickey and chop for the snarling young jaw with a fist the size of a grapefruit. I winced as Mickey went flying.

Brown stood and looked at me. "I'm not his brother, I'm his cousin," he said, as if defending himself. "And Brown's my right name. I went to see him in jail a week ago, and he swore you framed him. I came down here to see."

I remembered the gun in his tackle box. "And if you thought I had framed him?"

"You wouldn't have done any more framing, Mac," he said expressionlessly. He looked down at the unconscious Tate. "He's all yours, Mac. Maybe you can sell him for fertilizer."

He looked at Tate again, as if trying to think of a more scathing expression of contempt and disgust, then said to me—surprisingly, "You're a good joe," and turned and darted through the porch door.

This time, when I walked into "headquarters," herding the snarling Mickey Tate before me, Vance Chandler was in, and his jaw dropped so far it hid his tie. I shoved Mickey into the far corner. I wasn't interested in him just now.

"Vance," I said, "tell me yes or no, did you recognize George Brown as a relative of Mickey Tate, and did you think that George Brown was down here to get me because I had sent Mickey up the river?"

He didn't say yes or no. He didn't have to. The answer was plain in his face. He had known all along. I took a breath.

"Vance," I said heavily, "as of now I am unresigning as police chief, and you are resigning, as of now. I didn't think I was a good cop. I was squeamish. I'm not squeamish anymore. This town and every town needs a good cop. You're not a good cop, Vance. You're a lousy cop. I like this town and I don't like to think of it having a lousy cop. I am going to try to be the best kind of cop I know how. You're getting out, Vance, and you're not going to make any trouble, because if you do, I'll show you what trouble really is and ..."

I stopped. I couldn't kick a man when he was down. Vance wasn't going to make any trouble about resigning.

BODYGUARD

CHAPTER I

"GUILTY IN THE FIRST DEGREE!"

The jury plodded back into the courtroom with set faces, twelve zombies of justice. Frankie Melot crouched at the defendant's table like a cornered animal, and even from where I sat, I could see the cold sweat of terror that pebbled his face.

Suffer, rat, suffer, I thought with satisfaction. Because if anybody had it coming it was Frankie Melot, the punk kid brother of Big Lew Melot, rackets king of Tampa.

Frankie and another hood had shot it out on the corner of Broadway and Honduras Street, down in the Ybor City section. That's the Spanish quarter here in Tampa. The other hood got away clean, but Frankie took two in the leg. The real victim, however, was a twelve-year-old girl. She took one through the head. Frankie couldn't claim self-defense either. The little girl had been unarmed.

Big Lew never showed once in the courtroom, and the scuttlebutt was that two of his toughest bowers, Joe Cuba and TB Puys, were holding him in his Columbus Drive apartment at gunpoint.

I could believe that. The only one Big Lew had ever loved or ever would love was his little rat-brother, Frankie. Cuba and Puys didn't dare let him out of that apartment. He would have cleaned out the courtroom with a chattergun to get Frankie off the spot. The betting had been running two to one that the jury would rat out of it, that it would come up with a disagreement, and three to two that it would turn Frankie loose entirely. Such was the power of the Melot name in Tampa. A Melot had never even been arrested in Tampa, much less convicted, and all up and down Broadway the boys with the sharp eyes and the smart money were saying that the jury—just ordinary citizens, after all, not heroes—would be scared spitless of Big Lew Melot and would do everything but hang a medal on Frankie.

Now me, I'm an ordinary citizen, too. I'm a private eye, so that makes me a small businessman. This snoop and snitch isn't the babes-and-bullets racket the movies would have you believe. I had bet a sawbuck that the jury would convict Frankie for every volt that was coming to him. Maybe I'm an idealist, but I had faith that twelve honest men and women couldn't do anything else and still live with themselves afterward.

And nobody could look at the dead kid's father, San Martin, who'd been sitting there day after day in the front row, without wanting to walk up to Frankie and give him what Judge Lynch used to call a taste of law and order.

I don't know how much of the trial old San Martin actually heard, for most of the time he just sat there with his eyes closed and the tears running down his wrinkled, work-worn face, and if I'd been on the jury, every tear that rolled down his gaunt cheeks would have looked like blood.

The courtroom was so jammed that even the spittoons had been removed, and when the foreman of the jury rose to hand the verdict to the court clerk, a hush settled down like the pause before a requiem.

I'm supposed to be a pretty hard character, but my own pulses were hammering so hard in my ears that when the clerk started reading the verdict, everything was a mutter and a jumble until he came to the words:

"... find the defendant, Francis Melot, guilty of murder in the first degree, as charged."

That rang out like a bugle call!

I felt like shouting, and the courtroom went mad. Frankie Melot surged up out of his chair, his jaws working soundlessly with the scream that lay locked in his twisted little mind. His arms waved jerkily and he toppled straight forward across the table, out cold.

The dead girl's father, old San Martin, leaped to his feet, brandishing a cheap chrome revolver, crying hysterically: "I was going to kill him! I was going to shoot him down the way he did my little girl, if they had freed him!" He turned to the jury, "Thank you, thank you, oh thank you ..." Sobs shattered his voice and he covered his face with his hands.

The district attorney got to him with a fatherly, comforting arm a split-second before the flash bulbs started going off like the Fourth of July.

I got out of there before I got sick in somebody's lap. Frankie Melot was as good as dead, San Martin's terrible grief would burn a little less fiercely, and there was nothing left but the clowning and the jostling for position in the headlines. I went out to the courthouse steps for a breath of fresh air and a cigarette.

But in spite of all the hurdy-gurdy that the poignant drama of the trial was turning into, I felt clean and I felt like singing. American justice was still the shining sword our forefathers had forged, and without grandstanding, the D.A. had woven a net of electrodes around Frankie that even the dread name of Melot could not break. It was a good feeling.

Then somebody touched my arm. It was the whisper of a touch, the kind of touch that gives you the same sensation as walking into a face full of spider webs in the dark. I turned, and it was a little shyster everybody called Moxie—probably because he had a lot of it, all brass.

Except for one thing, Moxie could have been the greatest rackets mouthpiece in the country. He had all the instincts and no scruples, but fortunately for you and me and everybody else, he just plain didn't have the talent. He couldn't have convinced a jury of Eskimos that ice was cold. The sight of him always made me feel for the safety of my wallet.

He laid an insinuating forefinger on my arm. "Mr. Chastain," he beamed like a choirmaster at the sight of a new pair of legs among the choir girls, "might I have a word with you?"

Moxie's breath was always the first indication of the way the wind was blowing. For that reason and no other, I said coldly, "What's on your mind?"

"Money." His smile was as disarming as a pickpocket's fingers. "A lot of money. Are you thirsty? Suppose we run across the street and have a Juicer while we talk. Liquor is not the most cooling thing in the world, but it does change your attitude toward the humidity."

A Juicer is a lime and rum with pineapple.

"Fine," I said. "Who's paying?"

He enveloped me with his smile and murmured something about an expense account. Now ordinarily I would rather drink a nice private glass of hemlock than Scotch with Moxie, but they say curiosity killed a cat, and being bigger than a cat I was sure it wouldn't kill me. How wrong I almost was.

I let him steer me across the street to the courthouse hangout, Howard's Bar & Grill, where the Juicers were reputed to have the most rum and the least filler in the tallest glasses, and on a hot afternoon a Juicer was better than a Planters Punch, because you didn't have to be a garbage collector to get to your drink.

When we were finally settled in the farthest, darkest booth with a pair of Juicers before us, he came to the point in that roundabout way that even the worst lawyers seem to think make them legal beagles.

"Five thousand dollars," he said dreamily, "is a lot of money."

I yawned just to needle him. "Not if you want to buy a yacht," I said. "Or a few pounds of sirloin."

"Five thousand dollars will buy a lot of sirloin."

I had to agree that five thousand dollars would buy more sirloin than I could eat at a sitting. I was still feeling good over the conviction of Frankie Melot, and this was entertainment. He looked at me coyly from under his long, curling lashes.

"Without lifting a finger," he murmured, "you could have five thousand dollars."

I said I was feeling good, didn't I? Okay. I wriggled my fingers at him. "Point out the finger I wouldn't have to lift," I said.

That made him sore. I could tell by the way he waggled his fat fanny on the seat. To Moxie, there was nothing funny about money, and the more money, the less funny. He popped his eyes at me like a pair of boiled eggs.

"I'm laughing," he said, showing his teeth. "Ha, ha, ha!"

"Me, too," I said. "Ha, ha, ha. What's the pitch?"

"Does this look like a pitch?" He folded back his jacket and showed a sheaf of brand-new bills in the inside pocket. He riffled them with his finger. They were all C-notes, and my eyes spread like a catfish's at the sight of the biggest worm in the world. Moxie with more than a double sawbuck was enough to make anybody stare. But I could still count.

"That looks more like ten G's," I said.

He struggled with himself, then bitterly raised the ante to ten G's but, brother, how he hated himself for having riffled that moolah at me!

"All right," he said with difficulty, "ten G's." He pointed a plump finger at me and held it there for a moment for effect. "We," he said slowly and significantly, "are making an appeal for Frankie."

An appeal, in a murder case, is automatic. I had expected it. But getting it this way from Moxie, it was like a slap across the face with a wet fish. It meant the wheels within the wheels had started to turn again. The wheels you didn't see, the wheels that had always been there. Lew Melot's wheels.

The good feeling I'd had was gone. I could feel the skin tightening across my clenched knuckles.

"So you're making an appeal," I said. "What's that got to do with me?"

Moxie pursed his lips and beamed at me from over the little rosebud of his mouth. "Love," he said pontifically, "the sublime emotion that makes the world go round. Love. What would we do without love? Love is the flower, but"—he shook his finger at me—"marriage is the weed. Marriage takes money. It is rumored, Mr. Chastain, that you are contemplating the nuptial noose. Are my congratulations in order?"

I felt my face congeal. The whole pitch was clear to me now. Yes, it was love, but in the mouth of Moxie it sounded like something you could buy for two bucks down on Honduras Street. If I didn't reach across that table and take his fat throat in my fingers, it was only because I wanted to hear everything he had to say.

"What's your pitch, Moxie?" I croaked.

"A very simple one, Mr. Chastain. You are shortly to marry a Miss Peggy Whitney. Your prospective father-in-law must think highly of you, or he would not permit you to marry his only daughter. Your prospective father-in-law happens to be Lloyd Whitney, a judge in the court of appeals. We are going to make an appeal for Frankie. Ten thousand dollars."

He lifted it from his pocket and shoved it into my stiff hands. "Look at it, feel it. It's all yours. Your prospective father-in-law respects your opinion, and, all we want you to do is drop a word of simple truth here and there when you are with him. Just what a raw deal Frankie got, it should have been manslaughter instead of first degree, and it was an accident anyway, Frankie doesn't go around shooting kids, and think of poor Frankie, aside from the mental anguish he must suffer at having shot down an innocent child while engaged in protecting his own life, Frankie with two bullets in his leg, he'll have a limp for the rest of his life, and why should Frankie take the whole rap while the gunsel that tried to get him goes free ...

"I don't have to tell you what to say, Mr. Chastain. It's just the simple truth. Frankie was given the wet end of the stick and deserves a break, a new trial. All we want you to do is create a little natural sympathy for Frankie with Judge Whitney, that's all. All we want is for the judge to grant a new trial so we can bring forward our evidence and prove that Frankie did not kill that poor little innocent tot.

"We're not asking that you unduly influence the judge's decision, but merely that you show him that Frankie ..."

CHAPTER II

THE PELICAN CLUB

I smacked him. His head thunked against the back of the booth, his eyes rolled up and he slid gently from view beneath the table. I picked up the money, stalked over and gave it to the Spanish barkeep.

"For the Red Cross," I said. "For charity ..." and walked out.

Now I knew why some guys got sore when they were offered bribe money. It was a blow to their pride. It proved that somebody could have a low opinion of them. I hadn't gone three blocks when I discovered I had a tail—a dark-faced boy in a lavender sport shirt and chartreuse slacks.

I felt the back of my neck sprout like a scared cat's tail. That was Joe

Cuba, one of Lew Melot's toughest bowers.

He grinned and waved as my startled face showed over my shoulder, but he made no move to close the gap between us. He was joined a half block later by a tall, gaunt rack of bones with the pallor of death in his face, and they strolled along together behind me.

I stifled the impulse to run, to grab the nearest cop and hide behind him. The gaunt one was TB Puys, and now two of Lew Melot's prime hatchet men were stalking me. I stopped in the middle of the sidewalk and, my tongue shriveling in my mouth, waited for them to come up. They stopped abreast of me, and Joe Cuba gave me an angelic smile.

"What's on your mind, Joe?" I croaked.

"I can't answer a question like that without a lawyer, Chastain," he grinned.

"I think," TB Puys said gravely, "that perhaps Mr. Chastain has something on *his* mind. Is your conscience bothering you by any chance, Mr. Chastain?"

They just stood there and regarded me with amusement while my insides churned.

Joe Cuba murmured, "The barkeep didn't want that ten G's, Chastain." He patted his hip pocket. "He gave it back."

"He didn't appreciate your kindness." TB Puys looked sad. "He wants you to pay his dental bill."

"That's the thanks you get, Chastain," said Joe. "The guy loses some teeth, and right away he wants you to pay for them. He didn't know you were only kidding when you gave him that dough."

Suddenly I was sore. Just for the hell of it, they'd beaten up a guy who was nothing but an innocent bystander. I called them every blistering name I could lay tongue to, and wound up with, "And as far as Lew Melot's concerned, you can tell him to go to hell, too!"

Joe Cuba looked bored. "You tell him, TB," he yawned. "You ain't got much longer to live anyway."

"By an odd coincidence, Mr. Chastain," said Puys, his dull eyes momentarily gleaming, "we are on our way to Lew's apartment this very minute. Why don't you accompany us and deliver your message in person?"

"Why don't you point a gun at me?"

"On the public street? Tut, tut, Mr. Chastain. That's against the law."

"Take care of yourself, fella." Joe reached out and smoothed my tie. "Take *good* care of yourself."

I slapped his hand away, turned on my heel and walked into the gin mill behind me. They laughed.

Inside, I ordered a double Scotch, and don't think I didn't need it. My hands were trembling like a pair of cats in a dog pound.

The bartender started sympathetically. "What's the matter, mister? You look as if—"

"Don't talk to me," I warned him. "Don't even try to exchange the weather with me, or two guys are likely to walk in and knock your block off. I'm hard luck for bartenders."

He looked affronted and walked away. He didn't know I was doing him a favor.

Two double Scotches later I had started to think things over, and the more I thought, the screwier it got. Why should Lew Melot offer me, of all people, ten thousand clams to talk to Judge Whitney. He was Peggy's uncle, not her father, and he approved of me the way a fly swatter approves of a fly.

He wasn't her guardian, or anything, so he couldn't forbid her to see me, but he had made it pretty clear that I was about as welcome in his house as an attack of termites. He made no secret of this, so nobody in his right mind would offer me ten cents, much less ten grand, to put a soft word in the judge's ear for Frankie Melot.

It was the surest way I knew of to get Frankie electrocuted.

Which wasn't a bad idea.

I picked up Peggy up about eight that night. She was still upstairs, putting on the finishing touches, so I waited in the hall. I was standing there patting my tie before the mirror when the judge came walking through from the living room.

I said cheerfully, "Good evening, your honor."

He grunted and went by without even a glance. "Just for that," I said to myself, "you don't get my vote when you run for governor."

Maybe that was what it was all about. His dislike of me, I mean. He wanted to be governor, and maybe he thought that having a private eye in the family would cost him votes in the caviar belt.

He would make a very handsome governor. There was no doubt of that. He looked like Richard the Lion Hearted. If you picked them for looks, he'd make a wonderful governor. He was tall, with a very legal mane of white hair and gray eyes. He'd make the kind of governor whose face it would be a pleasure to see in the papers. My feelings in the matter were that a guy who's a private slob would be a public slob as well. Of course, I don't know very much about governors, so that's just my personal opinion.

Peggy came down the stairs, and the judge was out of my mind the minute I laid eyes on her. My heart did a couple of flipflops. She wasn't one of those patrician icicles. There was just enough Irish in her so that it showed in her red hair and blue eyes.

She came flying down the stairs, crying, "My golly, can't you be late for once? Darling!"

I was left dizzy by the pressure of her lips, the swirl of her perfume, the brief feel of her in my arms. And then she was walking down the hall to say goodnight to the judge. She was back a few minutes later with a puzzled frown on her face. She took my arm as we walked down the front steps to my car.

"What did you say to the judge, Micky?" she whispered. "He says you were impertinent."

"Me? All I said was, good evening, your honor. What's he want me to call him, your worship?"

"Oh, damn! I wish you two would get along."

"I wish he'd get to be governor and get it over with," I growled. "When are all us lucky people going to have the chance to vote for him?"

"Don't talk like that, Micky. This fall."

"Good, I said promptly. "Then he'll be so busy having his picture taken that maybe we can pitch our woo in peace for a while."

She murmured, "Poor Micky," and moved closer to me as I slid into the car behind the wheel.

We went to a movie, and afterward out to the Pelican Club on Route 541, where the rumba band didn't sound like a machine shop under full production. We danced, had a few frozen daiquiris, but mostly just sat at our table, smiled at each other, touched hands and said a lot of stuff that didn't mean anything except that just being with each other was the tops in any form of entertainment.

A shadow fell across our table. Literally.

A voice said, "Good evening, Miss Whitney. Good evening, Mr. Chastain. Welcome to the Pelican Club. I hope you plan to stay for the floor show. We have Zela, the new primitive dancer from Uruguay." It was a voice with a natural grate that even the best bourbon would never be able to smooth out.

I looked up expecting to see the manager or the MC or some other official baby kisser, but that face had never been designed for kissing babies—not those long alligator jaws, those hot black eyes, that harsh blue-black hair.

It was the face of Lew Melot.

My first impulse was to jump to my feet and put my hands up to defend myself, but he had a knuckly hand on my shoulder and he was smiling a reptilian smile.

"Are you enjoying yourself, Miss Whitney?" he was saying. "The orchestra is an importation from Puerto Rico. Later it will play some of its native music, some *pasodobles*."

Peggy looked from him to me, puzzled, uncertain whether to smile or answer or what. My face must have been showing.

"I didn't know the Pelican Club was yours, too, Melot," I managed to say finally, when I was convinced that momentarily his intentions were pacific.

"I don't own it. I just have an interest in it. I have an interest in a great many things. What did you want to see me about, Mr. Chastain?"

"*Me* want to see *you!*" It blurted out before I could stop it. "Uh-uh, Melot, not me."

"Well now, that's strange." He worked his long toothy jaws for a moment with private amusement. "Someone—I forget who—told me you had a message for me. That was this afternoon, I believe."

I felt a splash of cold prickles in my face. That afternoon? A message for him? Sure. I had told Joe Cuba to tell Lew to go to hell. But I had been sore then. Now I was just plain scared, but at the sight of that lizard face wordlessly commanding me to crawl, I got sore all over again.

"Yeah, I did have a message for you," I said, a little too loudly. "I gave it to a friend of yours. Didn't he deliver it? If he didn't, I'll be glad to repeat it. I said to tell you—"

His hand jerked as it tightened on my shoulder, and he interrupted quickly, "Oh, that? Yes. By the way, this is something that should interest you, Chastain. We have new evidence to prove that my brother did not kill that little girl. She was standing before a wooden fence when she was hit by one of several wild bullets. In the presence of several reputable witnesses, we dug three of those bullets from the fence and we are prepared to show that they did not come from Frankie's gun. That's rather conclusive, don't you think, Miss Whitney?"

At the table in front of us there was a fat little man with ear trouble.

Before Peggy could answer, I said, "Miss Whitney doesn't have an opinion, Melot. She's not very bright. She had a bad fall when she was a child. In fact"—I glanced at my wrist watch—"It's time for us to go home now and look at some picture books."

Melot laughed.

Peggy's face was furious as I steered her across the dance floor toward the hat check booth, followed by some two hundred interested pairs of eyes, but she waited until we were outside the club before she lit the fuse.

"Of all the things to say about me!" she exploded. "Was it a joke? Was it funny? Was I supposed to laugh? I was never so embarrassed in my life!"

"No, honey," I said soberly, "it wasn't a joke. How would you like to have seen something like this in tomorrow's papers: 'It is whispered that Peggy Whitney, niece of Judge (Appeals Court) Whitney, night clubbing with sleuth Micky Chastain last eve, handed down her opinion that the new evidence uncovered by the defense for Frankie Melot conclusively proves Frankie's innocence.'"

"I didn't say anything of the sort!" she cried indignantly.

"I know. But when Lew asked you that question about digging the bullets out of the fence and proving they hadn't come from Frankie's gun, what would you have answered?"

"Well, if the bullets didn't come from Frankie's gun—"

"That's all you would have to have said, honey. That little man at the table behind you was Bobby Hare, who happens to have a gossip column in the *Times* called 'Here And There With Bobby Hare.' Nuff said?"

"Nuff said," she agreed contritely.

"And furthermore," I said, "those bullets are as phony as a blue toupee. If they had been there during the trial, that tricky legal eagle Lew hired to defend Frankie would have had movies made of them and given three shows daily."

"Why am I so dumb?" Peggy said plaintively.

"And on top of that," I went on, "even if the bullets were the McCoy and not plants, I don't think it should make any legal difference. Frankie Melot had no license to carry a gun, and a private shindy between two mobbies doesn't spell self-defense in any language. Both of them are equally guilty of murder."

Peggy muttered, "Show-off," and walked toward the car.

CHAPTER III

A BRIBE

We drove over to Clearwater and looked at the Gulf of Mexico. But the business with Lew Melot had left a bad taste in our mouths, and after a while I took her home.

There was a Cadillac and a Lincoln parked in front of the house, and Peggy said, "Oh-oh, council of war or something! The judge's campaign managers must be sharpening their tomahawks!"

I thought for a minute. I didn't owe the judge a thing, but on the other hand I owed Lew Melot still less.

"I'd like to talk to the judge for a minute," I said.

She looked at me. "Go right in," she said ironically. "Walk right into the meeting. They'll be glad to see you. But you ought to dress for the occasion. You should wear a crash helmet."

"No." I took her arm and gently urged her up the front steps. "You just stand outside and put the pieces together as they come flying out."

"With pins," she hissed, "with pins!"

The conclave was in the judge's walnut-paneled study. I put my hand on the doorknob, blew a kiss to the round-eyed Peggy, then walked in, closing the door firmly behind me.

The three men turned sharply in their chairs. Two of them had the well-fed, cigar-studded faces of men who decide the destinies of states in back rooms. The third was the judge. He struggled with his apoplexy and finally managed to pant:

"Get ... out ... of ... here!"

I smiled all around and said, "Good evening, gentlemen," and walked down the room toward them, lighting a cigarette.

The two men gave the judge an annoyed, puzzled glance, and he leaped to his feet, his face furious. I held up my hand.

"This afternoon," I said, "I was offered ten thousand dollars by one of Lew Melot's errand boys to put in a good word for Frankie to the judge here. I thought you might be interested."

If you could have punched holes in the following silence, you could have used them for gun barrels, but you'd have needed a diamond drill to do it. The judge's jaws worked up and down.

"You're ... you're insane!" he gasped.

One of the other men said quickly, "Just a moment, Judge. This might be very serious. Who is this young man?"

"He ... he ..." The judge's face congested and he became incoherent. He had reached the limit of his descriptive vocabulary and could only spit.

"My name's Micky Chastain," I rescued him. "I kind of go around with the judge's niece, Peggy. I'm, uh, a confidential investigator. A shamus, if you go to the movies." I grinned.

The man who had spoken before said, "Oh, yes. My name's Barascule. I'm the judge's campaign manager. Tell me, Chastain, just who offered you this money?"

The judge turned angrily to him. "This is absurd! This man is—"

"Please, Judge, let me handle this ... You were saying, Chastain?"

"I wasn't, but have you heard of a shyster called Moxie? I don't know his real name. Everybody calls him Moxie."

Barascule nodded. "And he said he was acting for Lew Melot?"

"Not in so many words, no. But he had the ten thousand in cash on him, and where would Moxie get ten thousand clams?"

Barascule's eyebrows climbed his forehead. "Then you can't actually say the offer came from Lew Melot."

I looked pityingly at him. "I just did, didn't I? Have you ever heard of a fancy-dressed killer named Joe Cuba?"

His eyes sharpened and his head nodded just slightly.

"Or of TB Puys, another talented hatchet man from the Melot tong?" I went on.

"Well?"

"Well, after I poked Moxie in the schnozz, I gave the ten grand to the barkeep for the Red Cross, for charity. Ten minutes later, Joe Cuba and TB Puys caught up with me on the street. They're a pair of boys who don't always have to hammer you over the skull to put the fear of God into you. They gave me a once-over-lightly, letting me know I'd made a bum play and that there was a tall, dark man in my future."

I could see that Barascule was impressed, though the judge kept making outraged noises in his throat. Barascule, however, was the boss.

"Tell me, Chastain," he said, leaning forward, "what finally did happen to the ten thousand dollars?"

"Cuba and Puys took it away from the barkeep then, I imagine, and went back to Lew for further instructions. Then tonight I ran into Lew at the Pelican Club. He could have had a half dozen of his muscles work me over, but he didn't. He patted me on the shoulder and tried to get Peggy to say that their new evidence conclusively proved Frankie innocent."

Barascule said, "Hm-m-m," and unplugged his cigar. He looked at it very thoughtfully. He glanced up at the judge, who by this time was looking just a little sick. "I think, Judge," he said significantly, "that you owe Mr. Chastain your thanks for telling us this." That was an order.

The judge held out his hand as if he were sticking it into a blow torch and said with difficulty. "I want to thank you, Chastain—uh, Mick. I, uh, appreciate what you've done for me."

Just to see what it did to his face, I wagged his hand enthusiastically. It felt like a shad fillet.

"Not at all, Judge," I said heartily. "It's practically in the family, anyway."

He put his hand behind him as if he couldn't wait to get to the bathroom and wash it.

"Now I wonder, Chastain," Barascule gave me a hooded glance, "if you'd be willing to do us another favor?"

"Could be," I said warily.

"Stay away from the judge and this house until after election. Why not take a South American cruise—with all expenses paid, of course. How does that sound?"

"Wonderful," I said innocently. "I wasn't planning to get married that soon, but who could ask for a better honeymoon."

Barascule almost swallowed his cigar, and I grinned at him.

"No, no," he said hurriedly. "I mean alone. On no account must your name be linked with Miss Whitney until after the election. In fact, it would be better if you simulated a quarrel with her and severed all connections with this house."

"No, sir," I said. "I have only one love life, and a South American picnic without Peggy would be a hollow mockery."

Barascule was no fool. He knew damn well that all the love between the judge and me couldn't be fermented into a drink strong enough to intoxicate a fruit fly.

"Well," he said practically, "we can't coerce you. But I'd like to have you promise me one thing. Don't breathe a word of this to a soul. Keep it completely under your hat."

I said, "Yessir," and then with a grin at the judge, "In my circle—crooks and dips and stew bums—they'd think I was nuts for not grabbing those ten G's with both hands."

Barascule said drily, "I'm sure. But you won't regret this, Chastain. When the judge is governor, I'm sure a place can be found for you on the attorney general's staff."

"Look," I said, "I'll keep my mouth shut, but I don't want any handouts!"

I wanted them to know exactly how I felt. I walked out.

Peggy was waiting in the hall, fairly bursting with curiosity. I hadn't told her about the bribe offer. I gave her the bare bones of a grin and muttered, "Lead me to drink, honey. I need one, bad!"

We went into the dining room, and she took a bottle of Scotch and a tall glass from the Duncan Phyfe cellarette and started pouring. I didn't stop her till she reached the Plimsoll mark.

She scowled at the size of it and said, "Did you need it *that* bad?"

"Honey," I said, "I'm going to tell you a little story. Today when the jury convicted Frankie Melot, I had a good feeling—the kind of feeling you get when the band starts playing and the flag goes by. It lasted, I think, about ten minutes. People have been sticking pins in it ever since. Just now, I got another kick in the face. The judge is embarrassed, and do you know why he's embarrassed? I'll tell you why. He's embarrassed because Lew Melot has dumped a mess in his lap."

Peggy's eyes started to get flinty, and I recognized that look. She didn't like me to talk about the judge, and she didn't like the judge to talk about me. Nevertheless, I had something on my mind and I wasn't going to be able to sleep until I spilled it, come hell or high water.

"You don't have to look at me as if I'd drowned your kittens," I said. "I'm sore, too, and I'm going to tell you why those civic fathers in there have ants in their pants. When the appeal comes up, the judge is the one who's going to have to say whether or not Frankie Melot gets a new trial. Whichever way he jumps, he's going to lose votes.

"If he gives Frankie a new trial, he's a dead duck with the newspapers and the church crowd. If he doesn't grant Frankie another shot at it, Lew Melot goes on the warpath, and the Ybor City vote isn't the only vote that Lew has a finger in. He's got affiliations all over the state—he could cost the judge the election. So the problem is, how can the judge keep everybody happy?"

"And I suppose," Peggy said scornfully, "they broke down and told you all this!"

"No ma'am. They did not take me into their confidence. But when I told them that Lew had offered me a goodly sum to put in a kind word for Frankie, they did everything but stuff my throat with sugar plums to keep my mouth shut. In fact, they did offer a couple of sugar plums— a trip to South America and a job with the attorney general, if and when.

"And here's something I figured out with my own little brain. Lew Melot knew damn well I couldn't influence the judge one way or the other—*but he doesn't care.* All he wants is for me to accept that ten thousand."

Peggy was getting madder and madder. "As a gift, I suppose," she snapped.

"Nope. As an investment. It has been alleged that shortly I am to become the judge's nephew-in-law. So I accept a ten G's gratuity. The minute I wrap my hot little hands around that dough, it isn't a gratuity, anymore. It's a club. It's a club he can hold over the judge's head, because he knows the judge is going to find a way to grant Frankie a new trial, a way that will satisfy everybody.

"So here's the picture: The judge grants a new trial after I take ten G's to talk him into it, even though I hadn't. That's Lew's little club. No governor in the world could survive the scandal of his own nephew-in-law taking that kind of money. Believe me," I said, throwing down what was left of the Scotch in the bottom of my glass, "it's a wonderful world and it's so good to be alive!"

All of a sudden I realized that Peggy was not exactly applauding my keen, deductive reasoning. She stepped away from me with fire in her eyes.

"Wonderful," she said furiously, "marvelous! There's only one flaw in it—the judge is in absolutely no danger of getting a nephew-in-law!"

With one last bitter glance at me, she ran from the room, grinding her teeth in fine Irish style.

I felt suddenly very, very tired. I plodded out to my car and drove home. The apartment elevator wasn't working at this time of night, so I wearily climbed the two flights of stairs to my penthouse, opened the door and walked in.

Walked right smack into a stone wall, a stone wall with colored lights and a tunnel that roared like a subway train as I tumbled headlong into it.

It was tougher climbing out of the tunnel than it had been falling in. There was nausea and pain and it was an uphill climb. I don't remember getting into the bathroom, but there I was with the cold shower cascading down my neck and consciousness returning as reluctantly as an income tax rebate.

I had thoroughly soaked my tropical worsted, and the water was running down my legs, but I was upright and after a while I felt strong enough to reach out and turn off the water. I staggered into the kitchen and poured myself a prescription of fine whiskey.

Naturally, the first thing I thought of, when I was able to think, was Lew Melot and his merry men. Gripping a second glass of medicine, I plodded into the living room. There was nothing wrong with it, as far as I could see. Except that my portable typewriter was open, and in Florida you don't leave your typewriter open any more than you have to. Between the salt air and the sand, you'd soon be buying yourself a new one every six months.

So someone had used my typewriter.

I went into the bedroom. It was still there. I went through my chest of drawers. My gun was still there and the twenty bucks I kept hidden under my shirts for emergency.

There was nothing missing, not even the porterhouse I'd been hoarding in the refrigerator. So somebody had sneaked in just to practice on my typewriter. That made just about as much sense as two tails on an Airedale.

I thought about it. Dully. That smack on the head had left me very unstimulated. I was tired. I went to bed.

CHAPTER IV

BON VOYAGE

About nine the next morning I was awakened by a long buzz on my door buzzer. When I opened the door, there stood Judge Whitney, a little bigger than life because a good night's sleep made him look more like Richard the Lion Hearted than ever. But when he came in out of the hall, I saw that he hadn't had a good night's sleep after all, for his eyes were a little puffy and pink.

I said, "Good morning, your honor," and waited for him to hackle up like a gamecock.

Instead, he glanced here and there around my apartment as if looking for something nice to say but was finding it hard. He cleared his throat a couple of times, then looked at me.

"I want you to know, Chastain," he said frankly, "that I do appreciate your coming to us last night. I'm sorry if my manner was a little restrained, but ... dammit, sir, I can't like the business you're in!"

Straight from the shoulder, man to man.

"I know, Judge," I said. "There are crooks in my business, and there are crooks in your business, and it kind of makes it tough on the rest of us."

He breathed hard. He didn't like to be reminded that the judge business wasn't as lily white as nature had made the little snowflakes.

"Well," he said heavily, clinging to the olive branch with both hands to keep from using it as a club, "I hope in time we shall get to know one another better, Mick."

"I hope so, too—" I gave him a wistful smile—"Uncle!"

He winced. He turned red and cleared his throat again. I didn't want him to suffer any more than necessary, and in addition to that, I hadn't had breakfast yet, so I gave him a hand with his chore.

"You came to see me about something special, Judge?" I asked.

"As a matter of fact, I did, yes. I don't know if Mr. Barascule impressed on you the full gravity of the situation, but, my boy, it is of the utmost importance that no one, *no one* learns of Lew Melot's attempt to—ah—no one at all. It could be misinterpreted. I mean, gossip can be a vicious thing. You can understand that, of course."

"In plain English, Judge?"

"If word gets out, Chastain, somebody is sure to start saying that maybe you did accept that money, and the reflection of that on my reputation would be obvious."

I plucked a cigarette from the wilted package on the windowsill and stood for a moment looking down into the street as I lit it. On the sidewalk, a skinny, hound-type dog trotted eagerly toward the garbage can at the gutter, mounted to his hind legs and nosed into it. Twice a week this same hound came trotting just as eagerly to nose into the garbage cans. He never seemed to get any fatter.

"Okay, Judge," I said wearily, "I'll keep my trap shut, and nobody'll point any fingers at you. If that's what you want to know, there it is. But please don't let's talk about handouts again."

"Of course. But, Chastain, take care of yourself. Melot does not give up very easily."

"Sure, Judge, sure!"

He smiled uncertainly, then walked hesitatingly toward the door as if worried he had left something unsaid. He stopped at the door.

"Great Godfrey, I almost forgot!" he exclaimed. He took an envelope from his pocket and handed it to me. "Peggy asked me to give you this."

My heart took a sickening lurch as I felt something bulky in the envelope, and when I ripped it open, the ring I had given Peggy fell out. The note was very short and forthright.

> Dear Mick:
> I don't feel like wearing this right now. I'm going up to Jax to visit the Shelbys for a few days and think things over.
>
>   Peg.

I read it twice with the slightly frantic feeling that there was more but that I was missing it somehow. I looked at the judge and stammered, "When—when did she leave?"

"Last night." Then anxiously, "Is there something wrong?"

I ignored him and sprinted into the bedroom for the phone. I ate my fingers while long distance fuddled around and got Jacksonville. The operators tossed the number to and fro as if it were a basketball, and finally Mrs. Shelby's quiet voice came on.

"Can I talk to Peg, Mrs. Shelby?" I asked. "This is Mick."

"Of course, Mick. She's having breakfast. I'll call her."

I gulped air like a netted trout until Peggy's voice came over.

"Hello, Mick." There wasn't much expression to it. She sounded neither glad nor mad.

"Now, honey," I said, "what kind of a wingding is this?"

"No wingding, Mick. I just want to think things over."

"But there's nothing to think over, honey, nothing that has anything to do with you and me."

"Please, Mick, don't argue with me." She sounded tired. "It's a matter of loyalties, and I want to get them straight in my mind."

"What's there to get straight between you and me?" I was starting to shout. "It's always been straight—"

She hung up. I yelled into the phone and shook it, and if it had been a neck I'd have had a corpse in my hand. I slammed it down into its cradle. There was no sense calling her back. I knew Peggy. And there was no sense charging up to Jax to see her. She wouldn't see me.

The judge gave me a startled look when I stamped out into the living room again. The Chastains have an old-fashioned shanty-Irish temper, too, and it usually shows. He made a small gesture with his hand.

"At least, Chastain," he said, "we have one common bond. We both love her."

There was a real note of pathos in it, and I was so startled that I just gaped as he opened the door and walked out. It hadn't occurred to me before that he loved anybody.

I was sore, but it drained out of me and left me feeling empty. This was the first shindy Peggy and I'd ever had. I dressed very slowly. I didn't feel like eating breakfast, so I made myself an eggnog, added a splash of whisky, and drank it down, standing in the middle of the kitchen floor.

The door buzzed again. A voice called, "Western Union," and I opened the door quickly, thinking it was a telegram from Peg. It wasn't. It was a huge basket of flowers that almost filled the doorway, and tied to it was a wide white ribbon with gold letters that said, "Bon Voyage."

"What the hell's this?" I snapped.

"Flowers for Mr. Chastain," came the voice from behind the foliage.

Scowling, I backed into the room. The basket followed. The door closed and Joe Cuba and TB Puys, grinning, stepped out from behind the flowers.

"We hope you will have a very enjoyable trip, Mr. Chastain," said Puys solemnly.

I said, "Yeah? Where am I going?"

Puys took a ticket envelope from his pocket and pretended to glance at it. "Montevideo," he said, "on the S.S. *Maracaibo*. It sails at eleven this morning. Are you packed, you lucky man, you?"

Humor from him was like getting a hot foot from an undertaker.

I took an uneven breath and looked from one to the other. Their hands were in sight and empty, but their guns—and I knew damn well they packed—were a hell of a lot closer than the bedroom where mine lay in the dresser drawer under the shirts.

"You need a vacation, pal," said Joe Cuba. "You don't look so good ...

Does he, TB?"

"He could look worse, Joe. He could look a lot worse."

"You're right, TB. You're absolutely right. I've seen guys look worse. But they were kind of dead ... You'll look better after a nice boat ride, Chastain."

"Compliments of a friend," Puys added.

I raised a grin. It was hard, but I did it. I plucked a small brown zinnia from the basket and put it in my buttonhole.

"Let's get going," I growled. "I'm sick of this whole town and everybody in it!"

When I started around the basket toward the door, Puys blandly stepped back to allow me to pass. For a brief moment that huge bunch of flowers hid us from Cuba's sight, and before Puys could do anything effective with his hands, I drove my fist into the pit of his stomach and, whirling, shoved the basket into Cuba's face.

I sprang for the door and pelted down the corridor while he was still swearing and spitting gladioli from his mouth. I went down the stairs so fast that the beat of my feet against the steps sounded like the roll of a snare drum.

A big silver-and-blue interstate bus was just pulling up to the corner to discharge a few passengers from Georgia, and I jumped in before the driver could close the door. He was not supposed to pick up anybody in town, but before he could yap, I shoved a quick fin into his hand.

"Once around the park, my man," I muttered. "I want to watch the swans on the lake."

If he hadn't driven all night, if he hadn't been so tired, if he hadn't thought me a harmless souse, and if I hadn't gotten that fin to him before he committed himself out loud, he'd have made a good stab at heaving me to the wolves. And wolves are right, for a glance through the rear window of the bus showed me Cuba and Puys standing on the sidewalk looking up and down the street.

The driver looked up at me and said sourly: "Sit down and behave yourself."

I sat down and behaved myself. Hell, I'd have shined his shoes if he'd asked me. The bus moved majestically from the corner, leaving Cuba and Puys standing in front of my apartment, arguing angrily.

I got off six blocks down the line, grabbed a cab and went directly to my office on Florida Avenue before somebody got the idea ahead of me. The first thing I did was lock the door behind me, then I took my second gun from the file case and strapped it under my arm. I slipped it from the holster, checked the load and hefted it in my hand. It warmed up like a good friend, and I began to feel a lot easier.

I picked up the phone and called Lew Melot's Columbia Drive apartment. It was answered by some babe with a voice as sultry as a Spanish guitar.

"Put Lew on," I said shortly.

She laughed. There were bubbles in it. "Won't I do?" she asked throatily.

"With that voice, sweetheart," I said, "and at this hour of the morning, you probably look like Dracula's little sister. Put Lew on."

She laughed again and cooed, "You are so gallant, so masterful. You make my little heart go pitty-pat."

I heard a masculine voice growl, "Who is it?" and she answered carelessly, "Some jerk. Wants to talk to Lew."

"Find out who it is," the voice said.

She came back to the phone. "What's your name, Lover Lump?" she asked.

"Tell Lew it's Chastain."

"I might have known. A thick mick!"

She dropped the phone on some hard surface with a deliberate clatter, and I could hear her slippers go *slap-slap* across the floor. I waited for Melot pick up the phone.

There was a faint click and his voice came peremptorily: "What's on your mind, Chastain?"

I sat up straighter and gripped the phone. "Look, Melot," I said, "keep your dogs away from me, or they're going to get hurt."

"What's the matter with you? Are you crazy?"

"And it's not going to do your brother's appeal any good to have another Melot shooting spread all over the newspapers. Think it over, friend, think it over."

I hung up fast before he could answer, and sat there breathing hard. Then the humor of it hit me. Brother, was I a hero! Iron-guts Chastain, that's me. Just show me a phone and I'll pick it up and get tough with anybody. I took out my gun and pointed it at the phone.

"Bang," I said.

That made me feel better. Not a lot, but some.

CHAPTER V

A BANK DEPOSIT

But slowly I slipped back into the old slump. I wanted to talk to Peggy. I took a bottle of whisky from the bottom drawer of my desk, held it up to the light, then put it back again. I didn't feel that sorry for myself. The day dragged by. At noon I went down to the cafeteria and had a cup of coffee and a sandwich. I closed the office around three and went to a movie. I had dinner in a seafood den on the Bay, and when I got back to my apartment it was nine o'clock. The basket of flowers was still standing before the door in the living room.

I opened the kitchen window, made sure nobody was below, then tossed out the bouquet, geranium by geranium. The place still smelled like a funeral parlor, so I had a drink and turned on the radio. I felt as purposeless as a brassiere in a nudist camp.

There was some rumba music and I sat down on the sofa and crouched over my drink, getting a little maudlin over the memory of the last time I had heard rumba music with Peggy in the Pelican Lounge. Then all of a sudden the man on the radio was excited and his voice crackled away like a short circuit in an applause machine.

"... killed instantly as his car crashed into the concrete abutment of the bridge that crossed Sneary's Creek. Evans was the foreman of the jury that convicted Frankie Melot. There were no witnesses to the accident, and police say that Evans had been drinking ..."

I stopped listening as a cold little snake coiled sluggishly in the pit of my stomach. I didn't care what the police said—that had been no accident, and I wasn't the only one who was going to think that.

This was really putting Judge Whitney on the spot when the Frankie Melot appeal came up. It was a foretaste of what a second trial would be like. The new jurors would walk in fear of their lives, and if Frankie were convicted a second time, it would be a miracle. *If* he got a second trial. If.

Lew must have been out of his head to have pulled a trick like that. No matter what happened now, all hell was going to break loose. If Frankie were granted a new trial, the newspapers were going to scream like wounded eagles. And if Frankie were not granted a new trial, Lew Melot would be a madman.

I locked all my windows, bolted my door and went to bed with a gun under my pillow that night.

The next morning I picked up my mail in the apartment lobby, and when I got downtown the newsboys were screaming on the corners: "Melot files Appeal! Read all about it! Melot files Appeal!" I didn't take a paper. I didn't want to read anything about it.

I went up to my office and sat at my desk and looked at my fingernails. There wasn't any dirt under them, but on the other hand I hadn't been doing any work either. Maybe I should have taken either the vacation Barascule had offered, or the one Melot had bought. I felt tired and sick and just plain lousy.

I walked aimlessly over to the window and stood looking down into the street. There were cars parked all up and down the thoroughfare, but the one directly across from my office building had something special. It had a lavender sport shirt at the driver's window. There was only one guy I knew who wore lavender sport shirts and that was Joe Cuba.

My face hardened and I touched the gun under my arm. I may have done it the easy way, but I had meant every word I had said to Lew Melot. I was finished being pushed around.

I reached into my pocket for a pack of matches and felt the mail I had picked from my box in the apartment lobby. I went back to my desk and started opening it. It was something to do.

There were some bills, an advertisement from a diaper service—which, if things got worse, I might need—a notice that Dr. Morris Klugel, Chiropodist—he was notifying the right guy—had moved his offices; and a bulky letter from my bank.

I hadn't done anything to deserve a bulky letter from the bank, and I opened it with some curiosity. My bankbook fell out and there was a pink slip clipped to it. It said:

> Thank you for your deposit. Our Night Depository is open for your convenience every day from 3:00 P.M. until 10:00 A.M.

I picked up the bankbook very slowly and opened it, knowing very well what I was going to find, and there it was, initialed by the receiving teller: Deposit—$10,000.00.

The cute rats, I thought savagely. That's what the shenanigan was in my apartment when I had walked in and got smacked on the noggin. They had come for my bankbook. And remembering the typewriter, I knew what that was for, too. They had typed my deposit slip on my typewriter. That didn't mean very much, but if it ever came up, the typing had still been done on my machine and ostensibly by me. Pushed around again!

I reached for the phone, then slapped it away from me. The hell with hiding behind the telephone. I looked up Barascule in the book. This was his baby. Let him figure a way out. He was the one who wanted the judge elected, not me. He had an office on Florida Avenue closer to the middle of town than mine. It was a four-block walk, so I walked.

Joe Cuba wasn't alone in the car across the street. Puys was with him. They pulled out of their parking space and drifted down after me. I kept watching them, just hoping they'd make a play, but they didn't, and when I walked into Barascule's place—which was called the Barascule Building—they parked opposite and settled back to wait.

Their not making a play made me a little nervous, but I thought the hell with them, eyed the directory for Barascule's office, then took the elevator to the seventh floor. I pushed open the door marked "Barascule, Investments," and the wintry blonde at the reception desk gave me a glance that calculated to a thread the cost of my suit—$42.50. It would have been a waste of time talking to her anyway. I spotted the private office and barged in.

Barascule was working over a stack of papers behind a walnut desk, also suitable for ping-pong, and he looked up with irritated surprise when I slammed his door. I tossed my bankbook on the desk in front of him. "There's an interesting item on page two," I said. "Tell me what you think of it as an investment."

He picked up the book but kept looking at me. His aldermanic jowls did not look plump and pink this morning; they were pendulous and hog-fat white. His eyes were rimmed in red. He, too, had spent a bad night. He opened the book and his eyes spread at what he saw.

He started up out of his chair, snarling, "You damn little chiseling—" His face clotted and he clawed the air at me with a fat, half-clenched hand.

I said coldly, "Finished, friend?"

"Get out of here," he choked. "Get out of here!"

I didn't move. I just stared at him. He glowered back, then slowly sank back into his chair.

"I suppose," he said contemptuously, "that you have a proposition, or you wouldn't have brought this here. Well, let's lay it on the table. What is it?"

So, maybe you couldn't blame him at that. It was the kind of world he lived in. I remembered that good feeling I'd had at Frankie Melot's conviction. It seemed a long time ago.

I put both hands on Barascule's desk and leaned toward him.

"Two nights ago," I said, "somebody swiped my bankbook from my apartment. Today it came back through the mail from the bank, ten G's fatter. I don't want it, but it's your headache, so you figure out a way to get rid of it. But short of armed robbery, I don't see how you're going to get it off the bank's records."

He looked down at the bankbook. He sucked his cheek between his grinders and gnawed at it. If he could see a way out, he didn't look it.

"I know an answer to this," I said.

His eyes leaped at me. "Then for heaven's sake, man, give!"

"But," I grinned wolfishly, "you're going to have to throw over Lew Melot. You're going to have to knife him, and knife him hard. Forget the votes he controls and go after him."

He blustered, "What kind of nonsense is this?"

I shrugged. "Have it your own way. Clean up on Lew Melot, and I'll help."

Turning, I started toward the door. I hadn't gone two steps when he called me back. His eyes were two nail heads in a putty face. "What's your proposition?" he said expressionlessly.

"This," I said. "Frankie's appeal has been made. It's in the judge's hands now. That 'new evidence' of the bullets dug out of the fence is worth exactly what the judge will let it be worth. Have the judge prepare and sign a statement for the press, turning down the appeal, and as a rider have him take a blast at Lew himself. You give me the signed statement and I'll turn it over to the papers. Then I'll give evidence before the grand jury how Lew tried to buy me for ten G's to influence the judge. You'll sink him! The paper'll crucify him, and the judge'll be a hero!"

He shook his jowls and said impatiently, "It's not as simple as all that."

"What do you mean it's not as simple as all that?"

"You can't break Lew Melot by accusing him of bribing you. You have no official status. It's no crime to offer you money."

"But you'll crucify him in the papers. You'll win votes from Boca Chica to Chattahooohee. Judge Whitney—Richard the Lion Hearted, the People's Champion. Let the judge make one honest effort to get rid of Lew Melot and I'll campaign up and down this state for him if I have to hire an iron lung to yell louder."

His eyes veiled, Barascule stared down at the bankbook, tapping it thoughtfully with his forefinger. "You got something personal against Melot?" he asked slyly.

"No. I just hate his kind of guts, that's all. And maybe I kind of want my girl to have the kind of uncle she thinks he is."

He shot a glance up at me from under his brows. "Oh, yes—Peggy," he said. He put his hands flat on the desk and heaved himself to his feet. "I'm going to talk to the judge for a minute." He walked ponderously out of the office.

I sat on the edge of his desk and lit a cigarette, surprised to see that my hands were shaking a little. If they went after Lew Melot, it was going to be war. I had a shake or two coming.

Barascule was back in about five minutes, walking faster, looking worried.

"I can't get him," he said. "He went to Jacksonville to the Shelbys last night, but he should have been back long ago. We have an important meeting in about a half hour."

He snapped his fingers and turned back to the door. "Get me the Shelbys in Jax," he said sharply to the wintry blonde at the reception desk. He stood there at the open door for a moment, shaking his head, then turned and walked heavily to his desk.

Unaccountably, my heart was beginning to thump heavily in my chest. Barascule sat there drumming his fingers on the blotter, and when his phone tinkled, his hand pounced on it like a fat, white cat on a mouse.

"Mrs. Shelby?" he leaned back in his chair. "Barascule here. Can I talk to the judge for a moment? ... Oh. A message for you? ... Oh yes, he's right here." His eyes lifted at me over the phone. "Want to talk to him? ... All right, I'll tell him. Well, thanks a lot, Mrs. Shelby."

Slowly he hung up, took a deep breath and looked at me. I found myself gripping the desk until my fingers hurt.

"Well?" I demanded. "What is it?"

"Judge Whitney and Peggy left Jacksonville last night at eleven. She said that Peggy left word that if you called to tell you to call her here in Tampa, even if it was the middle of the night."

That jarred me and I could only stand there and yammer while the hot and cold prickles followed one another up and down my spine. Then suddenly I found voice and yelled at him:

"What are you standing there for! Something's happened, don't you realize that? Peggy would have called me hours ago. I'm getting over there right away!"

He mumbled, "Of course, of course," and padded after me as I strode for the door. He snapped at the frigid blonde to call his car, and when we got down to the street, there it was, waiting, the Cadillac.

"You'd better drive, Chastain," he panted. "And forget the police, just step on it They know my license plates."

CHAPTER VI

DOUBLE CROSS

The police knew it, all right. A couple of them made an angry start after us on their scooters, then turned off quickly as if embarrassed when they saw who it was. We made the judge's house so fast that the clock owed us minutes when we slewed to the curb.

The judge's sober black Buick was in the carport beside the house, and Barascule and I exchanged a glance as we trotted up the walk. I tried the front door, then thrust it open and walked in.

"Peg!" I called. "Judge!"

Barascule poked his head into the living room, then waddled down the hall toward the judge's study while I took the stairs three at a time to the second floor.

The judge, still in his pajamas, was lying on the floor just outside his bedroom. He was breathing harshly and my fingers found a small lump behind his left ear in the mastoid area. I knelt down beside him and went over him quickly, but there were no bullet wounds or knife slashes.

I heard Barascule panting at my elbow. I jumped up, thrust him aside, and ran down the hall to Peggy's room.

The covers and sheets, torn from the bed, lay crumpled on the floor. The closet door hung open and half her clothes were strewn around the entrance to it. The story was there. She had been snatched out of her bed.

I leaned against the door frame and clenched my hands until the white and red stopped flashing in front of my eyes. Then I whirled and sprinted down the hall, holding my gun under my arm so it wouldn't flip from the holster.

Barascule bleated after me, "Chastain, Chastain, come back here, you fool! You can't buck Lew Melot alone. This is a police matter. Come back here. This man needs a doctor!"

I swore at him and kept going. Police? He'd call the police the way I'd call Stalin. All I knew was that Lew Melot had taken Peggy—just as a little something to hold over the judge's head until he granted Frankie a new trial.

Crazy? Sure it was crazy. Whoever said Lew Melot was sane!

I dived into the Caddy at the curb. The keys were still in the ignition.

I needed that Caddy to move fast. The cops actually waved to me as I went by with the gas pedal to the floor.

The car with Joe Cuba and TB Puys had followed me for the first three blocks, but after that there was nothing but a blur and the road rushing at me with maniacal speed. I was at Lew Melot's Columbia Drive apartment before that powerful motor had even had time to really warm up.

I looked up at the gaudy Spanish pile of stucco, then ducked out of the car, holding my gun in its holster, and bounded across the sidewalk. I punched every button on the board except Lew's and went in when the front door started clicking.

Lew's apartment was on the top floor. I stopped for a flickering moment before his door, snapping back my hand from the buzzer before I pressed it. The hell with that. Why should I warn him? I took out my gun, held it inches from the lock and pulled the trigger. I was in the room before the smoke had cleared.

Lew, his alligator jaws clamped, was rising from behind a small desk, on which stood a regular battery of phones, his hand digging for the top drawer.

I yelled, "Hold it, Lew!" and scuttled to one side as a figure moved on the sofa. It was a girl, an ash blonde. "Both of you!" I waggled my gun. "I want to see four empty hands!"

Lew held out his hands, the fingers spread, but the girl just settled back into the sofa, folding her arms across her chest. She looked interested, but that's all. Lew lowered himself slowly into his chair behind the desk, still keeping his hands in sight.

"What's the beef, Chastain?" he asked evenly.

I jabbed my gun at him. "This time you're finished, Melot," I said. "This time it's the end. You've got nothing flat in which to tell me where you've stashed Peggy Whitney."

He jerked upright. "Where I've stashed who?" he said incredulously.

"Peggy Whitney—Judge Whitney's niece, pal, the judge you're trying to screw an appeal out of for Frankie."

Melot's eyes bulged and he shot up out of his chair. "What kind of damn fool do you take me for?" he roared. "Me put the snatch on—Where'd you get *that* from?"

"Time's running out, pal," I warned, tightening my hand around the gun.

The words he didn't care about, but the whitening of my knuckles around the gun he understood. The sweat stood out on his face, but his eyes glittered dangerously.

"Listen to me, Chastain," he said. "I don't know where this girl is. I don't know anything about this girl. And why should I pull a deal like that, anyway? Do you think I'm out of my mind?"

I said, "Yes."

His face was sheeted with sweat now. "For the love of heaven, man," he cried, "listen to me! I don't know—" He stopped and his mouth hung open. "There's more than that in your craw. What was that phone call about yesterday?"

"Ten thousand bucks you had stuck in my bank account," I snapped.

He yelled, "*What?*" and I thought he'd strangle.

"And," I said, "Joe Cuba and TB Puys trying to ship me off to South America. And Evans, that juryman, being knocked off last night." I leaned just a little toward him, and the gun in my hand became very still. "I want Peggy and that's the last word."

He just stood there making strangled sounds in his throat. He knew that in about five seconds that gun was going off. His teeth came together with a click.

"I don't know where the girl is," he said with finality, and clasped his hands behind his neck, waiting for the bullet.

No threats, no stalling, no nothing. It jarred me. Melot was the answer. He had to be. If he wasn't, then I was hung up, but good.

He was saying, quite calmly now, "I didn't stick any ten grand in your bank account, and I didn't have Cuba and Puys work on you, and I didn't have Evans, that juryman, bumped, and I didn't have that girl snatched. If you have personal reasons for shooting, go ahead and the hell with you. But you're not shooting me for being a damn fool!"

It came to me, sickeningly, that he was telling the truth.

I heard running footsteps on the stairs outside. I leaped to the right and quartered the gun on the whole room as Cuba and Puys burst through the broken door, their guns in their hands. They were half turned from me, facing Lew at the desk.

"Put them down, boys," I called. "I'm over here."

Puys' gun dropped immediately, but Cuba jerked twice—once as he started to whirl on me, and once as he stopped himself. Then his gun, too, thudded to the floor.

Lew Melot said, "Yours, too, Chastain."

With nausea, I realized that I had forgotten him for the instant in which Cuba and Puys were dropping their guns. I dropped mine and turned. He was standing behind the desk, a Luger held carelessly in his hand.

"Sit down, boys," he said to Cuba and Puys. "Chastain's got something on his mind. Get a load of it."

Cuba slanted a glance at Puys, then shrugged and sat down on the arm of the lounge chair, watching Lew with a mixture of boredom and insolence. Puys just stood and regarded me thoughtfully. Neither of them made a move to pick up his gun.

"Chastain," Lew went on, "has an idea I snatched some girl or other. What was the name, Chastain?"

That look of insolence on Joe Cuba's face told me something, and suddenly it was so plain that I started.

"They're crossing you, Melot," I said savagely. "They've been crossing you right down the line. That ten G's they offered me was not to persuade the judge, but to get him sore—to get him sore enough to judge Frankie's appeal on its merits and turn it down. Because they knew damn well what you'd do then. You'd try to blast Frankie out, and that'd be the end of you. They're getting ready to take over, Melot. You're half done, and you don't know it!"

Puys still regarded me thoughtfully, but Cuba yawned.

Lew said softly, "Just what was that ten G's all about, Joe?"

Joe looked resigned, like a martyr whose good intentions are being questioned. "This comedian's marrying the judge's niece, Lew," he said patiently. "We thought he'd be the right guy to put it to the judge for Frankie. Then he got balky, and we tried to ship him to South America."

"You knew it was in the bag for Frankie," Lew said. "You knew I made a deal with Barascule."

"I knew that? Who told me? A little blue bird? You keep an awful lot of stuff to yourself, Lew, then expect guys to read your mind."

Lew didn't answer immediately, so it was probably the truth, or enough of the truth to shake him a little.

Cuba pressed on. "I tried to tell you we were working on this clown, Lew. I brought up his name a couple times and you shut me up. TB and me, we talked it over. It looked good, so we did it. I still think it was the right play."

"And snatching Peggy Whitney was the right play, too?" I flung at him. "He's crossing you, Lew."

"Ah, hell," said Cuba, disgusted, "when did I have time to snatch anybody? I've been on your tail all day, Chastain, and you know it. You saw me a half dozen times, me and TB."

There was a lot of tension in the air, but it was all around me. All four of them—the girl on the sofa, TB, Cuba and Lew were looking at me with coldly murderous eyes.

Puys said gravely, "I think Chastain's going to be quite a nuisance, Lew. I think we ought to do something about that. If he goes around giving people wrong ideas, he can get to be a headache."

Lew nodded, fully convinced.

I started desperately, "I'm telling you, Lew, they're—" I stopped as it hit me—the real core of all this, the very first move that had put Lew on the spot. "Who was Frankie shooting it out with the day that little kid was killed, Lew?"

Lew shook his head. "The guy was in a car," he muttered, "Frankie couldn't see him."

"You dug some bullets out of a fence. Was that the McCoy?"

"I got one of them right here," said Lew grimly, tapping the desk. "And heaven help the guy whose gun it matches, if I ever match it."

"Then try those two guns," I flashed at him. "Cuba's and Puys'. The cops'll be glad to do a ballistics job for you."

The girl jerked upright on the sofa. Her hand shot out and she appeared to pluck a small gun from the air. It spat twice.

"Take him, Joe!" she screamed.

The gun spat again and I felt a slap against my left shoulder. I dropped as Cuba and Puys dived for their guns. Lew was leaning weakly against the wall behind his desk, pulling up his gun as if it weighed a ton. There were two holes in his chest.

Cuba snatched his gun and came up in a half crouch, just in time to catch Lew's first bullet in the face. It flung him up and backward, as if a giant spring had exploded under him.

Puys was pulling down on me. I was lying on my gun. I rolled frantically, pumping bullets in his general direction. He straightened up, looking mildly surprised, as if he had just discovered the answer to a puzzle that had been bothering him. Then he seemed to become disjointed and fell in an angular heap.

Lew was still leaning against the wall, breathing heavily, then suddenly he roared and shoved himself upright. His gun flamed three times, and three times the girl on the sofa was slammed back. Lew coughed, swayed, and dropped into the chair behind the desk. The trigger guard of his gun caught on his finger and dangled there.

I got stiffly to my feet. I walked over to the desk, picked up one of the phones and called police headquarters.

"I'm calling from Lew Melot's apartment," I said. "There's been a shooting. You'd better send the meat wagon and an ambulance."

I hung up. Almost immediately, the phone shrilled. I let it ring. I looked down into Lew's dark, staring eyes.

"It looks like everybody's been a sucker," I said, and walked out, holding my left shoulder. The wound was beginning to hurt.

I drove very slowly back to the judge's house. I saw the curtain drop back into place over the front window as I crawled out of the car and walked up the steps to the front porch. The judge, now a waxen replica of Richard the Lion Hearted, sat on the sofa, shaking all over.

Barascule came toward me, crying, "Thank God you're safe, Chastain! What got into you, man? You might have been—"

"Where's Peggy?" I interrupted woodenly.

He licked his lips and shot a quick glance at the judge. He made an apologetic gesture with his fat, white hands.

"The judge didn't pick her up at the Shelby's" he said. "We jumped to conclusions."

"He didn't pick her up? But you called Mrs. Shelby in Jax, remember, Barascule? You lying' rat!" I shouted. "There wasn't any call to Mrs. Shelby. You suckered me. You knew damn well what I'd do if I thought Lew Melot had snatched Peggy. You knew I'd go gunning for him!"

"You—you're making a mistake, Chastain," he stammered. "You—"

"Listen, you slimy political louse, you sent me out to kill Lew Melot— or get killed! You didn't care which. You wanted Melot out of the way. If I gunned him down, he was out of the way. And if he got me, he was out of the way, too, on a murder rap, because the public wouldn't let another Melot killer get further than the electric chair."

I was shouting too much, I was too noisy, and he knew I wasn't going to do any more than that. He recovered himself.

"Melot's dead, then," he said with satisfaction. "Good! You won't be the poorer for this, Chastain, I promise you."

Behind us a voice, thickened with blood, rage and hatred, said, "Another promise, Barascule? You're full of promises, full of deals ..."

The sound of the gun was flat and final. Barascule fell heavily into the cocktail table. The bottle of Scotch emptied itself on the rug beside his face. He didn't move.

I turned slowly. Lew Melot was leaning weakly against the living room archway, his fingers knotted in his bloody shirtfront. He gave me a grin, and there was blood on his teeth. "Suckers," he whispered, "suckers, everybody ..."

He turned and lurched drunkenly toward the front door. The sound of police sirens sang closer and closer.

I looked down at the judge, shivering wordlessly on the sofa. With Barascule, his campaign manager, dead under the gun of Lew Melot, and with the dying statement Lew would make, the judge wasn't going to be elected to anything, so something had come out of this mess, anyway. The voters were going to get a break for once.

I said, "So long, Governor," and walked toward the back door.

I didn't want any talk. I didn't want any questions. I didn't want any police. I just wanted Peggy. Jacksonville, praise be, wasn't at the other end of the world.

MAN WITH A REP

Dave Lait's face was normally cold and set, but now, at this minute, it felt pinched as his hand hovered indecisively over the phone. It was the house phone to the hatcheck booth downstairs.

Finally he jerked up his chin and asked shortly, "Did Hogan show yet, Dolores?"

"Not yet, Mr. Lait."

The girl lying on the chartreuse leather chaise across the office watched him narrowly as he dropped the phone back into its cradle. She was wearing a sea-green evening gown that covered her from neck to instep, yet she appeared naked. She was relaxed and quiet, but there was violence in every line of her, from the curve of her bold breasts to the full flame of her mouth. Her hair was a rich blonde and it burned like the corona of the sun. She sat up and swung her feet to the floor.

"Well?" she demanded.

Lait shook his head.

Her eyes narrowed. "How much longer are you going to stall around?" she asked angrily. "He's an hour late now. What're you waiting for, the end of the Truman administration?"

He said, "Shut up," but without conviction and looked down at his lean, bony hands.

She lunged up from the chaise and took two swinging steps toward the desk.

"Damn it, Dave," she said, "if a guy welches on a ten-G IOU in this town, you've got to do something about it or you're finished, done, washed-up. You know that. What're you waiting for?"

"I said, shut up."

"No, I won't shut up. Listen, Dave"—she was almost pleading—"let Zyla take care of Hogan. He'd love it, and he'll stay clammed forever. Give Zyla the word, and you'll have nothing to worry about."

This time he didn't answer at all, even with a shake of his head. He walked to the bar beside the window, turned his back to her and downed a pony of cognac. When he swung around again, she was gone. The office door closed as noiselessly as the door of a vault. But her violence still hung in the air, like the smoke after an explosion.

There were things he had wanted to say to her, things he had never said before. With them, it had always been Dave, tempered steel—and Tess, diamond hard. No sentiment. A pair of realists rather than two lovers.

But she was right. If he didn't do something about Hogan, he was finished. The Blues Club couldn't exist twenty-four hours without the roulette, the bird cage, the craps table, the blackjack. When the boys found out they didn't have to pay up, they wouldn't, and that would be the end.

He didn't even bother cursing Hogan. He had been taken, and he had been taken good. Ten G's worth. Hogan had always been loaded, always. But Hogan had shot his roll at Jamaica and had come into the game last night with the leavings. He would never forget the pallor of Hogan's face when he turned up four treys to Hogan's full house, aces up. Hogan had looked like a three-week corpse. A heart flush had been the biggest hand all night, and Hogan had shot the works—the works he didn't have—on that full house. Ten G's.

The office—the game was always in Lait's office—had been silent as a morgue when Hogan had spread his hand and looked sick as Lait turned over his four treys.

There had been five in the game—Johnny Michaels, Big Jim Farr and Aarons. Farr and Aarons had almost sweated blue, and Michaels had edged nervously toward the door. Dave's iron rule was No Credit. And Dave was supposed to be—well, tempered steel.

Hogan had stammered, "Tomorrow night, Dave. Tomorrow night at nine, I swear. It'll be right there on your desk. Ten G's." He shook as if he expected Dave to blast him down where he stood. He had asked for it.

But he had walked out, and the others had darted out after him, their eyes bright and a little gloating. Tough Dave Lait had been taken for ten G's. It was all over town by now.

Unless he did something about Hogan—something final and frightening, something that would keep the boys in line.

Dave was lean and over six feet tall, but he looked much less than that now as he slouched wearily in front of the tiny bar. The Blues Club was a gold mine, a kind of end-of-the-rainbow—and he was throwing it down the drain, because he didn't intend to do anything about Hogan.

He could give the word, and Hogan would be beaten and maimed. But that wouldn't be enough. Ten G's was important money. He'd have to go all the way with Hogan, and he wasn't going to. To hell with the Blues Club and everything else; he wasn't going to play God and order a man killed. He downed a quick cognac and wondered dully if it would have been different had it been Johnny Michaels. He liked Hogan, and he didn't like Johnny Michaels. Michaels was predatory and feral, ambitious. Hogan was well, a likable guy, that was all. A likable guy.

Johnny Michaels was a Hitler in miniature.

But even as the cognac inflamed him, he knew he would never have ordered Michaels killed, either.

He was glad he had canned Zyla. It removed the temptation. Zyla had the conscience of a grey wolf and sooner or later that would have spelled trouble.

He filled the pony for his third cognac, lifted the glass and said sardonically, "Well, it was fun while it lasted...."

The office door opened. Tess stood rigidly in the doorway, the ends of her mouth dipping at the sight of the glass in his hand.

"Getting soused?" she asked coldly.

He grinned, warming at the sight of her. His face, congealed by fifteen years of professional poker, suddenly started to feel warm and full again. It was over—and so what? He was glad. It had been a rat race from the word go. He was glad it was over now. He had enough money. Tess and he could take time out and go to Florida for the deep-sea fishing, or to California for the sights. They could get married and start out as humans. He stared at her as if he had never seen her before. He loved her! The realization flooded through him and made him feel like laughing, like bubbling over. Tough Dave Lait—that was all finished. He could be a human being. He could love and ask to be loved in return; he could make jokes; he could guffaw; he could *live!* And not worry about who was out to take him for a fast buck.

He started gaily, "Tess ..."

She interrupted abruptly, "I've taken care of it for you. You can relax." There was contempt in her face, but also a kind of fear.

He stiffened. "You what?" he asked carefully.

"Taken care of it for you," she cried shrilly, her hands clenching at her sides. "Did you think I'd just stand around and watch you take a nose dive? *I took care of it!*"

Then it penetrated, and very carefully he set down his pony of brandy. "And just how did you do that?" he asked.

"I called Zyla."

Her eyes widened. She thought she had seen every expression of which his face was capable, but suddenly it was all gaunt bones and harsh shadows, a death's head.

"And I'm supposed to thank you?"

Her hand flew to her mouth and her fingers trembled at her lips. She turned and ran.

He stared at the empty doorway, then furiously swung his arm and cleared the little bar of bottles and glasses. They tinkled and smashed and gurgled liquidly. He strode to the desk and snatched up the outside phone. He called Zyla's number and waited, freezing as it rang and rang and rang without an answer. Finally it was obvious, even to his forlornest hope, that Zyla was gone. He slammed down the phone and rounded the desk, jerking open the bottom drawer. He grabbed up a slim Luger and pulled out the clip. It was fully loaded. He dropped it into his jacket pocket and sprinted out of the office. He went down the stairs, two steps at a time. The doorman gaped after him as he leaped into his Caddy roadster, swung it around and sped down the driveway in a spray of flying gravel.

He clung grimly to the wheel with both hands and stamped the gas pedal to the floor. It was almost an hour's drive from Harwood Cliffs to Newark, where Hogan lived. He swept through the 9-W traffic, using his horn instead of his brakes. Through the towns he was grimly careful not to be stopped for a ticket, but once on the Pulaski Highway out of Jersey City he opened it up again.

He didn't blame Tess. She was protecting her capital. With the Club out of business, there wouldn't be any more mink, caviar or filet mignon. She'd have to rough it on hamburger. She had acted according to her pattern.

But he hated her, all the same. He hated the whole pattern, now that he'd had that brief insight into how it would be to be a human being again. Brief. Thirty seconds!

In thirty seconds he had lived and loved. For a normal person, living and loving meant a whole lifetime. He had done it in thirty seconds. He laughed insanely. That was the way to do it—fast. Get it over and forget it. Dave Lait, gambler. The turn of a card.

Only he couldn't. There were hooks. Hooks with barbs like fish hooks, and you couldn't shake them free. Tess still had her hooks in him.

But the greater urgency was the life of Hogan. He had to get to Hogan before Zyla did. He swore at a produce truck that momentarily barred the road, then clamped his hand on the horn and swept around it.

He was sweating. It was salty on his lips and it stung his eyes. He fanned his hand across his face. The road danced in front of him.

He drove mechanically, the roar of the tires filling his ears.

He had known, when he dealt his first card, that there was danger in it. But he had provided for all that. No Credit. If you paid up when you lost, that was the end of it, until the next time.

But Hogan had crossed him. Not willingly or intentionally. He was a likable guy, Hogan. If only Hogan had come to him at nine o'clock and said, "Dave, I can't pay. Give me time."

He would have given Hogan time. He knew Hogan would have kept his mouth shut. He would have given Hogan all the time in the world—if only he had asked. Swearing was futile.

Only one thing was important now—to reach Hogan before Zyla killed him.

He raced recklessly down McCarter Highway beside the railroad. Hogan lived in a dingy hotel on Mulberry Street.

Dave felt as if he were plodding through sand as he walked up the worn carpet to the desk.

If only he hadn't been such a phony. If only he hadn't pretended to be so tough. But, of course, if he hadn't, he wouldn't own the Blues Club, he wouldn't be in the chips. No one had ever called his bluff before—but that had been only a matter of propaganda. Zyla had always spread the word that you couldn't fool with tough Dave Lait. Tough. What a joke. But Zyla was smart and Zyla looked hard enough to back up anybody. And he was, too. Zyla couldn't think for himself, but he *was* hard enough to back up anybody once the word was given. Zyla was an animal. Zyla would kill and go on killing. He had to get to Hogan before Zyla did.

The sleepy-eyed, bored desk clerk said, "Hogan?" and turned languidly to look at the key rack behind him. He shook his head. "Nope. Sorry. He ain't in. There's his key. Wanna leave a message?"

"Yes, I do. Tell him Dave was here. Tell him it's okay. Tell him to wait in his room and let nobody in but me. You got that—nobody but me."

The clerk opened his eyes. His face became crafty. "What was the name?" he asked.

Dave got it. He threw a five-dollar bill on the counter. "Dave," he said. "Dave."

The clerk's hand hungrily covered the five. "Dave said stay in his room—right?" He leaned over the counter until his stomach bulged over the edge of it. "Is he wanted?"

Dave smothered his anger. "Nothing like that. It's a private matter. He'll understand. You'll be sure to tell him now, won't you?" At this point he couldn't afford to antagonize anybody.

The clerk shrugged, "For a V-note, I give him my own name." He shot Dave a sly glance and giggled.

Dave turned away, disgusted. Not that he had wasted his five. But if Zyla came along with a ten, the clerk would forget the five. That kind of thing belonged in the same category as ordering a man killed. It was a matter of—well, integrity, if you wanted to call it that.

But outside, on the sidewalk, his anxiety returned. Hogan. Where to look? Newark was a big place....

He forcibly calmed himself by holding a match to his cigarette until it curled in his fingers and burned his hand.

Finding Hogan wasn't so impossible if you put your mind to it. Hogan wouldn't run. He wasn't that kind. He wouldn't run and spend the rest of his life hiding. He was bold and reckless, willing to take a chance. He had grinned, even when he had seen Dave's four treys. He had grinned pallidly and turned green, but he had grinned. He wouldn't run. Nor would he crouch in his bed and shiver like a rabbit until the dogs came for him. Not Hogan.

But, with a flash of insight, neither could he see Hogan come begging for an extension of the IOU.

A voice called, "Dave. Hey, Dave."

Dave turned. Behind him, the lobby was empty. On one side of the hotel was a tailor shop, at the other side a dark parking lot. He walked over to the edge of the hotel, leaned against the corner and lighted another cigarette.

The voice said nervously, "I thought you'd show. I've been waiting for you. I got a little property you might be interested in."

Dave placed the voice now. Quiggy Moore. Quiggy, the little stoolie who had his ear at every rat hole. By "property" he meant information.

Without turning his head, Dave said, "How much?"

Quiggy stammered, "Fi-fi-fi-five C's." Then hurriedly, "It's worth it, Dave. It's worth it."

Dave went cold. Quiggy had never asked for more than a sawbuck at a time. Never. A five-C bite meant that Quiggy really had something special, something he knew Dave wanted badly.

Dave said tersely, "Shoot."

Quiggy said eagerly, "Skip town, Dave. Hit the grit, beat it and keep going. Zyla's Johnny Michael's right hand. Johnny wants the Blues Club. They're gonna hang the Hogan kill on you, being's everybody knows Hogan welched on that ten-G IOU—and Zyla's even gonna put the boots to you, if you're still hanging around. I'm leveling, Dave. Beat it."

Dave didn't ask where Quiggy had gotten his information. He didn't have to. Quiggy knew all the rat holes. Dave asked, "Did they get to Hogan yet?"

He could almost *feel* Quiggy shrug.

"A half-hour ago Hogan was down to the Shamrock Bar on Ferry Street, drunker'n a plumber's helper. Now that's worth five C's, Dave, ain't it? I coulda got better'n that from Johnny Michaels to clam up, but being's I'm a friend of yours ..."

Dave said savagely, "Okay, okay." He pulled five C-notes from his wallet, balled them and tossed them into the shadows. As he walked away he could hear Quiggy scrambling in the gravel for them.

Ferry Street. That was down in the Ironbound, down Neck, the tough section of Newark.

The back of his neck prickled as he braked the Caddy at the curb in front of the Shamrock. He looked up and down the shadowed street. Zyla could be anywhere, in any of those dark doorways, and Zyla would kill as a wolf kills—without fear, without heed, without even hate.

Dave wiped his shaking, sweating hands down his thighs, then slid out of the car and walked quickly into the tavern. His eyes quickly cased the smoky, noisy room. Zyla could be there, too. It would be a logical place, but Zyla wasn't. There was the usual border of rummies around the rim of the bar, and in back of them, about twenty muscular young kids in a state of high, boisterous elation because they had beaten the Ulster Club of Harrison, across the river, in a soccer match that afternoon. They were drunk and joyously ready for a fight.

Dave glided inconspicuously to the end of the bar. There was an empty space, but a beer sat on the bar before it, claiming it. A sullen-faced blonde squatted on the stool beside it, sucking at a cigarette.

The barkeep came down, and Dave said, "Hennessey." Casually, then: "Hogan come back yet?"

The barkeep looked back over his shoulder and shook his head. "He was hungry. He went out for some fish and chips. He's nuts about fish and chips. Hennessey?"

"I'm nuts about fish and chips, too. Where can I get myself a plate around here?"

"You can't, friend. The nearest is Harrison, across the river. You said Hennessey, didn't you, friend?"

"Yeah. But listen." Dave held out his hand. He went on quickly, "If Hogan shows while I'm gone, tell him to go back to his hotel and stay there. Tell him Dave said it's okay. Tell him Dave said—"

The blonde mashed out her cigarette on the wood of the bar and swung around, facing him.

"That wouldn't be Dave Lait, would it?" she demanded belligerently.

Dave nodded, then caught himself as her eyes blazed at him. She swung for his face with the back of her hand, missed and tumbled off her stool. The tavern went quiet.

The blonde shoved herself to her knees and screamed, "That louse is Dave Lait, the rat that's gonna put the boot to poor old Hogan." Her hand flabbily pointed at him. "That's the guy Hogan's been running from. C'mon, you lousy athletes—moider the rat! Break him up!" She swung her arm provocatively at the massed soccer players. "Moider 'im!"

Dave flattened against the wall. The kids were still for a moment, and then they grinned and their eyes shone. A fight. They surged toward him. Dave jerked the Luger from his pocket.

The barkeep, scared, yelled, "Hey!" and ducked down behind the bar.

Dave sucked in his breath and swept a tight quarter arc with the mouth of the Luger. The kids stopped. They had never faced a gun before, but they weren't afraid of it.

"Put it away, Hawkshaw," one of them called, "and I'll take you on alone."

The rest of them laughed and leaned toward Dave, anxious now and ready for the fight. They were between him and the door, and they weren't going to move until they were satisfied. Dave felt the sweat as it broke out in pebbles on his face. He couldn't take on the gang of them—for that was what it would amount to—and he wouldn't shoot them.

The drunken blonde was waveringly hauling herself to her feet, clinging to the barstool, screeching, "That's the son that's gonna knock off poor old Hogan. Kill the louse! Smear 'im!"

Dave hadn't said a word. The athletes took that for a sign of weakness and surged toward him again. Dave dropped the nose of the gun and fired a roaring shot into the floor at their feet.

"Scram," he snarled, for now he knew he had to say something.

They stared, aghast, then whirled and rushed for the rear of the tavern, smashing two tables and eight chairs, overturning the occupants and trampling them in the rush to get farthest from the open mouth of the Luger.

Dave jumped to the door and sprinted for the Caddy. Behind him, the blonde was still shrieking. Dave slid quickly into the front seat of the car and stamped on the gas pedal. The Caddy shot from the curb with an outraged roar. He went through two red lights, went over the Harrison bridge wide open, but he didn't begin to shake until the neon lights of central Harrison splashed the sky in front of him. Then he shook so hard that he had to pull to the curb. He took a bottle of Hennessey from the glove compartment, then angrily shoved it back without opening it. No. No liquor. He rubbed his lean, bony hand down his angular face. Oh, hell.

Those kids in there would have beaten the devil out of him. Three feet more and they'd have been all over him. Time. He didn't think about the beating he would have taken; he just thought about the time it would have taken. Time. Zyla. Hogan.

He stiffened his muscles and forced calm into his shaking hands. He stepped gently on the accelerator and prowled out from the curb. Up at the neon lights, he stopped in the middle of the busy intersection and waved his arm imperiously at the traffic cop in the booth on the corner.

The cop came out, sweating. He charged up to the open window, but his anger evaporated as Dave tucked a folded V-note behind his badge.

"If I were an Irishman in this town," Dave said, "where would I go for a plate of fish and chips?"

With a loving hand, the cop slid the bill from behind his badge and concealed it in his hand. He turned to the honking traffic and roared, "What're ya asking for, a ticket? Can'tcha see the man's wanting information? Come around and take it easy."

He turned back to Dave and spread his forearms on the window ledge. "So yer wantin' fish and chips, hey? And Irish?"

"Ulster," said Dave, gritting his teeth.

"Ulster? Well, now!" The cop laughed, turned and pointed straight up the street. "Right up there's where the boys is holding the wake, beaten as they was by the boys from Newark this aft in soccer. A terrible beating and tragedy it was. The Ulster Fish and Chip that's where ye'll find them. They tell me there's a crazy Irishman in there, buying fish and chips for all comers and paying on the line. I wisht I was able to get away meself. There's nothing I like better'n a dish of fish and chips, well doused in vinegar and salted down. The Ulster Fish and Chip, just this side the bridge between Harrison and Kearny. Maybe I'll see you there meself, if you stay long enough."

He turned and his arm shot out, holding up traffic until Dave rifled the Caddy up the street in full throttle.

Dave bounced the Caddy against the curb across the street from the Ulster Fish and Chip. It didn't look like a restaurant. The store front could have been that of a shoe store or a lingerie shop. A sway-backed Venetian blind hung in the window, and on the glass, in a circle, was painted—Ulster Fish and Chips.

Dave waited as a car careened dangerously down the avenue in front of him, then he sprinted for the opposite curb as another car zoomed toward him. Quite a town, Harrison. But he was too empty of emotion to feel very strong about it.

When within thirty seconds you have lived, loved and died, there was not much else to give a damn about.

Except the bone-breaking shock of a bullet from a gun held by Zyla. He might have lived and loved, but that harsh jangle in his nerve trunks told Dave that he hadn't quite died yet, no matter how else he felt about it.

He had suddenly discovered that he loved Tess, and the realization of it had been a warm fire heating a cold body. Now he knew she had not only sicced Zyla on Hogan, but she had double-crossed him as well.

Tess liked her mink. She liked her caviar and filet mignon. Tess had tipped off Johnny Michaels. Maybe she had even said in actual words,

"Dave Lait is chicken. Move in and the Blues Club is yours."

Johnny would have jumped at the chance. Johnny had been slavering at the chops for months for a chance at the Blues Club. Zyla was Johnny's man, Quiggy had said, and that was reasonable.

Dave sprinted for the doorway. He couldn't let himself be shot down by Zyla now, not before he had at least warned Hogan. He was not even noticed as he slipped inside and slammed the door behind him. It was a small room and it was crammed with young, muscular kids and their girlfriends. The din was terrific. The gaudy juke box blared its loudest, but no one paid any attention to it, for they were all furiously debating the soccer game they had lost that afternoon.

Dave spotted Hogan the minute he walked in. Hogan was standing up at the counter by the cash register, waving a crumpled handful of dollar bills over his head.

"Fish and chips for the house," he was shouting. He was grinning, but there was a far-away, doomed sadness in his eyes. "C'mon, step up and get your fish and chips!"

Then he caught sight of Dave. His jaw grew slack and he seemed to shrivel a little. Dave started slowly through the tightly packed crowd. A tall, red-headed kid, who looked like a young heavyweight, threw his arm around Hogan's shrinking shoulders and bellowed, "Yeaaaaaa for Hogan!"

The crowd stamped and whistled and shouted.

Hogan stood straighter and threw up his head. Dave stopped and felt a shiver go through him. All Hogan had to do now was point a finger and the fists would start swinging.

Hogan's face grew tight as Dave worked closer and closer to him. White-faced, Dave stopped within two feet of him.

He said, "Hi-ya, Hogan."

The big redhead sensed there was something wrong, and he looked from Hogan to Dave, then back to Hogan again. He nudged Hogan with his thumb and demanded belligerently. "Is he after you, pal?"

Hogan took a breath. When he let it out, it was a sigh. He shook his head. He looked sadly at Dave.

"I'm sorry, Dave," he said. "I just couldn't raise the dough."

"Why didn't you come to me and tell me?"

Hogan looked around the room. His mouth twisted. "I was having meself a last fling. I used to be a soccer player meself. Can I buy you a plate of fish and chips, Dave?" However drunk he had been earlier, he was cold sober now. He slipped from under the redhead's arm. "Let's go."

He started for the door. Dave crowded him and whispered angrily, "Do you think I'd have anybody gunned down for money? Why didn't you come to me?"

Hogan said incredulously, "You're gonna give me time?"

"All the time you want."

Hogan grabbed his hand, "Dave, I swear—"

"You're not out of the woods yet," Dave said grimly. "Johnny Michael's got Zyla after you, and I'm supposed to take the fall for it. Zyla's been on the prowl since ten. That's why I'm here."

Hogan nodded. "I thought Johnny was getting ambitious. He wants your spot, hey?" Then meekly, "What now, Dave?"

Dave stopped at the door, his hand on the knob, debating with himself. "The best thing, I guess," he said finally, "is to get back to the Club. We can straighten it out there among friends. Johnny won't throw any punches, once we got it settled."

He opened the door and took three steps out into the street. There was a cab at the curb. The door of it swung open and he grabbed wildly for his gun, throwing himself down and to the side, dragging Hogan after him. But it was Tess who exploded out of the cab.

She cried, "Dave!" and ran to him. Her face was as pale as death.

He rose, slapped the dust from his knees. "What happened, Tess—your conscience get too big?"

She made a small, appealing gesture with her hand. "I'm sorry, Dave. I didn't mean ... I thought I was doing you a favor."

"Doing me a favor, having a man shot?"

"I didn't think of it that way, Dave. I was only thinking of you. When you broke out of the Club, I knew you'd be going to Hogan's hotel, so I followed you. I wanted you to know that ... Damn it, Dave, when you're in love with a guy ..."

He stared at her in wonder. The tears were spilling naked and unshamed down her face. He laughed, empty, self-mocking laughter. What a pair they were, each loving the other, each too hard-boiled to admit it.

He put his arm around her. "Okay," he said. "It's okay, honey. But how'd you know where to find me?"

"Quiggy told me. He was at the hotel."

"Quiggy's making quite a night of it," he said drily.

He took her arm and ran her across the street to the Caddy. Hogan pounded after them. Dave didn't relax until he was on the Harrison Turnpike.

The parking lot was jammed when they reached the Club. The dance floor would be closed in an hour, but the gambling room would be open all night. Dave took them straight up to his office on the second floor.

He flipped on the light—then froze.

Johnny Michaels, wearing that small, tight smile of his, was sitting behind the desk. The heavy door closed behind them, and Dave whirled involuntarily. Zyla leaned against it, deadpan, hefting his gun in his hand. Hogan looked sick.

"Kind of thought you'd show up here, Dave," said Johnny softly. "And look who you've brought with you. Well, well, well. The gang's all here, hey, Dave?"

"You're sticking your neck out, Johnny," Dave said. "This is still my Club. My boys are downstairs ..."

"Sure they are," Johnny chuckled. "And when they come busting in here, they'll find all three of you nice and dead. And tomorrow they'll be saying: 'If Dave hadn't pushed Hogan so hard for those ten G's, the little jerk wouldn't have gone crazy and shot him and his girlfriend.' That's just what they'll be saying, Dave, and there'll be nobody to say different, because Hogan'll be cold meat, too. Now ain't that a shame...."

Hogan screeched and flung himself on Zyla, yelling recklessly, "Take him, Dave! Take him!" His arms flailed madly.

Zyla's gun roared. Dave dropped to the floor, smoothly sliding his Luger from his pocket. Johnny half rose from the desk, grabbing for the gun under his arm. Dave shot him in the face and without waiting to see him fall, turned toward Zyla. Bleeding down the side of the head, Hogan was clinging to Zyla's right arm with both hands. The big gunman shook him furiously, then raised his left fist and clubbed him behind the neck. Dave steadied his hand and shot Zyla through the knee. The man went down as if his leg had been cut off under him. Dave fired again, getting him in the right shoulder. Zyla fell back against the door and sat there, his eyes huge with sudden fear.

Hopelessly he watched Dave pick up his gun from the floor and straighten up.

Tess moaned, "No, Dave, no!"

He shook his head at her and bent over Hogan. Zyla's only shot had grazed the Irishman's skull, gouging out a shallow gutter, but otherwise had done no serious damage. Johnny Michaels had disappeared behind the desk.

Dave said heavily, "If he'd waited till morning, he could have had the Club a lot cheaper than that." He looked at Tess. "I'm through, honey. Done. Washed up. When the cops are finished pushing me around, I'm buying myself a little orange grove in Florida. If you come with me, it means no more mink, no more caviar, no more filet mignon ..."

She lifted her face. She was still shaking a little. "What's wrong with orange juice?" she asked defensively. "They say it's very healthy."

DON'T WAIT UP FOR ME

Clem Lasher was playing the piano when the apartment buzzer sounded off. He grimaced, slanted his eyes at the leggy girl curled on the sofa, and tilted his head toward the door. She assumed an expression of patient suffering and uncurled. She pulled her housecoat less revealingly around her and strolled toward the door as if the last thing she had in mind was letting anybody into the apartment that night. She was a handsome girl but with the kind of sulky face that all Clem's girls seemed to acquire after a while.

Clem missed three chords in the progression and went back over them, swearing softly. He was a big man with harsh red hair, a tough angular face and blazing greenish eyes. There was nothing delicate or poetic in his touch. He seemed to wrench the music from the piano with the sheer savagery of his attack. His fingers stabbed at the keys as if he were actually gouging the notes out of them. But there was more to it than just noise. It was music. It was angry, there was ferocity in it, but it was real. It was gutbucket. He always played gutbucket when he was "ironing out the kinks."

Two strangers from Duluth had taken him for eighteen hundred at stud that afternoon, and it was the same grinding run of luck that he he'd been having for the past month. There were kinks.

He played for twenty minutes after the girl brought two men back into the apartment with her, even though he knew they were there fidgeting on the sofa, but when he finished he had drained some of the furious frustration out of himself. He slipped a cigarette between his lips and turned on the bench.

One of the men on the bench was fat Ben Morgan, the theatrical agent, who was perspiring a little more than usual. The other was a quiet, compact man who right arm hung in a black silk sling.

"Say, that was okay, Clem." Morgan's smile was a very unstable commodity. "Ever think about playing professionally? You've got something."

"What I've got," said Clem dryly, "would get the piano abolished as a musical instrument. Nice of you to drop in at any old hour, Morg. Nice to see you, even if it is two A.M. Is there something on your mind, or did you just come up to show me how pretty your friend looks with his arm in a sling?"

The girl gave a short, brittle laugh. "I warned them," she said. "I told them exactly what to expect, but they didn't have sense enough to go home." She dropped into the lounge chair and threw her long, beautiful and very unreticent legs over the arm of it, staring at her fingernails as if wondering whether or not to sharpen them on the upholstery.

"Be quiet, Marthe love, or I'll boot your pretty little butt out of here. Did you say something, Morg?"

Morgan glanced at the compact man and licked his lips. "It's about Sonny Lind, Clem," he said.

"Oh yes, the kid with the voice. How's he coming?"

"Well," Morgan laughed nervously, "he isn't coming at all, Clem. He went."

"He did? Well!" There was a sharpening edge under Clem's polite tone. "Where did he go?"

"We don't know. Uh—this is Al Vance, Clem. He's a private detective. I put him on the job a week ago when Sonny disappeared." Morgan's voice became hurried. "We've been working every minute on it, Clem. We haven't left a stone unturned."

"Is that where you thought you'd find him," asked Marthe brightly, "under a rock?"

Clem ignored her and said to Morgan, "I seem to remember that Sonny Lind was to open in the Aztec Room in about a week."

"Tha—that's right, Clem."

"And I also seem to remember that I've got a thousand dollars invested in Sonny Lind, one way and another—singing lessons, clothes and so forth. But he seemed like a nice kid. I liked him, and he could sing. And it was on my say-so that Kraus was willing to give him a spot in the Aztec Room. If he flopped, okay; that was the chance I was taking. But when I invest a thousand dollars in somebody, and he just plain walks out without giving it a try, I think I have a right to be irritated, don't you, Morg? What I mean to say is, if you don't think I have a right to be annoyed, please tell me."

Al Vance, the private detective, smiled faintly; but Morgan was becoming increasingly nervous, and Clem's calm, polite voice did nothing to soothe him. Clem was not a calm man, and Morgan could feel the seething fury behind the big man's words. He made an aimless, helpless gesture with his plump hand.

"Listen to me, Clem," he pleaded, "just listen to me for a minute, please. This isn't the first time Sonny walked out. He did it twice before."

"Well, that changes everything—doesn't it? As long as it's only a personal idiosyncrasy, we can forgive him, can't we?"

"Just give me a minute, will you, Clem? Please? I didn't find out till too late that Sonny was a periodic lush. But this last time is something different. You tell him, Al."

Morgan sank back into the sofa cushions and shakily pulled the handkerchief from his breast pocket. He had dreaded this. He had dreaded this from the minute Sonny walked out. He had dreaded it, he admitted to himself, from the minute Clem Lasher had invested the thousand dollars in the kid. Clem wasn't a mob man or anything like that, but there was a wild violent streak in him, and you didn't want to be around when it erupted. He had gained a momentary respite, however, by passing the buck to Al Vance.

Clem turned on the piano, struck three harsh chords, and then brought his fists crashingly down on the keys. He jumped up and strode across the room to the cellarette. He clenched the neck of the Scotch bottle and stood staring down at nothing.

Every day, every day, every day he had been losing, for a month now, and the bankroll was showing signs of wear and tear, but that was all right. When you had a bad streak, you had to ride it out. You couldn't go off and sit in the park and wait for your luck to come back. You had to sweat, but you had to take it. You had to take it when you had three of a kind and the two pairs across the table turned up a third ace for the full house. Time and time and time again.

You had to take it, or the next thing you knew you'd be betting with scared money, and when you started counting your chips that way, your nerve was gone, and when that was gone you might just as well forget there's such a game as stud, and make up your mind that without your nerve you're only a half a man for the rest of your life.

But this Sonny Lind, this was something you could do something about. This was something you had to do something about. If you took this lying down, you were finished. When you put a thousand dollars in somebody and got him booked into the Aztec Room, he damn well opened in the Aztec Room on schedule or you knew the reason why, and if you could do something about it, you did it. And if you didn't do it, you got somebody else to shave you from then on, because you wouldn't be able to look yourself in the mirror. Marthe was on the verge of some more smart talk, but when she saw the thin set of his mouth she just murmured: "They can never say I didn't warn them."

Clem impassively filled the glasses and passed them around. He pulled over the piano bench and straddled it. He pointed a long bony finger at Al Vance.

"Give," he said.

Al Vance tasted his Scotch. He was as neat and economical as a cat in his movements. And as self-sufficient.

"I'm not a private detective," he told Clem in a matter-of-fact voice.

"So?"

"So I didn't want you to start off with the idea that I'm Bogart's little brother. I'm just a skip-tracer. I find people. That's all. I find deadbeats who try to run out on their bills. I usually work for the Central Credit Bureau. I just took this on as a favor to Ben Morgan."

"He's not paying you?"

"He's paying me."

"Then it's not a favor."

"It's still a favor. I've let my steady trade go for a week. There's no future in this wildcat stuff. That makes it a favor."

"What do you want me to do, send you a Mothers' Day card?"

"All I want you to do," said Vance calmly, "is to forget for ten minutes that you can lick any son of a bitch in the house and listen to what I have to say."

Clem looked at the compact little man and there was a gleam of admiration in his eyes. "I'll forget," he said. "Now what do you have to say?"

"I traced Sonny Lind to the Lyric Theatre in Hoboken. The Lyric is a burlesque house on Hudson Street. He was singing there. He was half swacked most of the time, but never so drunk that he couldn't go on. They told me that for the week he was there, he was almost as popular as the strippers, and that takes some singing in Hoboken."

"That takes some singing any place, including the Met. So he outshone the strip-girls?"

"Everybody liked him. He was a likeable kid. They called him Joe College because he looked like a college kid with his curly blond hair and baby-blue eyes."

Clem said sourly, "Yeah." He had invested a thousand dollars in the curly blond hair and baby-blue eyes. And the voice. The kid did have a voice. A genuine gold-plated larynx. Baritone. And a delivery as intimate as black lace panties, a real bedroom voice. But he wasn't a pantywaist. There was masculine timbre in that voice. Men liked him. There was no creepiness about Sonny Lind. Sonny was built like a fullback.

"So?" said Clem impatiently. "Why the buildup?"

"The buildup is to show you that everybody I talked to liked the kid. That was Tuesday, three days ago. Monday, Sonny disappeared."

"You mean he went someplace else and you haven't been able to find him!"

Al Vance picked up his drink with his uninjured left hand and took a sip. He looked at Clem over the glass. "Do you want to hear the rest of it?" he asked. "Or have you made up your mind to lick everyone in the house?"

"Keep that up," said Marthe, shortening the garter on her stocking, "and he will."

"Pay no attention to her," said Clem mildly. "She's just a sick friend I sit up with every once in a while, but I have an idea that shortly she will become permanently healthy ... So Sonny disappeared for the second time. You mentioned it as if there were something special about it."

"That's what I don't know." Al Vance did not look quite so self-sufficient; he looked puzzled. "Maybe he walked out, and maybe he was carried out. I don't know. On the Saturday before, after closing, he went to a party given by a Mr. DeGroot. Don't ask me who Mr. DeGroot is, because I don't know and I haven't been able to find out. I was able to pick up a few crumbs, but that's all. I got this from one of the chorus girls. Mr. DeGroot gives parties, apparently for business associates. He gets the girls for the parties from the burlesque house and pays them fifty dollars.

"Now if I were in a court of law, I wouldn't be able to swear to the reason he pays them fifty dollars for going to a party, so let's just leave it that he pays them the money to entertain his guests, possibly by singing and dancing. The chorus girl I talked to had never been at any of Mr. DeGroot's parties. She said virtuously that she wouldn't dream of going to one of his parties because she had *heard* things, but balanced against that was the fact that she was very homely, skinny and wore those things on her chest."

"Falsies," said Marthe. "But how did you know?"

"My sick friend," said Clem, "is getting healthier by the minute. Continue, Mr. Bogart."

The girl shot him a venomous glance and let her housecoat fall open, as if by accident, showing the high lift of her breasts and the smooth curves of her thighs.

"Who's for dancing?" she drawled, stretching her arms over her head. "These deep philosophical discussions bore the pants off me, which, believe it or not, is a hell of a thing."

Ben Morgan gave her a nervous, fascinated glance and looked quickly away—but the commercial part of his mind was rapidly cataloging the places in which he could sell a body like that. What would he call her? The Torso? Yes, that was a good one. The Torso ... But only after Clem Lasher had kicked her out, which would be in a very few hours. The Torso.

Neither Clem nor Al Vance paid any attention to her whatever. Vance went on calmly:

"I admit I blanked out entirely on the DeGroot parties. I couldn't get a thing out of any of the other girls, and DeGroot wasn't in any of the phone directories of Hudson, Essex or Bergen Counties, the three that converge on that area. But I did get this much. On Sunday, Sonny appeared with a terrific hangover, but he wasn't drinking. According to the manager of the Lyric, he was in a very subdued mood. He seemed to have something on his mind. His singing was lousy. He sang gutbucket down there, and when you sing gutbucket you can't have anything on your mind but gutbucket."

Clem said stoically, "Right," but there was another gleam of appreciation for this tight little man in his eyes.

"On Monday," said Vance, "Sonny disappeared. He was entirely sober. He sang in the matinee, but he never showed up for the evening show. Just plain disappeared. No trace, no nothing. Left his wrist watch, wallet and everything else in his dressing room. He never carried his wallet, so that doesn't mean anything, but he always carried his wristwatch in his pocket. Don't ask me why, but he did. He'd won it for basketball or something, and it wasn't like him to leave it behind, from what I hear. But he did."

"I remember that wristwatch. He showed it to me the first time we met. It was a trophy. He was state amateur heavyweight boxing champion," Clem remarked.

"And the first time he and *I* met," said Marthe dreamily, "he made a pass at me. When your back was turned of course, darling. It was right here in this apartment. You went to the bathroom to shave or something, and he made a pass at me. A very *hard* pass. To the day you die, you'll never know what I did about it." She smiled on Ben Morgan, as if she knew the commercial plans he had for her. "I don't know what it was he had, but he was willing to share it; wasn't he?"

Clem gave Al Vance the bare bones of a grin. "My sick friend has entirely recovered, I see. Pay no attention to her. These are merely the joys of complete rejuvenation. DeGroot. That's a Dutch name, isn't it?"

"Yes. I also looked up all the DeGroots in the New York directory. I can tell when some people are lying, but not everybody. DeGroot is a pretty common name, and there are DeGroots scattered from here to California. So which DeGroot gave the parties that included the willing little girls from the Lyric Burlesque Theatre? I don't know. I don't even know if it has anything to do with Sonny Lind's disappearance, or even what Sonny Lind's disappearance has to do with DeGroot. This is just information that I'm passing along to you."

Clem considered this, trying to keep his temper under control. His big, bony hands kept clenching and unclenching. This was something he was going to have to do something about, personally—to keep his self-respect, to keep his nerve.

"You're leading up to something," he said finally, in a controlled voice. "This has all been preliminary. Right?"

"Right."

"All right. Let me have it."

"You see this?" Vance leaned slightly forward and touched the arm in the sling.

"I see it. So?"

"I got a bullet through the shoulder."

"A special bullet?"

"A special bullet. Meant for me, personally. I have nothing to put my finger on, but I'm sure of it. I was staying in Burr's Hotel in Hoboken, and on Tuesday night I got a phone call. The man spoke with an accent, and he sounded as if he had a grudge. He said he'd heard that I was asking around about Sonny Lind—he called him Joe College—and he told me that if I wanted to know the score to come up to the park at the end of River Street at eleven o'clock that night. I was to tie my handkerchief around the top of my right arm so he'd know me. I was to sit on that bench on the little parapet facing the Hudson River."

Clem breathed, "Sucker."

"How was I to know? I know now, and so do you, but would you have known then? I doubt it. I was only looking for a runaway baritone, and who gives a damn about a baritone, except maybe a tenor or a basso. Me, I'm just a skip-tracer. So I went. I tied a handkerchief around my right arm, feeling as silly as hell, and sat on the bench facing the Hudson River. Well, I thought, if Hitchcock can do it in the movies, I can do it in Hoboken."

"But Hitchcock never had anybody shooting at him with anything but a camera. This character shot at me with a gun. He got me from behind, and it knocked me clean off the bench. That was Tuesday, three days ago, and I've been in the Hoboken clink for three whole days, trying to tell a roomful of very tough Hoboken detectives that I didn't crack the skull of the Dutch sailor they found in the bushes behind the bench I was sitting on. And do you know why it was such a tough job convincing them?" Vance asked with a sudden bitterness. "Do you know why?"

Clem said, "Yes."

"You know?" For the first time, Al Vance looked surprised at anything that happened. "Or are you guessing?" His eyes sharpened. "What do you mean, you know?"

"It's obvious."

"It wasn't obvious to me!"

"Think it over."

Al Vance thought it over. He nodded. The girl in the lounge chair laughed shrilly.

"He says, think, and you think, just like that!" she snapped her fingers. "Isn't he wonderful? That's why I'm crazy about him, all the time, twenty-four hours a day."

Ben Morgan, now safely out of it, watched her despairingly. With that body, he could do something with her. Make money for both of them. But if she insisted on needling Clem Lasher, she was going to have a body you wouldn't want to see on a dog. Why did she keep asking for it? Didn't she know Clem Lasher was nitroglycerin, and you had to handle it in specially prepared rubber kegs?

What was she asking for, a hole in the head? My God, a girl like that, with a talent for showing her legs and stuff, she should ask for a hole in the head! Two minutes alone, he could set her straight; but two minutes alone—with Clem Lasher sitting over there, his eyes like atom bombs—was out of the question. A pity. A real pity. A body like that. It was a real commercial body. There was money in it....

Al Vance said, "I was a sucker. But what would you have thought in my place?"

Clem shook his head. "I wouldn't have been in your place. If he called from a place from which he couldn't talk, he wouldn't have called from there. Too dangerous."

Al Vance hesitated, thought it over, and then said, "Right."

"Very well. So he said he would meet you at eleven that night. I gather that there was an interim of several hours. So why couldn't he have waited an hour, or two hours, before he called you, so that he could call you from a place that was safe? He could have done that very easily. And if he could have called you later, he could have given you all the information over the phone without all that abracadabra about handkerchiefs around your left arm and benches facing the Hudson River and parapets, and all the rest of it. That's the reason I said you were a sucker. When you consider how private a public phone booth really is ... Unless he asked for money. Did he ask for money?"

Al Vance said ruefully, "No, he didn't ask for money. But I thought—" He made a sharp gesture with his left hand. "Hell, Lasher, I was only looking for a squirt of a baritone on a toot, not a murderer, and with your permission, dear old pal," he showed anger for the first time, "I'm bowing out of this shenanigan. I've been shot through the shoulder, and I've had a rough time with the Hoboken cops for the past three days. I'm tired. I came up here tonight only because I wanted to help Ben Morgan. I don't like being shot at, and still less do I like being hit when I'm shot at, and still less than that do I like *you* after I've been shot!

You're a—"

Clem said, "Al—"

"Well?"

"You're hysterical."

Al Vance looked down at his shaking hands, at his empty glass, raised his head and gave Clem a cold grin. "I'm hysterical," he admitted. "I'm not a private detective, I'm not Bogart, but I've been shot and I don't like it. I've got a wife and two children, and they won't like that I've been shot, especially my wife. If I'm hysterical, I've got a good reason. I'm not accustomed to this. Most of the people I skip-trace don't shoot at me. They curse me and try to throw me down the stairs, but they don't shoot at me. There's something too damned final about a gun to suit me, so as I said before, I'm bowing out of this shenanigan, and if you and Ben Morgan want to carry it on, that's your business. Me, I'm going home to my wife!"

Clem said, "What was that character's name—DeGroot?"

"DeGroot," Vance said.

"And the manager of the Lyric Burlesque?"

Vance thought for a moment. "McNulty," he said.

"And McNulty likes gutbucket?"

"McNulty?"

"Yes, McNulty! He hired Sonny Lind, didn't he? And Sonny Lind sang gutbucket, didn't he? So McNulty must like gutbucket or he wouldn't have hired Sonny Lind. If you know of any reason why McNulty should have hired Sonny Lind without liking gutbucket, let me know before I start sticking out my neck!"

Al Vance looked at Clem with a new respect. According to Ben Morgan, Clem Lasher was merely the angel who had put up the thousand to get Sonny Lind going. But angels, even if they were explosive, only squawked to their lawyers. Here was a character who was going to stick his own neck out! It didn't add up, not in Al Vance's reckoning of Ben Morgan's clients. Clem Lasher didn't seem to fit into that niche.

Al Vance touched his sling significantly. "Before you start sticking your neck out," he said pointedly, "think this one over. Two inches to the left and it would have been the back of my skull. I have an idea they were only warning me to keep away, only warning me to—"

Clem's hand lashed out and swept the Scotch bottle and the glasses from the cocktail table that stood in front of the sofa on which the two men were sitting. He glowered at them, clenching his big hands.

"A warning!" he said heavily. "A warning. They tried to frame you for a murder and you call it a warning! If they hung you by the neck, I suppose you'd call that a warning, too! Or blasted your head off with a double-barreled shotgun, or wound you up with piano wire and sank you in the Hudson River. My God, how much of a warning do you need, or how are you going to interpret it? A warning to keep away! I thought you were smarter than that. That wasn't any warning, you damned fool! They meant business!"

Ben Morgan turned the color of veal fat, and made strangled, ineffectual noises in his throat. Al Vance held his wounded shoulder with his good hand, as if to reassure himself that he was still alive.

And before them were Clem Lasher's blazing green eyes. Clem leaned forward, his bony hands knuckled on his knees.

"I don't give a damn who they are. There's only one thing that matters to me. Two things. I sank a thousand bucks into this kid, and I gave my word to Kraus that he'd open in the Aztec Room a week from today. He's going to open in the Aztec Room one week from today, if it kills me!"

CHAPTER II

After Ben Morgan and Al Vance had gone, Clem stood at the hall door snipping pieces from his thumbnail with his teeth. His eyes were remote and cold, veiled with a kind of thoughtful blankness, the expression they habitually took when he sat down to a session of stud. His shoulders were hunched. He looked distastefully at the thumbnail he had been gnawing and shoved his hand into his pocket. A scowl deepened on his wide, thin mouth and he stared speculatively at the panel of the closed door.

He had a feeling that he had rushed Al Vance out of the apartment just a little too fast. There were things that had been left unsaid, unprobed. It was his own fault, of course. He had a quick, impatient mind that went leaping far ahead of plodders like Al Vance. He should have sat patiently and dragged every scrap of information possible out of the man.

"The hell with it," he said softly. He turned and walked quickly back through the living room toward his bedroom. Marthe was standing at the cellarette, pouring herself a drink of brandy. He gave her a casual nod as he went through the doorway. Bleakly, she watched him go, and then raised her glass. Her hand was shaking a little. She had gone too far tonight. She knew that. She had needled him just once too often. She drank down her brandy and shuddered as she replaced the glass on the cellarette. So this was the way it ended, not with fire and smoke, but with the impersonal chilliness of a good-by kiss in a railroad station. She walked across the room and stood in the bedroom doorway.

Clem had changed into battered tennis shoes and old blue jeans and was buttoning up a faded Army shirt.

"Going somewhere?" she asked. Her voice was very small.

"Fishing," he said, shoving the tails of the shirt into his jeans. He looked around the room as if making a last-minute inventory.

"Hoboken, Clem?"

He went to his chest of drawers and took out a handkerchief. "Could be." He whistled tunelessly as he gave the room another narrow sweeping glance.

She walked over to the chest of drawers and felt in the back of the drawer he had opened for the handkerchief. She brought up a short-barreled .38 and held it out to him.

"You're taking this, aren't you?"

"Hell, no."

She looked at him with growing wonder. "It could come in handy," she said, "even for Clem Lasher, the Great."

"I don't want it." He went to the chair over which he had folded his slacks and took the wallet from the back pocket. She followed him, still holding the gun.

"Just how tough do you think you are, Clem?" Her voice was incredulous.

"Exactly how tough do you really think you are? They warned Al Vance off with a bullet and he went. You're not the type to leave that early. I know you. Do you think the bullets are going to bounce off you? Do you think you're that tough?"

"Still needling, sweetheart?"

"No, I really want to know. I know you're tough, but I want to know how tough *you* think you are, going against people with guns with nothing but your bare hands. Or do you think the minute you walk into Hoboken they'll say, 'Oh God, here's Clem Lasher; back to the rat holes, boys.' Is that how tough you think you are? You're going to make a better target than Al Vance. You're bigger. And on top of that, your idea of getting things done is to make everybody furious within the first five minutes. I'll say this much for you—you are tougher than Al Vance. It's going to take three or four bullets to get rid of you. Maybe even five or six. You're going to make an awfully homely corpse, Clem."

Clem put two five-dollar bills in his pocket and threw the wallet on the bed. Despite his heavy losses during the past month, the wallet was still well filled.

"The apartment rent has been paid to January first," he said. "If you need any spending money, I think you'll find all you want in the wallet."

"So you're really running out on me."

"Not running, sweetheart—walking."

"You make it awfully easy for a girl to hate you, don't you, Clem?"

He shrugged and walked out of the room. She followed him. He went to the cellarette and took a pint bottle of whisky from the cabinet. He put it into his hip pocket. Marthe stood biting at her full underlip.

Suddenly her eyes flickered crazily and she jerked the gun up and thrust it against his stomach. Her knuckles whitened and her finger tightened on the trigger.

"Now let's find out how tough you are with a bullet in you!" she cried hysterically. "We might as well find out now and save you the trip over to Hoboken."

He looked down at the gun. "So long, sweetheart," he said. He turned his back to her and walked to the hall door.

She hurled the gun after him with a full overhand swing. It struck him between the shoulder blades and fell to the floor. He did not look back.

"Damn you, oh, damn you!" she screamed. "Look! Clem, just look!" She stood facing him with a high, hard lift of her chin. He had glanced back over his shoulder.

"Yes, look at me," she said in an ugly voice. "I used to be yours. But now I'm going to find somebody who hates you as much as I do, and I'm going to him. I'm going to him on the condition that he breaks you, one way or the other. I know you now, Clem Lasher. You're tough only because you're afraid of losing your nerve. That's the one thing you're afraid of. You're not tough; you're just plain scared!"

He nodded. "You could be right," he said thoughtfully, and walked out.

It was a short walk down Broadway to Times Square, where he took the subway to Cortland Street and the Hudson Tubes station. Hoboken was just across the river. He sat in the corner of the car with one leg thrown up on the yellow rattan-covered seat. He thought bleakly about Marthe. She was not the first who had lived with him, but she was a blueprint of all the others—cool, beautiful, insouciant girls. Expensive, but worth it—up to a point. Until they decided they had a proprietary interest. It had always ended in bitterness, hysteria, and jagged, ugly scenes. When they decided they knew all about him, they tried to devour him.

It was as depressing as any pattern repeated and repeated and repeated again, and he had a feeling that a man got the kind of woman he deserved. Except that with Marthe and all the others it had been strictly C.O.D. Clem didn't realize the train had stopped until the conductor plodded through the car and said wearily, "Hoboken, bud. All out. This ain't a hotel."

He walked up the stairs to the street level. There was a slight salty breeze coming in from the Hudson River, damp and a little chilly. The superstructures and booms of two freighters at the dock were gaunt, stiff silhouettes against the glowing New York skyline. Hoboken was asleep, and even the saloons were closed along the dark length of River Street. It was three-fifteen in the morning.

Clem had only a few meager bits of information. Sonny Lind had worked for McNulty, manager of the Lyric Burlesque House. McNulty lived in Burr's Hotel on Hudson Street, liked gutbucket, and his favorite gin mill was the Schiedam House on River Street. Not much to go on, but the swimming pool is always bigger than the springboard.

The old Lyric was just around the corner on Hudson Street, a few minutes' walk from the subway station. It had been a young theatre fifty years ago, but now the marquee that overhung the sidewalk had such a tired look that passersby often cast apprehensive glances at it. The title of the present show was *Guys and Gals*. The shadow boxes on either side of the doorway were plastered with publicity stills of girls as nude as the law allowed, and judging from the pictures the law was pretty broad-minded in Hoboken.

The star of the show was a plump Chinese girl named Soo Loo, and her picture left no mystery about her charms. Another featured specialty was a girl named So-So Dolan, who had a very wholesome grin on a pug-nosed Irish face. The rest of the girls were average showgirl types, a little too blond in the hair and a little too hard in the eyes and mouth.

So this was where DeGroot enlisted the girls for his parties. The photographs were the tip-off of the kind of parties they were. It was a cinch that nobody sat around sipping dry sherry, and if anybody held anything at these parties, it certainly wasn't a conversation.

Well, there it was. There was part of the answer on DeGroot. You gave rough parties for rough people. But what would that have to do with Sonny?

Clem scowled at the pictures and walked across the doorway to the other shadow box. His eyes widened. There was a picture of Sonny Lind. The name under the picture was Joey Smith, but it was Sonny Lind, all right. You could never mistake that All-American grin. Clem looked closer at the photograph. The eyes were very heavy-lidded in the picture and the grin was sloppy around the edges.

"Plotzed," muttered Clem disgustedly. Sonny Lind was advertised as the hottest scat singer in the country, part of the current show, *Guys and Gals*. Clem stepped back to look at the marquee again. The current show was *Guys and Gals*, and it would play through the following Saturday. If Sonny was in the show, he certainly couldn't have disappeared. How much can you disappear on a stage unless you're Houdini? Somebody was giving somebody the business.

Clem walked back to First Street, where he had seen the dismal lights of an all-night lunchroom across the way from the subway station. The counterman was leaning against the cash register yawning over a copy of the *Hudson Observer*. Two cops were hunched on stools gnawing at a pair of doughnuts and noisily slurping hot coffee. They gave Clem a disinterested cops' stare when he walked in, measuring him for a brief moment, as if filing his description away in their minds for future reference.

Clem said, "Coffee and a minute steak on a bun," to the counterman, and walked to the phone booth in the rear. He did not really want the steak, but it was an expensive item and his ordering it would tell the cops that he wasn't a bum. It would save questions and maybe trouble. Hoboken was a riverfront town, and in the small hours of the morning the cops were rougher on stray characters.

Clem called Burr's Hotel and crisply told the mumbling clerk that he wanted to talk to Mr. McNulty. He could hear the clerk yawn into the phone.

"Call him in the morning, mister, or leave a message. I can't wake him up at this hour."

"You can't wake him up at this hour," Clem mimicked him. "All right. I'll come down there and wake him up myself. Is that what you want? This is important. Put him on or I'll come down there and take care of it personally."

There was a silence and then Clem heard the buzzing ring of the house phone. Within a few minutes a sleepy voice came on.

"For God's sake," it said, "what now?"

"You McNulty?" Clem deliberately slurred his words.

"Yes, I'm McNulty, but there are times I wished I wasn't. Who's this?"

"Lemme ask you a question, Mr. McNulty. I just wanna ask you one question. You ever hear of Art Tatum, Mr. McNulty?"

"What is this, a rib?"

"No sir. Never rib when I'm talking about Art Tatum. Greatest piano player in the whole world, except me. Gutbucket piano, that's me. Best gutbucket piano you ever heard. You wanna hear the best gutbucket piano you ever heard? That's me. Want a job. Broke. I'll play you the best gutchbucket ... You come to the Schiedam House t'morrow. You hear what I'm saying? You come to the Schiedam House t'morrow and you'll hear the best buck bucket piano you ever heard. Now wait a minute, I wanna tell you something ..."

McNulty said disgustedly, "Ah, hell!" and hung up.

Clem was grinning a little when he walked back to the counter for his coffee and minute steak on a bun. McNulty was sore now, but musicians were supposed to be nuts. It was a trademark. McNulty would be in the Schiedam House when it opened the next day. This was a better way to get his attention than walking into the Lyric cold sober and asking for a job.

Clem straddled his stool and bit into his minute steak on a bun. He had expected a piece of fried armor plate, but it was good juicy beef. Both cops were watching him now.

One of them finally said, "Work around here, Red?" A flat suspicious question.

Clem nodded. "Lyric Burlesque. Just talked to McNulty on the phone. Go to work tomorrow. Hot piano. Taking Joey Smith's place."

The cops relaxed, looked at each other and winked, and one of them said, "Some guys have all the luck. What a way to make a living. Backstage with all them dames running around. How'd you like working in the burlesque, Al?" he asked the counterman.

The counterman said sourly, "I got a wife and kids."

The cop made a few good-naturedly obscene remarks about wives and kids, then asked casually, "Where you staying, Red?"

Just as casually, Clem said, "I was thinking of Burr's Hotel. Is it okay or is it a crumb trap?"

"It's okay, but don't try bringing any dames up to your room. They're fussy."

Both cops slid back off their stools, wiped their mouths with the flat of their hands, buttoned their tunics, yawned and straightened their caps. One of them patted Clem on the shoulder.

"Good luck, Red," he said. "But if we hear of any six-foot-two redheads with green eyes and an S-shaped scar on his right thumb holding up Al here for the cash in the till after we leave, we'll know just who to look for." He went, "Haw, haw!" but there was no humor in his flat gray eyes.

The pair of them marched out and a few seconds later the prowl car purred away from the curb like a stalking leopard. Clem looked at the counterman.

"What gives around here?" he asked. "They did everything but frisk me. Are they on the mayor's welcoming committee or something?"

"Or something," said the counterman. "They're on the prod. You're lucky they didn't take you down to headquarters just for the hell of it. They pulled two characters out of here at eight tonight—just for the hell of it."

"How come?"

"Another killing down in Hudson Park. It's getting to be a regular cemetery down there. Three days ago a Dutch sailor was knocked off, and tonight around seven another one was knocked off. This place is getting to be worse than it was during prohibition when all the Jersey beer came out of Hoboken. I worked in a deadfall on River Street in those days and believe me, we had fresh meat to cart off to the morgue. I got a funny feeling it's starting all over again."

Clem felt a familiar anticipatory tingle down his spine, that tingle that came when he had a queen in the hole, an ace-king-jack combo showing on the board and the last card about to be dealt with a top-heavy pot in the middle of the table.

"I don't get it," he said carefully. "Prohibition's long gone. You can even buy liquor in the drugstores these days. What's there to fight about?"

"Well, here's the way I figure it," the counterman spread his elbows on the marble top and lowered his voice confidentially. "You know what the taxes are on liquor? Eighty per cent, ninety per cent, and in some cases a hundred per cent, two and three hundred per cent. This is a shipping town, see. The freighters come in from South America. Okay.

"The customs go over them, but you know what a boat is. There are the big holds and the little holds and there are bulkheads and all that stuff. A captain or a chief mate that knows his stuff can hide an elephant in one of them boats and you'd never know unless it had pups.

"Now here's what I think, and here's what I know, too. Somebody's been bringing in tax-free liquor. South American rum, Spanish cognac, Scotch. Get the picture, Red? Without taxes on a case of cognac, you can clear a hundred bucks net on a case. That's big business. So who moves in? The musclemen, the hotrods, the boys with the organization. The next thing you know we're carting the fresh meat to the morgue again every day. Now I ask you, does that add up or don't it?"

Clem looked toward the door through which the two cops had marched. He remembered their flat, suspicious eyes—but he still couldn't buy this smuggled liquor idea. It took a lonely stretch like the Florida keys to bring in liquor in any paying quantity. The best you could do here in Hoboken, with all the official supervision, would be a few cases here and there. No, it didn't add up. There was something else, something not so bulky; something that could be handled much more easily.

But there was an organization working, all right. It had all the earmarks. Two killings within three days. It could be a coincidence, but then there was the shooting of Al Vance. He had only been winged, but it was still part of the setup.

The counterman dropped his voice another notch and said, "And you can't tell me, Red, that the cops don't know what's going on. I know cops.

I bet you they even know who knocked off that fresh meat up in Hudson Park. I'll lay money on that. But they have to make a show for the papers and they pull in a few bindlestiffs, show them the goldfish bowl down headquarters to schmooze the voting public and all the time they're being paid off by the boys with the organization.

"To tell you the truth, Red, I wouldn't of laid one to ten fifteen minutes ago that you wasn't on your way to the goldfish bowl. That short cop—Catlin, the one built like a billboard—he likes nothing better than sharpening his knuckles on somebody's noggin, some poor bird like those two they dragged out of here tonight. Know what I mean?"

Clem said slowly, "Yeah." The short, wide cop had had that look.

"Now just between you me and the lamppost," said the counterman, "if you don't have that job with the Lyric tomorrow, I'll give you a hunk of advice. Blow. Get out of here. Go to Jersey City or Weehawken, or someplace, but don't hang around Hoboken, because the first thing in the morning they're going to be checking with McNulty, and unless you like a mess of cops shoving their knuckles in your snoot, you'll blow. You don't have that job yet, do you? It don't make no difference to me, but when Catlin ast you that question, I could tell you didn't have no job with the Lyric. Maybe you braced McNulty and all that, and maybe you'll get the job tomorrow, but you ain't got it now. Either sew up that job first thing tomorrow with McNulty, or get the hell out of here while you still have two legs to walk on."

Clem finished the last of his coffee and stepped back from his stool. He wiped his mouth with a paper napkin.

"You ought to play poker, Al," he said.

"I did, Red. And that's why I'm a short order cook with a wife and kids today. Now don't get me wrong, kid. I like cops when they're people; but when cops start to act like cops, brother, you can have them. If you're short, I can let you have a buck or two to make Weehawken."

Clem laid one of his two fives on the counter and said, "Thanks. I'll keep it in mind."

He scooped up the change, knowing better than to leave a tip on the counter and walked out saying, "See you, Al."

Al said morosely, "Blow, kid, blow. There's nothing here for you but trouble. You got a trouble-face, and a face is the one thing you can't fool me on. You got a trouble-face."

CHAPTER III

Clem had a feeling when he walked out of the lunchroom, that the prowl car was lurking just around the corner, waiting to see where he would go and what he would do. He walked to River Street and turned north. The prowl car was not around that corner, and he realized that the corners were all in his mind, the result of the counterman's dark prophecies. But he did not try to fool himself that the two cops had forgotten him. Catlin, especially, had not looked like a cop who forgot very easily. Perhaps even now Catlin was checking up with McNulty in Burr's Hotel.

Thank God he had called McNulty, and thank God he could play the piano. There was that much if the prowl car came charging back and picked him up. He could always play the piano for them—if they didn't break his arms first.

River Street was dark and brooding. On the east side of the street was the high fence that guarded the warehouses of the steamship companies. It was a silent street of many saloons, old houses, and drunks sleeping in the shadowed doorways. A sheet of newspaper performed a slow, weird dance in the middle of the street as a puff of breeze from the river stirred it. There was no moon.

Clem strode northward. It was chilly and he walked with his hands in his pockets and his shoulders hunched. His mind was milling fiercely over the memory of that photograph of Sonny Lind in the shadow box beside the door of the burlesque house, and the first time his name was called he did not hear it. The second time it was called, he started and whirled. A man was running awkwardly toward him. It was Vance, holding his wounded arm tight to his body as he ran.

"I got something I want to tell you, Lasher," he panted.

Clem grasped him by the coat front. "And there's something I want to ask you," he interrupted, scowling. "I was just over at the Lyric. How come they're advertising Sonny Lind in the current show? His picture's up on the board."

"I know, I know. He was in the show when it opened, and they didn't change the billing when he skipped. That's all."

"That had better be all. How did you know I was over here in Hoboken?"

"I went back to your apartment. Your wife—"

"She isn't my wife."

Vance gave him a sharp glance. "She led me to believe—"

"I don't care what she led you to believe. She's not my wife. How did she lead you to believe?"

"She called you her husband and said you'd left right after we did and that you were going to call her back in about an hour and I could give her the message."

"So you gave her the message, I suppose," said Clem with thin sarcasm. "Anything else you gave her? Your wallet maybe? Or didn't she ask for it?"

Vance turned on his heel and started to walk away. Clem caught him by the left arm.

"Sorry—sorry," he growled. "But she milked you, that's what."

"Go to hell."

"I said I'm sorry, didn't I? I'll send you a singing telegram if you want, or would you rather sit in my lap?"

Vance jerked his arm from Clem's grasp, but he didn't walk away. "Well," he said finally, "for you, I suppose, that was a pretty handsome apology."

"Okay. I apologized, so let's forget it. What'd you tell Marthe? Anything important?"

"I told her I thought I had a line on De Groot."

"Why didn't you tell me when you were in the apartment the first time, damn it?"

"You practically kicked us out, that's why," said Vance coldly. "And it was only a hunch, anyway. It was something I got from one of the chorus girls at the Lyric, and after we left you I remembered it. I had to look it up to be sure."

"And you told it all to Marthe."

"Twice. She made me repeat it."

"I'll bet. And she probably wrote it down, too."

"She did."

Clem saw the stubborn set of Vance's chin and he said impatiently, "Okay, okay, nobody's blaming you, but you'd better let me have it before any more of my wives turn up."

"You're a daisy, Lasher, a real daisy. Here—" he took something from his vest pocket—"the darling wedding ring."

Clem reached for it and then stiffened. "Hold it!" he whispered.

A car had drifted up River Street and stopped at the corner of Second, a block back. A man darted from a doorway and ran to the car. He stopped for a moment at the driver's window, pointed up the street toward Clem and Vance, and then dived into the back seat. The car came rushing toward them with a surge of speed.

Clem yelled "Get down!" and dived for the sidewalk, trying to pull Vance after him. But he had grasped Vance's wounded arm, and the man jumped back with a cry of pain. At the very last moment he became aware of the speeding car. He took a panicky step and then flung up his left arm as if to protect his face.

A shotgun roared twice as the car swept by. There was a third blast and a crash as the slugs tore through the plate glass window of the tavern behind Clem. The car tore up the street to Fourth and disappeared around the corner with a scream of tires.

Clem cried "Vance!" and scrambled to his hands and knees.

Ten feet away, Vance was lying on his back. Clem leaped to his feet, took three steps and turned away, sickened. Vance had taken two loads of buckshot in the face and chest. Nobody, not even the undertaker, was ever going to be able to do anything for Vance now.

And then the deathly silence was pierced by the scream of a police siren. Clem threw up his head. The sound came from the south of town. He gave Vance a last glance and sprinted the block to Hudson Park. He ran in the shadows of the trees, keeping off the paths. He looked back over his shoulder and saw the sweeping headlights of the police car turn into the curb where Vance lay. A few moments later another prowl car turned into River Street from Third.

Clem cut diagonally through the park toward Hudson Street, running as hard he could. As he passed a low-hanging rhododendron bush, he tripped over something and sprawled headlong, rolling over and over. He caught a confused glimpse of someone leaping at him, arm upraised. He rolled again and lashed out with his feet. His right foot connected solidly and there was an agonized grunt. The man fell and curled, twitching, holding his groin with both hands.

Clem jumped up and ran on, swearing because he could not afford the time to see who his assailant had been. It took him over half an hour to reach the north end of Washington Street, keeping in the shadows, while the police cars rolled slowly by, the cops flashing their lights in every doorway. There was an open diner near the bus station at the head of Washington Street, and Clem slipped into it. If he were going to be picked up, it would be better to be picked up there instead of ducking around on the open streets.

A stout, gray-haired woman sat on a high stool at the cash register reading a copy of *Exciting Love* magazine. She took off her glasses and gave Clem a sleepy smile. On the radio Guy Lombardo and the Royal Canadians were playing "Because". Clem ordered a cup of coffee and a hamburger.

At least, he thought grimly, I'm being well fed tonight. But the hamburger gave him an excuse to hang around the diner longer. If necessary, he'd even eat a piece of pie.

As the woman turned tiredly away to flatten the hamburger on the grill, Clem took from his pocket the ring that Vance had thrust into his hand just before the shotgun blasts.

He held it on the palm of his right hand and scowled at it. It was a wedding ring, all right. A darling wedding ring, Vance had called it. Darling! Clem gave his head a little shake. Vance didn't talk like that. Maybe he had misunderstood. Maybe Vance had said Darline's wedding ring. Darline, the dame he had gotten it from. That would be more like it.

But there was something wrong with that, too. It wasn't Darline's wedding ring. It was Helen's. What Clem had first taken for a flowered engraving around the outside of the band was actually the girl's name. Helen.

That was a funny way to put a name on a wedding ring, around the outside. Most wedding rings had the name or initials inside—Bill to Mary, or WS to MG, 1955. There was nothing on the inside of the ring but 14-k. A cheap ring. He examined the ring more closely. It said Helen, all right, and the rest of the designs were shallowly engraved flowers. A hell of a wedding ring that was, with no husband's name. Maybe she didn't have a husband.

Anyway, there was the ring, and through it Vance had gotten a line on DeGroot. Probably through Helen, the chorus girl at the Lyric.

The woman served his hamburger and cocked her head at the sound of the police siren that had risen again.

"The Mickey Mice are having a busy night," she said.

"The what?"

"The Mickey Mice. The Cops. That's what we call them. Mickey Mice."

"What's going on?" Clem asked casually. "A riot or something?"

The woman answered just a little peevishly. "I don't know. Sometimes I think they play with them sireen things just to hear them squeal. Anything else? A piece of pie, a doughnut?"

"No thanks. How come you call them Mickey Mice?"

The woman shrugged. "I don't know. Maybe because sometimes they think they're so funny."

She plodded back to her stool at the end of the counter, back to her dream world between the covers of the *Exciting Love* magazine. She put on her glasses and very shortly a rapt expression flowed over her tired face like balm.

Clem finished his hamburger as slowly as he could. He could still hear the police cars working the town like bird dogs. He looked down at the woman. She finished her story. She closed the magazine, smoothed the cover with her hand, and put it carefully under the counter.

"Anything else now?" she asked him.

"Yeah," he said. "Is there a Salvation Army or something around here where I could bed down for the rest of the night?"

"What's the matter? Broke?"

He laid forty cents on the counter, just enough to pay for his hamburger and coffee. With his left hand, he worked a hole in his pocket, and then turned the pocket inside out for her to see the hole.

"That's the pocket I picked to put nine bucks in," he said.

Her eyes measured him and then turned to the open window, through which came the keening of the questing sirens. She tilted her chin toward the door behind the counter.

"There's an army cot back there in the storeroom where the cook sometimes flops when he's too soused to go home and face his wife. You're welcome to it."

Clem said gravely, "Thank you, miss."

She watched him with a kind of yearning approval as he ducked his bright red head to go through the low doorway. She cleared off the dishes, wiped the counter with a damp cloth and went back to her stool. This time she did not reach for her magazine.

The storeroom was a seven-foot cubbyhole just off the kitchen. Clem stretched out on the cot. He was tired, but sIeepless. Whenever he closed his eyes he could see that car stop again at the corner of Second Street, the man dart from the doorway and point up the street at him and Vance; and then the other man in the park at the north end of River Street.

That was organization, plugging River Street at both ends while they waited for the car and killers to show up. But he couldn't believe in that counterman's theory of liquor-running—even if you could clear a hundred bucks on a case of Spanish cognac, which he doubted. Liquor was too bulky to bring into a busy port like Hoboken. But what the hell were they bringing in? It had to be something big to support an organization.

He heard a masculine voice say noisily, "Hi-ya, lover girl," and he was out of the cot in a flash with his eye to the cracked storeroom door. He could not see much, but he caught a glimpse of blue cloth and brass buttons as the two policemen entered the diner.

The woman did not answer. The policeman laughed.

"We shouldn't of disturbed her, Joe. She hates to be disturbed when she's thinking about love. You should see some of the stuff she reads. *Exciting Love, True Love, Hot Love.* You wouldn't think it to look at her,

Joe, but she's a real lover girl."

The woman said woodenly, "In for the usual freeload, boys?"

"Uh-uh. Not tonight, lover girl. We're looking for a character. Have a character in here during the last hour or so?"

"What's he look like?"

"No description."

"What'd he do?"

"That's what we want to ask him."

"Well, as long as you don't know what he looks like and don't know what he did, I'll grab the next character that comes in and you can take him down to headquarters. You don't want a big one, do you? The little ones are easier to bounce off the walls down there."

"Come on, come on, sister, we're not kidding around. Anybody been in here during the last hour? If so, we want a description."

"Nobody's been here."

"Okay. I hope we never find out different, lover girl. Let's go, Joe."

Clem caught another glimpse of them as they walked to the door, and a few moments later he heard the *whirrr* of the prowl car starter.

The woman came within the range of his vision and he saw her lean on the counter. For a long while she stood there, unmoving, and then she turned and came heavily through the doorway.

When she opened the door to the storeroom, he was sitting on the edge of the cot, smoking a cigarette. He looked up at her. She was bulky, black and featureless, a silhouette against the light from the outer room.

"The cops were just here," she said tonelessly.

"I heard them."

"They were looking for you."

"I know."

She was silent for a moment and then said more warmly, "I had a feeling you wouldn't lie about it. Just as I had a feeling they were after you when you first walked in. There was dirt on your face and you were breathing like you'd been running. Did you shoot that fellow like they said on the radio?"

"No, but I was with him when it happened. They came down the street in a car and shot him as they passed."

"I don't want to know about it!" she interrupted hurriedly. "I don't want to know nothing. I didn't think you did it when I heard it on the radio. You're like my first husband. He wouldn't shoot you or stick a knife in you. If he wanted to beat you up, he wouldn't do it on a dark street. He wasn't very lovable, but I was crazy about him. He didn't look like you, but you're two of a kind. But you didn't have anything to do with it. You couldn't have, because you were sitting out there at the counter eating a hamburger when we heard the three shots. You can sleep here till you wake up. I'll leave word. I own half the place. You'll find a razor and comb on the shelf over the sink. Now you'd better get some sleep. And don't tell me nothing about nothing, cause I've done enough lying as it is. Get some sleep."

She went out and closed the door. Clem brooded down at the cigarette that was burning away between his fingers. Nobody had ever stuck out his neck to help him before, not this way. They had lent him money, sure, but they always expected it to be paid back. This woman didn't expect anything.

After a long time he fell asleep, but the kind of sleep that left him unrefreshed and tired when he awakened. The sun was on his face through the small window, and there was the sound of rattling pots and cutlery from the kitchen. He went to the small sink and washed, shaved, and combed his hair. He stared into the cracked mirror on the wall. His face looked gaunt and grim and there were shadows beneath his eyes, and when he grinned it was a wolf's grin. The savage bones were more pronounced in his hard jaw.

When he walked out of the cubby hole a thin man in a soiled chef's cap looked up from the gas range where he was cooking vegetables. He gave Clem a mild smile.

"Have a good snooze?" he asked. "Belle said to give you breakfast."

"Thanks, but I'm not hungry. What time is it?"

"About ten-thirty."

"Ten-thirty! I've got to beat it. Tell Belle thanks for me, will you?"

"She didn't do it for thanks, but I'll tell her. Sure you don't want breakfast? I got a nice ham slice."

"Thanks, but I have to see a man about a job, and I'm late."

"Luck."

He took a bus down Washington Street to Third and walked over to River Street. This was very close to the spot where Vance had been shot and he avoided looking at it. He turned right.

The Schiedam House was halfway down the block. A dapper little man with a clever simian face was standing at the bar drinking Holland gin from a cocktail glass. Clem had a hunch that he was either a racetrack character or McNulty, manager of the Lyric Burlesque.

Ignoring the sharp glance he got when he walked in. Clem shuffled to the bar and said thickly, "Gimme a shot."

He spread a dollar bill on the bar. He had two shots and the dollar bill disappeared. He looked around and saw the piano in an alcove at the rear of the room. He went over to it and sat down on the rickety stool.

His fingers trembled slightly as he reached for the keys. He stared at them. They were actually shaking. The tremor was visible. He was nervous. For the first time since God knew when, he was asking somebody for something; nervous because McNulty could give—or withhold—this lousy two-bit job. A gust of anger swept through him, and he plunged his hands at the white and black maw of the keyboard. The buzzing silence of the barroom was rocked under the assault of furious rhythm that beat from the piano. After he finished, he sat scowling down at his hands.

A voice at his elbow said dryly, "You're not better than Tatum. You're just louder."

Clem looked up in the face of McNulty. "Take it or leave it," he snarled.

McNulty's jaw dropped. He flushed, but instead of answering Clem, he turned to the barkeep.

"What do you think?" he asked. "This comedian calls me up in the middle of the night, wants a job, so I come down here to listen, then he tells me to take it or leave it. Now, honest, what kind of way is that?" he complained.

The barkeep chuckled. "If you give him the job, you better get him an armor-plated piano. Do that, Mac, and I'll come down to your lousy theatre just to see him tear it apart with his bare hands. He sure gives it hell, doesn't he?" There was a tinge of admiration in his voice.

McNulty turned back to Clem. "You sure do," he said. He was grinning.

Clem stood up abruptly. "Go to hell," he said, and strode toward the door.

McNulty ran after him and plucked at his sleeve. "Ah, now, wait a minute, bucko," he said. "If it'll make you feel any better, you got something. Don't ask me what, because I don't think there's a name for it, but you got it. The nearest I can come is, if the Dempsey-Firpo fight had been set to music, that'd be it."

Clem stopped. "Yes or no?" he demanded.

"I dunno, I dunno. I'm trying to make up my mind, so wait a minute, will you? But I'm telling you, bucko, you're a risk. When you really got into that piano, you made me feel like starting a riot. Not sore, mind you, just—well, violent. And me. I'm a peaceable guy. I'm afraid to think what'll happen when you start playing for a houseful of the kind of goons that come to see a strip act. Okay, okay, you're hired. Maybe they'll wreck the joint and I can collect the insurance. Now let's get back to the theatre and see where we can fit you."

As they left the Schiedam House Clem demanded, "What happened to that singer you had, that guy you called Joey Smith?"

McNulty grimaced with sour humor. "Where I come from," he said, "Joey Smith is a dirty word."

"Cut it out, cut it out. I asked a question. What happened to him?"

Trotting at his side, McNulty looked up at Clem with amazement. He said finally, "You do everything just the way you play the piano, don't you? Nothing happened to Joey Smith as far as I know. He borrowed dough from everybody in the theatre—he was into me for two hundred—and then took a powder. He was certainly a guy that was out for number one first, last, and always. You know him or something? He put the bite on you, too?"

Clem said shortly, "Never heard of him."

McNulty opened his mouth to retort, then closed it. He made a small gesture with his hands. It sure took all kinds to make a world. This one was a daisy, all right.

There was a black sedan parked in front of the theatre. The rear door hung open, and two men lounged against the front fender. One was thin and wore a light raincoat. His right hand was sunk in the pocket of his coat and was bulkier than a hand ought to be. The other man was a monolith of muscle. He fed a stick of gum into his mouth and his massive jaws moved stolidly.

As Clem and McNulty came around the corner to Hudson Street, the thin man leaned an eighth of an inch closer to his bulky companion and whispered liplessly.

The big man rubbed the palms of his hands down his thighs. He pushed himself away from the car and started diagonally across the sidewalk toward Clem and McNulty. He walked with his big head thrust forward, his eyes on the spot behind Clem's right ear where he would swing in with a looping left. He was as inconspicuous in bulk and intent as a Sherman tank on that drowsy sidewalk.

Clem saw him coming and stopped, shoving McNulty violently away from his side. The big man growled and, being single-minded, leaped in swinging a long left for that spot behind Clem's ear. Clem ducked and the curved arm scythed harmlessly over his head. He straightened and hit the man on the chin as hard as he could. The big man staggered back two steps, his arms flailing for balance. Clem hit him in the stomach with a hooking left, and then smashed up with his right fist as the man bent double, straightening him again. He seized him by the coat front and rushed him across the sidewalk toward the car where the thin one, swearing thinly, tugged at the gun in his pocket.

The gun whipped out and the man took a sideward step, yelling, "Hold it, Lasher!"

But he had waited too long, had been too confident, had relied too much on the muscles of his companion. The gun had barely cleared his pocket when he was smashed against the side of the car by the body of the thug. He uttered a bleating cry of pain as Clem jerked the heavy man away and slammed him back again. The gun clattered to the sidewalk, and Clem kicked it into the gutter. He reached around the big man and hit the thin one a glancing blow on the side of the head; but he had had to release the heavy man who, almost unconscious, sagged against Clem, clinching with the convulsive strength of an instinctive fighter.

The thin one fell to his knees, scrambled away from the car on all fours, and then bolted up the street, disappearing around the corner before Clem could untangle himself from the heavy man's frantic grasp. Clem hooked his fingers in the man's nostrils, pulled back his head and chopped him across the jaw. With an exhalation that was almost a sigh of relief, the big man slumped to the sidewalk and lay motionless.

Clem ran to the corner. There was no one in sight except two boys about ten years old pitching pennies to a crack in the sidewalk. He could see them eying him warily as he strode up.

"Which way'd he go?" he demanded.

The boys looked up at him with a bland shrewdness that was beyond their years, measuring him, classifying him. But there was something cowed about them, too.

One of them said brightly, "You lookin' for somebody, mister?"

And in the same spurious tone, the other piped, "A guy or a dame, mister?"

They backed away from Clem, standing separated, ready to dart left and right with the cunning of experienced street kids. They were as alert as little wild animals, young foxes of the alleys and backyards.

Clem dug into his pocket and brought out two crumpled dollar bills. "A buck apiece," he said. "Which way'd he go?"

The boys looked at each, other and mutely shook their heads.

"I'm not a cop," said Clem. "Do I look like a cop?"

"But you ain't from around here," said the farthest kid defiantly.

That was it. He was an outsider, a foreigner. He wasn't a local. It was a tip-off, all the same. The man he had chased was a Hoboken hood, and the kids knew him; or had recognized him. They wouldn't squeal to an outsider. But time had passed, and now it was too late. He balled the two bills and flipped them to the kids.

"If you were my kids," he said heavily, "I'd make you join the Boy Scouts and learn something."

He turned and strode back up the street, but he could not resist a glance over his shoulder. The kids thumbed their noses at him and jeered. "Aaaah, go soak your head, Brick-top!"

"Lookit the hair on him. His brain is rusty!"

Clem felt a passing gloom as if a dark cloud had momentarily obscured the sun, but he shook it off as he rounded the corner.

The heavy man was crawling aimlessly on the sidewalk like a blind mole, and McNulty stood to one side, watching him, an expression of shock blanking his clever face. He licked his lips and looked wide-eyed at Clem.

"What was all that?" he stammered.

Clem hooked his fingers in the collar of the crawling man's coat, and started dragging him toward the theatre.

"Open the door," he ordered McNulty.

McNulty fumbled a key from his pocket and opened the door to the lobby. Clem dragged the burly man inside. He looked around, saw the swinging doors to the auditorium, dragged the man through and into the dusty silence beyond the lobby. As the doors swung, creaking, he saw McNulty dart into the office beside the box office. He ran out and caught McNulty just as the theatre manager was lifting the phone from its cradle.

"I—I was just calling the police." McNulty sounded as if he were still in a state of shock.

Clem dropped the phone back into its cradle. "We don't need the police," he snapped. "I don't want them. This is personal. Come on."

He took McNulty's unresisting arm and marched him into the auditorium. The heavy man was crawling blindly across the carpeting, mumbling.

Clem shoved him into a sitting position against the barrier behind the last row of seats and snapped at McNulty, "Get me some ammonia or smelling salts."

McNulty scurried away and returned within a few minutes with a bottle of ammonia. Clem uncorked it and held it under the burly man's nostrils. The man's head jerked up. Clem pulled out his handkerchief, soaked it with ammonia and clapped it over the man's nose. The man pushed weakly against Clem's wrist. Clem took the handkerchief away.

"What's your name?" he demanded.

The man cringed. "Th—They mostly call me Pudge," he whimpered.

"Who was that guy with you?"

"I—I dunno. He just—"

Clem clapped the ammonia-soaked handkerchief over Pudge's nose and mouth and held it there with both hands.

Pudge fought feebly, but Clem bore down with muscle and weight until Pudge's eyes rolled up in his head. He pulled the handkerchief away.

"Now who was that guy with you?" he asked grimly.

"We—we call him Crackers."

"Crackers what?"

"I dunno. No … no!" He put up pawing hands to fend off the ammonia-soaked handkerchief. "Honest, I don't know. We just call him Crackers, honest. I dunno!"

"Okay. You don't know. What's the pitch on that caper you just tried to pull?"

There was a liquid, begging expression in Pudge's eyes. "I—I—"

Clem dug his thumbs savagely into Pudge's neck on either side, just at the hinges of the jaw.

"All I've got to do is push," he grated, "and you'll flip your lid. Give me the pitch!" He released the pressure slightly.

Pudge moaned and his trembling fingers fluttered at Clem's hard thumbs.

"I dunno," he whispered, "I dunno. I was playing pool down the Acme Bar. Crackers comes in and offers me a sawbuck to give a guy named Lasher a going-over and shove him in a car. He brings me here and you're the guy. That's all I know, mister, honest. That's all I know!" His voice rose to a terror-stricken scream.

McNulty cried hysterically, "Let him alone, Lasher. Let him alone!" He pulled at Clem's ropy shoulder with ineffectual hands.

Clem hunkered back on his heels, glancing up at McNulty. "Keep out of this," he said almost absently. He pulled the palm of his hand down the side of his jaw, scowling at the now thoroughly disorganized Pudge, who twitched fearfully every time Clem moved.

"This Crackers," said Clem, "he's a local hotshot, that right?"

"Yeah, yeah, that's right, that's right, that's right all right."

"Is he supposed to belong to a mob or something around here?"

"I—I never—"

Clem merely leaned a little closer and Pudge squealed and wrapped his arms protectively over his face.

"They—they said the Hudson Dusters!"

"The Hudson Dusters? What are you giving me? There hasn't been a Hudson Duster since eighteen ninety."

"It's just a name, mister. Just a name they use, and I don't even know if Crackers belongs. It's just what they say."

Clem muttered at McNulty, "That's kid stuff, Hudson Dusters. These days." He turned back to Pudge. "You're going to do a job for me."

"Sure, mister, sure. Anything you say!"

"But you're a little afraid of Cracker's gun, eh?"

"Well, sure, mister, if a guy's got a gun and—"

"I'm not afraid of Cracker's gun, and I'm going to show you something."

He dug iron fingers between the two bones of Pudge's elbow. The man arched and screamed. Clem released him immediately.

"That was nothing," he said. "I didn't even bear down. I just wanted to give you an idea. Now here's the job you're going to do for me. You're going to find out all you can about Crackers—his full name, the mob he's supposed to be tied up with, how many times he's been sent up and what for, and where he's living. Got it?"

"Yeah, yeah, I got it. I got it!"

"Smart boy." Clem sprang lithely to his feet, extended his hand and jerked Pudge to his feet. The man swayed, steadied himself on the barrier, looked apologetically at Clem.

"I—I'll get it for you, mister. I'll get it."

He sidled past Clem and lurched through the door held silently open by McNulty. Clem walked quickly across the back of the auditorium to the men's room. When McNulty walked in after him a few minutes later, he was bent over the sink, retching painfully. McNulty leaned against the doorframe.

"Well!" he said sardonically, "I didn't think anybody could be *that* tough!"

Clem raised his head from over the sink and looked at him.

McNulty said hurriedly, pushing the door open behind him, "Just kidding, Lasher. I was just kidding."

CHAPTER IV

Clem was backstage sitting on a prop bed used in one of the many bedroom skits, smoldering over a cigarette, when McNulty came through the wings from the opposite side of the stage with a ginger-haired, snub-nosed girl, whose generous mouth was pursed in lines of ironic patience.

McNulty introduced her as Ella Dolan, the chorus captain. "So-So Dolan," he amplified nervously. "She's got a specialty in the show."

Then Clem remembered. She was one of the strip-girls whose photograph was outside in the shadow box, the one who had looked so amused that anyone should pay good money just to see a few square feet of female skin, the wholesome looking one.

McNulty stammered to Ella, "This is—this is Clem Lasher. He plays a piano," and ducked out down the stairs beside the electrician's board.

Clem felt himself flush as Ella Dolan surveyed him from head to foot with that same air of ironic patience.

"That's all we need around here," she said at length. "Another of

Mac's protégés. What are you, a lush, a chaser, a hophead, or just a plain louse?"

Clem let his eyes rise from her feet to her ginger hair as slowly as a snake climbing a tree, and this time she flushed.

"Why do you like to strip in front of a lot of morons?" he asked deliberately. "Are you an exhibitionist, or have you done it so often here and there that it doesn't make any difference anymore?"

The blood ebbed from her cheeks. Her hand licked out and slapped him across the cheek. Her eyes glittered angrily, and his grin glittered back at her.

"We were even," he said, "'til you slapped me. I'm not a lush, a chaser, a hophead, or a louse. I might be an S.O.B., but I'm not a louse. Now, why do you strip for the goon-boys?"

"I like it. I like to take my clothes off. There's nothing I'd rather do!"

"You're a liar!"

His grin glittered again. His hand shot out, grasped her left wrist, twirled her, flipped her on her back on the bed beside him. He bent over her, kissed her—at first brutally, but then with a foreign softness. He released her and sat up, looking away.

"I'm sorry I did that," he said jerkily. "Not sorry because I kissed you, but I'm sorry. I apologize."

For a few moments she lay unresisting, soft, on the bed, staring at him with wondering eyes. Her hand rose shakily to her mouth and touched her lips. She pushed herself up, rested on her elbows. Something hardened in her face.

"That pays for the slap," she said. "With interest. Satisfied?"

He thrust himself away from the bed. She stood up.

"Let's start all over again," she said. "I'm Ella Dolan, and you're Clem Lasher. I'm pleased to meet you." She held out her right hand.

He hesitated and then took the offered hand. "Pleased to meet you, too, Dolan," he said.

She regarded him thoughtfully. "I can't believe that you came here to play the piano. You don't look like a man who'd be satisfied to make a living that way."

"What was that crack you made before about McNulty's protégés?"

"Poor Mac, he's always letting some talented heel talk him into something."

"Oh yes. He was telling me about a kid named Joey Smith."

"A kid!" Ella Dolan snorted bitterly.

"Joey Smith—if that's his right name—hasn't been a kid since the Hoover administration. He had everybody fooled with that big Eagle Scout grin of his. Everybody took him for a kid. Even I did, and I'm not easily fooled. But he was a little drunker than usual one night and he let it drop that he was born during the first World War. Figure it out for yourself."

Clem scowled. That made Sonny Lind around thirty-eight. He certainly wasn't any kid, though he had sure looked it with that curly hair and boyish grin.

"What kind of heel was this Sonny—I mean, Joey Smith?" he asked.

"He was a revolving heel. He was a heel no matter how you looked at him. When he walked out of this theatre, he took almost a thousand bucks with him. Not bad for a week's work, eh?"

"What do you mean? He tapped the till? He knocked off the box office?"

"It wouldn't have been as bad if he had. He suckered all of us with that All-American grin of his. He took poor old Mac for a pocketful, he cleaned out the stage hands with a pair of dice that could do everything but whistle Dixie, and even I lent him fifty. Me! Picture that. And I'm supposed to know my way around. What gets me sore is that he didn't even have to pick our pockets. He just asked us for it and we gave it to him."

"He sounds like a smooth operator."

"He was smooth, all right. He let drop that he had taken some sucker over in New York for a thousand, too. For singing lessons, no less. That guy must really have been a sucker. But the worst he did around here," she added broodingly, "was to Helen."

"Helen!"

"Yes. One of the chorus girls. She was crazy about him. L-o-v-e— love— the real thing. She had two hundred in her grouch bag, and he took that. But that wasn't enough for Joey Smith. He really put the slug on the poor kid in the end. She got tight with him one night and woke up the next morning in a hotel room with a big fat old Dutchman, who, it turned out, had slipped pal Joey a hundred to fix it up for him. Helen was almost crazy when she got back to the theatre that day. She was going to fix Joey. I told her to forget it, but if I'd known what she had in mind, I'd have stuck to her like tar to a fender."

"Just what did she have in mind?" asked Clem carefully, fingering the wedding ring in his pocket.

"She jumped in the river," said Ella flatly. Her eyes narrowed. "Hold everything, Lasher. You've been pumping me for the past ten minutes. What's your interest in Joey Smith?"

Clem said grimly, "I'm the sucker from New York, the one he took for a thousand bucks for singing lessons."

Ella whistled.

"You're not my idea of a sucker," she said.

"I won't be Sonny Lind's idea of a sucker, either, before I get finished. That's another one of his names—Sonny Lind."

Ella said eagerly, "He's still around Hoboken, Lasher. I saw him yesterday on Ferry Street in a gray convertible longer than Methuselah's beard. He had a couple of public enemy type citizens with him. For a minute I had the wild hope that they were taking him for a ride, but no such luck. They were laughing and joking like happy politicians."

"Good. I wouldn't want anything to happen to him."

"Let me help, Lasher. I'll do everything I can. First just give me time to get the nearest baseball bat. I just want to be around to see the expression on his face. That is, if you leave enough of a face for him to have an expression."

"This is all under your hat, Ella Dolan— As far as anybody else around here is concerned, I'm just the piano player, understand?"

"Anything you say, Lasher. I'd give an arm and a leg to get Joey Smith or Sonny Lind or whatever his name is over a barrel. But do you mind if I say something?"

"Go ahead."

"Those two citizens in the convertible with him. They weren't anybody's playmates. If you played with them, you'd stand a good chance of going home feet first. Be careful."

"I will."

"No, you won't. You'll charge in with your chin out, swinging with both hands. Mac told me about that hassle you had out there on the sidewalk. You were just plain lucky, Mac says, that the man in the raincoat didn't get his gun out a split second earlier. Mac picked that gun up out of the gutter where you kicked it. Make him give it to you ... What's the matter?"

Clem muttered. "Be right back." He ran across the stage, out through the stage door and up the alley to the front of the theatre. The black sedan was gone.

McNulty was standing in the lobby, watching him. "They took it away about fifteen minutes ago," he said. "Two characters the size of boxcars. I didn't argue with them."

Clem slapped his fist into the palm of his right hand. "There isn't any chance that you took the license number, is there?" he demanded.

"Not a chance in the world," said McNulty promptly. "You as good as told me to mind my own business, and this was one time, bucko, that I was only too pleased to."

Clem eyed him hotly, but this time he kept his mouth shut.

McNulty went on conversationally, "You know, bucko, I'm not a bad guy. I don't know what kind of trouble you're in, and I'm not asking. If you want to tell me, okay; if you don't want to tell me, okay, too. But sometimes it's nice to have friends, if you know what I mean."

Clem said shortly, "I'm doing all right."

McNulty shrugged and turned away to greet a squat man, who was walking diagonally across the street toward the theatre. "Hi, Catlin," he said. "How's the boy?"

Catlin tilted his chin at Clem. "This monkey play the piano for you, Mac?" he demanded in a hard, flat voice.

McNulty shot Clem a swift glance and answered, "That's right, and he's pretty good, too."

Catlin swung around on Clem. "Where'd you go after you left the lunchroom last night?"

Clem recognized Catlin as one of the two cops he had seen in the lunchroom just before meeting Vance.

"I went up Hudson Street to Burr's Hotel," he said.

"You're a liar! I just checked with the hotel and you was nowheres near it, then or ever."

"I didn't say I went in, did I? When I got there, I found I didn't have the price."

"You're a liar again! Al down at the lunchroom said he gave you change for a five."

Pulling out the lining of his pocket, Clem twiddled his fingers in the hole he had made there the night before. "That's where it went—right through there. I had forty cents left, and I went down to that diner by the bus station at the other end of Washington Street. I asked the dame there if she knew of a Salvation Army where I could get a flop for the night, and she let me use a cot in the back room. Now what the hell is this all about? If somebody held up the lunchroom, it wasn't me."

"Don't get tough. What time did you get down to the diner?" Catlin still sounded hard, but not quite so sure of himself.

"I don't know. I lost my watch in a crap game in Albany. Wait a minute. Right after I walked in, we heard three explosions, and the dame said, 'There goes the gasworks again,' or something like that. That help?"

Catlin pressed his thin lips together. Then with an air of great cunning, he shot out, "When was the last time you saw Alfred Vance, wise guy?"

Clem let his face go blank. "Who's he?" he asked.

Catlin stepped close to Clem and gathered his shirtfront in a big fist. "Don't lie to me!" he grated. "You lied twice, and I don't like it. I've got a good mind to take you down to headquarters and sandpaper you down a little just for the hell of it."

McNulty saw Clem's eyes narrow, and he sprang across the sidewalk, thrusting his thin body between the two men.

"Now, wait a minute—wait a minute," he begged. "We don't have to have any trouble. Hell, Catlin, Lasher's story should be easy enough to check. If it doesn't check, that's the time to get tough. But I've got an idea it's going to check. He'd be a damned fool to give you a story like that if it wouldn't check, wouldn't he? Let's be sensible."

Catlin pushed out his jaw at Clem. "You'll be awfully easy to find if you ain't here when I get back," he said heavily. He turned and walked up the street, his heels hammering the sidewalk with barely suppressed fury.

McNulty looked at Clem and said ironically, "So you're doing all right, eh? You're doing just dandy, if you ask me. In just about a whisper you two would have been rolling all over the sidewalk. Don't you know it's against the law to smack a cop in this town, no matter how wrong he is? You'd better file that for future reference. The food in the local hoosegow is lousy, they tell me."

Clem looked up the street after Catlin, without answering.

McNulty said, "That was a straight story you gave him, wasn't it?" He looked a little worried. "That Catlin's a mean one, bucko, and from here on in, right or wrong, he's going to hate your guts. You'll be better off if you're right."

But Clem was not listening. He was thinking of that woman in the diner and how she had said she would give him the alibi because he reminded her of her first husband or something. She had seemed sincere, but now he could not help wondering how she would feel about it in the cold light of day, with a hardboiled cop like Catlin just aching to take her apart and doing his damnedest to break her down. It was a chilly feeling.

CHAPTER V

Clem had two spots in the show, neither of them a solo. He played the music for what McNulty called the parade-in-one, which was nothing more than four chorus girls walking listlessly up and down the apron of the stage in front of the curtain, while the stage hands changed the scene for the next skit. There were two parades, one just before the intermission, and one just before the big production number that closed the show. There was no piano on the stage, so he had to play from the orchestra pit. He played angrily and undoubtedly with effect, because later one of the chorus girls, lightly clad in a few strips of nylon, went backstage where he was sitting on a prop trunk, smoking. She leaned against his knee and moaned that she would just love to have him do the music for her specialty next week, and maybe they ought to get a few rehearsals in ahead of time.

He took the cigarette from his mouth. "Do what?" he demanded.

"Th—the music for my specialty next week," she stammered. "Mac's letting me do a strip number. H—he lets the girls take turns. Like Ella Dolan this week. You could do the music. I mean," her voice turned sultry again, "if we could get in a few rehearsals, Mac would let us have the key to the theatre in the mornings and we could kind of get the number in shape...."

He looked up into her slow, insinuating eyes. "Why don't you go and put some clothes on?" he asked.

Her eyes widened and she backed away from him. "Well, pardon me for living!" she said haughtily, and walked across the stage, switching indignantly.

Ella Dolan's strip number closed the first half of the program. Wrapped in a white terry robe, she went back to Clem.

"I'll bet you didn't even catch my number," she accused him.

"Sorry," he said, "I was thinking."

She put her hand on his arm and smiled. "To tell you the truth, Clem," she said, "I like you better for that. I like you better than if you'd been in the wings with your eyes standing out on stalks the way some of the characters we've had in here do. What did The Heat Wave want with you?"

"The who?"

"The Heat Wave. That chorus girl, Eve Barnett. I saw you give her the brush-off."

"Oh her. She wanted a rehearsal or something."

"Rehearsal!" Ella chuckled. "There's a girl who'd rehearse with anything in pants. Have you found a place to stay yet?"

"McNulty got me a room in Burr's Hotel."

"Good. Well?"

"Well what?"

"Aren't you going to ask me to have dinner with you between shows? They serve a nice seafood platter down at the Clam Broth House."

Clem shook his head. "Sorry, honey, but I've got some looking around to do."

"What are you worried about, Clem?"

"I'm not worried."

"If you're not worried, you're certainly practicing to be. What is it? Is it that cop, Catlin? Don't scowl at me like that; Mac told me all about it. He's worried, if you're not. Catlin's something to worry about. He's poison mean. He was a local jerk before they gave him a gun and a badge, and now he's got delusions of grandeur. Watch out for him, Clem."

"I'm not worried about myself, I told you!" Then he added heavily, almost reluctantly, "I'm worried about a dame who stuck her neck out for me. She had no reason to, either. I didn't ask her. She's an old dame, around fifty. I reminded her of her first husband or something. I didn't get it then, and I still don't get it."

"Never mind. She's probably got an angle. Everybody has an angle."

"Beat it, will you?"

"All right. You rassle with it for a while. Sure you won't take me down to the Clam Broth House for dinner?"

"Beat it!"

"See you tonight, Clem."

He lit another cigarette and stared introspectively through the veil of smoke.

After the matinee—or rather, directly after his number—he left the theatre, walked up to Washington Street and took a bus to the north end of town. There were several customers at the counter of the diner, and the gray-haired woman, Belle, was drawing two cups of coffee from the shiny urn. She started and spilled a little of the coffee into the saucers when she saw Clem sitting at the end of the counter. She looked away from him and kept her head down as she went back to the grill and made a Western on rye.

It was five minutes before she was able to get away from the trade to take a cup of coffee up to him.

"There was a policeman up to my apartment this afternoon about you," she whispered.

"I know. He saw me first. Did he give you a bad time? Did he get tough with you?"

"He—he asked me all kinds of questions I couldn't answer. I just told him you were in here when we heard the shots. I don't think he believed me. He made me go over it again and again and again, but I told him the same thing all the time—you were in here when the guns went off."

"He didn't get tough, did he?"

"No, nothing like that. But when he left, he said he'd be back. He sounded real nasty."

"Listen," Clem plucked a menu from between the pepper and salt shakers. "If they really come after you, pull your neck back in. Tell them I pointed a gun at you. Tell him I made you say those things. Tell them I scared you."

"But—you didn't shoot that fellow, did you?"

"No, but I was right there when it happened, and they might be able to prove it. I don't want you to get it in the neck just because you tried to do me a good turn. Understand?"

"I—I'm scared," she confessed in a barely audible voice. "He scared me. He was more than nasty. He was—I don't know—all I know is I knew I'd scream if he kept it up another minute."

"All right," said Clem with unaccustomed gentleness. "If they come to you again, just tell them that I threatened you with a gun. They won't do anything to you."

"I—I'm sorry. I thought I could stand up against them, but I can't. I didn't know what it would be like."

"That's all right. Stop worrying. You may never see them again. Now get me a breaded veal cutlet."

There were tears in her eyes when she turned away and walked hurriedly up the counter. She disappeared through the door to the kitchen instead of calling the order through the small cutout, and it was several minutes before she reappeared.

Now, he knew, it was up to Catlin. What way would the Catlin jump? He smiled grimly at the pun. He didn't think there was much real bloodhound in Catlin, but there could be a lot of bulldog. He might hang on. It could be bad if he did. That would mean a bad session down at headquarters. But on the other hand, Catlin had not shown back at the theatre, and there had been plenty of time.

He ate quickly, and went out without talking to the woman again. He gave her a wink when he paid the check and left.

He was standing just outside, lighting a cigarette, when the gray convertible came rolling down Fourteenth, turned into Washington and picked up speed. He dropped his cigarette and took two steps after it, staring. Two big muscular men were in the front seat, Sonny Lind was in the rear seat—and beside Sonny lolled Marthe!

She turned her head at the sound of Clem's roar from the curb. She looked directly at him, raised her hand in a mocking salute, and deliberately turned away, whispering something to Sonny Lind. A moment later, the car disappeared into the moving wall of the heavy traffic.

Clem looked wildly around for a taxi stand, and then ran across the sidewalk to a bus driver who was lounging against the side of his bus, smoking.

Clem bellowed, "Damn it, aren't there any cabs in this town!"

The bus driver snatched the cigarette from his mouth, startled. "Next corner, mister," he said.

Clem sprinted up the sidewalk, scrambled into a cab and snapped, "Down Washington Street. See if you can spot a gray convertible."

But it was five-thirty, and the late afternoon traffic was pouring into the city from the Lincoln Tunnel, from Weehawken, from Union City. Big, high-sided trucks hemmed them in more effectively than a herd of elephants, and even the agile cab had to crawl at a pedestrian pace while Clem fumed impotently in the back seat.

They went all the way to Ferry Street, at the southern end of Washington, without another glimpse of the convertible. Clem ordered the cabbie to go back by the next street north, and he sat tensely on the edge of the seat. His head swiveled from one side to the other, watching the parked cars as well as the steadily growing stream of traffic.

They were wedged in a school of faster moving lighter cars and small trucks when Clem caught sight of the convertible drifting eastward away from the curb, but it was half a block before the sweating driver could dart between two panel trucks to the side of the street to let Clem out. Clem flung him a crumpled bill and shouted for him to wait.

The convertible was gone by the time he reached the cross street, and the crowds were so thick that he had to do some nimble broken-field running to get through to Washington Street. He climbed high on the City Hall steps, but he could not see the car in either direction, north or south, though with its top down it would have been easy enough to spot in that host of business traffic. He plodded back to his waiting cab.

"We're going up and down every street in this damned town," he grimly told the cabbie. "I've got a feeling they're in here for the night, and we'll find them."

The cabbie looked at his wild red hair, his bleached army shirt, his disreputable jeans.

"That'll cost you, mister," he said flatly. "You got the dough?"

Clem gave him five out of the money McNulty had advanced, and the cab nosed out into the traffic, beginning what was to be for Clem five of the most frustrating hours he had ever spent. It was almost eleven o'clock that night when he climbed stiffly out to the sidewalk before the old-fashioned brownstone front of Burr's Hotel.

"Thanks for the buggy ride," he said sourly to the hackie. "We should have brought a picnic lunch."

The night clerk was drowsing at his desk in the dim lobby. The stairway to Clem's room on the second floor smelled like old books kept too long in a closed closet. Burr's was a preserved relic of the 1890s.

Clem opened his door and his hand froze on the knob, the knuckles whitening. Propped up comfortably with two pillows on his bed, smoking a slim, freckled panatella, was Sonny Lind.

CHAPTER VI

Sonny grinned lazily and waved the cigar. "Come in, Lasher, dear old pal," he drawled. "Pull up a chair and let's gum over the dear dead days beyond recall."

Clem closed the door very slowly. He took the key from his pocket and locked it. His eyes were icy. "I've been looking for you, Lind," he said evenly.

"Well if that isn't the darnedest coincidence, dear old pal," Sonny's voice was airy and faintly derisive, "I've been looking for you. But that's life for you, isn't it? Ships that pass in the night."

Clem ignored the flippant tone. He was feeling that stern exhilaration that sometimes comes to very good prize fighters who have gotten, their opponents into an inescapable corner. He locked his hands behind him and looked down at the bed.

The bedside lamp threw a strong light on Sonny Lind's face and Clem could see now that the man was older than he had supposed him. It was the big grin that erased the years, and Sonny was only smiling faintly now. The laugh lines at the ends of the eyes and from the sides of the nose to the ends of the mouth now became creases. Sonny looked hard-bitten, callous, and cynical. He also looked prosperous. The Glen plaid suit he was wearing had cost between two-fifty and three hundred, the nylon shirt around twenty-five, the tie about fifteen, and the bench-made Scotch grain brogues another fifty. Counting the wristwatch, the cuff links and ring, he was wearing about a thousand dollars' worth of haberdashery and jewelry. He was a big man, an inch shorter than Clem's six-foot-two, but heavier.

"The only reason I'm not beating the face off you," said Clem with controlled anger in his voice, "is because it has a certain commercial value. But don't count on it."

Sonny reached out a long arm and pulled the straight chair to the side of the bed. "Sit down, friend Lasher," he said soothingly. "Let's talk about a few facts of life, and maybe after it's all over we'll be soulmates." He gave Clem that big All-American grin, but this time Clem could see there were teeth in it.

As Clem sat down in the chair, Sonny dipped his fingers into the breast pocket of his jacket, took out a folded wad of bills and dropped it into Clem's lap.

"Eleven hundred iron men, dumb chum," he said. "Your original thousand plus ten per cent interest. Now we're even."

Clem counted the bills. There were eleven crisp C-notes. He put them in his pants pocket. "Not quite," he said. "I gave my word to Kraus of the Aztec Room that you'd open there next week, and you're going to open if I have to drag you in with your ears nailed to a wheelbarrow. That's a fact of life, and don't think it isn't."

Sonny looked mildly interested. He drew at his cigar and savored the smoke before replying. "Oh, Lasher, Lasher," he sighed, "you act tough, but I'm afraid at heart you're just another beautiful dreamer. Of course I'm not going to open in the Aztec Room next week or any other week. My boss wouldn't like it if his sales manager exhibited himself in a common saloon."

"Sales manager? What do you sell, Lind—cancer?"

A flash of pure viciousness slashed across Sonny's face like a lightning stroke. "I can sell, Lasher," he spat. "I can sell anybody anything. I promoted a grand out of you, and I sold myself into the job I got. I'm not just a male thrush, and don't you forget it! I can promote anything, anywhere, any time!"

"Yeah," Clem nodded, "and you even promoted two hundred bucks from a kid named Helen down at the Lyric Burlesque." The singer became very still. The smoke was a straight thin ribbon from his cigar. "What's that supposed to mean?" he asked woodenly.

"They found her in the river."

"So? I threw her in?"

"No, but just as good as, when you walked out on her and peddled her when she was plotzed to a fat kraut. I'll remember that one, Lind. And another fact of life that I'm keeping in mind is Al Vance. Vance had some kind of line on you, and they tore him apart down on River Street last night."

"Al Vance had no kind of line on me at all. I didn't have anything to do with that!" He squirmed up from the bed on a hip and an elbow and gestured agitatedly with his free hand. "I had nothing to do with that, nothing!"

"No? Maybe it was your boss, then. DeGroot."

"Who?" Sonny Lind looked genuinely puzzled.

Clem repeated, "DeGroot," and narrowly watched Sonny's face for a flicker of recognition, but there was none.

Sonny relaxed back against the pillows. "Wake up, Lasher," he said, "wake up. You're asleep in the deep. There isn't any DeGroot, I didn't knock off Al Vance, Helen Swensen was a neurotic squarehead, and I'm not going to sing in the Aztec Room or any other room from now on except in my bathroom. So take your eleven hundred bucks, count the extra hundred as sheer profit, and write it off the books."

Perhaps it was the smug complacency, or perhaps it was the underlying sneer in Sonny Lind's voice. Whatever it was, at the sound of it, fury shot up in Clem and he lunged out of his chair with a guttural snarl. He seized Sonny by his hand-stitched lapels, shoved them up under his chin, thrusting his head back into the pillows at an agonizing angle, and ground his knuckles into the straining throat.

"Nothing gets written off the books, Lind," he panted, "until you open at the Aztec Room. And after that—" he tightened his savage grip—"I'm going to take you apart like an Erector set. Now listen to me"—Sonny Lind made strangling sounds. He arched violently on the bed and struck at Clem's head, but Clem's spread elbows broke the blows in the middle.

The closet door opened behind the chair that Clem had just vacated. A thick-bodied man stepped out noiselessly. In his hand he held a twelve-inch length of garden hose, stuffed with birdshot and plugged at both ends. The thick-bodied man leaned over, raised the blackjack, and brought it down with dispassionate force just behind Clem's right ear. Clem collapsed across Sonny Lind's chest. Sonny swore, thrust him away, and squirmed out from under and up to his feet. He stood breathing painfully, and then reached down, tangled his fingers in Clem's harsh red hair and twisted brutally.

The thick-bodied man said stolidly, "He is unconscious, boss. He cannot feel. If you so wish, I will make it that he will scream when he recovers his senses." He slapped the shot-weighted length of garden hose against his broad palm. "It will not take much. Just a tap here and there, but I know how to do it. He will scream and beg to be killed."

Sonny thrust Clem's head back against the mattress and shook his head, smiling thinly. He shook from his hands the strands of red hair that stuck between his fingers.

"No, Piet," he said. "We've got other ideas for our dear old pal here. He's going to be the knot that ties up a little package that's been lying around open since last night. He's going to be the fall guy. That's an Americanism, Piet."

"I know what a fall guy is. The victim, no?"

"No, he's not the victim, Piet—you have no sense of finesse. First comes the victim, and then comes the fall guy." Sonny had recovered his airy jauntiness. "The fall guy trips over the victim or rather, he doesn't trip; he's pushed. That's a joke, son."

"A joke?" Piet wrinkled his forehead. "I do not think Grotius would appreciate a joke. I think Grotius would prefer this carrion out of the way."

Sonny slapped Piet's beamed shoulder and chuckled. He was in a thoroughly good humor.

"Don't you worry your little pointed head about Dexter Grotius. Dexter and I see eye to eye. Say, there's an idea for a lyric. Dexter and I see eye to eye and we'll all have pie in the sky by and by. I'll have to write music to that."

Piet scowled, and then said impassively, "I think we go now back to Grotius. I do not think he will like this leaving this garbage alive."

"You do not think, period," grinned Sonny.

CHAPTER VII

Clem heard them go out of the room. He heard the heavy, guttural voice of Piet, though he could not distinguish the words, and he heard the door slam. He was not entirely unconscious, but every sense had been paralyzed by that experienced tap from the shot-filled hose. It was a long time before he could even groan. The room was nothing but a luminescent fog with no clearly defined outlines. When he was finally able to move one hand, it was as if an anvil had been shackled to it with anchor chains.

His brain would not work. He was numb. With more effort than he had ever expended before on anything, he was finally able to move both hands. It exhausted him. His face felt as if it were grinding into the mattress of the bed. Slowly, one by one, his muscles began to function. His mind was a pulsating field of darkness. It was nothing but the basic instinct of self-preservation that caused him to roll from the bed, hitting the floor with a bony jar, and crawl feebly toward the door of the room.

When Sonny and Piet slammed the door in leaving, the ancient, unoiled catch had failed to snap into its slot and the door had bounced back a good three inches. Balancing precariously on hands and knees, Clem nosed open the door with the side of his jaw to allow him passage through. There was no deliberately planned progression, but his instinct told him to get out of that room.

He felt the harsh jute threads of the carpeting in the hallway under his fingers and he turned left toward the end of the hall, away from the stairway. There was no thought in this either. It was instinctive memory. At the left end of the hallway was the fire escape. Twice his arms collapsed under him, grinding his face into the rough carpet; twice, with infinite effort, he raised himself and continued his snail pace toward the fire escape.

He remembered later, chiefly from the bitter bite of iron against his lips, gums and teeth, falling against the iron grillwork of the fire escape, pushing himself up again on shaking arms and legs, crawling down, down, down, licking the taste of rust and flaking paint from his mouth. But mainly there was no memory, except that of movement—movement away from that room, and down to the foot of the fire escape.

He did not pass out entirely when he fell from the end of the fire escape into the alley at the side of Burr's Hotel. His mind had begun relentlessly turning again, and when he felt hands hook under his armpits, he reached back weakly tried to claw them away. When his fingers failed, he tried to turn his head and bite. He could not let himself be dragged so helplessly.

A voice murmured soothingly and pleadingly at his ears—but Sonny Lind's voice had murmured soothingly—and he tried to fight even when a cool hand was pressed to his cheek and forehead and something warm and wet dropped against his face. He was dragged up, shoved and propped, and something slammed against his right arm.

The next sound he could identify—the rhythmic burbling of a car motor. He was in a car, then, a moving car. He was beginning to see a little, to think a little. A hand swam up toward his face and there was a small half-pint flask in it.

A voice in which the hysteria was barely submerged said, "Take a drink, Clem! Take a drink, then let me have one. Are you hurt?"

He clasped the bottle in both hands, held it to his numbed lips and let the liquid pour down his throat. At first it had no taste, no flavor, no bite, but then suddenly he felt it, a warmth spreading in his chest like feeler roots, spreading down into his legs and up into his arms, into his throat and head, giving him strength.

He swallowed, coughed, and swallowed again. He turned his head and saw Ella Dolan crouching over the wheel of the old car, her face strained.

"Here," he said, holding the flask to her lips.

She drank, sucking air on the sips. She pulled back her head, and he took the flask away, corking it.

"Feel better, Clem?" she asked shakily. "You looked like death when I dragged you out of that alley."

"Alley?"

"Yes. Next to Burr's. You came down the fire escape. But thank God you did. All the police in Hoboken are out after you. I got you away just in time."

Memory came back with a rush. "Sonny Lind!" he said tersely.

"I don't know about that, but they're after you for killing a man named Vance on River Street last night. Clem—"

"What?" he asked harshly.

"Will you tell me the truth? Wait a minute before you get mad. I'm getting you out of Hoboken because—God help me—I think I'm in love with you. Clem, you didn't kill him, did you?"

"No! I wish to hell people would stop asking me if I did." He clenched his hands on the edge of the seat on either side of his thighs, bent his head and took several deep breaths to relax himself. Ella didn't speak.

They were out of Hoboken now and were climbing a steep winding road. Clem looked through the window.

"Where are we going?" he asked.

"Jersey City. I swapped apartments with Sam, the electrician. Don't worry about Sam," she added. "He doesn't know I'm taking you there, and anyway he owes me some good turns."

The apartment was on Ditman Street, on the brow of the hill overlooking Hoboken. Clem stood in the window and looked down at the city. He could hear the faint banshee wails of the police sirens and see the lights of moving cars. Ella came out of the kitchen with a bottle of bourbon and two glasses. She smiled wanly at him.

"I think both of us could use a drink," she said. She crossed the room and dropped onto the sofa. She wore a belted camel's hair topcoat, and when she crossed her legs he saw a flash of long, well-curved thigh, as if she were wearing nothing under the coat.

"Sit down. Clem," she said, patting the cushion beside her. "You're getting yourself all wound up prowling up and down the room like that."

He grimaced and sprawled on the sofa. As he did, some loose change fell out of his pocket. Ella bent to pick up a coin that had rolled against her foot, and when she straightened, her eyes were distended. In her hand she held the wedding ring that Vance had given Clem. She shrank away from Clem.

"Where—where did you get this?" she whispered.

He looked absently at the ring in her shaking fingers. "It was given to me."

"It's Helen's!"

"I know. Her name's on it." He was still brooding over Sonny Lind.

Ella stared at him with growing horror. "She—she was wearing this the night she disappeared, and the next day she was found in the river." The words came out jerkily.

He scarcely heard her. She sprang to her feet, her features distorted.

"You were with her that night!" she shouted hysterically. "You were with her, because she was wearing this when she left the theatre that night. What did you do to her, Clem?"

He looked up, scowling. "Do to who?" he demanded.

She put her hand to her mouth, moaned and backed away from him. She turned and ran for the door. It was locked, and she tugged frantically at the doorknob. He jumped up, strode across the room, and pulled her away from the door. He held her by the shoulders and shook her.

"What are you trying to do?" he growled. "Wake up everybody in the neighborhood? What's the matter with you?"

She beat at his chest with her fists. "Let me go! Let me go!"

"Go where?"

"The police, that's where! Let me go!" She bent and bit his hand.

He snatched it away, caught her up in his arms, strode back across the room and threw her onto the sofa. "Now what the hell's the matter with you?" he snapped, standing over her.

She thrust Helen's ring into his face. "That's what's the matter with me," she cried shrilly. "That! What did you do to her that night, Clem?"

He stared at the ring, uncomprehending.

"Me?" he said. "Me?"

"Now I'm beginning to see it. She didn't jump in the river. She didn't commit suicide. You killed her!"

"I—*what!*" His jaw tightened. "Have you gone crazy? I haven't killed anybody. I never even knew the girl. The ring was given to me by Al Vance the night he was shot. He seemed to think it had something to do with Sonny Lind."

He prowled to the window and brooded down at the lights below. What could that ring have had to do with Sonny Lind? Had Al Vance been killed because of the ring? And Helen? Suicide was too pat, and the river too handy. He swung around.

"Did you ever hear of a guy named DeGroot?" he demanded.

Ella shook her head.

Clem swore. "Damm it, he's in it someplace. Vance was told by one of the chorus girls that DeGroot threw some interesting parties."

Ella faltered, "If it was Helen who told him, he might have misunderstood. She used to speak with a strong Swedish accent. We kidded her about it. We called her smorgasbord. Clem"—she looked pleadingly at him—"I'm sorry I threw that wingding."

"That's okay." He began to pace the room. "Did you know about these parties the burlesque girls went to? They were paid fifty dollars."

"I knew about them," she said almost inaudibly. "I—I even went to one of them. They were awful." She began to cry. "Clem, I'm so sorry I said what I did to you."

He cut her off with an impatient wave of his hand. "I said okay, didn't I? Let's forget it. I want to know about the guy who ran those parties. Are you sure it wasn't DeGroot?"

Ella sat huddled on the sofa, her hands limp in her lap. "It was a foreign name, but it wasn't DeGroot," she said dully. "I don't remember what it was. They called him Dex. He was some kind of bigshot. A businessman. I didn't stay around long enough to find out anything. When I saw what kind of party it was, I got out."

"What kind of business was he in?"

"I don't know. Something to do with shipping, I think. Most of the men at the party were from the North Dutch Steamship Company. I didn't understand what they were saying most of the time. They spoke Dutch."

Clem stopped and snapped his fingers. "This Helen," he said, "are you sure she was Swedish, not Dutch?"

"She was Swedish. Helen Swensen."

"But maybe she could understand Dutch?"

Ella looked up and regarded him, openmouthed. "Why yes," she said, "yes, she could. She could speak Swedish, French, Spanish, Italian, Dutch, and German. We used to laugh about it. We used to say she could speak every language in the world except English."

"Now we're getting someplace!" His lips pulled back in a mirthless grin. "Helen overhears something at the party. She's nuts about Sonny Lind. She tells him what she's overheard, and the next thing we know Sonny Lind is in the chips. But in the meantime he gives her a rough time, and in revenge she hints something about this stuff to Al Vance. Not very much, but enough to scare Sonny and the guy he's working for, so they get rid of Helen. Then they get rid of Al Vance. Does that sound to you as if it adds up?"

Ella covered her ears with her hands and cried hysterically, "Stop it!"

His head jerked up and he eyed her with astonishment. Then, in two swift strides, he crossed and sat down beside her. He put his arm around her.

"I'm sorry, honey," he said in a softened voice. "I'm all wound up, I guess."

Ella turned her face into his shoulder and clung to him. "You kept hammering at me," she whimpered.

"I know, I know. I'm sorry. I'm an ingrate. You do me a good turn, and I kick you around."

"No, you're worried, that's all."

"Worried hell! I'm sore. I've been pushed around and I don't like it. So what do I do?" His mouth curled in disgust. "I take it out on a girl who's trying to give me a hand. Brother, am I a prize package!"

"No, darling, no!" She raised her face, smiling through a glistening of tears. "You're just not used to having people help you, that's all. You've always been—self-sufficient."

He laughed shortly. "That's just a nice way of saying I've been an arrogant bastard. It's just come to me that ever since I've hit Hoboken, I've been helped by all kinds of people. I wouldn't have gotten to first base with my alleged self-sufficiency. The counterman at the lunchroom wanted to lend me money; that woman in the diner covered for me with the cops; McNulty gave me a job; you got me out of a bad spot. I've been kidding myself all my life. I can do all right, all by myself. The hell I can! The hell anybody can. Even poor Al Vance gave me a hand. Lasher the Great Lasher—the great jerk!"

"You're tired, darling," she touched his cheek. "You're just tired."

"Tired? Yeah. Sick and tired. Sick and tired of me."

"Let's go to bed. I'm worn out and so are you. Forget about it all until tomorrow. We can't think straight anymore...."

He took a deep breath. Fatigue was like a heavy hand pushing him deeper into the cushions.

"Okay," he said. "I'll sleep out here on the sofa."

"You don't have to. There are two beds."

He smiled tiredly. Forget! Just as if it were some books he had brought home to work on, the way he used to in the old days when he was a hungry certified public accountant.

"Yes," he said with a gentleness that was more familiar now than it had been, "we'll forget all about it until tomorrow." He kissed her lightly on the cheek and rose to his feet. "Now, where's the sack?"

"That room." She pointed. "I'm going to take a shower. Do you want to take a shower?"

"After you," he said sleepily.

She turned off the light and he fumbled into the bedroom in the darkness. He quickly stripped off his clothes and dropped into the bed. His mind was churning, but there was a heaviness. He closed his eyes.

They opened with a jerk when he heard her come into the room. The room was not as black as it had been when he had first come in, still dazzled from the light. There was a glow from the thin horned moon. He saw her throw off the topcoat she had worn. She had nothing on underneath except the beaded G-string and the wisp of brassiere that she wore for her specialty in the theatre. She was not beautiful the way Marthe was. Marthe's beauty was diamond-hard perfection; Ella's had a radiant warmth, deep-breasted, full-thighed. Clem closed his eyes again.

A moment later the covers lifted, and he heard the whisper of her body against the sheets.

CHAPTER VIII

An alarm clock awakened Clem the next day. Ella, again wearing her belted topcoat, was standing in the doorway of the bedroom with the tinkling clock in her hands. "I thought you'd be mad if I didn't wake you, darling," she said apologetically. "It's two in the afternoon." There was something tremulous in her smile.

He said, "Oh Lord!" and sat up, but then he remembered that dawn had been lifting in the eastern sky when they had gone to sleep that morning.

"Come here," he ordered.

She came hesitantly across the room. He took her wrist and pulled her across him, dipping over her, brushing her lips with his.

"I'm crazy about you, but I suppose you know that by now," he said in an accusing voice.

She raised her fingers and touched his lips lightly. She smiled. "I was afraid you weren't going to say that," she whispered.

"Well, you're going to hear a lot more of it from now on!"

He kissed her again and pushed her away. He rolled from the bed, wrapping the blanket around him, toga fashion.

"I'm going to take a shower," he said. "Then let's find out what the score is."

She darted out into the living room ahead of him, and when he followed she was hurriedly gathering up a newspaper that was scattered on the sofa.

He watched her for a moment and then said, "Let me take a look at that for a moment."

"Take your shower first, darling." She gathered up all the papers in an untidy bundle in her arms.

"I'll take a look first." He took the papers from her.

She watched him bleakly as he sat down in the lounge chair at the window and spread the paper on his knees. His eyebrows went up at the sight of a two-column picture of himself at the top of the front page.

The accompanying story really did a job on him. He was wanted for "questioning" in the murder of Alfred Vance. That was expected, but the body of the story was a shock. Somebody had been very, very smart. There was a statement from Benjamin Morgan, a New York theatrical agent.

"According to Morgan," the story read, "he and Vance paid a visit to Lasher, a notorious New York gambler, on the eve of the killing. Vance and Lasher quarreled violently over a debt which Vance refused to pay, claiming that the card game in which he lost the money had been dishonest. Morgan alleged Lasher told Vance to get up the dough, or else.

"After leaving Lasher's apartment, Morgan said, he persuaded Vance to pay the debt for his own sake, and lent him the money to do so.

"When they called Lasher to settle the debt, they learned that Lasher had left to sit in on a floating poker game on River Street in Hoboken. Vance, fearing Lasher's notoriously violent temper, wanted to settle the debt that night, and went to Hoboken to find Lasher.

"I wish now I had gone with Vance," Morgan said, "for when next I heard of him, he was dead."

The story ended with the statement that Officer Frank Catlin had broken Lasher's alibi for the time of the killing and concluded with a quote from Police Chief Sullivan: "Lasher is armed and dangerous. If you recognize him on the streets, phone your nearest precinct station. Do not attempt to apprehend him without police aid. He is violent and will shoot to kill."

Clem whistled and looked up at Ella.

Her face was white. He grinned at her.

"You don't believe this stuff, do you?" he asked.

She shook her head. "No, but I didn't want you to see it. At least not till you had something to eat."

"That's female logic for you. Don't give a man bad news on an empty stomach. Come here." He held out his hand down into his lap. "It's rough, honey," he said soberly, "and it might even get rougher. I want you to go back to the theatre. I don't want you mixed up in this. And no arguments." There was a thin gold chain around her neck, and he twisted it on his finger. "I might as well tell you now there's a dame mixed up in this. Her name is Marthe, and I went with her for a while. We never did hit it off. This story in the paper is her doing. She's getting even. She—"

He stopped and stared at the chain wound around his finger. There was a wedding ring at the end of it, a duplicate of the other, except that this one had Ella's name on it instead of Helen.

"Where did you get that?" he demanded.

"That?" she looked down, bewildered at the sharp change in his voice. "That's—that's what they gave all the girls at the party. Each of us got a wedding ring with her name on it. Just a kind of souvenir. We all thought it kind of funny, but kind of nice, too."

Clem said exultantly, "That's the first real line that I've gotten. These rings had to be specially made. I'll find out where they were made, and then I'll get a line on DeGroot, or whatever his name is!"

"How will you do that?"

"Stop in at a few jewelry stores. The name on the ring doesn't mean anything, but the floral engraving is probably a stock design. Somebody might recognize it."

"You're not going out of the apartment! Oh no, Clem! They're looking for you. Your picture's in the paper. Clem, listen. Let me—"

"I will not let you!"

He lifted her from his lap and as he started to gather up the newspaper, when his eye fell on a small item:

Hit-and-Run Victim

> The body of a man identified as Vincent "Pudge" Riordan was found on Ferry Street early this morning.

He saw Ella watching him narrowly, so he grimaced and threw the paper into the chair as he got up. "Lousy picture of me," he said. "The photographer tried to make me grin like an ape."

"Don't go out, Clem. Please don't!"

"I've got to, honey. I can't spend the rest of my life here." He turned and went into the bath to take his shower. She didn't try to stop him again, but when he was ready to go, she handed him a hat. "It's Sam's," she said. "You've got to cover that red hair of yours, darling. It stands out like the San Francisco fire."

It was half a size too large, but a strip of newspaper in the sweatband remedied that. He kissed her and walked swiftly to the door. He turned and grinned at her. She was standing before the large mirror that hung over the dropleaf table across the room. She looked so forlorn that he went out quickly before he weakened and stayed with her.

There were many jewelers in Union City and Jersey City, but both those places were uncomfortably close to Hoboken. His best bet would be Newark. The trip took him three quarters of an hour in Ella's old Chevvy. He left the car in a parking lot and walked up Market Street.

A newsboy ran by him, holding aloft the latest edition of the *Newark Times* and shrieking, "New victim in gambling kill. Read all about it. New victim in gambling kill—"

Thinking first of Ella, Clem felt the cold touch of dread. He suppressed the wild urge to shout after the boy, who was already halfway down the street, and walked to the next corner. He stopped beside a newsstand to light a cigarette.

The sense of relief was so flooding that he felt weak for a moment. It was not Ella—it was Ben Morgan. He was able only to glimpse the story over the match he held to his cigarette, but the whole story was in the lead. Morgan had been shot and killed in his own apartment as he was in the very act of calling police headquarters. For protection, authorities believed.

My God, he thought, walking away, how big was this thing, and what was at stake? This made the sixth killing, including the two sailors. What could be worth all this butchery? Morgan had not been killed merely to hang another murder around Clem's neck. Morgan was timid—that was the answer. He had always been afraid of Clem, and with Clem still free he must have been frantic to recant—despite what payment he had gotten from DeGroot & Company.

But now the police of two states were looking for him. With another killing chalked up against him, Clem knew his time was running out. The chips were down and still he held no playable cards!

He went into the first small jewelry store he came to and laid the "Helen" ring on the counter. "I'm getting married next week," he said. "I got this for the wife. She thinks it's okay and she wants me to have one with my name on it for one of them double ring ceremonies. Can you fix me up?"

The jeweler took the ring in his hand, gave it a brief glance and dropped it contemptuously on the counter again. "Cheap novelty," he said. "I only handle quality merchandise. Just look at the engraving on that. So shallow you could scratch it on with a pin. Here, let me show you something fine." He dexterously snatched a tray of wedding rings from the case and set it before Clem. "First class goods and I bet you I sell for less …"

"I know, but she likes this."

"So she likes that. All right. I can have one made up for you."

"Special?"

"Sure it has to be made special."

"I can't afford that. I got this in Seattle. They had them in stock and it only cost five bucks extra to have the name put on. Sure you don't have nothing like that in stock?"

The jeweler started toward the back of his shop, sneering over his shoulder, "Go back to Woolworth's. Maybe they have some left."

Clem flushed and walked out, curbing his temper.

Clem was given similar treatment in several jewelry shops, but stubbornly, he continued to trudge along. It was eight o'clock and quite dark when he plodded into a tiny shop at the south end of Broad

Street. He put the ring on the counter and mechanically repeated his story. The old man behind the counter looked with interest at the ring and shook his head.

"No," he said, "no, I'm sorry. Where did you get this one, young man?"

Clem said wearily, "Seattle."

"Ah yes, perhaps that is the reason."

Clem looked up sharply. "The reason for what?" he asked.

"I handled these about a year and a half ago. A salesman came through and left me a few samples. When I tried to order some, I got no response from the company. They probably moved out west."

Clem's hands tightened on the edge of the counter. "Do you remember the name of the company?"

The old man thought for a few seconds. "No, I'm sorry I can't help you, young man. I threw the salesman's card away, not having any reason to keep it."

"But can you remember where they were from?" Clem asked desperately.

"Hm. Yes. I think I can. They were from Hoboken. Yes. that's right. Hoboken. But I'm afraid that won't be much help to you, young man. I wrote to them several times and received no answer. I don't want to give you any false hopes."

Clem backed toward the door. "Thanks," he said. "Thanks a lot!"

He took a cab back to the parking lot. He wanted to stop and call Ella, but he didn't know Sam's last name. He knew she would be worrying. It irked him to have to stay under the speed limit across the Turnpike, but it would have been insane to risk being stopped for speeding. He parked in front of Sam's apartment and ran up the steps eagerly, with a sense of anticipation. He wanted her in his arms again. He waited impatiently until the front door clicked open in answer to his ring.

The apartment door was standing partially open, and he started in, calling, "Honey—"

He saw just the barest flicker of movement in the mirror over the dropleaf table, a movement behind the door he was opening, a figure bulking larger than Ella. Without halting his stride, he gripped the doorknob and flung himself sideways into the door, smashing it into the man who stood behind it. He rounded the edge of the door in almost the same motion, this time slamming it shut. He hooked twice into the jaw of the figure that staggered against the wall.

The man fell limply against him. Clem hit him once again on the jaw and stepped back as the man sagged to the floor. A gun skittered across the wooden flooring. Clem snatched it up. The man on the floor rose shakily to his hands and knees, toppled and rolled over on his back. It was Sonny Lind.

"You rat!" Clem said softly, and hit him behind the ear with the flat of the gun.

He straightened and looked around. "Ella!" he called anxiously. "Ella—" He ran into the bedroom. She was spreadeagled on the bed, her wrists tied to the headboard, her feet to the footboard. A towel was stuffed into her mouth. Her topcoat had fallen open. Her eyes filled with thanksgiving at the sight of him.

Clem pulled the gag from her mouth and snapped the ties that bound her to the bed. She flung her arms around him and clung convulsively to him.

"Did he hurt you, honey?" he asked tightly. "I'll kill the—"

"No, no, Clem. He didn't lay a finger me, except to tie me up. But he was going to kill you. Oh, darling, I almost went out of my mind!"

"I'll take care of Sonny Lind!"

"No, darling, no. Please!"

"I don't mean that way," he soothed her, kissing her. "He's going to be a big help to us. I've got a lead. Where's the telephone directory? Look, while I'm wrapping up that little bundle of joy outside, you start going through the Hoboken directory for wedding ring companies. I'll explain when I get back."

There were no more ties left on Sam's meager tie rack, but Clem stripped off Sonny's belt and strapped him to the radiator. Sonny's eyes opened glassily and he groaned as Clem pulled the belt tight.

"That's only the beginning, friend," Clem told him grimly.

Ella came out of the bedroom. The topcoat was once again wrapped concealingly around her. She heard Sonny's groan and cried, "Clem!"

"I'm not hurting him, honey—not yet. He's opening in the Aztec Room next week. I gave Kraus my word and I've never broken my word yet. What'd you find in the book?"

"N-nothing yet. I'm worried about Sam. What did he do to Sam, Clem?"

Sonny said, "Nothing. Just tied him up. Honest, I didn't hurt him! The minute I found you'd swapped apartments with him, I just tied him up."

Clem said shortly, "You'd better be right, pal. Now, if you feel like talking, you'll save yourself a lot of grief."

Sonny clamped his teeth tight. "I'm not talking," he said.

"You'll talk."

Ella looked up from the phone directory. "I've got two, Clem," she said.

"Fine," he said with his eyes on Sonny Lind. "What are they?"

"The Forget-Me-Not Company on Hickory Street and the Darling Wedding Ring Company on Elm Street."

Clem saw Sonny's jaw sag when Ella read off the name of the Darling Wedding Ring Company. He remembered what Al Vance had been saying just before the death car had swooped down on him. "The darling wedding ring—"

"That's the one," he said with satisfaction. "The Darling Wedding Ring Company."

Sonny strained against the belt that strapped him to the radiator. "Wait a minute, Lasher," he said desperately. He was sweating. "You can do yourself a lot of good—"

"With two murder counts against me?" Clem mocked him.

"They can be quashed. Just let me talk to a certain guy on the phone. He can show you more money than you've ever seen before in your life!"

"The way he showed Ben Morgan, for instance? No thanks, dumb chum. But is there anything you want to tell me, pal?"

"Yes!" Sonny spat viciously. "You'll be dead before morning."

He reached out and brought up his fist to the point of Sonny's chin. Ella gasped. Clem looked at her.

"Don't feel sorry for a rat like that, honey," he said somberly. "I should have taken him apart. Is there something we can tie him up with?"

"There's a clothesline in the kitchen."

"Let's go."

Ten minutes later, Clem slipped out through the back entrance of the apartment with the bound and gagged Sonny Lind over his shoulder, while Ella drove the car around to the side street. Clem dumped Sonny on the floor of the back seat and covered him with a blanket he had brought down from Sam's apartment.

It was a tense and silent ride back to Hoboken. Clem stopped the car a block north of the Darling Wedding Ring Company on Elm Street. "Go back to the Lyric," he whispered to Ella. "Park behind the theatre. Give me an hour. If I don't see you or call you by then, call a cop."

"But what do you expect to find, darling?"

"God only knows," he muttered. He leaned through the open window and kissed her. "Remember. Give me an hour."

He turned and walked down the street while the car turned east toward Hudson Street.

The Darling Wedding Ring Company was in a red brick factory building on the corner. On the main floor was the Marple Import & Export Company. The second floor was occupied by the Darling Wedding Ring Company, Wholesalers. Clem scouted the building very carefully. There was a loading platform on Steuben Street, the main entrance on Elm Street, and another side entrance down the alley. There was a light in the basement where the night watchman was probably having a snack, but the barred windows were so dirty that Clem couldn't see through them.

But the thing that impressed Clem was that none of the glass-paneled doors showed any of the distinctive cross marks of a burglar alarm, a strange thing for a building that housed a wedding ring company with an inventory of gold. All the first floor and basement windows were barred, however. At the far end of the alley a fire escape zigzagged up the side of the building to the roof.

Clem eyed the fire escape. By climbing to the top of the first-floor window, he would be able with a jump and some luck to reach the supports of the first landing of the fire escape. To pull down that rusty ladder for an easy ascent was out of the question. It would scream in its rusty grooves like a thousand strangling cats.

The climb to the top of the window bars was easy, but once there, he had to turn cautiously and crouch, holding on with the fingertips of one hand. He took a breath and leaped, reaching desperately for the narrow angle of iron. He wrapped one hand around it, swung, feeling the iron bite into his palm, and then clawed himself up for a grip with the other hand. He hung resting, and then raised himself as if he were chinning the bar, hooked an elbow over the edge of the grilled platform and pulled himself silently up to the level.

He sat for a moment with his head against his drawn-up knees. He had to wait until the lights stopped flickering before his eyes. He touched his back pocket to reassure himself that Sonny's gun was still there, and then began the stealthy climb to the roof. He stopped at each landing to try the windows, but they were all locked.

He prayed as he went over the lip of the roof. If the entrance to the roof was by a door, he would have to smash a lock, and noise had been the one thing he had dreaded. He looked around swiftly. There were several chimneys, but no curving hooded form of a door leading down into the factory. He breathed more easily. That meant that there was merely a scuttle. He found it beside a chimney, an oblong wooden frame covered with asbestos shingle to keep out the rain. He lifted it cautiously, laid it to one side, and crouched over the opening, listening.

There was no sound from below, no footsteps of a night watchman making the rounds. He lit a match and held it down into the blackness. Twelve feet below was the floor. A ladder leaned against the wall, but he couldn't reach it. He would have to drop, but if he hung by his hands from the scuttle, it wouldn't be too far.

Clem rubbed his hands down his thighs and lowered himself over the edge of the scuttle until his legs dangled free. He rubbed his hands again on his shirt, gripped the edge and hung free. It was an eerie sensation, dropping into that pit of darkness with nothing below to see but the empty blackness. He let go. The drop was really short, but it seemed that he fell forever, and then his feet hit hard. A board in the flooring gave way with a soggy crunch, and he fell sideways, clawing desperately, knowing that the four-story stairwell was to his right.

He struck the railing around the stairwell with the small of his back. It gave, and for a moment he thought it would splinter and hurtle him down into that lethal darkness. But it held.

Then, far below, something crashed on the lowest floor. Even before he reached for his back pocket, he knew what it was. Sonny's gun had twisted from him. He flattened on the floor. The boards smelled wet, like the underside of a flat rock, old and rotting. He heard a door slam open far below, and voices. A light sent shadows dancing up the stairwell.

He heard a grumbling voice, "Now, what the hell?"

And another voice, "Take the doors—I'll take the windows."

Running footsteps went pounding, receded, gradually returned, and the voices coupled again.

"Okay with me. How's it with you?"

"Nothing busted. Nobody came in."

"This place gives me the willies. Every night something comes apart. One of these times the whole damn joint's coming down. Want me to tell you something? It's been condemned four times, and each time the boss—"

The voices diminished again as their owners stamped resentfully down the stairs to the basement, the door slamming shut this time. Clem breathed again.

He raised himself cautiously. The boards did not creak. They were beyond the creaking stage. They were sodden with wet rot. He was on the fourth floor of the factory building. The thin horned moon threw a discouraged light through the grimy window at the far end of the hallway. Now he could see the stairway downward, and the doors on either side of the narrow passage. He swore softly, remembering the gun, but he walked toward the first door. It opened easily and showed a large empty room, lighted by dirty windows. The second door showed another large empty room. He crept down to the third floor. It was a duplicate of the fourth, both in layout and emptiness.

He scowled in bewilderment. What the hell was this? Hoboken was a shipping city, with floor space at a premium even in so dilapidated building as this. This floor space could have been rented not by the foot, but by the inch. Yet here were two entire floors as empty as a chorus girl's mind.

He listened over the railing of the stairwell. The only sound was a muted drip-drip-drip of defective plumbing. He descended to the second floor, the floor that housed the Darling Wedding Ring Company, testing each tread before he let down his full weight. But these steps were no longer capable of creaking.

The first door, another duplicate of the doors of the third and fourth floors, let him into a large room filled with machines. Milling machines, engraving machines, polishers, lathes, a small smelting furnace—all the equipment that might be expected in a jewelry factory.

At the end of the room was a plywood partition between the shop and the office. Clem felt his way down the room toward the office. The machines or their benches did not feel clean and dry as machines and benches should feel in an active shop. They were furry with thick dust, as if they had been unused for months. The office, by contrast, was clean and neat. The windows shone from the street light on the corner, and he did not have to light a match to see his way about. There was a large desk, a bank of new filing cabinets, and a large safe.

Obviously, the shop outside had not been used for a long while. Nothing had been manufactured there, except possibly the souvenir rings for the party. But the office had probably been used that very day.

He went to the files and in the A-B drawer he found the books. His eyes lighted. Here was something he could understand. The books showed the pulse of the business.

He carried the books to the desk, pulled out the chair and sat down. There was a curious feeling of going back ten years, going back to the starvation days of his C.P.A. service. He shook his head and lit a cigarette. He opened the books.

De Groot, or whatever his name was, used a simple double-entry bookkeeping system. The Darling Wedding Ring Company was a wholesaler, and the Accounts Receivable ranged from coast to coast, name after name, wholesaling on a big scale. It was not until Clem leafed through to Accounts Payable that his eyes really opened. During the past year, the Darling Wedding Ring Company had purchased over seven million dollars' worth of gold from licensed refineries, at the legal rate of thirty-five dollars an ounce.

Clem stared at the figures and whispered to himself, "*Seven million!*" That meant that the Darling Wedding Ring Company had bought over six tons of gold during the past year!

Looking for a pencil and paper, Clem pulled open the middle drawer of the desk. There he found a small package of business cards that described one Dexter Grotius as president of the company. That fitted. Ella had said that the man who had given the parties had been called Dex. Dexter Grotius. D. Grotius. This was the elusive DeGroot. A girl with a heavily laden smorgasbord accent might easily make D. Grotius into DeGroot.

The books were very simple, and within twenty minutes Clem figured that after deductions for overhead, payroll, manufacture and distribution, the Darling Wedding Ring Company had made a net profit of thirty-five thousand dollars. That wasn't bad going, but it certainly was no important money, not important enough to—

Manufacture!

Clem sat bolt upright and turned his head to stare at the doorway to the shop. The last entry in the ledger bore the date of that very day, yet it was obvious that the shop had been unused so long that dust had settled thickly over the machines. There hadn't been any manufacturing. If that one item was false, the whole bookkeeping system was fake.

He jumped up and strode to the filing cabinet, and the first thing he found, filed under "L", was a loaded Luger; but he wanted to see the orders received for non-existent wedding rings.

It was not until he ran across an order from K. Feinsod, Jeweler, South Broad Street, Newark—the shop that had told him it had written several times and had received no answer—that Clem realized this impressive stack of orders and accounts was stuffed with dummies.

The Darling Wedding Ring Company had purchased over seven million dollars' worth of gold, but it had no customers and manufactured nothing....

The door opened behind him, and he whirled. The man was two paces into the room before he saw Clem. His jaw dropped and he stood for a paralyzed instant as Clem dived at him. He cried out and took a step backward, clawing for the gun under his left armpit. He tripped over the doorsill, his arms flailing in the air. Clem hit him on the point of the chin with a hard right, then twice again as he crumpled.

Clem dragged him into the office, ripped off his tie and belt, and bound his wrists and ankles behind him. He snatched the gun from the watchman's shoulder holster and crouched beside the door, waiting for the second watchman, who would surely come after having heard the sounds of the scuffle. He held his breath, but all he could hear was the water drip. After an eternity, he heard heavy footsteps on the floor below, followed by the slam of a door. The quiet, except for the dripping water, was absolute again. The second watchman had gone back to the basement.

Clem ran lightly down the stairs and listened at the door to the basement. There was a muffled metallic crash as if the watchman had thrown something into a garbage can. Clem stamped heavily on the floor and then flattened against the wall. The watchman came running up the stairs and when he burst through the doorway, Clem slapped him across the back of the head with the flat of his gun. He went down as if his legs had been cut off at the knees. Clem trussed him as he had done the first watchman and took his gun, shoving it into his own back pocket. Though he was sure there had been only two watchmen, he went cautiously down the steps into the basement.

The lighted room was about thirty feet square, and piled in front of the doors of the freight elevator were about twenty bulky wooden crates. They were all addressed to a Z. Van Der Sluys, Rotterdam, Netherlands, and lettered on the sides was the notice: Machinery—Proof Presses—Handle with Care.

Clem looked quickly around the room and found a pinch bar hanging on a nail beside the elevator. He stripped off the side of one of the crates, splintering the wood. It contained a dozen proof presses, bench models. Clem knew enough about printing and presses to know that they were authentic.

It was a simple piece of machinery, about twenty inches wide and forty inches long. There was a bed on which the type-filled chase was laid, and a heavy cylinder that rolled on a track to make the impression from the type to a sheet of proof paper. At one end was the inking slab, a thick flat sheet of steel about fifteen by twenty inches.

It was obvious to him now that the Darling Wedding Ring Company had rented the two upper floors of the building and kept them empty to conceal the fact that no rings were being manufactured on the second floor. That fact had led him to the conclusion that the Marple Import & Export Company on the first floor had to be a dummy of the Darling Company. It was possible, of course, that the Marple did make authentic exports, but—

His eyes narrowed. His hand shot out and he felt the thickness of the inking slab at the end of the proof press. It was three inches thick, and solid. It shouldn't have been solid; it should merely have been a steel shell. In inking type to make a proof, a printer used a light rubber roller, and the inking slab didn't have to sustain any real weight. But this was solid—and three inches thick.

Clem grinned, and slid the edged tip of the pinch bar diagonally across the plate. The dull steel finish curled up from it like a potato peel, and as the pinch bar moved across the slab it left behind the broad shining gleam of yellow gold. The inking slab was pure gold!

He felt rather than heard the humming sound—or rather, he felt the cessation of humming, as if a powerful motor had suddenly been shut off. He ran to the window, scraped an inch of dirt from the glass with his fingernail, and noiselessly peered out to the sidewalk. A long black limousine had stopped at the curb, and men were spilling out of as speedily as ants from a trampled ant hill, and as noiselessly.

He ran up the stairs, bypassing the unconscious watchmen, to the fourth floor. He was sure that the men at the door below were not police—police did not ride around in limousines. He was just as sure that all exits from the first floor were covered. His only hope was the roof, and he didn't know how much of a hope that would be.

He took the ladder from against the wall, staggered a little under its soggy weight, and thrust it up into the oblong of the scuttle to the roof. He scrambled up to the roof, and as he turned to haul the ladder up after him, something exploded against the back of his head and he felt himself tumbling head first into the midnight cave below the scuttle.

Clem came out of unconsciousness coughing and fighting the ammonia fumes from a rag held against his nose.

A voice said peevishly, "That's enough, that's enough. Don't choke him to death."

The shadowy half-world swam into focus. He was back in the office of the Darling Wedding Ring Company, seated again at the desk. Standing across the room, facing him, was a plump, slightly bald, middle-aged man in horn-rimmed glasses.

"You have caused me a good deal of trouble, Mr. Lasher," he said accusingly. "You have made yourself a general nuisance for the past twenty-four hours."

Clem was still thick-witted from the effect of the blow on the back of his head and he mumbled something unintelligible.

The man remarked, his voice still peevish, "The watchmen have orders to call me every hour and report. When they did not do so, well—" he waved his hand—"you can see for yourself."

Clem shook his head. His eyes cleared. Standing against the wall behind the middle-aged man was Marthe, her eyes wide with a dawning fear, her hand to her mouth. To Clem's right was the thin gunman Pudge had called Crackers. Crackers was still wearing his raincoat. To Clem's left was the thick-bodied Piet, a stranger to Clem. Both Piet and Crackers held guns.

Clem looked at the balding man and said, "You're Grotius—Dexter Grotius?"

"Yes, but that is of no importance at the moment. What is of importance, Mr. Lasher, is that you have been going through the company's books. You discovered something?"

Clem saw the journal and ledger still lying open on the desk before him. He flipped them with his hand and laughed.

"You call these books?" he asked recklessly. "A second-year student in a commercial high school would see through these books in half an hour. They're pitiful."

"So?" Grotius frowned. "And what is so pitiful about them? I keep the books myself, and so far, the auditors have not been able to find anything wrong with them."

"If they didn't find anything wrong with them, they must have been awfully anxious to get out for a beer. I spent twenty minutes on them, and I discovered that you were buying gold and black-marketing it abroad. I haven't worked at accounting for ten years, so you can see what a real auditor could do to you."

Grotius licked his lips. "That's nonsense," he said defensively. "You found the gold in the basement. You saw the proof presses—"

Clem grinned as he leaned over the edge of the desk. "But why did I go down to the basement to look at the proof presses, Grotius?" He slapped the books with the back of his hand. "The whole story's right here!"

He was bluffing, but he could see he had Grotius scared—Grotius was a fair bookkeeper, but unacquainted with accounting. But Clem also knew that death lurked at both elbows in the persons of Crackers and Piet, but the gamble of it sharpened his wits. He pointed a long finger at Grotius and said scornfully:

"For instance, take your cost-system—" He started out on a long line of technicalities, hardly pausing for breath.

It was all gibberish, but Grotius stared at the books as if they had suddenly sprouted horns, hoofs and a pointed tail.

Grotius was sweating, and the sudden death at Clem's elbows was receding. Grotius was sold. Clem shot out his finger again to clinch it before anybody could speak and spoil it. He had Grotius panicked and hypnotized, and Clem wanted to live long enough to get out of the factory.

"Here's the way the figures shape up, according to your books," he lied. "You buy seven millions of gold at thirty-five dollars an ounce. You resell them to the European black market at from seventy to a hundred dollars an ounce, a profit between a hundred and two hundred percent. Right?"

Grotius said mechanically, "But there are expenses—"

"All right, all right," Clem interrupted. "But that much profit is worth protecting, isn't it?"

"Yes—yes."

"Okay," Clem spread his hands. "Why not take me in and let me protect it for you?"

Grotius was nodding assent when the office door slammed open. Clem's eyes widened. McNulty, the manager of the Lyric Burlesque, strode in—not the McNulty Clem had known, but a sharp-eyed, dangerous McNulty.

Grotius bleated, "Mr. McNulty, the books. He says ..."

"Shut up, you kraut-headed jerk!" McNulty's cold eyes darted at Clem. "What kind of bill of goods you selling him?"

"Strictly borax," said Clem coolly.

"I might have known. I should have had you cooled the first time I laid eyes on you, Lasher. I could see you were trouble!" He turned on Marthe. "I thought you were going to deliver him registered mail, insured."

Marthe looked pleadingly at Clem. She tried to speak, but couldn't. Clem tried to divert McNulty's attention.

"*You* sent Sonny Lind after Ella and me," he said.

McNulty said contemptuously, "What the hell did you think I was going to do, let you go to the cops and send me valentines? When she ran out on the show, I knew she was going to you."

"And you knocked off Helen Swensen, Al Vance, and Ben Morgan."

"Cut it out, Lasher, cut it out, or there won't be a dry eye in the house. But in case you're interested, the Ben Morgan end of it was your pal Sonny Lind's idea." He swung around on Grotius. "I work like hell to make an organization and keep it together. I'll admit Sonny Lind was my mistake. I thought he had something on the ball. But this smooth-talking jerk! I told you to get rid of him, didn't I? Okay, let him have it, Piet!"

Grotius croaked piteously and crossed his arms before his face. Piet stolidly shot him through the head. The bullet slammed Grotius back against the wall and he fell to the floor.

"Now the dame," said McNulty metallically.

Marthe cried out. Clem flung himself at Piet. Crackers shot Marthe, then leaned across the desk chair and hit Clem across the side of the head. Clem dropped, clawing down the sides of Piet's legs, but he managed to keep his consciousness.

He sat on the floor and grinned fiercely at McNulty.

"You'll have to think of something special for me, Mac," he giggled almost drunkenly. "You'll have to think of something very special. Half the people in Hudson County know I was out after the Darling Wedding Ring Company. Protect your profitable investment, McNulty."

McNulty regarded him stonily. "Brother," he grated, "I'd give half that investment to have Piet break every bone in your body, one by one, slowly."

"Go ahead, Mac, go ahead."

McNulty flapped his hand sharply at Piet. "Get him on his feet," he ordered.

Clem almost screamed as Piet tangled his thick fingers in his hair and pulled him upright.

"Shove him against the filing cabinets," said McNulty. "And get out of the way. When the police walk in, he's going to be found right there, robbing the joint, shot down by the watchman."

Clem steadied himself against the cabinets. "Don't you want my fingerprints on one of the drawers, pal?" he taunted McNulty. "It might come in handy. The police sometimes get nosy about things like that. They say fingerprints don't take after death. Try to make me put my prints on one of the drawers!"

"I can make you do it, all right." McNulty regarded him with an icy smile. "Piet here knows some very useful tricks. Two minutes with Piet and a mother would eat her own baby, fried. But here's one of your own, Lasher, the one you tried on Pudge Riordan, the fingers in the throat at the sides of the jaw. Give him that one Piet. The top of his head will come off!"

Clem cried frantically, "No, McNulty, no! I'll give you my prints. Look, I'm opening a drawer ..."

He jerked open the "L" drawer. He snatched out the Luger from behind the file of fake orders and dropped to the floor, blasting the first bullet up into Piet's broad, unmissable chest. He squirmed over on one hip and snapped the next shot into Crackers, who flew back against the wall as if jerked by a rope. Clem dived flat for the floor as McNulty's shot slammed over him. He came to rest on his elbows, peering into McNulty's lowering gun, his own gun pointing up into McNulty's face.

"A showdown," said Clem evenly. "Go ahead—pull your trigger. I'm watching your finger. When you pull, I pull. Let's see who gets out of it alive."

McNulty crouched not six feet away, his gun pointing down at Clem, who lay prone on the floor, his gun as steady as if set in concrete. They faced each other, immobile. It was McNulty who broke first.

"I'll make a deal with you, Lasher," he said. "There's plenty in this for both of us."

At that moment there rose the wail of a police siren. McNulty's face twitched. Clem shot him through the right shoulder, lunged forward with a shove of his legs, and scooped up McNulty's gun. He glanced at the clock.

"Right on the dot!" he grinned. "I gave Ella an hour to call the cops...."

The Aztec Room was filled to capacity. Clem and Ella had a ringside table. The third chair at the table was occupied by a man with a cold, still face. His name was McNamara and he was from the FBI.

"Listen, Lasher," he said impatiently, "we appreciate what you've done in breaking up this gold smuggling ring, but we want this missing witness and killer you've been hinting at. Bringing me here tonight—"

Clem interrupted him with a wave of his hand as Kraus, who was not only manager of the Aztec Room but his own M.C. as well, ran out to the middle of the floor carrying a microphone.

"Ladies and gentlemen, fellow Aztecs and other savages from the wilds of Jersey," said Kraus. "Tonight we are introducing a new singing sensation, Sonny Lind."

Clem leaned over the edge of the table. "I'll give you your witness and killer after this number," he said to McNamara. "I gave my word to Kraus that Sonny Lind would open here tonight, and I've never broken my word yet."

He grinned over at Ella, and reached for her hand.

THE END

LORENZ HELLER BIBLIOGRAPHY
(1910-1965)

As Frederick Lorenz

Novels:
A Rage at Sea (Lion, 1953)
Night Never Ends (Lion, 1954)
The Savage Chase (Lion, 1954)
A Party Every Night (Lion, 1956)
Ruby (Lion, 1956)
Hot (Lion, 1956)
Dungaree Sin (Chariot, 1960)

Stories:
Backbite (*Justice*, Jan 1956)
Big Catch (*Justice*, July 1955)
Living Bait (*Justice*, May 1955)

As Dan Gregory

Three Must Die! (Graphic, 1956)

As Laura Hale

Novels:
Wild is the Woman (Rainbow, 1951)
Lovers Don't Sleep (Falcon, 1951)
Kiss of Fire (Rainbow, 1952; reprinted in Australia as *Kiss Of Death*, Phantom, 1953)
Woman Hunter (Falcon, 1952; reprinted in Australia, Phantom, 1953)
Desperate Blonde (Beacon Australia, 1960)
Lessons in Lust (Beacon, 1961; re-write of *Woman Hunter*)
Sensual Woman (Beacon, 1961; re-write of *Lovers Don't Sleep*)
The Zipper Girls (Beacon, 1962; re-write of *Wild is the Woman*)
The Marriage Bed (Beacon, 1962; re-write of *Desperate Blonde*)

As Larry Heller

Novels:
I Get What I Want (Popular, 1956)
Body of the Crime (Pyramid, 1962)

Story:
Blood Is Thicker (*Guilty Detective Story Magazine*, Mar 1957)

As Larry Holden

Novels:
Hide-Out (Eton, 1953)
Dead Wrong (Pyramid, 1957)
Crime Cop (Pyramid, 1959)

Stories (alphabetical listing):
...And Death Makes Ten (*Detective Tales*, June 1947)
Another Man's Poison (*Shadow Mystery*, Apr/May 1948)
Any Corpse in a Storm (*Dime Mystery Magazine*, Aug 1949)
Anybody Lose a Corpse? (*Mammoth Detective*, Aug 1946)
The Big Haunt (*10-Story Detective Magazine*, Oct 1948)
Blackmail Means Homicide (*15 Story Detective*, Feb 1950)
Bloody Night! (*Dime Mystery Magazine*, Oct 1949)
Bodyguard (*Thrilling Detective*, June 1951)
Bullets for Beethoven [Dinny Keogh] (*Mammoth Mystery*, June 1946)
Coffin Key (*Detective Tales*, Oct 1951)
A Corpse at Large (*Ten Detective Aces*, July 1949)
Corpse in Waiting (*New Detective Magazine*, Nov 1950)

BIBLIOGRAPHY

A Corpse to His Credit (*Dime Detective Magazine*, May 1947)
Criminal at Large (*Suspense Magazine*, Summer 1951)
The Crimson Path (*Detective Tales*, Sept 1947)
Cry Murder (*New Detective Magazine*, Oct 1952)
The Crying Corpse (*Ten Detective Aces*, Sept 1948)
Death Brings Down the House (*10-Story Detective Magazine*, Apr 1948)
Death Carries the Mail (*F.B.I. Detective Stories*, Aug 1950)
Death for Two! (*Detective Tales*, Dec 1952)
Death in Dirty Linen (*Shadow Mystery*, June/July 1947)
Death in Six Reels (*Doc Savage*, July/Aug 1948)
Death in Thin Ice (*Shadow Mystery*, Feb/Mar 1948)
Death Is Where You Find It (*Suspect Detective Stories*, Nov 1955)
Die, Baby, Die! (*Detective Tales*, June 1948)
Don't Crowd My Shroud (*10-Story Detective Magazine*, Dec 1948)
Don't Ever Forget (*Detective Story Magazine*, Mar 1953)
Don't Wait Up for Me (*Triple Detective*, Fall 1955)
The Eighteen Screaming Corpses (*Detective Tales*, Jan 1948)
The Expendable Ex (*Dime Detective Magazine*, June 1952)
Face in the Window (*Detective Tales*, June 1951)
Fall Guy (*Detective Tales*, Aug 1953)
Forger's Fate (*Dime Detective Magazine*, Apr 1951)
The High Cost of Chivalry (*Dime Detective Magazine*, Dec 1951)
Home for Christmas (*Thrilling Detective*, Dec 1947)
House of Hate (*10-Story Detective Magazine*, Apr 1949)
Humpty-Dumpty Homicide (*Detective Tales*, June 1949)
If the Body Fits— (*Dime Mystery Magazine*, Dec 1947)
If the Frame Fits— (*Detective Tales*, Dec 1951)
I'll Be Home for Murder! (*Detective Tales*, Apr 1948)
I'll See You Dead! (*Detective Tales*, May 1947)
In Her Mother's Best Bier! (*Detective Tales*, Dec 1948)
Keeping Honest (*Doc Savage*, Winter 1949)
Kickback for a Corpse (*All-Story Detective*, Apr 1949)
Killer's Kiss (*Detective Tales*, Aug 1949)
Lady in Red (*Detective Tales*, Oct 1948)
Lady-Killer (*Dime Detective Magazine*, Dec 1952)
Lethal Boy Blue (*Detective Tales*, May 1949)
Love Me, Love My Corpse! (*Detective Tales*, Aug 1948)
Make Mine Mayhem (*New Detective Magazine*, Jan 1949)
Man with a Rep (*Detective Tales*, Dec 1949)
Mayhem at Eight (*New Detective Magazine*, May 1950)
Mayhem's Mechanic (*Detective Tales*, Sept 1946)
Morgue Bait (*New Detective Magazine*, Dec 1951)
Murder and the Mermaid (*Dime Detective Magazine*, Oct 1952)
Murder Never Gets Too Old (*Private Detective*, Jan 1950)
Never Dead Enough (*New Detective Magazine*, Sept 1947)
Never Turn Your Back (*Mike Shayne Mystery Magazine*, July 1959)
Nightmare (*Detective Tales*, Oct 1952)
No Dead End (*Triple Detective*, Spring 1955)

On a Dead Man's Chest (*Thrilling Detective*, Apr 1953)
One Dark Night [Dinny Keogh] (*Mammoth Mystery*, Dec 1946)
One for the Hangman (*Suspect Detective Stories*, Feb 1956)
Operation—Murder (*F.B.I. Detective Stories*, Aug 1949)
Orphans Are Made (*Mobsters*, Feb 1953)
Out of the Frying Pan... (*15 Mystery Stories*, Oct 1950)
Port of the Dead (*New Detective Magazine*, July 1947)
Prelude to a Wake (*Dime Detective Magazine*, Feb 1952)
Red Nightmare (*Dime Mystery Magazine*, July 1947)
Sailor, Beware! (*Detective Story Magazine*, May 1953)
Save Me a Kill (*New Detective Magazine*, June 1953)
Self-Made Corpse (*Detective Tales*, Apr 1949)
She Cries Murder! (*New Detective Magazine*, June 1952)
Sing a Song of Murder (*Dime Detective Magazine*, Aug 1952)
Snow in August [Dinny Keogh] (*Mammoth Mystery*, Aug 1946)
The Spice of Death (*Private Detective*, Dec 1950)
Start with a Corpse [Dinny Keogh] (*Mammoth Mystery*, Jan 1946)
There's Death in the Heir [Dinny Keogh] (*Mammoth Mystery*, Aug 1947)
They Played Too Rough [Dinny Keogh] (*Mammoth Mystery*, Mar 1946)
This Shroud Reserved (*New Detective Magazine*, Oct 1951)
Those Slaughter-House Blues (*Mammoth Detective*, Feb 1947)
A Time for Dying (*Dime Detective Magazine*, Aug 1951)
Too Many Crosses [Dinny Keogh] (*Mammoth Mystery*, Feb 1947)
Tragedy in Waiting (*Invincible Detective Magazine*, Mar 1951)
The Trouble with Redheads (*Mike Shayne Mystery Magazine*, Apr 1959)
Two-Headed Killer (*15 Mystery Stories*, Feb 1950)
Undressed to Kill (*New Detective Magazine*, Sept 1949)
Vicious Circle (*Detective Tales*, Nov 1949)
The Voice That Kills (*15 Mystery Stories*, Aug 1950)
Wake of the Ermine Chick (*15 Story Detective*, Dec 1950)
When Cops Fall Out (*Detective Tales*, June 1953)
With Hostile Intent (*Fifteen Detective Stories*, Dec 1954)
With Love and Bullets! (*Detective Tales*, Feb 1953)
Written in Blood (*Ten Detective Aces*, May 1948)
You Can't Live Forever (*New Detective Magazine*, Aug 1952)
You Die Alone (*Fifteen Detective Stories*, Oct 1953)
You'll Die Laughing (*Detective Tales*, Oct 1950)
You're Killing Me (*Detective Story Magazine*, Sept 1953)

Dinny Keogh series:
Start with a Corpse (1946)
They Played Too Rough (1946)
Bullets for Beethoven (1946)
Snow in August (1946)
One Dark Night (1946)
Too Many Crosses (1947)
There's Death in the Heir (1947)

BIBLIOGRAPHY

As Lorenz Heller

Novel:
Murder in Make-Up (Messner, 1937)

Stories:
Blood Money (*Suspect Detective Stories*, Nov 1955)
A Tasty Dish (*Suspect Detective Stories*, Feb 1956)
Twilight (*Short Stories*, Nov 1956)
The Hero (*Mystery Tales*, Dec 1958)
The Last Hunt (*Adventure*, June 1959)

As Burt Sims

Television Scripts:
1953: "Death Does a Rumba" (Season 2, Episode 12, *Boston Blakie*)
1953: "Island of Stone" (Season 2, Episode 1, *Chevron Theater*)
1954: "Tailor-Made Trouble" (Season 1, Episode 11, *Waterfront*)
1956 - 1959: Seven episodes of *Sky King*
1958: "Beautiful, Blue and Deadly" (Season 1, Episode 14, *Mike Hammer*)
1958: "Texas Fliers" (Season 1, Episode 18, *Flight*)

Rediscover the hard-hitting, character-driven fiction of

Lorenz Heller

The Savage Chase (as Frederick Lorenz) · $19.95
Three 50s noir thrillers in one volume. "...a sexually frank, violence packed thriller with vividly crisp dialogue."—*GoodReads*.

A Rage at Sea / A Party Every Night · $19.95
"Lorenz's characters are what keep the pages turning."
—Alan Cranis, *Bookgasm*.

Dead Wrong · $9.99 · Black Gat Books #26.
"These interesting, well-developed characters propel this rather standard crime-noir plot into something special and unusual."—*Paperback Warrior*.

Hide-Out / I Get What I Want · $15.95
"In Lorenz's fiction, it feels like he moulds the plot from organic character confrontations, his writing is electric and alive with unpredictability."
—Paul Burke, *CrimeTime*.

Crime Cop / Body of the Crime · $15.95
"One of the better entries, outside of 87th Precinct, in the paperback police school." —Anthony Boucher, *New York Times*

Woman Hunter / Kiss of Fire · $15.95
"What makes this one ding is not necessarily the plot, but the great characterizations which serve to humanize all the players. A terrific read."—Dave Wilde

Hot / Ruby · $17.95
"[Heller] writes in a hard, fast, crisp style and he has a feel for colorful language and characters that makes the story sing."
— *Mammoth Mystery*

Stark House Press, 1315 H Street, Eureka, CA 95501
griffinskye3@sbcglobal.net / www.StarkHousePress.com
Available from your local bookstore, or order direct via our website.

www.ingramcontent.com/pod-product-compliance
Lightning Source LLC
LaVergne TN
LVHW021809060526
838201LV00058B/3298